Praise for Val McDermid's Lindsay Gordon series

"One of my favorite authors."   —Sara Paretsky

"Val McDermid is an inspiration."
                    —*Herald* (Scotland) on *Common Murder*

"Another winner . . . One of the best women's mysteries in a long time."   —*Booklist* on *Booked for Murder*

"Funny and scary by turns, always sharp."
                    —*Daily Telegraph* (UK) on *Booked for Murder*

"McDermid not only keeps you guessing but keeps you interested."   —*Sunday Telegraph* (UK) on *Hostage to Murder*

"Neatly constructed and splendidly sarcastic."
                    —*Daily Telegraph* (UK) on *Hostage to Murder*

"McDermid cannot write an uninteresting sentence."
                    —*Women's Review of Books* (UK) on *Final Edition*

"McDermid's snappy, often comic prose keeps the story humming."   —*Publishers Weekly* on *Common Murder*

"Lindsay Gordon is smart, tenacious, daring, lusty, loyal, and class-conscious to the bone."
                    –Barbara Neely, author of the Blanche White series,
                                        on *Report for Murder*

BOOKED FOR MURDER

AND

HOSTAGE TO MURDER

Also by Val McDermid

A Place of Execution
Killing the Shadows
The Grave Tattoo
A Darker Domain
Trick of the Dark
The Vanishing Point
Northanger Abbey

TONY HILL/CAROL JORDAN NOVELS

The Mermaids Singing
The Wire in the Blood
The Last Temptation
The Torment of Others
Beneath the Bleeding
Fever of the Bone
The Retribution
Cross and Burn
Insidious Intent

KAREN PIRIE NOVELS

The Distant Echo
A Darker Domain
The Skeleton Road
Out of Bounds

KATE BRANNIGAN NOVELS

Dead Beat
Kick Back
Crack Down
Clean Break
Blue Genes
Star Struck

LINDSAY GORDON NOVELS

Report for Murder
Common Murder
Final Edition
Union Jack

SHORT STORY COLLECTIONS

The Writing on the Wall and Other Stories
Stranded
Christmas is Murder (ebook only)
Gunpowder Plots (ebook only)

NON FICTION

A Suitable Job for a Woman
Forensics

VAL McDERMID

BOOKED FOR MURDER

AND

HOSTAGE TO MURDER

Grove Press
New York

Booked for Murder was first published in Great Britain in 1996 by The Women's Press Ltd.
Paperback edition in 2005 by HarperCollins UK. First published in the United
States in 2005 by Bywater Books.

Hostage to Murder was first published in Great Britain in 2003 by HarperCollins UK.
First published in the United States in 2005 by Bywater Books.

Printed in the United States of America
Published Simultaneously in Canada

Text Design by Norman Tuttle at Alpha Design & Composition
This book was set in 11.5 Bembo with Charlemagne
by Alpha Design & Composition of Pittsfield. NH.

First Grove Atlantic edition: March 2018

Library of Congress Cataloging-in-Publication data is available for this title.

ISBN 978-0-8021-2778-5
eISBN 978-0-8021-6554-1

Grove Press
an imprint of Grove Atlantic
154 West 14th Street
New York, NY 10011

Distributed by Publishers Group West

groveatlantic.com

18 19 20 21   10 9 8 7 6 5 4 3 2 1

INTRODUCTION TO
THE GROVE EDITION

I grew up reading mysteries. From Agatha Christie to Ruth Rendell, from Rex Stout to Chandler and Hammett, I devoured them all. But what started me working on the first Lindsay Gordon novel, *Report for Murder*, in the mid-1980s was the chance to march to a different drum.

There was a new wave breaking on the shores of crime fiction, and it was led by women. Even though there had never been any shortage of female protagonists in the genre, you'd have been hard pressed to find many you could call feminists. But by the early '80s, a new breed of women had emerged.

They were mostly PIs, though there were a few amateurs among them. What marked them out was their politics. Whether they called themselves feminists or not, they were strong, independent women with a brain and a sense of humour, but most of all, they had agency. They didn't shout for male help when the going got tough. They dealt with things on their own terms.

Another key difference was that these stories were organic. They weren't random murders bolted on to a random setting. The crimes grew out of their environment—the particular jobs people did, the lives they led, the situations and recreations they were involved in.

I devoured every one of those books I could get my hands on. Sara Paretsky, Barbara Wilson, Sue Grafton, Marcia Muller, Mary Wings, Katherine V. Forrest and a dozen others showed me how to write about real lives within the framework of murder and suspense. Their protagonists took on the male establishment when they had to, and they didn't back down. They didn't shy away from confronting difficult issues either. I loved them.

I wanted to write my own version of those women. A Scottish version, a woman as firmly rooted as her American sisters, but one who would have to accommodate different laws, different customs, different politics and different histories. I didn't have the nerve to make her a PI because I didn't know any at the time. And I suspected women PIs in the UK would have very different professional lives to their US counterparts.

What I did know was journalism. I became a journalist after I graduated from Oxford, just to bridge the gap until I could support myself writing fiction. (I always had the absolute conviction that day would come, a conviction not shared by anyone else back then . . .) I thought if I made my character a journalist, I'd be on safe ground. I knew what journalists were capable of and how we went about circumventing the doors that were closed to us. I knew the rhythm of our working lives and what made a good newspaper story.

In other respects, Lindsay Gordon has congruences with my own background. She's Scottish, she shares my politics, and she's a lesbian. It would, however, be a mistake to conflate us. Our personalities are quite different. (Except that we both have a fondness for fast cars and good whisky . . .) She's far more headstrong and stubborn than I am, for example, and much more willing to take risks.

I'm proud to say that Lindsay was the first out lesbian protagonist in UK crime fiction. It never crossed my mind that she wouldn't be a lesbian, because those American novels had given me permission to put whoever I wanted centre stage. But the books were never "about" being a lesbian. Lindsay doesn't wrestle with her sexuality or her gender, nor does she ever apologise for it. It's only one part of her identity and it's not one she has a problem with. The gay characters in the books are part of a wider landscape, one that accommodates all sorts and conditions of people.

That was a very deliberate choice on my part. When I was growing up on the East Coast of Scotland, there were no lesbian templates for my life. No books, no films, no TV series, and certainly no lesbians living open lives. I decided that if I was going to write fiction, I was going to give the next generation of gay women a character they could celebrate. I never describe her physically and that's deliberate too. I wanted her to be a chameleon, to take the form of whatever her readers needed. They could identify with her if they wanted. They could fantasise her as lover or friend or colleague.

Report for Murder was published in 1987 and the Lindsay Gordon books have never been out of print in the UK. I think those early choices I made go some way to explaining why the books have remained so popular. This series is all about character and story, not special pleading or righteous argument.

Each of the books is set in a different world—a trick I learned from reading P. D. James! My own experiences were the springboard for my imagination in the creation of those environments. *Report for Murder* is set in a girls' boarding school; *Common Murder*, at a women's peace camp; *Final Edition*, in the world of newspapers; *Union Jack*, in the milieu of union politics; *Booked for Murder* in publishing; and *Hostage to Murder* moves between Glasgow and St Petersburg in the course of a tense kidnap and murder thriller.

I never intended to write so many Lindsay Gordon novels. Originally I planned a trilogy. (Mostly because the book I really wanted to write was the third one but I couldn't figure out how to get there without writing the first two.) I even packed her off to live in Half Moon Bay with a view of the ocean so I wouldn't be tempted to write about her any more. But she wouldn't let me go. As soon as I'd despatched her, I had a great idea for another book that gave her the starring role. And then another, and another . . .

Lindsay Gordon took a hold of me and for almost twenty years, she wouldn't let me go. I hope she has the same effect on you.

Val McDermid, 2017

BOOKED
FOR MURDER

For Jai and Paula.

They know why.

ACKNOWLEDGEMENTS

Readers often wonder how much research writers do in the pursuit of our plots. I used to think that the only way to do it was over a beer or a meal. That was before I discovered the Internet and the wonders of e-mail.

This time around, I'd like particularly to thank Kathryn Skoyles, whose knowledge of the seamy side of commerce was invaluable, and Janet Dawson and Chris Aldrich, who kindly prevented me from committing an assortment of transatlantic solecisms. Others who contributed in varying degrees, wittingly or unwittingly, were Lee D'Courcy, Frankie Hegarty, Brigid Baillie, David Byrne, Chaz Brenchley, Jai Penna and Sharon Zukowski.

Setting a book in the publishing industry holds certain dangers for an author. In a bid not to become what the Americans now term "dispublished," I'm bound to say that none of the editors, agents or publishers depicted in these pages bears the slightest resemblance to the people I actually work with. Except the dog.

PROLOGUE

Murder, she felt fairly sure, was not the kind of "Purpose of Visit" calculated to speed her through the notoriously difficult US immigration channels. "Pleasure," she ticked, deciding it might not be entirely a lie. At least no one would suspect the truth that lay behind the occupational description of "systems consultant." In spite of the books and films that indicated otherwise, hers was not a job people expected to be carried out by a woman.

She finished filling in the form and looked out of the windows of the jumbo jet. They had chased the sunset west across the Atlantic, and now it was firmly dark blue night out there. Streetlights formed a glittering web when they passed above small towns. Over bigger cities, the lights seemed to be enclosed beneath a dimly glowing bowl that held them trapped, the highway lights leading away from them like chains of refugees. Somewhere out there, her target. Watching TV, eating dinner, reading a book, talking to her lover, gossiping on the phone, composing e-mail. Whatever it was, she wouldn't be doing it tomorrow. Not if the woman was successful in her mission.

She turned away from the window and pulled her paperback novel out of the seat pocket. She opened it where she had carefully dog-eared a page to mark her place and carried on reading *Northanger Abbey*.

A change in engine note signalled the start of the descent into San Francisco. It was a sign she noted with relief. A trans-atlantic, transcontinental flight was quite long enough for her body to feel permanently realigned into the shape of the aircraft seat. That might be just about bearable in first class, but back in anonymous economy it provoked the irresistible fear that she might never walk properly again. The woman stretched her spine, thrusting shoulders back and chest out. The sleeping man next to her snorted and shifted in his seat. Thankfully, he'd been like that for most of the flight. She never liked talking on public transport unless she had instigated the conversation, usually for professional reasons.

She couldn't believe how quickly she cleared immigration. It had been half a dozen years since she'd last set foot in America, and her abiding memory of arrival had been spending the thick end of an hour shuffling forward foot by foot in an endless queue that snaked across the concourse while sadistic immigration officers with faces impassive as hatchets questioned every new arrival. As she collected her luggage, she wondered idly what had brought about the change. It couldn't be that the Americans had become less xenophobic or less paranoid about terrorism, that was for sure, especially after Oklahoma. She only had to think about the drop in the numbers of American tourists to Britain in the wake of the IRA's abandoning of their precarious ceasefire.

Slinging her suit carrier across her shoulder, the woman headed for the taxi rank and gave the name of the hotel where she hoped a room would be waiting for her. Even though she'd been up all night, she feared that sleep would abandon her as soon as her head hit the pillow. It didn't matter. She had time. According to her briefing, the best opportunity she'd have wouldn't come before six in the evening of the following day.

She'd heard about the fog rolling in across the bay in the late afternoon, but she'd never quite believed it could be so tangible a phenomenon. She sat among the Sunday tourists in one of the Fisherman's Wharf cafés and watched the bank of fog envelop the rust-red curve of the Golden Gate, leaving the twin towers stranded above and below. She stirred the last inch of her cappuccino. It had been about the only thing she'd recognised on a list of beverages. They didn't have iced mocha latte in the coffee bar where she picked up her morning carton of steaming pale brown liquid that smelled mostly of its polystyrene container. She supposed this was what they called culture shock.

She'd spent the morning on a whistle-stop sightseeing tour of the crucial highlights. None of her clients had ever sent her to San Francisco before, and she always liked to make the most of her trips at other people's expense. Her one regret was that she hadn't had time for Alcatraz. Now she was reading through her brief one last time, making sure there wasn't something important she'd failed to notice. But it was all as she remembered it. The photographs—well, snapshots really. Directions to the target's home. Suggested lines of approach. And the number to call when she'd achieved her mission.

The woman swallowed the dregs of her coffee and headed back to her hire car, shivering as the damp air hit her. She was wearing only a light cotton shirt over the linen shorts she'd bought for last year's Greek island holiday. It had seemed an appropriate outfit for the warm sun that had beaten down on her earlier. It was California in July, after all. Now the weather had turned into English autumn, she was hopelessly underdressed. She wondered whether she had time to slip back to her hotel, but decided against it.

Ten minutes out of the city, and she was as glad of her decision as she was of the car's air conditioning. The fog that had chilled her was so localised that half a dozen miles away people were still sweating in the same heat that had engulfed her earlier in the day. But at least the air conditioning meant she was clear-headed enough to pay attention to the road signs, making

sure she ended up heading down the coast on Highway 1. She
drove cautiously, aware that a speed limit lower than the UK's
would be easy for her to breach without realising. Attracting
the attention of the Highway Patrol would definitely not be a
good idea.

The road curved across the peninsula past the vast suburban
tract of Daly City, then swerved towards the ocean, the blue
swell coming properly into view as she rolled down the hill and
past the boxy condos of Pacifica. According to the map she had
unfolded on the passenger seat, she was nearly half-way there.
Once the map ran out, she had a hand-drawn map of her exact
destination, courtesy of her client.

She appreciated the need for the detailed map as soon as
she turned off the highway into Half Moon Bay. She found
herself in a grid of streets between highway and ocean, quiet
residential streets where a strange car cruising slowly and making wrong turns would probably be noticed before too long.
Following her directions, she turned on to a road fronting the
Pacific. The houses were detached, two storeys high, covered
in either carefully tended white or pastel siding or natural wood
protected from the climate by heavy coats of sealant. Several had
verandas along the front that looked out across the calm ocean
towards the eventual sunset. The houses looked like money.
Not excessive, obscene, vulgar amounts, but substantial, two
professional income levels. As she approached the house where
her target lived, she was careful neither to speed up nor to slow
down, but she slewed her eyes left as she passed and registered
a battered black convertible in the drive. According to the client, that was the target's car. As expected, she wasn't home. But
this wasn't an appropriate place. Too easy for her target to avoid
what came next.

The woman carried on to the end of the road and turned
left on to the rough, unmetalled track that led across the few
hundred yards of greenish-brown scrub that lay between the
houses and the dunes that edged the beach. As she drew nearer,

she could see what had looked like a gentle swell breaking on the sand in a white frothing surf. Where the track ended there was a clear area, and, as instructed, she parked her hire car there, a short distance from the two other vehicles already facing the pounding waves.

She got out of the car and ignored the hard-packed path that led from the car park to the beach. Instead, the woman walked about half a mile north across the scrub before she chose another route down to the beach. She didn't go all the way down, halting at a point where, if she hunkered down, she would be invisible both from the beach and the flat scrubland above. She settled behind an outcropping of gritty sandstone and surveyed the long sweep of the strand. She'd never seen so spectacular a beach that wasn't scarred with serried ranks of sun loungers, parasols, cars and bars. The beach was wide and flat, sweeping round in a long white arc. From the air, it would look more like a crescent than a half moon, scything a thick line between the dark blue sea and the brown land.

She took a small pair of green rubber binoculars from her satchel and scanned the beach from north to south. Luckily for her purpose, there were surprisingly few people, and those there were clearly didn't belong to the bucket and spade brigade. Every time the woman's binoculars picked out a dog, she paused and took a careful look at the animal and its owner. There was no sign of her target.

The woman lowered her binoculars and waited five minutes before repeating the exercise. On the third sweep, she picked out the black Labrador frolicking in the waves. In spite of his playfulness, he was clearly no puppy. She felt a frisson of excitement. Forcing herself to be patient, she continued her slow scan. A couple of hundred yards behind the dog, a figure jogged slowly. A finger nudged the focus wheel and the face came into sharp focus. There was no doubt about it. It matched the pictures supplied by her client. The dog was a six-year-old Labrador cross called Mutton. The woman was a thirty-seven-year-old

journalist with a reputation for stirring up trouble. Her name was
Lindsay Gordon. If the observer was successful in her mission,
tomorrow someone else would have to walk the dog.

With infinite care, the watcher returned the binoculars to
the backpack. It was time to do the business.

1

Lindsay Gordon jogged gently along the hard sand at the edge of the Pacific surf on Half Moon Bay. Against the rhythmic beat of Air Nikes on wet sand and the thud of blood pulsing in her ears, the waves crashed less regularly. Ahead of her, Mutton chased the foaming surf as it retreated across the sand to be sucked back into the vast body of water, occasionally pausing to bark a deep protest as some bubbles he'd been particularly attached to disappeared. Other joggers might have Walkmen clamped to their heads, shutting out everything except their chosen sounds. Lindsay preferred a more natural music, particularly on a day like today when she had death on her mind.

The day had given no indication that it was going to bring tears before bedtime. She'd got up with Sophie and they'd eaten breakfast on the deck together—peaches, bananas, grapes and walnuts chopped up and sprinkled with Grape Nuts, freshly squeezed orange and grapefruit juice and, for Lindsay only, the industrial-strength coffee she still needed to kick-start her day. It didn't matter how healthy her diet and her habits became; she had grown up on a high-voltage caffeine jolt first thing in the morning, and herbal tea was never going to boot her synapses into activity. Later than usual, because it was Sunday and she was only on standby, Sophie had headed north to the hospital in the

Bay Area where she worked with HIV-positive mothers, leaving Lindsay to her computer. She preferred to work when Sophie was on duty so she could enjoy their time off together without guilt. Consequently, she didn't mind settling down with more coffee and a pile of photocopied newspaper cuttings next to her keyboard.

Six years before, she'd stopped practising journalism and started teaching it. Not a day had gone by when she hadn't congratulated herself on her decision. Now, thanks to the "publish or be damned" demands of her boss at Santa Cruz, she'd been catapulted into her past life. A persuasive editor had talked her into a publishing contract for a book on the decline of British tabloid journalism from 1980 to 1995. It was supposed simultaneously to be a penetrating political analysis and an entertaining romp for the general reader. "Define oxymoron," Lindsay muttered as her machine booted up with its usual mechanical grumbles. "The demands of a publisher's editor. On the one hand, deep and insightful. On the other hand, shallow and superficial."

Today, the Falklands conflict. Not the battles between the Argentinian and British soldiery, but the rows that raged between government censors and militant journalists betrayed by proprietors who caved in under pressure. And the *Sun*'s shameful "Gotcha!" headline on the sinking of the *Belgrano*. It was more than enough to keep her absorbed in her screen until late afternoon, apart from a quick break at noon to walk Mutton around the scrubland and eat a chicken Caesar salad.

By five, she'd had enough. Whistling the dog, Lindsay had fired up her battered black Caddie and headed inland to a grocery store a few miles away that carried a stock select enough to satisfy the most discriminating California foodie. Lindsay's freezer was empty of bread, and she needed to stock up on ciabatta with olives, with artichokes, with sun-dried tomatoes and just plain. The challenge was always to get it home without tearing lumps out of it *en route*. While she was there, she raided the deli counter for grazing material for the evening. It was that once-a-month night when Sophie would be out with her doctor friends putting the world to rights, so Lindsay could veg out on the sofa and watch the *Inspector Morse* episode she'd taped the week before, with occasional trips to the kitchen to stack up another plate of nibbles. Bliss.

Her plans died when she got back to the house and finally got round to opening the morning paper. She idly flicked over the front page, breaking off a piece of artichoke ciabatta. *Darkliners Author Dies in Freak Accident* seemed to separate itself from the rest of page three and rise towards her like a macabre magic carpet.

"No," Lindsay breathed as she started to read.

(London, AP)

Penny Varnavides, best-selling author of the Darkliners series of novels, died yesterday as the result of a freak accident while on a trip to England. She was killed when a bottle of beer exploded in the kitchen of the apartment in London, where she was living temporarily.

The body was discovered by a neighbor, alerted by the open door of her apartment. It is thought Ms Varnavides had just returned home when the accident occurred.

According to police sources in London, Ms Varnavides bled to death when a shard of glass from the explosion penetrated her carotid artery. The unusually prolonged hot summer weather this year in England, where some areas have not had rain for over five weeks, is being blamed for the accident.

A police officer said, "The beer in question was apparently a kind which contains live yeast. In the warm weather, it must have started a secondary fermentation, and so the pressure inside the bottle would have increased enormously. The slightest vibration could have triggered the resulting explosion.

"It was a freak accident. Ms Varnavides was alone when it happened. If someone else had been present, it's possible she might have survived. But there are no suspicious circumstances."

Ms Varnavides was in London to complete research on her latest book, said to be a departure from her award-winning Darkliners series of fantasy novels for adolescent readers. She was rumored to be working closely with her British publishers, Monarch Press, on a "women in jeopardy" thriller aimed at the adult audience.

A member of the Monarch editorial team said, "We're all devastated by Penny's death. She was in the office only hours before she died. It's a tragic loss."

Ms Varnavides, 42, grew up in Chicago and studied at Northwestern and Stanford. After graduating, she worked in the computer industry. Her debut Darkliners novel, The Magicking of Danny Armstrong, *was first published in England because she couldn't find a US publisher. But its runaway success was repeated all over the world and she became a full-time novelist ten years ago. She was unmarried and lived in San Francisco.*

The apartment where the tragedy took place is the home of a British academic who exchanged it with Ms Varnavides' duplex in Noe Valley for the summer.

The piece of bread never made it to her mouth. Lindsay sat down suddenly on a kitchen chair and reread the article, tears pricking her eyes. Mutton slumped against her leg, butting his head against her sympathetically. Lindsay's hand went to the dog's head in an automatic movement, rubbing her fingers over the silky ears. Her other hand traced the outline of the newsprint. Penny was dead.

The tears spilled over and trickled down Lindsay's cheeks. Less than five weeks before, Penny had been sitting on their deck knocking back Sierra Nevada amber ale and bemoaning the end of her relationship with Meredith Miller, the woman she'd been seeing for the previous five years. It had been a shocking conversation. If anyone had asked Lindsay who were the couple most likely to make it work, she'd have answered without hesitation, "Meredith and Penny." They'd always seemed entirely compatible, a marriage of equals. Even Penny's need to remain in the closet because of her huge market among teenagers in middle America hadn't been a bone of contention; it was matched by Meredith's own requirements. A computer scientist with a defence contractor, she had top-secret clearance, a grading she'd lose immediately her sexuality became known to her professionally paranoid bosses.

The two women had shared a tall Victorian house that had been divided into a duplex; Meredith lived in the two lower floors, Penny above. But the terraced garden at the back was common, allowing them to move freely from one section of the house to the other without being overlooked. So they'd effectively lived together, while maintaining the fiction of being nothing more than friends. In San Francisco, Lindsay had realised a long time ago, it wasn't always easy to tell who were lovers and who merely friends. It was so easy to be out that everyone assumed anyone who wasn't had to be straight and sadly lacking a partner.

Although it had been clear from the tone of the conversation that it had been Penny who had given Meredith her marching orders, she had spoken with deep regret about the ending of the relationship. "She left me with no choice," she'd said sadly, head leaning against Sophie's shoulder as Lindsay tended the barbecue. "Right from the start, we always had borderlines, you know? We had common concepts of what was acceptable in a relationship and what wasn't. Fidelity was an absolute. She must have known she was leaving me no option, doing what she did." She took another pull on her beer and stared into the sunset.

"Maybe she was testing you," Lindsay had tried.

"I don't think so," Penny said. "I think she was in self-destruct mode. And you can't stop somebody who's that determined."

"No, but you don't have to give them a shove in the wrong direction," Lindsay muttered, knowing she wouldn't be heard over the hissing of the marinade she'd just used to baste the salmon.

By the end of the evening, Penny had had enough bottles of the dark golden ale for Sophie to insist she stayed the night and Lindsay had had enough of Penny's grief to slip away on the excuse of checking her e-mail. "Tactless toerag," Sophie had muttered as she'd slid into bed beside her later.

"How can I be tactless from my study?" Lindsay asked plaintively.

"Have you forgotten who taught you to be computer literate? Who showed you how to surf the Internet?"

"Oops," Lindsay said.

"Oops is right. You going off to collect your e-mail was the signal for Penny to slide right over into maudlin tears and reminisce about Meredith turning the lesbian community cyberpunk."

"But only if they let her wear a bag over her head," Lindsay responded. "You know, I couldn't do a job where I had to stay in the closet."

"No," Sophie sighed. "You have many fine qualities, Lindsay, but discretion isn't even in the top forty."

And now Penny was dead. Lindsay kept staring at the newspaper. She had no idea what to do next. She supposed she should call Meredith in San Francisco, but she didn't have any enthusiasm for it. It wasn't that she didn't want to be supportive, rather that she knew she was more use at the practical rather than the emotional side of things. In their partnership, it was Sophie who did emotional support.

Impatient with herself, Lindsay wiped the tears from her face. She'd take the dog for his evening run, then she'd call Meredith. "Penny would have taken the piss mercilessly," she told Mutton as she walked up to the bedroom and changed into her running uniform of shorts, T-shirt and crosstrainers. "'Whatever happened to the tough journalist?' she'd have said. 'Thought you could face out anybody? You scared of a bit of raw emotion, Lindsay?' She'd have been a proper monkey on my back, dog," she added as Mutton licked her knee.

Lindsay jogged up the street, then cut across towards the beach, avoiding the wiry grasses that would whip her legs raw within minutes. Once on the sand, she headed for the water's edge, turned her back on Pillar Point and let her rhythm gradually build to a place where it became a part of her she didn't have to think about. There were fewer people than usual on the beach that evening but Lindsay didn't notice. Penny Varnavides was at the centre of her mind's eye, caught in a slo-mo memory replay, playing beach volleyball with Lindsay, Sophie, Meredith and half a dozen other women last Easter. Lindsay could see the ponytail of glossy black hair switch across Penny's tanned shoulders as she leapt for the ball, the sun glinting on dark eyes and white teeth as she soared into the sky, fingers stretched to the limit to nudge the ball upwards again for one of her teammates to sweep back over the net.

Never again, Lindsay thought, bitter and sad. Next time they all trooped down to the beach, they'd be one short.

Although she wasn't consciously checking out her surroundings, part of Lindsay's mind was on alert. Her evening routine with the dog had been going on sufficiently long for her to be familiar with other locals who ran or walked by the ocean. A stranger was enough in itself to register with her. A stranger walking a north-westerly line that looked as if it were chosen to intersect inevitably with her southerly one was enough to take her mind momentarily off Penny. Lindsay slowed slightly and stared at the approaching figure.

A woman. Height around five six, hair shoulder length and mid-brown. A large leather satchel slung over one hip. Shorts, lightweight shirt and sandals, but the skin too pale to be a Californian. Mutton bounded up to the woman, barking cheerfully. At once, she stopped and crouched to pat him. "English," Lindsay grunted to herself. She slowed till she was barely faster than walking pace. The woman looked up, met her eyes and straightened up. By then, only a dozen yards separated them.

"Lindsay Gordon." It was a statement, not a question. Two words were enough to confirm Lindsay's presumption that those pale limbs didn't belong to an American. Mutton dropped on to his stomach on the sand, head down between his front paws.

Lindsay paused, hands on hips, breathing slightly harder than she needed to. If she was going to have to take off, better that the other woman thought she was more tired than she was. "You have the advantage of me, then," she said, a frosty imitation of Mel Gibson's proud Scottish dignity in *Braveheart*.

"Meredith Miller sent me. I . . . I'm afraid I have some bad news."

The accent was Estuary English. It had never been one of Lindsay's favourites, always reminding her of spivvy Tory MPs on the make. Distance hadn't lent it enchantment. She wiped away the sweat that had sprung out on her upper lip. She cocked her head to one side and said, "I know Penny's dead, if that's what you mean. It made the papers. Who *are* you?"

The woman opened her satchel and Lindsay rose on to the balls of her feet, ready for fight or flight. The past she'd tried so hard to bury in California had conditioned her responses more than she liked to admit. Especially when she was dealing with people with English accents. But nothing more threatening than a business card emerged from the bag. Lindsay took it and read, "DGM Investigations. Sandra Bloom, senior operative." There was an address with an East London postcode that would have rendered the whole card a joke before Canary Wharf started to fill up. Now, it signalled that Sandra Bloom's company thought they were out at the leading edge of private investigation, light years away from the bottle of bourbon and the trilby.

"DGM?" Lindsay asked.

Sandra Bloom's mouth twisted in a wince. "Don't get mad?"

Lindsay nodded. "Must have seemed like a good idea at the time. So what's all this about, Ms Bloom? What are you doing here? What's your connection to Meredith? And why are we standing in the middle of a beach when we live in a world that has more phones, faxes and modems than hot dinners?"

Sandra looked faintly embarrassed. "I don't know exactly what it is that Ms Miller does for a living . . ."

Lindsay interrupted with a snort of ironic laughter. "Join a very large club."

". . . but whatever it is, it's made her rather paranoid about normal methods of communication," she continued regardless. Lindsay nodded. "Right. I remember the lecture. Menwith Hill, Yorkshire, England. One of the biggest listening posts in the world, run to all intents and purposes by the US government. Who routinely monitor phone calls, faxes and computer traffic. I've always found it hard to get my head round the idea. I mean, the sheer volume of it. Some days I don't have time to read my own e-mail. The thought of ploughing through everybody else's . . . Anyway, yeah, it's starting to make sense. Okay, I understand why Meredith wouldn't want to entrust anything sensitive to any form of telecommunication. And given the news in today's paper, I don't have to be what's-her-name with the crystal ball on the national lottery to figure out it must be something to do with Penny. So what's going on?"

Sandra pushed her hair back from her face in what was clearly a regular time-buying gesture. "Ms Miller and her lawyer have sent me over from London . . ."

"Hang on a minute," Lindsay butted in again. "What's with the 'lawyer' bit? I didn't even know Meredith was *in* London, never mind that she'd got herself a lawyer."

"Ms Miller has a lawyer because she seems to think she's about to become the police's number one suspect in their inquiry into the murder of Penny Varnavides," Sandra blurted out in a rush, clearly deciding it was the only way to tell Lindsay anything without interruption.

Lindsay found herself staggering slightly at the abrupt news. Mutton scrambled to his feet and thrust a wet nose into her hand. "Can we walk while we talk? My muscles need to warm down properly or I'll cramp up," she stalled, turning so she and Sandra faced back up the beach. Sandra fell in by her side. A few steps further on, Lindsay said, "The paper here said there were no suspicious circumstances. What changed?"

"The police found out about the murder method in Ms Varnavides' new book."

"Which is?"

"The killer reads a warning in the newspaper from a chain of—is it 'convenience stores' they call them over here?"

"That's right, if you mean off-licences."

"This warning tells customers to keep wheat beer refrigerated in prolonged spells of warm weather to prevent secondary fermentation and possible explosive accidents. So the killer puts half a dozen bottles of wheat beer on top of the fridge at head height. Then he knocks one to the floor, where of course it breaks explosively. He snatches up a shard of glass and when his victim comes rushing through to see what's going on, he thrusts it into her neck. Then he pulls it out, wipes it clean of his fingerprints and lets her bleed to death. Then he shakes up another bottle and opens it so that she's sprayed with beer as if she'd been caught in the actual explosion." Her delivery was precise and measured. That made it easier for Lindsay to tune out the thought that it was her friend who had been killed in this ruthless way. She imagined Sandra's reports would be masterpieces of concision.

"Yeah, right," Lindsay sighed. "I can see why they might have changed their minds. But that still doesn't explain what you're doing here, stalking me like some trainee assassin," she added, trying to get rid of the sinking feeling in her stomach with smart-mouthed defiance.

"I'm here to bring you back to England," Sandra said baldly.

Lindsay shook her head. "No way." She'd been right to feel apprehensive. For once, being right didn't make her feel any better.

"Ms Miller has hired me to persuade you to come back and help her," Sandra said woodenly.

"So far, you're not doing too well. What does she need me for? She's already got a private eye."

"We don't do this kind of work. Our speciality is white collar fraud. I wouldn't know where to begin on a murder investigation. Ms Miller seems to think you would."

Lindsay shook her head. "I'm not a hired gun. I'm a journalist, not a private eye. Besides, I've been away from England a long time. I'm not what Meredith needs."

"She thinks you are."

Lindsay shook her head violently. "No way. You've had a wasted journey, Ms Bloom." Then she turned away and started to run back towards the safety of her own four walls.

2

The high whine of the jet engine dropped a little as the plane hit its cruising height and levelled out. Lindsay pressed a button in the armrest and exchanged the operatic aria in her headphones for contemporary Irish music. At least flying Aer Lingus meant there was a decent choice of in-flight music, she thought. And the music was the perfect distraction to avoid having to think about why she had agreed to a marathon journey back to London, changing at Dublin, in the charmless company of Sandra Bloom.

Ten minutes after Lindsay had made it back home, the dogged private eye had rung the doorbell. Lindsay had tried to ignore it, continuing on her journey to the fridge for a cold beer, but Mutton refused to play. He ran to the front door, snuffling eagerly round the edges, then barking loudly, tail wagging as he scented his newest friend. He turned to look expectantly at Lindsay, uncapping her beer and ostentatiously ignoring the dog. He gave a soft whimper then turned back to the door, outlining its edges with anxious snorts and anguished yelps.

"All *right*," Lindsay sighed. She took a long swig of beer, then crossed to the door. She yanked it open and immediately said, "I told you no, and I meant it."

Sandra Bloom nodded agreement. "I know. But Ms Miller is adamant that you're the only person who can help her. She stressed that she wants you to come not only because of your investigative skills but also because you're a friend and that means she can trust you with things she'd be wary of explaining to a stranger."

Lindsay cast her eyes upwards. "Emotional blackmail now, is it? I suppose you'd better come in. The neighbours think we lower the tone enough as it is without having private eyes leaning on the doorbell."

Sandra Bloom had been an investigator for long enough not to care how ungracious an invitation might be as long as it was forthcoming. She followed Lindsay inside and took in a living area with polished wood-block floors, dark squashy sofas and brilliantly coloured Georgia O'Keeffe prints splashed across white walls. She decided not to comment on its attractiveness, knowing instinctively her target would dismiss it as merely another ploy. "I realise you feel pressured," she said as Lindsay threw herself down on the nearest sofa, scowling.

"Good."

"But Ms Miller is in a very vulnerable emotional state. Her lover—"

"Former lover," Lindsay interrupted.

"Her lover until very recently," Sandra Bloom corrected her precisely, "has been murdered in a particularly calculated and cold-blooded way. She's on her own in a strange city, thousands of miles from her friends. And as if that isn't enough, she's a suspect in the murder inquiry. And you're the only person she thinks can help her."

"But I'm not," Lindsay protested. "What has she told you about me?"

"Very little. She did say that although you weren't a detective, you'd solved murders before."

Lindsay took another long pull at her bottle of beer. "Look," she said. "I'm a journalist by trade. I don't even do that any more. I teach kids how to be journalists because I realised I couldn't do the job any more. It was costing me too much to burst into people's lives and turn them upside down. Yes, I got caught up in murder investigations a couple of times and managed to uncover some stuff that the police didn't. But none of that makes me competent to sort out Meredith's problems."

"You're probably right," Sandra Bloom said sympathetically. "It takes a lot of skill and experience to be a good detective. You might have the rudiments of the skills, but you certainly haven't got the experience. Frankly, I think Meredith Miller would be better off hiring almost any private investigator in London. That's what I told her lawyer. But Ms Miller wasn't having any. It was Lindsay Gordon or nobody."

Lindsay's scowl deepened. "I told you, emotional blackmail doesn't work."

"Fair enough." Sandra Bloom's smile was placatory. "And I fully appreciate why you don't want to get involved. It can get hairy out there on the streets. You don't want to be out on the front line unless you really know how to handle yourself. No, better Ms Miller has nobody out there batting for her than she has somebody who doesn't know what the hell to do next."

The smile was starting to make Lindsay feel patronised rather than soothed. "I didn't say I was totally clueless," she muttered.

"Of course not," Sandra continued blithely. "But you said yourself, you're a long way off being a pro. But you appreciate I had to come and double check." She took a step towards the front door. "I can go back now with a clear conscience. Once she realises that she can't count on having an investigator who's one of her closest friends, I know she'll settle for a regular firm of private investigators. I know a couple we can recommend to her. Thanks for your time, anyway." Another step towards the door. "I'll tell Ms Miller that you fully sympathise, but you're unable to help."

Lindsay dropped her empty bottle on the floor with a clunk. She sighed. "Okay. You win. I'll come back. You can stay here tonight, and first thing tomorrow, we'll sort out a flight."

Sandra Bloom's smile quirked upwards at one corner. It was the only sign that she'd succeeded in a carefully worked-out plan. "Not quite," she said. "I've got reservations for an overnight flight."

Lindsay looked at her watch. "Tonight? No chance. I've got to discuss this with my partner, I've got to pack, I've got arrangements to cancel . . ."

"And Ms Miller could be under arrest by morning."

Lindsay stood up and glowered at Sandra Bloom. "Have you ever met my partner? Sophie Hartley?"

Sandra Bloom shook her head, puzzled. "Why? Should I have?"

"I think the two of you took the same guilt-tripping course," Lindsay growled, picking up the bottle and stomping through to the kitchen.

Five hours later, she was in flight. Because college had broken up for the summer, she had no teaching burden to rearrange. Writing the book could wait; she'd reached the point where any distraction was welcome. It had taken less than half an hour to pack the assortment of light and heavy clothes an English summer normally demands. Lindsay's attempts to contact Sophie had taken rather longer since Sod's Law—anything that can go wrong will go wrong—was the only exception to itself, operating like clockwork as usual. Inevitably, Sophie and her cronies hadn't been in their usual restaurant, so Lindsay hadn't been able to speak to her lover. She'd ended up leaving a written explanation stuck to the tin of chamomile tea that she knew Sophie would hit as soon as she came home. Hopefully, Sophie wouldn't be too upset, given that their own summer trip to the UK was due to start in a week's time anyway.

As the night slipped away under the plane's wings, Lindsay wondered what she would find at the end of her journey. One thing was certain. Her own mourning had to go on hold if she was to be any use to Meredith at all. And in spite of her initial resistance to Sandra Bloom, Lindsay wanted to do what she could for Meredith. She'd always had a soft spot for her, not least because of Meredith's response to her techno-fear.

It had happened after her last brush with murder. She and Sophie had been telling the story to Meredith and Penny one weekend when the four had been camping down at Big Sur. By lantern light, Sophie had revealed how, without her computer expertise, Lindsay would never have uncovered the truth behind the death of trade union boss Tom Jack. Both Meredith and Penny had been open-mouthed with astonishment to discover that someone who worked in the communications industry was a virtual electronic illiterate.

"Doesn't make me a bad person," Lindsay had mumbled uncomfortably.

The others hooted with laughter at her discomfiture. "You don't have to be a nerd to know a bit from a byte," Meredith told her. "Hey, it's only scary because you don't understand it."

"I've tried to teach her," Sophie said.

Meredith snorted. "That's like husbands teaching their wives to drive. Never try to teach your beloved anything technical. It's the fast lane to divorce. Nah, Sophie, leave it to me. I'll have her writing code by the end of the year."

It had never gone that far, but Meredith had taught Lindsay more about hardware, software, hacking and net-surfing than she'd ever needed to use. The only question it had left unanswered was what exactly Meredith did for a living that meant she had all this stuff at her fingertips. There was no secret about who she worked for—a software and electronics complex in Silicon Valley, south of San Francisco, whose income, everyone knew, came from the Pentagon. Whenever Lindsay or anyone else asked for something approximating a job description, Meredith would simply smile and shake her head. "I kill bugs. You want more details, you have to need to know, babe," she'd say. "And just being curious don't count as a need." Lindsay had sometimes wondered if even Penny had known.

Somehow, though, Meredith's silence about that crucial area of her life hadn't been a barrier between her and Lindsay. While Sophie was undoubtedly closer to Penny, Lindsay and Meredith forged a complicit bond where they played the childish role to the other pair's sensible maturity, running off to play computer games or to chase the dog along the beach when the conversation grew too serious for their mood.

But it wasn't all frivolity between them. Meredith regularly printed out obscure snippets and articles from the Internet that she thought might interest Lindsay, and often as they walked along the sand the two had debated the thorny issues around freedom of information and the preservation of personal privacy. From theoretical debate, their dialogues had moved to the personal, each sharing issues in their relationships with lovers, friends and colleagues. While Lindsay was unequivocal in her conviction that Sophie was her closest friend, she knew too that Meredith had an important place in her life. "I have to have somebody to whinge about Sophie to," she'd said once, only partly joking. She might have few complaints about her partner, but she knew herself well enough to realise that the way to keep them in perspective was to release them to someone who could point out that she was overreacting. For Meredith, coached in a life of secrecy both professionally and personally, talking to Lindsay, no matter how sparingly or obliquely, was often her only outlet. It wasn't so surprising that she had sent Sandra Bloom after her.

Remembering what Meredith had taught her about the relentless logic of computers, Lindsay sifted through the little she knew about Penny's death. She sighed and shifted in her seat. "How did the police get on to the idea that it wasn't an accident after all?" she asked Sandra Bloom.

The detective looked up from her copy of *Sense and Sensibility*. "The murder method was identical to the one outlined in Ms Varnavides' new book," she said, her tone patiently condescending.

"Yeah, I got that first time around, thanks. What I mean is, what tipped them off to the fact that Penny died the same way as her fictional victim? I'm having some trouble getting my head round the idea of some cop sitting down with Penny's laptop and scrolling through her files on the off chance of finding something that would turn an accident into a murder inquiry. It's usually the other way round, isn't it? Ignore the suspicious circumstances, call it an accident, it doesn't half cut down on the paperwork."

Sandra Bloom breathed heavily through her nose as she listened to Lindsay's irony. "According to Ms Miller's solicitor, Ms Varnavides' agent called the police. She'd read a synopsis of the book and she believed it was more than coincidence that her client should die in an identical way."

"Her *agent*? Bloody hell, that's one way to make sure you maximise your ten per cent!"

"I think that's a pretty harsh judgement," Sandra said stiffly.

Lindsay snorted. "Easy seen you've not encountered many literary agents. Think about it. Penny's death is going to increase sales anyway. But murder? That's a whole different ball game. Tie your dead author in to a gruesome murder mystery that's linked in turn to her books and you've hit the jackpot. Penny Varnavides is probably going to sell more books dead than she ever did alive. But I don't suppose any of that even crossed her agent's mind when she rushed off to perform her civic duty." Her Scottish accent intensified with her sarcasm.

"It was bound to come out sooner or later," the detective said. "I expect her publishers will be doing their bit to cash in too. Somebody will presumably have to finish her final book so they can publish it. So they'd have been bound to make the connection."

"I suppose so."

"And by that stage, the waters would have been muddied by the passage of time and it would have been that much harder to nail the killer," Sandra observed calmly.

Lindsay nodded. "You're right. In fact, you seem to be pretty good at this being right business. I don't suppose you'd want to stick around, help me out with the investigation?"

Sandra Bloom gave the first spontaneous and open smile Lindsay had seen so far. "With someone as awkward as you? No offence, Lindsay, but life's too short."

Put in her place as firmly as few had ever managed, Lindsay grunted and squirmed round in her seat, tucking her pillow under her head and pulling her blanket over her shoulders. "Wake me for breakfast. Not before," she said firmly.

You could never confuse the approaches to San Francisco and Heathrow, Lindsay thought as she stared down at the chequerboard of small fields and housing estates. Having dozed fitfully some of the way across America and the Atlantic and read the rest of the time, she'd been stupefied with lack of sleep during the transfer at Dublin Airport. At one point she'd found herself wandering dreamlike into a Doc Martens shop and trying on a pair of shiny gold boots. If it hadn't been for Sandra Bloom looming over her at the crucial moment, she might even have bought them. But now she was grittily awake, feeling faintly sick and aware that the long flight had just been a way of putting things on hold. In a few minutes, they would land, and she'd be in the thick of things. Penny's death, Meredith's grief and someone's guilt would have to be dealt with. She wished she'd waited for Sophie.

Baggage reclaim, customs and immigration were swift and painless. The two women emerged into the main concourse, Lindsay apprehensive, Sandra relieved. Straight ahead, Meredith bent one arm at the elbow in a half-hearted wave. The forlorn gesture knocked Lindsay on her heels with its pathos. Then she surged forward, leaving Sandra to take charge of the abandoned luggage trolley, and swept Meredith into her arms.

For a long minute, the two women rocked each other back and forth wordlessly. For Lindsay, who knew the pain of losing a lover to death, it was as if Meredith's agony was seeping into her by osmosis, taking her back to a place she thought she'd left far behind. All Meredith was aware of was the comfort of a familiar face, a familiar shape in her grasp.

It was Meredith who pulled back first. "You'll never know how much this means," she said, her voice cracking.

"Couldn't just abandon you," Lindsay said. As soon as the words were spoken, she knew they were the truth. There had never really been any chance of Sandra Bloom coming back empty-handed. "I'm so sorry," she added.

Meredith nodded, biting her lip, clearly battling tears. Lindsay put her arm around her and they moved away from the incoming passengers and their meeters and greeters. Out of the corner of her eye, she was aware of Sandra Bloom conferring with a woman in a dark trouser suit, a mac thrown with stylish lack of care over her shoulders. Where Lindsay and Meredith moved, they followed.

Lindsay steered Meredith into a chair in a quiet corner away from the crowds. "Okay?" she asked anxiously, watching Meredith blow her already red nose and dab at puffy eyes with a crumpled tissue.

The woman in the suit stepped forward. "I'm Geri Cusack," she said, the soft blur of an Irish accent still evident enough almost to swallow the vowel on the end of her first name. "Meredith's solicitor."

More sexily slurred vowels, Lindsay couldn't help noticing. She'd also taken in the straight shoulders and the gentler curves below, the reddish hair and hazel eyes set in a face shaped like a Pre-Raphaelite maiden. The features, though, were far too strong to appeal to any painter whose idea of womanhood fell on the submissive side of the fence. Geri Cusack, Lindsay decided, was not a woman to mess with. Wherever Meredith had found her, it hadn't been first pick in the Yellow Pages. "It was good of you to bring Meredith to meet me," she said. "We'll manage now."

"I don't think you appreciate the gravity . . ." Sandra Bloom started. Geri Cusack raised her hand in a warning gesture and the detective's words trailed off.

"Sandra, would you wait with Meredith a minute? Me and Ms Gordon need to have a word."

Lindsay, half in love with the lawyer's voice, followed her meekly for a few yards. "I meant it," she said. "We'll manage now."

"That's fine. I understand you need to ask her things it would be as well I didn't know the answers to. That's the way it goes in difficult cases like these. I don't have a problem with it. I just wanted to fill you in on where we're up to. Saturday evening, she was arrested and taken in for questioning. They were concentrating on establishing that she knew about the murder method in the book, and on where she was at the time they think Penny was killed. She doesn't have anything approaching an alibi. But they've got nothing on her except the thinnest of circumstantial evidence so they've released her on police bail."

"They wouldn't want the custody time to run out without enough evidence to charge her," Lindsay said sourly.

"You know how the Police and Criminal Evidence Act works? That might come in handy. Anyway, she's been advised not to attempt to leave the country and to report back to the police station on Friday morning. Just so's you know."

"And you want what, exactly?"

Her wide mouth twitched in what looked like a half-smile, half grimace. "My client's instructions were to get you here so you could establish her innocence. I think I'd settle for that."

"Nothing too difficult, then," Lindsay muttered.

"Not for you, according to Meredith." Her eyebrows rose momentarily. If it hadn't been a wildly inappropriate moment,

Lindsay would have been convinced she was flirting. As it was, she decided, it was simply part of a formidable armoury Geri Cusack dedicated to the greater good of her clients. "I'll let you get on," the lawyer said.

Lindsay stayed where she was for a moment, watching Geri Cusack say farewell to her client and scoop Sandra Bloom up in her wake. Then she moved across to Meredith and sat down beside her, taking her hand and squeezing it gently. Meredith stared bleakly at Lindsay with the red-rimmed eyes of a sick and bewildered child. "I didn't kill her," she said. "God knows, I felt like it, but I didn't do it."

3

The service flat in St John's Wood was a reminder to Lindsay that Meredith and Penny inhabited a different financial dimension from her and Sophie. While Meredith was making coffee, Lindsay prowled the room, noting the deep pile of the carpet and the expensive brocade of upholstery and curtains. The weekly rate was probably about double the monthly mortgage on the house in Half Moon Bay. Whatever had brought Meredith to England, it was clearly something she valued.

It hadn't been difficult to persuade her that the arrivals lounge at Heathrow wasn't the best place to deal with her grief. Stifling her Calvinist conscience at the thought of the expense, Lindsay had followed her to the cab rank, secretly grateful that she wouldn't have to lug her bags any further than absolutely necessary. They hadn't said much on the stuttering journey through west London's heavy traffic, contenting themselves with superficial conversation about San Franciscan acquaintances and Lindsay's flight. It had been a relief to escape from the stuffy cab and feel able to talk openly.

Meredith carried through a tray with mugs and milk jug grouped around a steaming cafetière and placed it carefully on a footstool large enough to accommodate a pair of seven league boots. As she poured, Lindsay looked at her more closely. Meredith's dark blonde hair was ratty, pulled back into a ponytail held by an elastic band. Her eyelids looked bruised and puffy, and dark pouches had appeared under eyes whose grey irises swam in a background of red and white craquelure. The skin on her face and neck seemed to have sagged and crêped overnight, and her lips were chapped and split. Passing her in the street, a casual observer would have assumed the expensive clothes, carefully chosen for their flattering cut and colour, belonged to someone else. Lindsay had always thought Meredith attractive; now she understood that it was only the spark of her liveliness that had made her so. With Penny dead, the light in Meredith's face had died, leaving her damaged and ordinary.

"I appreciate you coming," Meredith said. "I didn't know if you would."

Lindsay felt a pang of guilt that she'd even considered refusing. "Yeah, well, we've been friends a while now."

"I haven't behaved much like a friend since Penny and I split up. I didn't return your calls, I didn't come round."

Lindsay shrugged. "I assumed you weren't ready to talk about it. I wasn't offended."

Meredith sighed. "It wasn't just that I wasn't ready. I knew Penny was seeing Sophie. I saw Sophie pick her up one night around dinnertime and drop her off a couple of hours later. I figured you'd have heard Penny's side of it. Which would not have been a pretty story. I didn't expect you'd be too bothered about the case for the defence."

"You should know me better than that."

Meredith acknowledged her reproach with a sad smile. "I know. But I haven't been thinking too straight."

"That's what I'm here for now. But if you're serious about wanting me to investigate this, you're going to have to give me a free hand."

Meredith nodded, cradling her coffee in her hands as if it were precious and fragile. "You got it," she said.

Lindsay nodded, her lips tight in anticipation of awkwardness. She pushed her hair back from her face and said, "It means I have to ask difficult questions. You probably aren't going to want to answer some of them, but it's important that you tell me the truth, okay? Even if it's something that makes it look bad for you, you have to tell me. I'm not going to misunderstand the way your lawyer might, because I *know* you couldn't have killed Penny." Well, not like that, she added mentally. Not with that degree of premeditation.

Meredith stared into her coffee. "I don't have anything to hide," she said, her voice flat as a synthesised answering machine. She looked up, her eyes blank. "I didn't kill Penny. I don't know who did. That's what I need you to find out."

"I'll do my best. So, when did Penny actually arrive in Britain?"

"She'd been here a day or two under three weeks."

Lindsay jotted a note on the fresh pad she'd dropped into her backpack in Half Moon Bay. "I knew she was coming over, of course, I just wasn't sure exactly when she'd left. It was Sophie who spoke to her last. And you were due to come too, is that right?"

"I guess you remember how carefully she liked to plan things, and she'd been organising us both for this trip for months." Meredith sighed. "Originally, the plan was that I was going to join her for a couple of weeks near the beginning of her stay, then I was coming back towards the end for another ten days. After we split up, she decided it would be good for her to go ahead with the trip anyway, only alone."

Lindsay nodded. "But you decided to come regardless?"

"I couldn't leave it be. It meant too much for us to walk away from it. Hell, you know how much we loved each other. You and Sophie, you were there right from the start. Ruby's birthday dinner at Green's. The lights shining on the bay, only all I had eyes for was Penny . . ." Meredith's voice tailed off and two fat tears spilled down her pale cheeks.

Lindsay leaned forward and put an awkward hand on Meredith's arm. "I remember. She was the same. I couldn't get a word of sense out of either of you. If there hadn't been a table between you, you'd have been arrested for indecency in a public place."

A sad smile curled the edges of Meredith's lips. "Yeah. Feels like ancient history now, though." She rubbed the tears away with an impatient hand. "That said, I still cared about Penny too much to want to let her go. I figured I had a chance if I could only get her to listen to me. So I came on after her. I'd already booked the vacation time, it was just a matter of arranging a base for myself."

"And when did you get in?"

"Exactly a week ago."

Lindsay gave the room a quick scrutiny. "You dropped lucky with your digs."

"Pardon me?" Meredith looked puzzled.

"Sorry. Soon as I get back on British soil, I become more idiomatic than the natives. I was saying, you lucked out with the apartment."

Meredith looked round her vaguely. "This place? The company has a deal with the management here. This is where we always stay when we're over on business. It's easier to be private for meetings and stuff in an apartment like this than in a hotel. I just asked our travel department to book me a place and bill me direct."

Lindsay leaned back, relieved that her ploy had loosened Meredith up a little. "Going back a bit," she said casually. "To when you split up. That was about five, six weeks ago, am I right?"

Meredith's eyes went back to her coffee cup. "I guess," she said.

"I'm not entirely clear what went wrong."

Meredith made a choking sound that Lindsay translated as a bitter laugh. "The chapter and verse is clear enough. But why it escalated the way it did, that's the obscure part." She stood up abruptly and walked across to the window to stare out at the canopy of trees. "Do you have a cigarette?" she demanded, turning back into the room.

"Meredith, you know I quit years ago," Lindsay protested.

"I know, I just figured you might have brought some in tax-free for somebody. Friend, family, I don't know."

"You quit too. About six months after me. Don't do it, Meredith. Don't let the bastard kill you as well as Penny," Lindsay said passionately.

With an impatient gesture, Meredith freed her hair from the elastic band and let it fall around her face in a limp curtain. "Oh, fuck it!"

"You going to tell me what happened?" Lindsay said quietly, not taking her eyes off Meredith's face.

She threw herself into a large wing chair opposite Lindsay. "It all started with Penny deciding it was time she got out of the closet on her own terms before some smartass decided to out her."

"Was that likely?"

"You better believe it. There are a lot of militants out there who think that people like Penny owe it to the lesbian sisterhood to be out and proud. No compromises accepted. Never mind that Penny's been doing more good by keeping her sexuality to herself and providing positive images in her books. The politically correct know there's only one way to be and that's in people's faces." Meredith shook her head angrily. "Don't they understand that when you out somebody like Penny, all it means is that every right-wing parent in the country stops buying her books? As long as she looks as straight as a Midwest momma, they're never going to look inside the covers to see what their kids are reading. Soon as she's out, they'll be burning her books regardless, because she's a dangerous dyke poisoning the minds of their children."

Meredith's tirade left Lindsay momentarily without words. Compulsory outing was one of the few subjects on which she didn't have definite and strong views. She was for it when it came to hypocrites who abused their power over the lives of others, like politicians who failed to support gay rights issues and churchmen who preached one thing and practised another. But when it came to people who merely happened to have become celebrities, she was considerably less certain. She'd heard all the arguments about role models, but what message was being sent by a role model who had to be dragged kicking and screaming into the daylight? Clearly not one Meredith relished. "Mmm," Lindsay eventually muttered. "And Penny thought it was going to happen to her?"

"She'd already been threatened. We were at a party about three months back at Samoa Brand's house. Samoa has this new baby dyke lover, just graduated from college. And since she's twenty years younger than Samoa, she gets indulged all she wants. So this moron comes up to Penny and starts in on her with, 'My kid sister's read all your books. Don't you think it's time to pay back? People like you should be outed, don't you think? Shouldn't we show the world we've got a middle class too?'"

Lindsay raised her eyebrows. "That's just one motor-mouth kid, though," she said. "Surely Penny wasn't getting herself in a state over that?"

"She didn't think the kid was going to do anything, but it made her start to wonder how long it would be before somebody did. So she decided the best way to deal with the fallout was to take control and out herself. She knew there would be a lot of publicity round the new book, with it being her first adult novel. She figured that would be a good time to spread the word." Meredith rubbed the palms of her hands over her face.

"And you didn't think it was a good idea?"

Meredith sighed. "This is really difficult for me. No, I didn't think it was a good idea. I knew it would hurt her sales, but that would've been her price for her choice. That wasn't what it was about for me. I told Penny she was forgetting something important. She was forgetting there were two people in this relationship."

"But her coming out wouldn't automatically implicate you, would it? You didn't technically live together. You have separate postal addresses, separate front doors. Your lives are legally detached," Lindsay protested.

Meredith shook her head. "You don't understand the kind of job I do. Every damn year, I get vetted. That's why you never see me the second half of March and the first half of April. That's when it's my turn, so I have to look like Little Miss Prim around then. I *need* top security clearance to do my job. Soon as it became public knowledge that the person who lives in the other half of the house is a lesbian, they'd start to look a lot more carefully at me. If you know what you're looking for, you'll find it. Besides, you know what it was like for Pen. She wasn't some literary writer that nobody's ever heard of. She was a celeb. There isn't a literate teenager in America who hasn't read a Penny Varnavides Darkliners novel. She comes out and there's going to be media interest. And they're going to want to know exactly who her lover is. I had no chance of surviving if she came out."

Lindsay closed her eyes momentarily. "I'd avoid saying that to the police, if I was you," she sighed. "So, Penny was talking about coming out and you were trying to dissuade her. That about the size of it?"

"I guess."

"So how did you get from there to splitting up?"

Meredith looked away. "The whole thing was so dumb." Her voice was bitter.

"It usually is," Lindsay said.

"We were fighting a lot. That's something we'd never done before. Things never used to escalate like that between us. But it seemed like every time we were together we ended up fighting about whether she should come out." Meredith ran her hands through her hair in a gesture of frustration. "It was driving me crazy. I need to be clear-headed at work, I need to be able to think straight. And Penny was making me nuts. She just wouldn't be logical about the situation."

Lindsay waited. Eventually she said, "It's a lot of pressure, when things start going wrong between you and your lover. Something's got to give."

Meredith nodded. "It did. I slept with somebody else. I was out of town, we had dinner together. She was all the things Penny used to be with me—warm, funny, sympathetic. And I slept with her. I didn't even need a few drinks to get me there, I went sober and willing."

Lindsay thought back to a time when infidelity had been something infinitely casual to her. It was so alien to her relationship with Sophie, it felt like a past life experience. But memory helped her construct a glimmer of what that urge to betrayal felt like. "You're not the first and you're not going to be the last. There are other kinds of treachery that cause just as much damage. I take it Penny found out and confronted you?"

"I told her," Meredith said bleakly.

Oh, great, thought Lindsay. Why couldn't she have been a Catholic and off-loaded the guilt to a silent priest? "You didn't think she'd take it badly?"

"I knew she'd take it badly. That's why I told her. I figured it would make her realise how upset I was about her plan to come out. I guess I thought she'd realise that if I felt backed into a corner so far that I had to do something that went so fundamentally against everything our relationship was about, it was real serious and she should think again about what she was doing."

"And that's not what happened."

Meredith snorted ironically. "You got it. She could not see past her own concerns. All she could see was that I'd been unfaithful to her. She didn't stop to think why I might have felt driven to do that. She just didn't get it. Far as she was concerned, I'd committed one of the cardinal sins against the relationship. She was judge and jury and there was only one sentence she could pass. Had to be the death sentence. No mitigation."

"Didn't you try and explain?"

Meredith leaned forward, elbows on knees, hands clasped. "What do you think?"

Lindsay gave a wry smile. "I think you showered her with flowers and cards, filled her answering-machine tape with messages and kept a constant watch on the deck so that if she so much as stuck her nose out the door of an evening, you'd be able to saunter casually up to her and throw yourself at her feet and beg for mercy. That's what I think."

"Not far off the mark."

"And she ignored all your messages, dumped the flowers on your doorstep and didn't set foot outside from the moment you came home from work to the minute you left again in the morning?"

"She tell you all this?" Meredith asked, resigned to embarrassment.

"She didn't have to. Like you said earlier, I've known the pair of you right from the start. So you followed her over here to try and change her mind?"

Meredith nodded. "Waste of time and money. She'd have no more to do with me over here than she would back home. I guess she just about wore me down. The day she died, I left her another message on the answering machine. I swore it was going to be the last, and I told her so. I said it was her last chance to put it back together, otherwise I was going to assume she meant what she said and take appropriate action."

"Ah."

"Exactly."

"I was wondering how the cops got to you so fast."

"Wonder no more," Meredith said wryly. "I left the number, of course."

"And you knew all about the plot?"

"Oh, sure. Penny used to discuss her plots with three people—her agent, her editor and me."

"Is that all?" Lindsay asked, dismayed at seeing her circle of suspects shrink towards zero.

"She ever talk about them with you and Sophie?"

Lindsay shook her head. "She once asked Sophie for some background information about HIV, but even then she didn't explain why she wanted to know. We had to wait till the book came out before we knew what it was all in aid of."

"Exactly. She always said if she talked about it too much, she got bored with the story, then she couldn't be bothered to write it." Meredith's words clearly jogged a painful memory, for her eyes glittered with tears again. "I can't believe it, you know? It's like some sick joke. Like the phone's going to ring and she's going to say, 'Hey, have you suffered enough yet?'" She clenched her eyes shut, but tears still seeped through.

Unsure what to do for the best, Lindsay stood up and crossed to Meredith's side, putting a careful arm round her shoulder. "I know," she said softly. "Just when you think you've learned everything there is to know about pain, something creeps up on you and lets you know you're only a beginner. And everybody tells you you'll be all right, that time's a healer. I'll tell you something, Meredith. I don't think it ever gets better. It just gets different."

Meredith half turned and buried her face in Lindsay's chest, her body jerking with sobs. As she wailed, Lindsay simply held her close, one hand rubbing her back, trying not to think about Penny. Or her own Frances, all those years ago. It couldn't last forever, she told herself.

Eventually, cried out, Meredith pulled away and blurted, "I miss her so much," her voice choked with emotion. She pulled herself upright and staggered across the room into the hallway. Lindsay, hesitantly taking a step or two after her, was reassured by the sound of running water. She went back to her seat and waited. Long minutes passed, then Meredith returned, her eyes even more bloodshot, her face glowing from the scrubbing she'd clearly given it.

"Okay," she said briskly. "This is not getting you any closer to finding Pen's killer. What do we do now?"

"Who had a motive?" Lindsay demanded. "Apart from you, that is?"

4

Lindsay hadn't expected London temperatures to be nearly as high as California's. She was still dressed for the air-conditioned coolness of the plane, she thought, shrugging her shoulders to unstick shirt from skin. In this heat, jeans and cotton twill were not the ideal outfit for climbing four flights of narrow, dusty stairs with the smell of urine from the entrance still pungent. She wondered how many prospective clients were put off by the approach to Catriona Polson's office. Then she remembered that those climbers would be pre-published authors full of hope. "None," she muttered under her breath as she rounded the curve of the stairs and reached the final landing.

In contrast to the understated brushed-steel plaque on the downstairs wall and the ambience of a stairway which clearly doubled as a hostel for the homeless, the offices of Polson and Firestone indicated that somewhere on their client list there were some major earners. Even when Lindsay had left Britain, before Soho went up-market and sexually ambivalent, office suites in the area had commanded high rents. Now that the district was almost chic, it must take a sizeable bank balance to secure the whole top floor of a building with a view of Soho Square.

The offices lay behind tall double doors of pale grey wood and brushed steel. Lindsay opened the right-hand door and walked into a reception area that was still lurking in the previous decade. The bleached grey wood was the keynote, looking like the ghost of trees. What wasn't wood was leather or brushed steel. Including the receptionist, Lindsay thought grimly. She was glad she'd employed a ruse to ensure Catriona Polson would be in. Looking at hair blue-black as carbon steel and a jaw with a higher breaking strain than a girder, she knew she was about to be given the brush-off for having the temerity to arrive without an appointment or three chapters and a synopsis. The sweat on her forehead from the sudden transition to air conditioning didn't make her feel any more confident of success.

Lindsay had felt slightly guilty about ringing up and pretending to be an American publisher's assistant breathlessly booking a noon phone call to Ms Polson, but not guilty enough to miss making sure she wouldn't have a wasted journey. The receptionist's grim glare gave her immediate absolution. She smiled. Nothing altered. The receptionist continued to stare at the screen of her computer. Lindsay cleared her throat. The receptionist's plum-coloured mouth puckered. Lindsay found herself irresistibly thinking about cat's bottoms. Then the lips parted. "Can I help you?" haughtily, in a little girl voice that would have shattered crystal.

"I'd like to see Ms Polson. No, I don't have an appointment. I know she's in the building and I'm absolutely positive she's not in a meeting." Lindsay's smile grew wider as her voice became more honeyed.

The receptionist's whole face tightened, eyeliner and mascara almost meeting in a smudge of black. "I'm sorry," she said smugly. "She's expecting an important phone call."

Lindsay assumed her Southern belle accent. "I know, cher. I was the one booked the call. I just wanted to be good and sure Miz Polson would be here to see me." Then she grinned. "Would you tell her I'm representing Meredith Miller?"

The receptionist did her cat's bottom impression again. But she condescended to pick up the phone. "Name please?" she demanded as she keyed in a number.

Resisting the temptation to respond with her Sean Connery impersonation, Lindsay simply gave her name. The receptionist spoke into the phone. "Catriona? I've got a person here called Lindsay Gordon who says she's representing Meredith Miller. She also says she made a hoax phone call to us earlier, booking your call from New York . . . She says she wanted to make sure you'd be here . . ." She flicked an ostentatious glance up and down Lindsay's outfit. "No, she's definitely not from the tabloids . . ." A malicious smile crept across her face at those final words. She replaced the handset. "Ms Polson will be right with you."

Lindsay perched on the edge of the desk to irritate the receptionist while she searched her business card wallet for something appropriate. When she found it, she slipped it into her breast pocket for later. Just then, the inner door opened. Now Lindsay realised why all the doors in Polson and Firestone reached right up to the Victorian ceilings. Any lower and Catriona Polson would have been perpetually banging her head. She was one of the tallest women Lindsay had ever seen, and she must have been aware of the effect she had on people meeting her for the first time. Yet there was nothing apologetic or clumsy about the way she carried her six feet plus. Lindsay imagined with relish the effect on some of the more effete males of the publishing world whom she'd met. She wore a swirling skirt of Indian cotton, flat strappy sandals and a loose embroidered cotton camisole. Flyaway blonde hair was cut in a twenties bob and framed a round face that looked as if its normal expression was cheerful and welcoming. Right now, wariness was the predominant aspect.

She peered down at Lindsay without stooping. "Ms . . . Gordon, was it?"

Lindsay nodded. "Catriona Polson?"

"That's me. When you say you represent Meredith Miller, in what capacity are we talking here?" Her voice was firm and clipped, her accent straight out of a girls' school story.

Wishing she had a discreet card saying, "Private Investigator," Lindsay said, "I think it would be better if we conducted our business in private."

Catriona frowned. "I'm not at all sure we *have* any business. All I know about you is that you perpetrated a time-wasting hoax on my company and you claim to 'represent' someone who is not one of our clients and who, as far as I am aware, has nothing to do with publishing."

It was hard not to feel intimidated by the whole package. Lindsay struggled to maintain any sense of control over the confrontation. Just then, the outside door opened and a middle-aged man in a leather jacket came in. Shit or bust, she thought, dredging up an ancient memory of an interview with a private eye. "I'm a legal agent acting on Ms Miller's behalf," she said firmly. "I'm trying to conduct this matter discreetly, but if you prefer to discuss business matters in the lobby, that's fine by me. You are Penny Varnavides' literary executor and my client is her residuary legatee. My client wants to know what exactly . . ."

Before Lindsay could say more, Catriona had stepped back and was holding the door open for her. "This way," she said, her voice ten degrees frostier than the air conditioning.

Once she'd ushered Lindsay inside, Catriona stepped in front of her and led the way down a corridor lined with framed book covers. A couple were prize-winning Penny Varnavides Darkliners titles. At the end of the corridor was another steel and wood door which led into a small boardroom. The table and the chair frames were the now familiar ashen wood. Lindsay began to wonder if they'd taken over the offices from some failed financial consultancy. More book covers lined the walls, interspersed with author photographs. Penny was still there, in the centre of one of the side walls. Catriona walked determinedly to one end of the table and sat down, stretching her long legs in front of her and crossing them neatly at the ankles. "So," she said. "Why are you really here?"

Lindsay pulled out a chair a couple of seats away from her and sat down. "What makes you think I'm not here to talk about your executorship?"

"Pointless before probate's granted," she said dismissively.

"So why march me in here?"

"When people waltz into my office intent on causing trouble, I prefer not to give them the satisfaction of an audience." She dug into a pocket of her skirt and pulled out a packet of the mild cigarettes Lindsay had only ever smoked when she was kidding herself she was about to give up. As she lit one, she kept an eye on Lindsay. "So who are you, and what are you really doing here?"

The best lies, Lindsay knew, were the ones closest to the truth. "I'm an investigator. Meredith Miller is innocent, and she's engaged me to make some inquiries about the death of Penny Varnavides. I'm here to talk to you about Penny," Lindsay said, watching the smoke curling upwards and remembering how the business of smoking had always made her feel much better than the physical sensation.

"What makes you think I've got anything to say?"

"You had plenty to say to the police. And you were quick enough to say it."

Catriona leaned back in her chair and stretched for an ashtray sitting on a sideboard. "The police are the appropriate people to talk to when one believes a crime has been committed. And given Meredith's status as prime suspect, I'm not at all sure it would be appropriate for me to talk to you. Besides, there's an issue of client confidentiality here. Penny was my client, and I'm not inclined to breach our professional relationship."

"As soon as probate is granted, it'll be Meredith who benefits from your work even more than you will yourself. She will, in effect, be your client. Don't you think it would make life a little easier for everyone if you cooperated with me?" Lindsay tried.

"If Meredith did kill Penny, she won't be earning a shilling from the estate, will she?" Catriona inhaled, then released what was left of the smoke from her nostrils. It was hard not to read self-satisfaction into the gesture.

It was clear that Catriona and Lindsay were never going to become friends. With nothing to lose, Lindsay went on the attack. "But you will, won't you? Ten, twenty per cent of what Penny earned must have made you a lot of money while she was alive. Dead, she's going to generate a small fortune, isn't she? Even if it was just an accident, her sales are going to climb. But if it's a particularly gruesome and mysterious murder, using the very method outlined in her next book, her sales figures are going to go through the roof."

Catriona's eyebrows furled together in an angry frown. "That's an outrageous suggestion. You take my breath away, Ms Gordon."

"You're not the first woman who's said that," Lindsay said suggestively, gambling that Catriona was straight.

"How dare you!" Catriona said with contempt.

"Penny used to say it all the time," Lindsay continued blithely. "I wasn't entirely candid with you, Catriona. I live in California, you see. Penny and Meredith are very old friends of mine. I know a lot more about you than you do about me. I know, for example, how much you'd hate a story in one of the middlebrow newspapers that pointed out how much you stand to gain from your little trip to the police station. And how, when it actually comes down to it, you knew much more than Meredith about the murder method. She'd only heard Penny talk about it, but you'll have read it. And if we're talking *cui bono* . . ."

"My God," Catriona said, voice dripping contempt, "I didn't know private snoopers like you knew *cui bono* from Sonny

Bono. Ms Gordon, to kill Penny Varnavides for the income generated by one short burst of sales would be akin to killing the goose that laid the golden eggs in the hope of pushing the market price of gold higher. I stood to earn a lot more cash from Penny Varnavides alive than I could ever hope to gain from her death."

"Maybe so. But it would still make a nice tale in the tabloids. I'm not asking you to breach commercial confidentiality. All I want is some answers to a few innocuous questions. I'm not the one who got heavy here."

"I despise blackmail," Catriona said, lighting a second cigarette.

"Me too," Lindsay said cheerfully. "It doesn't half get results, though."

"You must go down like a cup of cold sick in a euphemistic society like America."

"They love it. Penny used to call me a breath of fresh effluvium. They think all the Scots are brutally frank. They've been watching too many historical Hollywood epics. So, are we going to talk to each other, or am I going to talk to the tabloids? Did I mention I used to be a national newspaper journalist?" Lindsay's smile alone would have been accepted by any court in the land as sufficient provocation for GBH.

Catriona fiddled with her cigarette. "There's so little to say that it's not worth arguing over. I'm far too busy to have to deal with muck-raking journalists as well as interfering busybodies."

It wasn't a graceful climbdown, but Lindsay wasn't proud. "Thanks," she said. "I know Penny would have wanted you to help."

Catriona looked as if she'd bitten into a profiterole and found a slug. "Such convenient knowledge," she muttered.

"You've been Penny's agent right from the start, am I right?"

"Since before she was ever published. She brought *The Magicking of Danny Armstrong* to me after it had been rejected by all the major American houses and her agent in New York had let her go. I was able to place it for her over here, and the rest, as they say, is history."

Lindsay took out her notebook, more for show than necessity, and scribbled a note. "This latest book? Very different, I hear."

"Penny decided she wanted a challenge. She was doing three Darkliners titles a year, and she wanted to break out of what had started to feel like a rut. *Heart of Glass* was going to be her first adult thriller. It was very *noir*, very passionate and very powerfully written. I had great hopes of it."

"How much of it was actually finished?"

"Penny had written about three-quarters of it. She came over here to do some research she needed for the last part of the book, and to finish writing it. I read what she'd completed before she arrived. But within days of getting to London, she announced she was doing a major rewrite. I was surprised, because what I saw was very good. But Penny was adamant that it needed some substantial alterations."

Lindsay frowned. "She wasn't going to change the murder method in the book, was she?"

"Not as far as I'm aware. From what she said to me, it was the characters she planned to work on, not the plot or the structure."

"Was there anything in particular that she mentioned?"

Catriona stubbed out her cigarette. "Nothing specific," she said.

"Have you got a copy of the manuscript?"

Catriona sighed heavily. "Unfortunately not. Penny took it away with her. She said she wanted me to come to the rewrite with as fresh an eye as possible, not to be able to compare it with what had gone before. She was always quite fussy about retrieving first drafts. Almost neurotic."

"She was a perfectionist," Lindsay said sadly, stricken by memory of her friend. "She hated the idea of anyone revealing her early drafts to the world after she'd gone. I remember her talking about it one night."

"I don't even have a current synopsis," Catriona said, sounding more cross than sad. "If Meredith should come across the manuscript of *Heart of Glass*, or the computer disk it's on, I'd really appreciate it if she could pass it on to me."

"Why?" Lindsay asked, suspecting she already knew the answer.

"The 300 pages I saw were publishable quality," Catriona answered, confirming Lindsay's guess. "If they came with a synopsis, her editor could probably cobble together an ending in an appropriate style."

"Oh, great, just what Penny would have loved," Lindsay said sarcastically. "A load of cobblers."

"I think I have more right to be the judge of that," Catriona said stiffly. "If Penny had doubted my judgement, she would hardly have granted me so much power as her literary executor. Penny wanted to show the world that she was more than just a writer of teenage fiction. What I've seen of *Heart of Glass* demonstrated a formidable talent, and she deserves to have that credited to her reputation. That's what she really wanted, Ms Gordon. She wanted it so badly she could taste it."

Lindsay looked away, realising that Penny had wanted it so badly she had even been prepared to jeopardise Meredith's career just to generate more publicity. That indicated a raw ambition Lindsay had never recognised in Penny before. She could understand her desire for acknowledgement; what she couldn't relate to was her willingness to sacrifice her emotional happiness and security for the fickleness of reputation. "Yeah, well," was all she said.

"I'm not really the person you should be talking to about this," Catriona added casually as she lit another cigarette. "Penny spent a lot more time with her editor than she did with me this trip."

"And her editor is?"

"Belinda Burton. Baz to her babies. Baz would have had a much clearer idea of where she was up to and where she was going. They were very close. It was a large part of the reason behind Penny's success. The relationship between an editor and a writer is crucial. Different people work in different ways. When you link an editor and writer whose minds run along the same tracks and who like to work at the same level of detail, you've got a match made in heaven. A mismatch and everybody's life is an absolute bloody misery. It's part of my job to marry up writers with appropriate editors. Baz and Penny fit like a matching plug and socket," Catriona said expansively.

"You wouldn't be trying to divert me, would you?"

Catriona laughed. "No. But if you're still fixated on the profit motive and you think that Penny dead is an appealing moneymaker, you really would be better employed talking to Baz. Penny's royalty is ten per cent, so my cut is around one and a half per cent of the retail price. Monarch Press, on the other hand, are picking up between ten and forty per cent on every book sold. As they say on your side of the Atlantic, go figure."

Lindsay stood up. She wasn't entirely convinced she'd got everything out of Catriona Polson that there was to be had, but she didn't have the right questions to elicit more. Perhaps after she'd spoken to Baz Burton, she'd have more ammunition to fire at the agent. "Fine," she said. "I'll talk to her. Now, wasn't that painless?"

"Painless but not a terribly productive use of my time," Catriona said dismissively, leading Lindsay out of the room and down the corridor. "I'm bound to say, I hope your client is paying you up front. I suspect she may end up wasting all her available cash on defence lawyers. I think you're backing the wrong horse, Ms Gordon. Always a mistake to let sentiment stand in the way of reality, however unpalatable that may be."

For once, Lindsay refused to let herself be wound up. She contented herself with, "As Arnie says, hasta la vista, baby." On her way out of the front door, she took out the card she'd put in her shirt pocket earlier. It was about ten years old, but that didn't matter. She flicked it across the desk to the receptionist. "Have a nice day, cher," she said in her best Bayou accent. She didn't wait to register the response to a card that read, "Lindsay Gordon, Staff Reporter, *Daily Nation*."

5

When she left Catriona Polson's office Lindsay felt a strange sense of dislocation, a combination of sleep deprivation and an awareness that there had been changes in the street ambience of Soho in the six years she'd been away. Seedy sex tourism had given way to café bars with fashion victims spilling out on to pavement tables, braying loudly. Surely, Lindsay thought, there couldn't be *that* many jobs for film critics? What she needed was a space to call her own, somewhere she could spread her things around her and feel grounded. Meredith had offered her the second bedroom in her apartment, but Lindsay didn't want to be constantly bound to Penny's death.

She found a phone box near Tottenham Court Road, checked her personal organiser and punched in a local number. "Watergaw Films, how can I help you?" she heard in a bright Scottish accent.

"I'd like to speak to Helen Christie," Lindsay said. "The name's Lindsay Gordon."

"One moment please." Then what sounded like *Eine kleine Nachtmusik* played on penny whistles. Lindsay gritted her teeth and waited. It would be worth the assault on her eardrums if this call gave her what she needed, and she didn't anticipate denial. Helen had lived with Sophie for years, but she'd been Lindsay's friend long before that. The two women had linked up years before at Oxford, the only two working-class women in their college's annual intake. The recognition had been instant, forging an immediate friendship that time, distance and lovers had never threatened. They had discovered their common sexuality in tandem, been paralytically drunk and terminally hung over together, wept over broken hearts and celebrated famous victories by each other's side. No matter how long the gap between their encounters, Lindsay and Helen invariably fell straight back into the easy camaraderie that had marked their relationship right from the beginning.

"Lindsay?" It was Helen's familiar voice, Liverpudlian crossed with Glaswegian, untouched by anything south of the M62. "How're you doing, girl?"

"Off my head with jet lag, but otherwise okay. Listen, Helen, I need a bed a few nights sooner than we anticipated."

"What do you mean, jet lag? Are you here in London already?"

"Yes. Just me. I'll explain when I see you, it's too complicated over the phone. Is your spare room free?"

"Course it is. The whole house is a total tip, though, on account of I wasn't expecting the pair of you till next week, but if you don't mind a bit of chaos and no milk in the fridge, move on in. Sophie'll go nutso when she sees the state of the place, but I've had more important things on my mind than tidying and Kirsten wouldn't notice if the council started emptying bins into the living room, bless her," Helen gabbled.

"Sophie's not with me," Lindsay cut in as soon as Helen paused for breath.

"Aw, Lindsay, you've not done one, have you? I know you, first sign of trouble and you're off over the horizon. You should stay and talk it over, you know you should. You're a million times better for her than I ever was."

Lindsay laughed. "Give me some credit. I have grown up a wee bit in the last half-dozen years. There's nothing wrong between me and Sophie, I swear. The reason I'm here early is something else entirely. Look, I'll explain when I see you, okay? I'm running out of money here."

"All right. Listen, can you get yourself round to the office? Only I've got to leg it to an important meeting, but I can leave the spare set of keys with reception, and you can sort yourself out, is that okay?"

"That's fi—" The money ran out and Lindsay found herself talking to dead air. She hailed the first cab that passed and asked him to wait outside the warehouse in Camden occupied by Watergaw Films while she picked up the keys. They stopped at Meredith's to collect Lindsay's luggage, then carried on to Helen's terraced house in Fulham. As the black taxi juddered through the early afternoon traffic, Lindsay pondered her next move. Collecting keys and luggage had reminded her that she needed to check out the flat where Penny had been living.

Dredging her memory for details of a half-forgotten dinner conversation with Penny and Meredith, Lindsay recalled that Penny had swapped her house for a flat in Islington belonging to a friend of Sophie. An academic, Lindsay recalled. A philosopher? A psychologist? A philologist? Something like that. The Rubik's cube of memory clicked another turn and the pieces fell into place. A palaeontologist attached to the Natural History Museum. Called . . . She pinched the bridge of her nose in an attempt to awaken her protesting brain as the taxi rattled along Fulham Road. They turned into a side street wide enough for cars to double park without obstructing the road, then rounded the corner into a street of three-storey terraced villas, their stucco in varying states of repair that reflected whether they were single residences or split into rented flats. As the taxi squealed to a halt, Lindsay suddenly realised she didn't really need to remember his name. He was the man living in Penny's house, at the end of a phone whose number she knew almost as well as her own.

Feeling triumphant, she paid off the taxi and staggered wearily up Helen's short path with a bag that felt heavier with each step. She unlocked the three mortises that fastened the front door of the sparklingly painted house and keyed the last four digits of the phone number into the alarm pad to silence the high-pitched squeal of the warning klaxon. Then she stumbled into a living room that could have been sold to the Tate Gallery under the title of *Installation: Millennium Chaos*. There were piles of newspapers and magazines in a haphazard array by the chairs and the sofa. The coffee table was invisible under an anarchy of used crockery. A spread of CDs was strewn in front of the stereo and tapes were tossed randomly on the shelves to either side of it. Books teetered in tall pillars against the wall. The only remotely ordered area in the room was a cabinet of videos that seemed to be arranged according to some system, though there were gaps in the rows and half a dozen unboxed tapes were piled on top of the TV. A tabby cat sprawled on one of the two video recorders, barely registering Lindsay's arrival with a flicker of one eyelid.

Lindsay closed her eyes briefly. She'd had her moments in the untidiness rankings, but she'd never come close to this. Helen had been right. Sophie would go absolutely nutso. Grinning, she gripped her suitcase and staggered upstairs. The spare room was considerably clearer than downstairs. On the floor next to the ironing board was the biggest pile of clean but crumpled clothes Lindsay had ever seen, but that apart, the room could have been almost anyone's guest room. What marked it out as belonging to Helen were the framed TV and film stills featuring actors she'd placed in her previous career as a casting director. Though she'd progressed to producer/director in her own independent production company, it was clear she hadn't forgotten how she'd started in the business.

Lindsay dumped her case on the floor, not even bothering to open it, and headed back downstairs. There had to be a phone somewhere. She tracked it by the flashing light on the answering machine. A glance at her watch told her it would be just after eight in the morning in San Francisco. She didn't even have to feel guilty about calling too early. On the third ring, a voice said, "Hello?"

Foiled in her hope that he'd identify himself, Lindsay blundered on regardless. "Hi," she said cheerfully. "It's Lindsay here. Sophie's partner?"

"Oh, hello," said the precise voice she remembered from phone calls she'd answered previously. "How are you?"

"I'm fine. And you? Settling in okay?"

"Well . . . Everything was going splendidly and then I had some rather terrible news about . . . well, about our flat and the woman we swapped with."

"I heard about that," Lindsay said sympathetically. "That's actually why I was ringing, Brian." Brian! It had suddenly come to her in mid-sentence. Brian Steinberg, married to an anthropologist called Miriam. Grinning with relief, Lindsay said, "I know this probably sounds a bit weird, Brian, but did you happen to leave a spare set of keys with anybody when you left?"

"Keys?" he echoed.

"Yeah, for the flat." When in doubt, gabble. It was a lesson Lindsay had learned from Helen years ago, and she'd just had the refresher course. "The thing is, Penny's girlfriend, Meredith, is in a bit of a state, as you can imagine, and I'm over here in England with her trying to get things sorted out. You know what it's like, all the bureaucracy. Anyway, I'm just trying to sort out the practical stuff, and Penny's agent is desperate to get hold of the manuscript of Penny's last book, and it's stuck on the hard disk of her computer, which of course is in the flat, and the police are being really difficult about letting anyone in, so I thought if I could get the keys and just nip in and out . . . I mean, you know me, you know I wouldn't be doing anything I shouldn't be doing . . ."

"I don't know," he said hesitantly. "If the police don't want you to go in . . ."

"There's no reason for us not to go into the flat. It's not as if the police have any objections, it's just that they're being really awkward about fixing up a time when we can go and sort it out. I don't have to tell you about bureaucracy, you're dealing with American academia."

"Yeah," he said, with feeling. "Oh, I suppose it'll be okay. I can't see any real problem, and the police have had days now to do whatever it is they have to do. I left a spare set with Miriam's sister. She lives up in Hampstead." Brian gave Lindsay the address and promised to phone his sister-in-law right away to warn her Lindsay was on her way.

What felt like a lifetime later, Lindsay emerged from the rancid stuffiness of the tube into sunlight at Highbury Corner. Even though it was laden with traffic fumes, the air was still fresh enough to rouse her from the virtually catatonic state she'd reached underground thanks to the combination of heat, jet lag, lack of oxygen and lack of proper sleep. She hoped her exhaustion wouldn't make her miss anything in the flat. Probably it could have waited till the following day, but Lindsay had never liked leaving till tomorrow what could be thrashed out today. Besides, this was a good time to make an unauthorised entry. At the end of the working day, all sorts of people were going in and out of buildings where they didn't necessarily live.

To guard against her potential for carelessness, she stopped at a chain-store chemist for a pack of disposable latex gloves. A few minutes later, she turned into the street where Brian and Miriam occupied the middle flat in a converted Georgian terraced house. Even though she was pretty certain the police would have finished by now with the scene of crime, that was no reason to take chances. She walked right to the end of the street, then kept turning right till she'd done a circuit of the block and was back where she'd started. She'd seen no sign of any police officers, nor did there seem to be any twitching curtains or faces at windows as she strolled down the street for the second time.

Deciding it was clear, she turned nonchalantly into the entrance of Brian and Miriam's house. She climbed the four steps up to the front door and hastily sorted through the bunch

of keys until she found the ones that fitted the two locks on the
heavy street door. Inside, she closed the door smartly behind
her. Ahead lay a dim carpeted hallway, a flight of stairs at the
far end. Cautiously, Lindsay made for it and climbed to the first
landing. There was a sturdy door facing her, crisscrossed with
yellow plastic tape that proclaimed Police. Keep out. The flat
was still officially a crime scene.

Pulling a face, Lindsay pulled on the gloves, then fumbled
with the locks until the door swung free. Then, with a quick
look round the corner to check the stairs above were still clear,
she ducked under the tapes and into the flat. This long after the
killing, she couldn't believe she was going to affect any crucial
forensic evidence.

She found herself in a corridor which opened out into a
large, high-ceilinged room whose walls were hung with richly
coloured fabric panels. The soft furnishings were low, squashy
and oatmeal-coloured, coordinating with what could be seen
of the room's paintwork. Face down on a low table whose legs
were carved African fertility goddesses was an open paperback
of a Robertson Davies novel. Beside the nearest chair was a
bowl of grapes starting to go mouldy, a thick A3 pad of scrap
paper and, inevitably around Penny, a couple of autopencils.
Caught momentarily off guard, Lindsay was ambushed by her
grief. Suddenly, she couldn't see through tears, and the lump in
her throat threatened to choke her. Subsiding into the nearest
chair, she set her sorrow free, her shoulders shaking with sobs
as memory flooded her.

Eventually, the wave of pain receded, leaving her beached
in a corner of the enveloping sofa. She rubbed a hand across her
face, forgetting about the gloves until the latex skidded across
her tear-streaked cheek. With a watery grin, Lindsay pushed
herself out of the sofa and forced herself to work.

There wasn't much more in the living room to mark Penny's
presence, apart from a postcard of the Golden Gate Bridge from
Meredith, wishing her a safe arrival. Interesting that she hadn't

binned it, Lindsay thought. Perhaps Penny hadn't been as adamant in her dismissal as she had seemed to be.

Lindsay crossed the hall into the kitchen. While the lounge looked as if its resident had popped out for a minute, the kitchen made it plain that she wouldn't ever be coming back. On the cork-tile floor was a reddish-brown stain like a giant Rorschach test. Spatters of dried blood afflicted everything else in the room, from cupboard doors to kettle, their sizes ranging from pinpricks to bottle tops. There was even what looked like a thin drizzle in one corner of the ceiling. On every surface, the bloodstains were half obscured by fragments of glass and fingerprint powder. Looking at the room, it was hard to imagine how it had got like this. Logically, Lindsay knew that when an artery was pierced, blood spurted and sprayed like an out-of-control fountain. But this was beyond that. It looked as if someone had shaken a jeroboam of blood-coloured champagne and sprayed it joyously round the room, like a driver winning a murderous Grand Prix. And then thrown the bottle after the foam.

She took a deep breath. There was a faint metallic smell of blood but it was overlaid by the sour smell of spilt beer. Lindsay looked around at the arena of death, taking in the outline marked on the floor like a scene from a bad Saturday Night Mystery Movie. She noted the fridge, tall for a British one, its top standing just under five feet above floor height. On top of it, three bottles of German *Weissbier* remained standing. In spite of her reputation among her students and former colleagues as a cold-hearted bastard, Lindsay didn't expect to drink wheat beer ever again.

It was easy to see how the first assumption was of accidental death. A bottle exploding under pressure at that height could easily drive flying glass slicing through soft tissue. To have imagined it was murder would have seemed perverse without Catriona Polson's information. Even so, there were no signs of another's presence. No alien footprints, no tell-tale bloody handprints on the door jamb. Nothing that didn't tally with the hypothesis of accident.

Sighing, Lindsay backed away from the kitchen and started to search the rest of the flat. In the bedroom, she found nothing unexpected. Penny's suitcases were under the bed. Her clothes occupied one half of the wardrobe, Brian and Miriam's, presumably, the other half. The chests of drawers told the same story. In one, Lindsay recognised Penny's T-shirts and swimsuits. In the other, unfamiliar clothes were stuffed into overcrowded drawers. The bedside table held a notepad and autopencil, a battered copy of W. H. Auden's *Collected Poems* and an alarm clock.

She had higher hopes of the study when she saw the papers strewn across desk and table, but even a casual scrutiny told her there was little of interest there. There were a couple of scribbled lists of Stuff To Do along the lines of "Imperial War Museum, tampons, Tabasco, *Brewer's Dictionary*, ???video store???, bread, grapes, ???Calistoga???" Under a paperweight there was what looked like a reading list—*The Ghost Road, The Invisible Man, The High Cost of Living, The Information, Crime and Punishment*. An odd selection, but other people's reading tastes never seemed normal, in Lindsay's experience. Most of the rest of the sheets contained single handwritten paragraphs of description of individual characters. These ranged from highly stylised and polished pen portraits to scrawled sentences like "looks like Larry, broods on imagined slights, has the dress sense of a color-blind hobo in a thrift shop." Lindsay couldn't help a smile escaping as she skimmed them.

Eventually, she found a dozen pages with the header *Heart of Glass*. Judging by the page numbers, they were from the first couple of chapters, though not all the pages were present. She searched those of the desk drawers that were unlocked, but found no more of the supposed 300 pages that Penny had completed. As she shifted the desk away from the wall to search more thoroughly, she discovered something more chilling than the missing papers. The power socket behind the desk contained a plug with a cable that led into a transformer which stepped down the voltage from 240 to 12. A second cable led from the transformer to nowhere. But Lindsay knew what would normally be attached to that particular cable.

"'The curious incident of the dog in the nighttime,'" Lindsay muttered as she cast around the room for any possible remaining hiding place for a laptop computer and a fistful of floppy disks. It was conceivable that the police might have taken the manuscript away with them for further scrutiny once murder had been alleged. But she found it hard to believe that even the most dim-witted of detectives would have taken the laptop away for further study without the source of its power. Admittedly, it ran off batteries too, but not for long enough to scrutinise every file on the hard disk.

The absence of the laptop was a serious problem. Lindsay had hoped it would still be here, not least because Penny and her computer were virtually joined at the hip. Unlike most authors, who seemed content to use their machines merely as word processors on which to write their novels, Penny fed everything into her machine—accounts, diary, notes, scanned photographs of Meredith, her friends and her beloved garden. Lindsay had expected to find answers to almost all of her questions nestling somewhere in the massive memory of a machine that weighed little more than a bag of sugar. To find it gone was more than a setback; it was a puzzle.

Whoever had taken it was no petty thief; the printer, for example, was still sitting on the floor under the table. Lindsay decided the chances were it had been taken by someone who knew a little about computers, since there wasn't a floppy disk in the place. After a painful episode in the early days of her computing life when a hard disk had crashed and Penny had lost seventy pages of a new book, she had been particular to the point of paranoia about making copies of all her material on floppy disks. Given that her motto when working was "Back up early and back up often," it was inconceivable that there were no floppies to be found.

The only reasonable conclusion seemed to be that the killer
had known Penny's habit of storing every piece of her personal
and professional data on her computer and had needed to make
sure some incriminating piece of information was gone forever
with the absence of her hard disk and every floppy in the place.
Whoever killed Penny Varnavides had not only known about
the murder method outlined in her book. They had also had
to possess a considerable amount of information about her life.
Lindsay rubbed her tired eyes and sighed. If she hadn't been
representing Meredith, she'd have been her prime suspect.

She had a last trawl round the flat, checking she hadn't
missed the laptop and the back-ups. Finally, she was forced to
admit failure. Wherever they were, it wasn't in the flat. And
there was nothing else to be found here.

Dispirited that she had learned so little, Lindsay made sure
she'd left nothing tell-tale behind, then let herself out of the flat.
As she turned the top mortise lock, she heard footsteps coming
up behind her on the stairs.

"Excuse me," a man's voice said officiously, "but what
exactly do you think you're doing?"

6

Limited options flashed across Lindsay's mind as cold sweat sprang out along her spine. Her escape route was cut off by the man filling the stairwell behind her. She could whirl round and catch him off guard, banking on one swift push toppling him and being able to get clear by jumping over him. She could pretend to be connected to the police, mutter something obscure, finish locking up and leave. Then she remembered Sandra Bloom's briefing what felt like weeks ago. The murder had been discovered by the upstairs neighbour. Since this was probably the man who had found Penny's body, she realised that whatever she did, she needed to find a way to talk to him.

Lindsay swung round and gave an alarmed smile to the man, who stood frowning a couple of steps below the landing. A thatch of greying, mousy hair jutted out above a high forehead that narrowed to a pointed chin. Round, intelligent blue eyes flanked a beaky nose that overhung a small, feminine mouth whose lower lip bore the indentations of two front teeth. He reminded Lindsay irresistibly of a cartoon octopus.

"God, you nearly gave me a heart attack," she said as lightly as she could manage while desperately dredging her memory for his name.

"Sorry," he said automatically. "I just wondered what was going on. That's a crime scene, you know."

"That's why I was in there," Lindsay said, holding up her gloved hands for his inspection. "Just checking up on one or two details for my boss." She grinned disarmingly, still reaching for a name.

"You're with the police?" he asked, still an edge of suspicion in his voice.

"How else would I have the keys?" she parried. If she managed to avoid making any firm statement, it would be that much harder afterwards to make a case against her for impersonating a police officer. "I wish everyone was as civic-minded as you, Mr Knight." She'd summoned up a mental picture of the names by the bells on the front door jamb; she prayed she'd gone for the right one.

The man relaxed visibly. She'd got it right, and her knowing his name immediately made the rest of the scenario credible, even though it was a picture almost entirely of his own painting. He smiled back at her. "Well, you can't be too careful, can you? How's the investigation progressing? I heard on the news that you'd released the woman you were questioning."

"That's right. We need to build a more solid case before we can think about charging anyone."

"I can imagine," he said. "But you're pretty sure you've got the right person, are you?"

Lindsay winked. "Obviously that's not something I could comment on, sir. But we're not expanding our circle of inquiries any wider just as yet, if you get my meaning."

"I only wish I'd actually seen her leave, been more help," he said wistfully.

"You've been very helpful already, sir. Without your intervention, who knows how long Ms Varnavides might have been lying there?"

He shrugged, his expression a cross between smug self-satisfaction and embarrassment. "I'm a great believer in taking social responsibility."

Now she remembered another snippet from Sandra's briefing. Derek Knight was a manager in one of the new hospital trusts. As caring as Mr Gradgrind, if what she'd read in her imported *Guardian Weekly* about the new breed of health service bosses was anything to go by. "I suppose you have to be, in your job," Lindsay smarmed. "Actually, I was hoping to catch you. There were just one or two points I needed to clarify with you."

"Was there some problem with my statement?" he asked anxiously.

"No, no problem at all. It's just that in the light of subsequent interviews, my boss wanted me to come back and go over some of the details in your statement. Just to check there's no possibility of error."

He nodded magisterially. "I understand. Iron out any potential contradictions."

"I wouldn't say contradictions, exactly . . ." Lindsay hedged. "Perhaps if we could go upstairs? More private than here?"

"Of course, of course. If I could just . . . ?"

Lindsay squeezed into the corner to allow him to pass her and turn the corner to the upper flight of stairs. She followed him into a flat whose layout was similar to the one below, save that Derek Knight had left the wall of the corridor intact. Combined with the lower ceilings of the top floor, it made his living room seem significantly smaller and more claustrophobic than Brian and Miriam's, an impression compounded by the dark brocade curtains and upholstery. The room managed to be both fussy and impersonal. It looked like the province of a much older person, as if it had been decorated and furnished by his mother and he hadn't dared impose his own personality on it, Lindsay thought.

Knight dropped his briefcase by the door and gestured towards one of two wing chairs facing each other across a gas fire that was the double of one Lindsay had lived with as a student nearly twenty years before. It hadn't been new then. Beside it, incongruously, was a set of antique brass fire irons. Obediently she sat, and he settled in opposite.

"You'll have to bear with me," Lindsay said. "I only had the sketchiest look at your statement before the boss whipped it off me, so I'm probably a lot less *au fait* with what went on the other night than you are."

"Well, as you'll have seen from its brevity, there wasn't a great deal your colleagues considered to be significant," he said primly.

"You came home at . . . what time would it have been?"

"The usual time. Just like tonight."

"So . . . around half past seven?"

"Between twenty-five and half past seven. It depends on the tube."

Lindsay nodded, her notebook out and her pen scribbling. "And you noticed nothing at the street entrance to indicate there might be any problem, is that right?"

"No, no, that was the first sign that things were not as they should be. I said so in my statement," he said plaintively, as if dealing with a stupid and recalcitrant child.

Thinking furiously, Lindsay gave it her best shot. "The lock?" she hazarded.

"Exactly. The mortise was unlocked. It was only the Yale that was engaged. As if someone without a key had just slammed the door shut behind them. Well, I knew the Thomases on the ground floor wouldn't dream of leaving themselves so vulnerable. I had had occasion to mention the importance of it to Ms Varnavides, but since then she'd been quite reliable about it, so I was rather upset." He pursed his lips and sighed through his nose. "I assumed she'd just been remiss again. As I think you were today?"

Lindsay looked surprised, recalled she hadn't locked a mortise behind her as she'd come in and smiled sheepishly.

"I thought as much. Of course, I had no idea there was more to it than carelessness."

"Of course not," Lindsay said, trying to keep the irritation out of her voice. "Thinking back, was there anything that struck you as being out of place? Sometimes, with the passage of time, things become clearer to us . . ."

Knight crossed his legs at the knee, revealing an inch of bony, milk-white leg between grey sock and grey trouser cuff. He knitted his fingers together in his lap and pondered, clearly revelling in self-importance. "Nothing springs to mind," he eventually said reluctantly.

"Never mind. So you climbed the stairs and saw . . . ?"

"The door to the Steinbergs' flat was open." He gave a tight little smile, as if imagining the impact when he imparted this in the witness box.

"When you say open, do you mean ajar, or standing wide open, as if someone had flung it back?"

A momentary flicker of a frown tugged at the skin round Knight's eyes. "Are you sure you read my statement?"

Lindsay willed herself to relax and smiled. "Like I said, I just had time to glance at it. We like to do these follow-up interviews without too many preconceptions. A fresh eye on the subject, you know?"

"Hmmm. Waste of time, more like," he muttered. "I wouldn't stand for a waste of resources like this in my hospital."

"The door?" Lindsay prompted, biting back a sharp comment about patients being shunted from one hospital to another in the futile search for an intensive care bed before they died in the attempt.

"It was half open. Considerably more than ajar, but not wide open."

"As if someone had come out in a hurry?"

He pulled a face Lindsay recognised. It was the same one her chemistry teacher had used whenever he'd been asked a question he didn't really know how to answer. "I wouldn't really have thought so," he eventually said. "The Steinbergs have one of those thick-pile carpets in the hall, so the door doesn't swing free. If someone had yanked it open in a rush, it would have been wider than it was."

Lindsay filed the incongruous detail away for further consideration, marking it with an asterisk in her notes. "So, being
a good neighbour, you went in?"

"I knocked on the door," Knight corrected her. "I called out,
but there was no reply. I was starting to feel a little concerned."

"And so you went in?" Lindsay prodded.

He nodded, a prurient gleam in his eye. "I knew something was wrong as soon as I got inside. The place smelled like
a brewery crossed with a butcher's shop. I could see there was
nothing amiss in the lounge, but when I got to the kitchen
doorway . . . Well, I don't have to tell you what it was like," he
said, an obviously spurious delicacy giving him pause.

"Just for the record?" Lindsay asked, pen poised.

"Blood everywhere. On the floor, on the walls, all over the
worktops. And glass. There was broken glass scattered around.
And in the middle of it all, Miss Varnavides. It was obvious she
was dead. No one could lose that much blood and still be alive."

There was no compassion in his voice, Lindsay thought
bitterly, only the self-satisfied confidence of a man who thinks
he knows what he's talking about. "Indeed," she said, her voice
dry and emotionless. "Did you actually go across the threshold
into the kitchen?"

"Of course not. These days everybody knows you mustn't
interfere with the scene of a crime and I could see that something terrible had happened. I assumed some intruder had hit
her with a broken bottle. That was the only explanation I could
come up with, seeing all the blood and the glass. Your people
thought it was an accident. But it turns out I was right after
all." He smirked.

"Mmm," Lindsay said noncommittally. "So you came
upstairs and called the police?"

"Well, yes. I didn't want to use the phone down there in
case the last number Miss Varnavides had called was a clue."

"Not very likely if she'd been killed by an intruder," Lindsay said quietly as she made a note.

"She might have been trying to call the police," he said defensively. "She might have panicked and rung 911 instead of 999, being American."

It was, she supposed, a reasonable point. "And then our lads arrived," she said.

Knight gave her a curious look. "Sorry?"

"And then our lads arrived. The police. After your 999 call. The boys in blue."

"That's right," he said slowly. "Very quick off the mark, your detective inspector."

Lindsay smiled. "He doesn't hang around."

Knight got to his feet. "I'm sorry," he said. "I'm being very inhospitable here. I just realised how thirsty I am. You must be too, in this heat. Can I get you anything? Tea? Coffee? Mineral water?"

Lindsay shook her head. "I'm fine, thanks. I'll need to be on my way soon. I've just got a couple more questions about visitors to the flat . . ."

"I'll be right back, if you'll just bear with me a moment." He cleared his throat noisily. "Desperate for a cup of tea. Terrible frog in my throat." Knight smiled ingratiatingly as he sidled out of the room, closing the door behind him.

Lindsay sat still for a moment, wondering what she'd said to unsettle Knight so obviously. Then, faintly, she heard the electronic exclamations of a touch-tone telephone. "Ah, shit," she murmured, stealthily easing out of the chair and edging towards the door. Half-way there, she noticed there was a phone on a side table just within reach of Derek Knight's preferred armchair.

She sidestepped the chair and reached for the phone. One hand gripped the handset, the other wormed its way under the earpiece until it was pressed down over the black plastic trigger that replaced the old-fashioned cradle. She lifted the handset to her ear, still keeping the trigger firmly depressed. She wrestled one-handed with the handset until her thumb was pressed hard against the mouthpiece, effectively cutting off any external sound, then put the earpiece to her ear. With slow and infinite care, Lindsay gently and gradually released the black trigger.

Derek Knight's voice was loud in her ear, waspishly impatient "... asked to be put through to Inspector Nicholson."

"This is Detective Constable Partridge, sir. I'm one of the inspector's team. How can I be of help?" a more distant voice rumbled. Lindsay's chest tightened. If Knight was calling the police, there could only be one reason. He'd sussed her.

"I don't wish to appear rude, officer, but I've already had dealings with Inspector Nicholson on the Varnavides case, and it would save time all round if you'd just put me through to the correct extension."

Good sense would take her feet out of there as fast as they could go, Lindsay knew. But good sense had never been her first choice when curiosity was one of the other available options. She wanted to know what had triggered Derek Knight's suspicions of her. Then she'd leave, and only then.

"I'm afraid that won't be possible," DC Partridge said, his voice placatory. "Inspector Nicholson isn't in the station right now."

"When will she be back? This is urgent, officer!"

She, Lindsay thought ruefully. What a time for her to be hoist on the petard of sexist assumption. The police had been "the lads" for so long, it hadn't occurred to her that the officer in charge of a murder hunt could be a woman. And everybody else had been so busy being politically correct that no one had mentioned it to her.

Lindsay was so busy mentally cursing herself that she missed the officer's reply. But she heard Derek Knight's response loud and clear. "Well, in that case, you'll just have to do. Are you familiar with the Varnavides case?"

"I'm the officer who took your statement, Mr Knight," Partridge said heavily.

"Fine. Well, I've got a woman in my flat impersonating a police officer. I caught her coming out of the murder scene and when I challenged her, she claimed to be with the police. She said she had some more questions for me, but I was suspicious. Then I tricked her into revealing that she thought Inspector Nicholson was a man."

"And this person is still in your flat, sir?" Suddenly Partridge sounded alert and interested.

"Oh, yes."

"Do you think you can keep her talking until we can get a car there?"

"No need for that, officer. I've locked her in."

Lindsay closed her eyes and swore silently. Then she gently depressed the phone button and replaced the receiver as silently as she possibly could. She crept to the door and depressed the handle. Nothing happened. Derek Knight hadn't lied. She was locked in his living room three floors above the Islington street.

7

Within minutes, the police would be on the other side of the door. Lindsay doubted whether they could touch her for violating the crime scene since she had the tacit permission of the house-holder to be there. But from what she'd heard Derek Knight say, he'd be going in hard on the angle that she'd lied to convince him she was a police officer. He'd have to, she realised. She'd barely known him half an hour, yet she knew that in a tight corner, the most crucial issue for Derek Knight would always be saving face.

"This isn't the time to stand about thinking," she muttered angrily to herself. "Shit!" She looked round the room in desperation, hoping something would inspire her to find a way out. At a pinch, she supposed, she could use the fire irons to batter the wooden door to splinters, but she didn't imagine she would have time for that. Besides, the last thing she needed was a charge of criminal damage to add to everything else. She swung round and stared at the door, willing it to open. Then she noticed the butt end of the hinges.

Probably as old as the late Georgian building, the hinges were substantial. But unlike the door, they were free of genera-tions of paint. Lindsay stepped closer and scrutinised the polished brass. "Yes," she said softly. She hurried over to her chair and grabbed her backpack, delving into the front pocket to emerge triumphantly with her Swiss Army knife. Then she picked up the poker from the fireplace. She crossed back to the door and pulled free one of the knife's blades. It was a narrow spike that extended about two inches from the middle of the knife, forming a T-shape. Lindsay placed the tip of the spike against the bottom edge of the linchpin of the upper of the two hinges. It was difficult to get much of a back-swing on the poker so close to the door, but she did her best. Using the heavy brass knob on the end of the poker as a hammer, she hit the back of the knife in a bid to force the pin free of the hinge. The first blow made the hinge creak, but nothing shifted. The second whack coincided with a screech from Derek Knight of "What the hell are you doing?" The third bang of poker on knife drove the spike into the centre of the hinge, thrusting the linchpin a good three inches clear of the top of the hinge. "Yes!" Lindsay exclaimed. She knew she could pull the pin clear easily now.

Turning her attention to the lower hinge, she repeated the process, ignoring Derek Knight's frantic yells. This time, she pulled the pin completely clear, then worked the top pin free. Now, only the lock held the door in place. Gripping the edge of the door with her fingertips, Lindsay inched the hinge side of the door back from the frame. The tongue of the lock creaked against its socket, but she managed to pull the door back sufficiently far to clear the jamb. Then, one hand on the handle, the other on the hinge side of the door, she slid the whole thing sideways, pulling it neatly free of the lock.

Derek Knight was standing in the hall facing her, his mouth open and his eyelids as wide as they could go without surgery. Lindsay stepped through the doorway, leaning down to pick up her backpack. "Sorry, got to go," she said.

He lunged at her, mouthing something incomprehensible, but Lindsay sidestepped neatly and rushed for the door of the flat. She took the stairs two at a time, the blood pounding in her ears, obscuring any sounds of pursuit. She didn't even bother closing the street door behind her, sprinting down the street in the opposite direction to the tube station. At the corner, she turned left at random, cutting diagonally across the road and jinking into a mews court that ran between two parallel streets.

At the end of the mews, she stopped running. She wasn't dressed for jogging and no one on the Islington/Canonbury border ran except joggers and muggers. As she turned left into the next street, she heard the whooping sirens of police cars nearby. On the corner was a pub. Lindsay breathed deeply to calm her thudding heart, walked straight through the doors and ordered a pint of bitter.

The first drink had gone down so well, Lindsay hadn't had to work hard to persuade herself that she deserved a second. She'd found an unobtrusive corner, hidden by a raucous group of youths wearing sweat pants, sports shirts and training shoes that had never seen activity more strenuous than the game of darts their owners were throwing. Lindsay kept her head down and thought about the little she'd learned from Derek Knight before she'd given herself away in so embarrassingly inappropriate a fashion.

What stuck in her mind were his comments about the doors. From the moment Sandra Bloom had revealed that Penny's death was murder, Lindsay had recognised it as a carefully planned, premeditated crime, based as it was on the plot in Penny's own book. According to Derek Knight, the flat door was ajar, but not flung wide, which tied in with that supposition. It wasn't left that way in a panic, but deliberately. It also indicated that the killer wanted the body to be found fairly quickly.

However, the mortise lock on the street door had been left undone. That suggested either that the killer didn't know the residents routinely kept it locked or that in his or her haste to get away from the scene of the crime they hadn't been able to find Penny's keys. It was confusing. On the one hand, it had been made to look like an accident; on the other hand, like murder.

Lindsay sighed and finished her second pint. It was nearly nine o'clock, and she felt like she hadn't slept properly for days. In the ladies', she splashed water over her tired eyelids, then set off on the long journey across London to Helen's. Outside the pub, to be on the safe side, she set off on a wide detour that would bring her via side streets to the top end of Highbury Fields, so she could approach the tube station from a diametrically opposite direction to Penny's flat. Better safe than sorry if the cops happened to be keeping an eye open at the station.

Her route took her down the side of the park, past tall, narrow houses that looked out across the variegated greens of trees and grass. It was a view she knew well. There had been a time when she had regarded one of those tall houses as her home. It had belonged to her lover, Cordelia. When Lindsay had moved in with her after their relationship had pushed her into abandoning her old life in Glasgow, she had thought that love was enough and forever. "How wrong can you get?" she muttered under her breath as she passed what had been her front door during what she looked back on as the time of the Great Illusion. Neither love nor Cordelia had proved to be what they seemed, and Lindsay still carried the scars. It had been a nice view, though, she thought fondly, wondering who lived there now and if it still belonged to Cordelia, the rent funding her permanent exile.

As the station grew nearer, caution forced nostalgia to the back of her mind. With sinking heart, Lindsay noticed there were a couple of police officers talking to a *Big Issue* vendor on the station approach. Slipping her backpack off her shoulder, she carried it by her side like a bag and walked briskly into the station, looking neither right nor left. As she turned to go down the stairs, she risked a quick glance back. Neither police officer was looking in her direction. Grinning to herself, Lindsay trotted down to the platform and waited for her train. The only way they were going to catch up with her now was if they still had her fingerprints on file. After all these years, she doubted that. Even paranoia had to call it a day sometime.

By the time she made it back to Helen's, reaction had set in, perfect partner to her growing jet lag. Her knees felt disconnected from her legs, her hands had a tremble she couldn't be bothered trying to control and her eyes felt grittier than they did on days when the wind whipped the sand on Half Moon Bay into a hazy cloud. "Oh, God," she groaned, closing the front door behind her and leaning against it.

A woman in faded 501s and a white T that told the world "My grannie was working class" pressed "pause" on the video remote control and looked across at her, dark blue eyes crinkling in a smile. "You'll be Lindsay," she said. "I'm Kirsten." She jumped to her feet and thrust her hand out.

Lindsay pushed off from the door and dragged her weary body across what felt like miles of carpet, dragging Kirsten's details up from the dim recesses of her mind. Freelance radio journalist. A few years younger than Helen, from somewhere in the West Country. They'd met at Pride two years before, had been living together around eighteen months. Sophie and Lindsay had missed meeting her on their last trip home because she'd been off covering some obscure opera festival. "Good to meet you at last," Lindsay said, taking Kirsten's hand and letting herself be drawn into a welcoming embrace.

"You look completely shattered," Kirsten said sympathetically. "Come on through, have a drink, something to eat. Helen's in the kitchen."

Lindsay was past independent thought. She let Kirsten lead as they threaded a staggering path through the chaos of the living room into the kitchen.

Helen jumped to her feet and greeted Lindsay with a huge bear hug. "Hey, Linds, it's great to see you, girl. And now you've met Kirsten in the flesh. Isn't she drop dead gorgeous?" She took one arm away from Lindsay to draw Kirsten into the cuddle.

"Behave," Kirsten protested. "You're embarrassing me!"

"Impossible, you're a journo. And she was one for too long to believe in the possibility of another hack getting a red neck over a compliment," Helen teased. She stepped back, looking critically at Lindsay. "Where you been till this time? You look like last orders in the dyke bar. We were going to wait to eat till you came back, but we couldn't hang on, we were starving. But there's loads left," she added, waving a vague arm at an array of foil takeaway cartons that covered half the available worktop space. "Just load up a plate and smack it in the video cooker."

"I'm too tired to eat," Lindsay said, disengaging herself from Helen's arm and slumping into the nearest chair. "Thanks for letting me stay here. I really appreciate it."

"I'm made up you're here. I'd have been really brassed off if I'd found out you were staying someplace else!" Helen opened a cupboard and took out a wine goblet, picked up a bottle of red that was sitting beside the pile of papers she was working on and glugged out a glassful. "Get yourself wrapped round that and tell me what you've been up to. Oh, by the way, Soph rang earlier. I don't think you're top of her Christmas card list right now."

Lindsay took the glass and swallowed a mouthful of something that reminded her of a pit bull terrier—warm but with a bite that didn't let go. "She want me to call her back?"

"She said she'd ring again." Helen glanced at her watch. "In about half an hour. So what have you been up to? What's going on? Soph said something about some friend of yours being murdered. What's the score?"

"Helen," Kirsten protested. "Let her get her second wind."

"It's okay, I'm used to her appalling manners," Lindsay said.

"Only because I learned them off you!" Helen roared with laughter.

Fortified by the wine, Lindsay gave Helen a succinct outline of recent events. "I'll colour in the picture when I've had a kip, okay?" she wound up.

"You just can't keep away from it, can you?" Helen said.
"We're two of a kind, you and me. We can't just sit on our hands
when something needs sorting."

"Mmm," Lindsay grunted, reaching for the bottle and
pouring a second glass. "So how's the film business?" She needed
to keep awake for Sophie's phone call, and listening to Helen
seemed a less taxing option than doing the talking herself.

"If I'm honest, Linds, it's actually a bag of shit right now."

"What's the problem?" Lindsay slurred through a mixture
of drink and exhaustion.

Kirsten groaned. "Don't encourage her. We'll be here all
night and I need my beauty sleep."

"If anyone needs their beauty sleep around here, gorgeous,
it's not you. The problem, Linds, is Guy. Well, it's not really
Guy as such, it's Stella. You remember the set-up at Watergaw?"

Lindsay remembered. Helen and Guy had set up their independent film-making company three years earlier. Before that,
Helen had worked in theatre administration, then run her own
casting agency, working for TV and film companies initially in
Britain and later across Europe. Guy had been a TV director
and producer first of current affairs and later of high-profile
documentaries. Together they'd decided to create Watergaw
Films to take advantage of new EU funding geared towards
community groups who wanted to develop TV and film projects, both dramatic and documentary. "How could I forget?"
she said. "Straight partnership, down the middle, you and Guy.
Best buddies, known each other since school, both gay, both
refugees from New Labour, both filled with the burning desire
to make meaningful TV."

"That's what I thought too," Helen said bitterly. She ran
a hand through her mop of flaming red hair. "Turns out I was
well wrong. On pretty much every count. I could just about
live with the way he's turned into the worst kind of exploitative
capitalist, because I could always weigh in and get the balance

straight again. But now he's got that bitch Stella on board . . . I
just don't know how much more of his shit I can take."

It had to be serious for Helen to be badmouthing another
woman like that, Lindsay realised with a jolt. Normally first to
the barricades when sisterhood came under threat, it took a lot
for Helen even to admit a woman was in the wrong when there
was an available male to be blamed. "Who's Stella?" Lindsay
asked as Kirsten moved behind Helen and started to massage
the back of her neck and shoulders.

"Oh, that's wonderful," Helen purred, rolling her head back.
"The bitch goddess from hell joined us about a year ago. We
needed someone else on board with directorial experience, and
she came highly recommended. Plus she had a bit of capital which
we needed right then, so she bought in at twenty per cent of the
company. What was supposed to happen was that she would do
the bread and butter stuff for Guy and work with me on projects
where I was producer. What wasn't supposed to happen was Guy
rediscovering his lost heterosexuality and climbing into bed with
the scheming little minx," Helen said. Not even Kirsten's massage
was enough to subdue the anger in her voice.

"Oh."

"Yeah, 'oh.'" Helen reached behind her and gently disengaged Kirsten's hands. "Thanks for the thought, K, but you're
wasting your energy. That pair have got me so wound up . . ."

"Well, don't talk about them, then," she said reasonably.

"As well as tell a river to stop flowing downhill," Lindsay
muttered.

"Exactly. And as if it's not enough that he's sleeping with
her, he's taking professional decisions with her. To all intents
and purposes, she's in control. Whatever she wants, Guy
backs her. Whenever there's a difference of opinion, whether
it's about company strategy or something as minor as how a
sequence should be filmed, Guy sides with her every time, and
I'm the one left out in the cold. I feel like I'm being frozen

out of my own company, and it's really pissing me off. Things get decided when I'm not even there—like as not between the sheets. But it's more than just being sidelined that bugs me. They're changing the culture of the company, and I'm spending all my time and energy running to try and stand still instead of moving us forward. It's not what I came into this business to do, but I just don't know how the hell to beat this bitch at her own game." Helen drained her glass and emptied the last of the bottle into it.

Lindsay rubbed her eyes with her knuckles and tried to straighten out of the slump that was spreading her upper body over the table top. "There's got to be some dirt," she managed to say.

"You what?"

Lindsay dragged herself upright and yawned hugely. "You don't get to be queen bitch at your first attempt. If she's such a smooth operator, there's got to be bodies buried somewhere."

Light dawned in Helen's eyes. "Hey, why didn't I think of that!"

Those were the last words Lindsay heard as she drifted into a limbo between sleep and waking. "Mmm," she murmured as she slipped away.

It didn't last long. Before she could fall far enough for dreams to capture her, the shrill chirrup of a telephone cut into her unconsciousness. "Huh? . . . wha'? . . . what is it?" she gabbled as her head shot up and her eyes snapped wide open and staring. She registered Helen reaching over to grab the phone that was buried under some papers inches away from where Lindsay's ear had been.

"Hiya, Soph. All right? . . . Yeah, she's here. All seven dwarfs rolled into one—Sleepy, Grumpy, Dopey, Snorey, Guilty, Boozy and Sexy." Helen roared with laughter.

Lindsay, pitying Sophie's eardrum, said, "You've been practising that line all night. Gimme the phone." She stretched her arm out, beckoning with her fingers.

"Here she is. See ya, Soph." Helen grinned, handed the phone to Lindsay and grabbed a bundle of papers before sweeping out of the kitchen.

Lindsay cleared her throat. "I know. If I was home, I'd be sleeping with Mutt. In the doghouse."

"No, if you were home, you'd be where you're supposed to be," Sophie said, sounding more exasperated than angry. "How do you get into these things?"

"Natural talent?"

"Natural stupidity, more like."

"I couldn't just leave Meredith to it, could I?" Lindsay said plaintively.

"I don't see why not," Sophie grumbled.

Even with a continent and an ocean separating them, Lindsay could tell her heart wasn't in it. "The woman you fell in love with wouldn't turn her back on Meredith."

"That was then. Things that are endearing in the first flush of passion can lose their charm, you know," Sophie pointed out, a warning creeping into her voice. "This isn't just about Meredith, is it?"

"Yeah, all right. Partly it's for me. I cared about Penny. We both did. I've tried to keep my nose out when people I care about have died before, and I never managed it. I thought this time I might as well be honest right from the start and admit that I know I can find out things the police won't get to hear in a million years."

"I thought it might be something like that. Is that why you didn't wait until I got home? Did you really think I'd try to talk you out of it?"

Lindsay thought she detected a trace of hurt under the warmth in Sophie's voice. "I wanted to wait till you came home, but the plane tickets were already bought and booked. I didn't feel I had the right to go wasting Meredith's money. I did try to call you at Crazy John's, but they said you guys weren't in and didn't have a table booked. I didn't know where else to try.

I'm sorry if you feel I didn't take you into account. That wasn't what I had in mind."

Sophie sighed. The silence stretched and Lindsay couldn't avoid filling it. "Anyway, you'll be here next week. Things'll be sorted by then. We'll have our holiday just like we planned."

Another sigh. This time Sophie followed it up with words. "If you're still in one piece," she said gloomily.

"No reason why I shouldn't be," Lindsay said. "Come on, I know how to take care of myself."

More silence.

"I've done this before, you know. I did it before I had you fussing around like a nursemaid. I'm not a child, Sophie. I'm not helpless."

"I didn't say you were, my love. I just worry about you, okay? I know it's totally unreasonable of me, but I do worry."

"You don't have to. I'm too much of a coward to get damaged."

In her office with its view of the Oakland Bridge, Sophie Hartley grabbed her greying curls with her free hand. Lindsay might have chosen to forget, but she could never lose the knowledge of how dangerous her lover's favourite game could be. "I hope you're right," she said softly. "I really hope you're right."

8

Lindsay stirred the warm grey liquid that passed for coffee in the supermarket café and stared across the car park at the row of converted mews cottages that housed Monarch Press. Nothing was moving so far. But that was hardly surprising of a publishing house at five to nine in the morning. In an ideal world, she'd still be tucked up in bed letting her body recover. But Helen had never mastered the art of rising quietly and unobtrusively. If she was awake at seven, the rest of the house was guaranteed to be awake by five past, their ears possessed by Radio Four at full volume. Helen liked to hear the morning news wherever she was in the house, including the shower.

Lindsay had staggered downstairs at ten past seven, lured by the smell of coffee. She'd found Kirsten reading the *Guardian* in her dressing gown, her short dark hair sticking up in a Fido Dido crest, hands wrapped round a mug of very black coffee. The room was an oasis of relative quiet, the radio there being silent. "Plenty in the pot," Kirsten mumbled. "Croissants in the oven. A couple of minutes yet."

Lindsay tried moving a mouth that seemed to be lodged in a concrete face. "I can't believe you got her to switch off the radio in here," she managed as she helped herself to coffee.

"I don't mind bringing work home with me. But I'm damned if I'm going to wake up to it as well. I told her, it's the *Today* programme or me."

"It must be love," Lindsay commented.

Right on cue, Helen bounced into the room swathed in a kimono, her marmalade hair in damp coils to her shoulders. "Sleep okay, Linds?" she demanded, sweeping past them both and yanking a tray of hot croissants and *pains au chocolat* out of the oven.

"Yeah," she said. "Could have done with a few more hours, but . . ."

"Don't be daft," Helen said, dumping the croissants on to a plate and balancing it on top of the papers she'd been working on the night before. "Never mind Tulsa, you're back living on Tulse Hill time," she continued, breaking into song and playing air guitar in a bad imitation of Eric Clapton.

"Helen," Kirsten groaned plaintively.

"Best cure for jet lag," Helen persisted. "What've you got on today, K?"

Kirsten frowned momentarily. Then her face cleared. "Doing a piece for Radio Bloke about holiday reading. One last interview to do, then I can cobble it all together."

"Radio Bloke?" Lindsay asked faintly.

"Five Live," Helen informed her. " 'Twenty-four hour news and sport from the BBC,' " she mimicked, helping herself to a croissant.

"I do bits and pieces for them, but mostly I work for Four," Kirsten said, her warm radio voice re-emerging from the early morning gravel. "Arts and media stuff."

"That's handy," Lindsay said, perking up as the coffee worked its way through to her brain.

"Watch out, K," Helen cautioned through a mouthful of pastry. "When this scally starts to take an interest, there's always an ulterior motive. She'll be after borrowing some fancy recording equipment or something, just wait and see."

Reaching for a *pain au chocolat*, Lindsay shook her head. "You know me too well, Helen."

"You can't scam a scammer," Helen said.

"Is there something I can help you with, Lindsay?" Kirsten asked between mouthfuls.

"I don't honestly know," she said. "Maybe. Do you know anything about Monarch Press?"

Kirsten nodded. "As it happens, yeah. *Kaleidoscope* did a feature on their tenth anniversary. I wasn't producing, but I went along to the party. Lemme see . . ." Her dark eyes focussed on the middle distance as Helen leaned across to refill her coffee cup. "Thanks, love. Now, lemme get this right. The guy behind the company is an East End wide boy called Danny King. He's a proper cockney, one generation away from a barrow boy. Though that's being a bit unfair. His dad actually got off the barrows and worked as a printer in Fleet Street."

Lindsay groaned. "Bigger highway robbers than Dick Turpin."

"Yeah, well, old man King retired to Spain on his redundo some time in the mid-eighties, leaving his wife behind."

"How did you find all this out?" Helen demanded. "I know you're nosy, but that's ridiculous!"

Kirsten grinned. "I was standing next to his dad during the speeches, which were mostly the kind that can only be improved by talking through them. He told me his entire life story, most of which, thankfully, I have managed to erase from the memory banks."

"So how did an East End cowboy get to be a gentleman publisher?" Lindsay asked, trying to keep the conversation on track.

"Who said anything about gentleman?" Kirsten said, eyebrows steepling. "Danny's mum was a great believer in self-improvement, and she was always encouraging her little lad to read. When he ducked out of school, his dad called in a few favours and got him a job in the print works of one of the big

publishing houses. From there, Danny parlayed himself a job as
a sales rep. Supposedly he was a very good one. Then he won
the pools."

"You're kidding!" Helen exclaimed. "How much?"

"A mill and a quarter. Which was a lot of cash eleven or
so years ago."

"It's a lot of cash now," Lindsay pointed out. "And he set up
a publishing house?" The incredulity in her voice was matched
only by the expression on Helen's face.

"That's right. He announced to a waiting world that nobody
was publishing the books he'd wanted to read as a teenager, or
the books he'd wanted to sell, or the books he wanted to read
now, and he was going to fill the gap in the market. Everybody
laughed at him, of course. Publishing was in a decline, the market was shrinking, there were too many books and not enough
buyers already. And of course, he was a toerag from the wrong
side of the tracks without the requisite English degree. But he
proved them all wrong."

"So what kind of stuff does Monarch publish? Apart from
Penny's Darkliners series?" Lindsay asked.

Kirsten dug a packet of cigarettes out of her dressing-gown
pocket and lit up. "It's a pretty eclectic list. Mostly fiction, mostly
by young writers who don't come out of the sausage factory of
university and journalism. The keynote is that it's all slightly off
the wall, out of the mainstream. Cult fiction. Acid-head doleite
narrators. Travel guides to places you didn't know you wanted to
go to till you read the book. Their slogan is, 'Fact or fiction—in
your face.' Your friend Penny was his first big success, but there
have been others since."

"How did he do it? What made it work?" Lindsay asked.
Her curiosity was pricked now, and it was nothing to do with
Penny.

Kirsten shrugged. "He was one of the first to abandon
hardback publishing and go for good-quality softback originals
that were only a pound or two more expensive than mass-market

paperbacks. The books had a strong corporate image, so they stood out on the shelves. He hired people who weren't afraid to back their hunches on new writers. And he marketed the books with a bit of chutzpah. They advertised in music mags, style mags, top-end women's glossies—places where publishers hadn't gone before, except with individual titles. It wasn't any one thing—it was the way he combined ideas."

"He took the right risks," Lindsay said.

"That about sums it up. And now Monarch has got a real brand identity with its readers. People read a Monarch title and they like it, so they try another one. Pretty soon, they start to buy the new titles automatically."

"Sounds a bit too much like a dream come true," Helen said sceptically.

Kirsten rumpled her hair. "You're just a twisted old cynic. Not every business has a skunk like Guy and a snake like Stella."

Lindsay nodded. "Maybe you should pitch Danny King into the film business, Helen. Sounds like he's got the golden touch."

Helen snorted. "Spare me any more boy wonders." She glanced up at the schoolroom clock on the wall. "Speaking of which, I'd better get my skates on before I find we're contracted to make a soap for satellite."

After Helen had gone, Lindsay said, "Did you happen to meet Baz Burton? She was Penny's editor."

"Can't help you there. After I disentangled myself from Danny's dad, I was doing the rounds of the authors, trying to see if I could pick up any programme ideas. I didn't actually talk to anybody from Monarch. Sorry."

Then it had been Kirsten's turn to leave. Even after Lindsay had loaded the dishwasher and put the remains of the previous night's takeaway in the fridge, it was barely eight o'clock. Showered and dressed, she'd been on the street by half past and in the supermarket opposite Monarch's Shepherd's Bush office twenty minutes later. Now all she could do was wait for the publishing day to begin. At least, for the first time in her life,

she was on surveillance somewhere with an unlimited supply
of coffee and, more importantly, a toilet.

By ten fifteen, Lindsay reckoned that anyone who was planning
on coming to work at Monarch was probably there. Besides, the
table clearer in the café was starting to become restive, sighing
heavily every time she passed Lindsay's table with its coffee
cup still half full. She picked up her backpack and strolled out
into the car park, where the warmth hit her, a shock after the
air-conditioned cool of the store. "Just like being at home," she
muttered. At least she was dressed for it today, in Bermuda shorts
and a sleeveless tunic with a mandarin collar.

As she got closer, Lindsay could see that the ground floors
of five of the mews cottages had been knocked together to give
a semi-open-plan appearance to Monarch's ground floor. The
reception area, in the middle cottage, was decorated in the same
sunshine yellow and forest green as the distinctive livery of the
imprint's paperbacks. The receptionist sat behind a high yellow
desk like an airport check-in. Her acid fuchsia T-shirt clashed
magnificently with the decor. Clearly not a place to work if
you were prone to hangovers or migraine, Lindsay thought as
she approached with a smile. A green sign told the world the
twenty-something receptionist's name was Lauren. Somehow,
she looked like a Lauren. She had long hair the colour of set
honey, big blue eyes and a bone structure that hollowed her
cheeks. In spite of the right components, she somehow missed
being beautiful. "Good morning, Lauren," Lindsay said. "Is
Baz Burton in?"

The receptionist dragged her attention away from something behind the desk that Lindsay couldn't see. "Is she expecting
you?" she asked, her voice a disappointing nasal south London
whine.

"I don't have an appointment. But I'd really appreciate it
if she could spare me a few minutes." She smiled ingratiatingly.

"Can you tell me your name and what it's in connection with?" was the bored reply as the eyes strayed back beneath the counter top.

"My name is Lindsay Gordon and it's in connection with Penny Varnavides. I'm representing Meredith Miller."

That got Lauren's undivided attention. "Right," she said, her voice approving and interested. "Let's see what we can do, eh?" Her hand appeared above the counter clutching a phone and she keyed in a number. "Susan? It's Lauren at the front desk. Someone here for Baz . . . No, but I think Baz will want to see her . . . Penny Varnavides . . . No, she's not press, she says she's representing . . ." Her voice trailed off and she looked questioningly at Lindsay.

"Meredith Miller."

"A Meredith Miller . . . Right." She replaced the phone and gave Lindsay a friendly smile. "Ms Burton's assistant is going to check if she can see you."

"Thanks." Lindsay strolled over to a wall display of book jackets, her eyes automatically seeking out Penny's titles. A phone rang and Lauren answered it. "Monarch Press, how may I help you . . . You want to leave a message for . . . Certainly. And you are . . . ? Could you spell that . . . ? T-a-v-a-r-e? Fine, Mr Tavare, I'll see he gets the message."

As the phone went down, a scarlet-faced woman with a disturbing resemblance to a hamster marched round the end of a partition and into the reception area. "How many times do I have to tell you?" she hissed at the receptionist. If it was meant to be out of Lindsay's earshot, she'd failed. "People who arrive without an appointment get shown the door. You do *not* buzz through and put Susan on the spot, is that clear?"

Lauren flushed. "But Baz . . ."

"I don't want to hear buts. It's a simple enough procedure, surely you can manage it? Or do I have to talk to Danny?"

Lauren, who had clearly learned her lesson from the Princess of Wales, dropped her head and looked up at Baz from under her eyebrows. "I'm sorry, Baz, okay?"

"And while I'm on the subject of simple procedures, how come an urgent set of proofs that gets biked round to me yesterday morning doesn't make it on to my desk till ten minutes ago?" The woman's voice rose in pitch and volume. "Do you know what the word urgent means, or do I have to buy you a bloody dictionary?"

Before Lauren could answer, Lindsay jumped in. "Excuse me, but am I in the wrong place? I thought this was a publishing house, not a casualty ward. I mean, how urgent can a set of proofs be? You know, every time you get wound up like that, it takes days off your potential life span." She smiled disarmingly. "I'm Lindsay Gordon. You must be Baz Burton."

Baz gave Lauren a final glare, then swung round with a broad smile towards Lindsay. "Pleased to meet you." She didn't offer her hand. "Sorry about that. You know what they say—you just can't get the staff. My assistant tells me you're representing Meredith Miller. Can I ask in what capacity?"

"Can we talk somewhere a little more private?" Lindsay said, stepping to one side to avoid a pair of young men walking through reception deep in discussion about book clubs.

"Is this going to take long?" Baz asked, glancing ostentatiously at a Mickey Mouse watch. "Only, I've got an important meeting in twenty minutes, so if you need longer, I'd suggest you make an appointment for another day."

"Let's make a start with that twenty minutes, then," Lindsay said firmly. "If we need more time, I can always come back later."

"Fine," Baz said curtly. "Follow me."

She led the way round a room divider and into a small office partitioned off the larger room, where people sat at computers and piles of manuscripts. Baz settled into a leather executive chair behind a desk cluttered with papers. She didn't invite Lindsay to sit, but she did anyway, noting that the visitors' chairs were significantly lower than the edge of the desk. The room had no door, and Lindsay felt strangely exposed with her back to the entrance.

Baz tilted her head to one side, frankly studying Lindsay. Lindsay returned the compliment, taking in a hennaed urchin cut over straight brows and eyes the same muddy colour as the supermarket coffee. Her plump, jowly cheeks were at odds with a neat frame whose slimness was accentuated by the tight black jeans and vest she was wearing. Her shoulders were as pink as her cheeks and showed all the signs of peeling from too much sun. In her left ear was a single earring in the shape of an axe. In her right, a line of half a dozen silver studs marched upwards from the lobe till they met a pair of ear cuffs. "Sorry about that business out there. It's not that I didn't want to talk to you. It's just that I am literally snowed under with work, and that idiot girl on reception keeps on funnelling wannabe writers through to me as if I'm running a counselling service for failures," Baz said to break the silence.

"All the more thanks for giving me some time," Lindsay said noncommittally.

"You still haven't answered my question, though," Baz said with a teasing smile that completely altered her face, reminding Lindsay that hamsters could be cute. She leaned forward with her elbows on the desk and gazed at Lindsay.

"At Meredith Miller's request, I'm investigating Penny Varnavides' murder."

Baz looked incredulous. "*You're* a private eye?"

"Not exactly. But I have had some experience of murder inquiries."

"And Meredith's hired you to clear her name, is that it?"

"Sort of." For no reason she could put her finger on, Lindsay was reluctant to reveal how much she knew about Meredith or Penny. Admitting she was working out of friendship would be to give too much away.

"Fine. I'm all for Meredith's name being cleared. It's absolutely ridiculous that she's even come under suspicion." Baz spoke vehemently, her voice rising. "Anyone with half a brain could see that Meredith would never hurt a fly. She's one of the gentlest people I've ever met."

There were a lot of words Lindsay would have applied to Meredith before she got to gentle. "Have you known her long?" she asked.

"Almost as long as Penny. Which makes it about eleven years. I met her the first time I went to San Francisco. And I've seen her quite a bit over the years, both in the US and here in England. When she's in town on business, we sometimes have dinner. I really hope you can get the police off her back," she added, beaming a wide white smile at Lindsay.

"You knew right from the start they were lovers?"

Baz's lips quirked in a half-smile. "You know what they say. It takes one to know one. It took Penny about four years to tell me the big secret, but I sussed it from day one. But why all the questions about Meredith?" she demanded, suddenly suspicious. "I thought you were supposed to be on her side?"

"I am. Just background, that's all. I'm told that you had seen a lot of Penny this trip?"

"I wouldn't have said 'a lot,'" Baz objected. "We met a few times to discuss the progress of her new book."

"Did you normally do that?"

"Not with the Darkliners series, no. Pen could knock them off standing on her head with one arm tied behind her back. She'd just send me a two-page synopsis so the art department could get busy with the cover and we could do the jacket copy. Then twelve weeks later, like clockwork, another fifty thousand words of Darkliners title would drop through the letter box. Then we'd have a meeting to sort out the edits, and that was about it, really. If she was over here anyway, we'd do lunch or dinner, but for pleasure, not work."

"But this time it was different?" Lindsay prompted.

"Inevitably. *Heart of Glass* was a very different book from anything Pen had attempted before." Baz gave Lindsay another dazzling smile. "I wanted to give Pen all the support she needed

to complete it." Sensing her facial expression was inappropriate, Baz swiftly changed to a suitably sad look. "Tragically, that
didn't happen."

"How was the book progressing?" Lindsay asked briskly,
refusing to be sidetracked into a sharing of sorrow.

"Very well. About 70,000 words on paper." Baz had suddenly become abrupt, her previous chattiness vanishing as if it
had never been.

"Do you have a copy of the manuscript?"

"No. I don't have any text. I don't even have a synopsis.
Pen was guarding this one with her life." As she realised what
she had said, Baz's mouth fell open.

"So it would seem," Lindsay said grimly. "So what exactly
was it that her killer didn't want the world to read?"

9

Baz's mouth was moving but no sound was coming out of it. "There must have been something," Lindsay persisted. "Nobody has a copy of the book—not you, not her agent, and certainly not Meredith. Her laptop and her back-up disks have gone missing. There must have been something in there that someone wanted to keep hidden."

"That's ridiculous," Baz finally said. "It's only a novel, for God's sake. Nobody thinks fiction's important enough to kill over it!"

Lindsay shrugged. "Why else use such an outrageous murder method? It's ridiculous. Who'd go to all that bother when they could just have picked up a bottle and cracked her over the head with it? It's as if the killer was leaving a message: 'Anybody else in the know that's thinking about messing with me, don't do it!'"

"You're wrong," Baz said desperately. "You've got to be wrong. There must be something else behind it."

"Convince me. What's *Heart of Glass* about?"

"It's a thriller."

"About?"

Baz sighed. "It's a really complicated plot with a lot of psychological suspense that centres around a writer. Every time this guy imagines something, it happens. So he decides to try and see if he can get rid of all the people he hates by writing their deaths into his books. In parallel with that, you've got a surgeon who is a particularly gruesome killer. And their two lives collide via the surgeon's wife, who is the writer's editor. It's 'a roller-coaster ride of horror,' according to the catalogue copy I wrote six weeks ago. Which reminds me that I have a bloody big hole to fill in next spring's list." She poked around among the papers on her desk, as if to indicate that she had far more important things to do than talk to Lindsay.

"Sounds like it would have walked straight on to the best-seller lists. What a pity Penny isn't going to be able to finish it," Lindsay said ironically. "But that still doesn't answer why someone would want the book suppressed. Was there anything in it that seemed potentially libellous to you?"

Before Baz could answer, there was a tap on the partition behind Lindsay's head. She turned to see a man's face grinning at her. "Sorry to butt in," he said in a strong London accent. "Whenever you like, Baz."

"Be right there," Baz said, getting to her feet.

The man moved into the doorway. He looked to be around forty, with dark wavy hair that needed trimming and creamy white skin that showed no trace of the freakishly sunny summer weather. His smile was cheeky and cheerful, the lines in his face revealing it as a familiar expression. It was his eyes that caught the attention, however; the same blue as the denim shirt he wore, they sparkled like sapphires even in the artificial light of the office. He angled his head to one side, like a bird listening for underground movement, and said, "And you must be the mystery visitor who's come to talk about Penny's tragic death, am I right?"

"Ms Gordon was just leaving," Baz said repressively, hast-ily moving across the room to cut off the line of sight between Lindsay and the man. "And we've got marketing strategies to discuss." She put a hand on his arm, which he ignored.

"Hell of a thing," the man said, shaking his head. "She was the last person you'd expect to die like that. She was lovely, you know? It's hard to imagine how she could drive someone to kill her."

"I know what you mean," Lindsay said, pleased to find herself talking to someone who seemed to have valued Penny for the person she was rather than for the profits she could generate. It made a welcome change.

"I loved her work," he continued. "Always so sharp, so bright. Just like she was, really."

"We're keeping everyone waiting," Baz said, trying to edge him out of the doorway.

"It won't kill them," the man said negligently. He held out a hand to Lindsay, who was by now also standing. "Since Baz seems to have lost touch with her manners, I better introduce myself. I'm Danny King. I'm the publisher. And you are?"

"Lindsay Gordon. Meredith Miller's asked me to investigate Penny's murder. To clear her name. She didn't do it, in spite of what the police might think."

He nodded. "You're preaching to the converted here, Lindsay. According to Baz, Meredith could never have harmed a hair on Penny's head. And I trust Baz's judgement implicitly. As long as it keeps making me a profit," he added with another grin. "So how are your inquiries coming along?"

Lindsay pulled a face. "Early days. What would really help would be a copy of Penny's manuscript."

Danny cast his eyes up and tutted. "You and me both," he sighed. "Baz tells me there was enough there for us to craft some kind of an ending. I really want to get this book out there—not just because it'll be a good seller, but because it's a helluva book and it's the only way we've got of paying some kind of tribute to the great writer Penny was. But we haven't got a copy and neither, apparently, does Penny's agent. I don't suppose you know where we could locate one?"

Lindsay shook her head. "Sorry."

Danny grinned and gave her arm a quick squeeze. It was clearly a gesture of farewell.

"Maybe I should get you on the payroll too, see if you can come up with the goods? Anyway, nice to meet you, Lindsay. If you need any help from anybody here at Monarch, all you've got to do is tell them Danny sent you." He winked and ushered Baz ahead of him into the main office.

"I'll see myself out, shall I?" Lindsay said to the empty cubicle. Unfortunately, it was too public to search the desk, so she followed the other two on to the editorial floor. She was in time to see them vanish up a flight of stairs. She sighed. Without knowing who was who, there was no point in trying to screw information about Penny or her book out of Baz's colleagues and minions. Feeling as if she'd wasted a golden opportunity, Lindsay walked back to reception.

As she passed the reception desk, Lauren glanced up. Seeing who it was, she leaned forward and said, "You got a minute?"

Lindsay stopped. "Of course."

"That was really cool, earlier, when you dived in like that with Baz."

"No sweat. She's obviously got a lot on her mind."

A sly smile spread across Lauren's face. "You don't know the half of it."

"You going to tell me?"

"Might do. You a private eye?"

"Sort of."

"That means you get expenses, right?"

Lindsay snorted with laughter. "You watch too much telly." Lauren looked disappointed. Lindsay relented. "I can probably run to a few quid."

"Okay, you know Riverside Studios?"

Lindsay dredged her memory. "Other side of the Hammersmith gyratory?"

"That's right. None of this lot can be bothered to walk that far at lunchtime. I'll see you in the café there about quarter to one. Okay?"

"You're not taking the piss?"

Lauren repeated her sly smile. "Believe me, you won't be wasting your time or your money."

Before Lindsay could say any more, the phone rang. As she left, she could hear Lauren saying, "You want to leave a message for Paddy Brown? Yes . . ."

With the best part of two hours to kill, Lindsay consulted her A–Z, then headed down through the artificially bright shopping mall on the traffic island at the heart of Hammersmith towards the river. She turned right under the bridge, where she found a sudden splash of colour against the relentless urban grime. Settling down on a bench in a patch of shade in the lush rose garden, Lindsay took her laptop from her backpack, opened it up and switched it on. With plenty of pauses to contemplate the faded houseboats straggling along the riverbank, she typed in all the information she'd gathered so far on Penny Varnavides' murder.

It didn't take long.

Lauren was right on time. Lindsay bought them both salads and bottles of mineral water and they settled at a table in a quiet, gloomy corner of the café. Lindsay poked at her salad with a fork. "Pretty bloody dreary," she muttered. "Amazing how quickly you forget."

"Forget what?" Lauren asked, shovelling tuna into her mouth like an apprentice bulimic.

"Forget the sorry mess of tired vegetation that passes for salad in this country. When I rule the world, the person who developed iceberg lettuce will be first up against the wall. No wonder when I come home I live off junk food. No shocks that way. It's the one thing that I actually expect to be as bad as it is."

"What d'you mean, when you come home? Where else do you go?"

"For some strange reason, I still think of Britain as home, even though I've lived in California for the last six years."

Lauren's eyes opened wide. "You live in California? Excellent! How did you manage that?"

"My partner got offered a job over there, so it was go with or split up. I was having a pretty shitty time over here, apart from our relationship, so I went with. Got a job, got a doctorate and stayed."

"Wow! Cool!"

"Better than Shepherd's Bush," Lindsay said drily. "You should give it a whirl if you're that keen."

Lauren's mouth turned down at the corners. "I ain't got the skills, have I? Bit of word processing and GCSE Spanish."

"You never know. Being bilingual in English and Spanish isn't a bad start in southern California. Don't put yourself down." Lindsay gave Lauren an encouraging grin. "And they love Brits."

"Yeah, well. Fantasy Island, that is. Anyway, daydreaming about California's not what I came here for. What's it worth to you, the dirt on Baz and Penny?"

Lindsay shrugged. "I don't know what it's worth until I know what it is, do I? Look, why don't you tell me what you know and I'll see you right?"

"How do I know I can trust you?" Lauren demanded, scowling.

"You don't. But right now I'm the only show in town, so you might as well skin me for what you can get while you can get it." Lauren looked unconvinced, so Lindsay tried another tack. "Look, Lauren, I was Penny Varnavides' friend. Her and Meredith used to come round our house at least once a month. We played beach volleyball together, we climbed mountains together, we saw the New Year in together. This isn't just a job for me, it's personal."

"Yeah, okay, you talked me into it," Lauren said, trying and failing to sound tough and worldly wise. "I've been working at Monarch for two years, right, so I'd met Penny a few times. I got talking to her one afternoon when she'd come in to see Baz and Baz was late getting back from lunch. I told her how

I'd read all the Darkliners books when I was a teenager, and how much I'd loved them. She was great. She laughed her head off and said she didn't think publishers employed anybody that actually *liked* the books they produced. And after that, every time she came into the office, she always brought me some book or other that she'd seen in America and thought I'd like. She's the only author I've ever met who remembered my name without having to read the plaque, never mind what I liked to read. So I always paid attention when she was around."

So like Penny, Lindsay thought with a pang. She'd always been a woman who paid attention to the seemingly insignificant people. It was why she always got the best table in her regular hangouts, why her newspaper was never dumped on the step to become a soggy mess, why the local second-hand bookstore always remembered which titles were on her want list. Little touches of consideration that made her life run smoothly. Not that that was why she'd done it, Lindsay reminded herself. Just that she was the kind of person who noticed details. "Was she like that with other people in the office?" she asked at last, forcing herself back into the present.

"She didn't really have much to do with anybody except Baz and her assistant, Susan. If she had, they might not have got so pissed off with her."

"Pissed off with her? Who got pissed off with her? Why?" Lindsay asked.

"A bunch of them in editorial. The PC brigade. If that lot went on a march, they wouldn't go, 'Right, left, right, left,' they'd go, 'Right on, right on.'" Lauren grinned.

"And what had Penny done to upset them?" Lindsay asked.

"It was about her being gay. I never even knew she was till that lot started going on about it. It turns out they were put out because she'd been in the closet all those years. They kept going on about it being hypocritical not to be out, and how she'd only stayed in the closet for the sake of her sales figures. Which I thought was a bit of a liberty, really. I mean, it's nobody's business who she goes to bed with if she doesn't want it to be, is it?"

Lindsay sighed, lacking the energy for that particular conversation. "Did anyone make any specific threats, or was it generalised grumbling?"

"Just grumbling, really. People who haven't got anything better to do except indulge in petty jealousy and poison. And nobody had the bottle to front Penny up about it, either." Lauren frowned. "Although . . . maybe that's what it was went wrong with her and Baz."

"Something went wrong? When?"

"This last trip. When I first met Penny, her and Baz got on really well. They were always laughing and joking together, teasing each other, taking the piss, that kind of thing. They'd always go out to lunch or dinner together. More than just duty, like they really enjoyed each other's company. But this time, it was different. They were dead polite to each other, you know?"

"Formal?"

"Yeah, like they hardly knew each other. Awkward. Like it was uncomfortable to be with each other. Penny was in and out a few times, and every time they were dead stiff with each other."

"As if they'd had a row?"

Lauren frowned. "Not exactly, no. More like they were sniffing round each other. Like they were trying to avoid a row, almost. Anyway, the upshot was that Penny comes to me and says can I let her into the office last thing at night, once everybody else had gone home. She said she'd make it worth my while. Well, it was no problem for me, was it, on account of I've got a full set of keys so I can get in in the mornings. And nobody notices what time I go home, so long as it doesn't inconvenience them."

Lindsay stared at Lauren, food forgotten. "Did Penny say why she wanted to get into the offices?"

Lauren shrugged. "Not exactly. But she wanted to know if I knew if the computers were on a network and if people like Baz and Danny had their own separate terminals. I said I didn't know what the exact set-up was, but I sussed she was only mentioning Danny as a sort of diversion. It was Baz she was really interested in. I didn't give a toss anyway. I mean, you've seen what a shit that Baz can be. So I said all right, I'd hang on late one night and I'd let her in. We agreed that she'd lock up and drop the keys back round my flat when she'd done."

"And did it all go off smoothly?"

"Course it did. She made it worth my while, didn't she?" Lauren said pointedly. Lindsay pulled out her wallet and looked inside. Apart from traveller's cheques, she had about fifty pounds in cash. She took out a twenty and slid it across the table. Lauren looked at her pityingly. The second twenty followed, Lauren pointedly staring into the wallet as Lindsay dug it out. She continued to look expectant as she picked up the second twenty.

"Tube fare, Lauren," Lindsay said. "I need tube fare. If your information pans out, I'll get you some more money from Meredith, okay?"

Lauren sighed. "I suppose."

"What time did Penny bring the keys back?"

"It wasn't that late. About half ten, I suppose."

"Had she found what she was looking for?" Lindsay asked.

"Don't know. She never said. And I didn't ask, neither. She must've left things the way she found them, though, because nobody said anything about somebody raking through their stuff or buggering up their computer."

"Did she come in the office after that? I mean, officially."

Lauren frowned as she gobbled the last of her lunch. "Yeah, now you come to mention it, she did. The day before she died. She had a meeting with Baz late morning. But Baz was out. Susan said there wasn't anything in the diary and Penny said Baz must have forgotten to write it down. Penny was a bit put out. She said it had messed up her whole day's writing, so Susan got Danny to take her out to lunch. He had a face like fizz when he came back, so I suppose it screwed up his day too. He gave Baz a right gobful, told her Penny Varnavides was a lot more

valuable to Monarch than she was and next time she made an
appointment with her, she'd better not forget it unless she wanted
to start looking for another job." Lauren sniggered. "Baz had a
gob on her like a dried prune."

"And that was the last time Penny was in the office."

Lauren nodded. "Far as I know."

Lindsay drank her water and wondered what to ask about
next. Then she remembered the crucial question. "Do you do
the incoming post?"

"Nah. That's Gary in the post room."

"So you wouldn't know who had access to the manuscripts
that Penny sent in?"

Lauren shook her head as she lit a cigarette, leaking smoke
from her mouth like a damaged flue. "No idea. Sorry. Why
d'you want to know? I mean, maybe I could find out for you."

"You know how Penny was murdered the same way one
of the victims dies in *Heart of Glass*? Well, I'm just trying to find
out who exactly knew what happens in the book."

Lauren gave a knowing smile. "You don't need to talk to
the post room to find that out. Everybody knew."

"What? About the beer bottle exploding?"

"Yeah, everybody knew about *that*." Lauren looked very
pleased with herself.

"How?"

"They had a bit of an argy-bargy about it. They were talking to Nigel, who does the covers, about what was going on
the front of *Heart of Glass*. Penny told Nigel about the murder
method and said the cover should be just the title and her name
and a splinter of glass, all on a black background. And Baz said
no, she'd been meaning to talk to Penny about that, and the
whole thing was just too far-fetched and she didn't believe in it
and she wanted her to come up with a different idea. And Penny
said no way, José, it was perfectly feasible and she thought it was
dramatic and ironic and it was staying."

"They got heated?" Lindsay asked eagerly.

"Not really. It was like it was part of the whole arm's-length thing. Baz just wasn't prepared to go head to head with Penny. She just backed down and said okay, if it was that important to Penny it could stay. Everybody was gobsmacked, because Baz never backs down with her authors. Like, never. That's why it stuck in my mind. So you see, everybody at Monarch knew about the murder method. And God alone knows who they went home and told."

10

Lindsay sat in the swaying tube train, her thoughts swirling in confusion. At breakfast, she'd had two suspects—three if she'd been prepared to include Meredith. But thanks to Lauren's revelations, she now had dozens. The publishing world was so riddled with gossip that if anything could be guaranteed, it was that half London would know Penny Varnavides and her editor weren't seeing eye to eye. The disagreement over the bottled beer murder method would have been discussed avidly among publishers, agents and, by now, probably authors too. Rather than narrowing down her list of suspects, Lindsay's visit to Monarch had swelled it a hundredfold.

As if that wasn't bad enough, she didn't have the faintest idea what to do next. But if six years in California had taught her anything, it was that there weren't many problems that couldn't be eased by some judicious retail therapy. For some, that took the form of trawling the department stores and boutiques for designer clothes at charity shop prices. For others, the gourmet food stores were the fount of all comfort. For Lindsay, shopping paradise took the form of second-hand book and CD stores, where she could browse for hours, then emerge with some obscure gem that cost next to nothing. It didn't matter when Sophie pointed out that in the time she had taken to find that single specimen,

Lindsay could have written an article that would have earned enough to buy a dozen brand-new CDs or hardback books. The hunt was the fun as much as the purchase, and fun was what Lindsay needed in her present mood.

However, given Sophie's decidedly stiff manner on the phone the previous evening, Lindsay realised a serious peace offering was going to be required at the airport when Sophie arrived the following week. There was nothing more calculated to win her round than some obscure object to add to her collection of historic obstetric instruments. Lindsay could hardly look at them without wincing and crossing her legs, but they fascinated Sophie. And if her memory served her well, one of the antique shops in Camden catered for such perverse tastes. Lindsay could find something for Sophie, then indulge herself in the second-hand stores around Camden Lock. And if she was really lucky, maybe the logical part of her brain, left in peace, would come up with a possible new direction for her investigation.

Just over an hour later, she emerged from the antique shop with an 1860s variant of a Higginson syringe, a fearsome object used by surgeons for aborting the unwanted foetuses of the gentry as well as for routine internal spring-cleaning. Just listening to the shopkeeper describe its function made Lindsay's flesh creep.

As she walked towards the canal, she started to review what she had learned earlier. She'd got as far as rerunning her conversation with Baz when a hand clamped heavily on her shoulder. Her stomach lurched, seized by the same panic she'd felt escaping from Derek Knight's flat. Startled, Lindsay swung round on the balls of her feet, ready to push her assailant away and run for it.

Familiar red curls swirled in front of her. "What are you doing here?" Helen demanded. "I thought you were off in darkest Shepherd's Bush making citizen's arrests on publishers."

Lindsay closed her eyes and let out the breath she hadn't even realised she was holding. "Don't ever do that again," she said. "Jesus, Helen, I've eaten too much cholesterol over the years. Another shock like that and I could drop down dead."

"You know, sometimes I forget you were a tabloid hack for a million years. Then you go and sound like the front page of the *Sun* and it all comes flooding back to me. Never let the truth get in the way of a good exaggeration, eh? So what are you doing over here?"

"I decided I better arm myself for Sophie's arrival," Lindsay said, unwrapping her package and waving it under Helen's nose.

"Yeuuch! That's disgusting. Take it away, you revolting little toerag. And don't tell me what it's for," she warned.

"It's a peace offering."

"A peace offering? Bloody hell, Lindsay, I know they do things differently in California, but I didn't realise the sex was that bizarre!"

"It's for Sophie's collection," Lindsay said, casting her eyes upwards in mock exasperation.

"I know that. So, you finished over at Monarch, then?"

"I'm finished. Don't take it personally, but I really don't want to talk about it just now. This is one of those cases where the more I find out, the less I know. And now I come to think about it, what are you doing walking around the streets instead of looking important in your office?"

Helen scowled like a child caught playing truant. "I reached the point where if I'd stayed there a minute longer, even you wouldn't have been able to get me off a murder charge. Come on, I'll treat you to something long and cold and you can listen to me moan." Without waiting for an answer, Helen linked an arm through Lindsay's and dragged her into a nearby pub which promised air conditioning.

"If you called this air conditioned in California, you'd get lynched," Lindsay remarked as they stood at the bar. The stale air was admittedly a couple of degrees colder than the street outside, but it reeked of smoke and dead beer.

"I'd heard that about the American justice system," Helen said sweetly, catching the barman's attention and ordering without consultation two bottles of Belgian raspberry beer. Lindsay looked dubiously at the brownish-red liquid in her glass, shrugged resignedly and sipped.

"I've tasted worse," she muttered as she followed Helen to a quiet corner booth.

"I picked up a tasty bit of goss this morning that might interest you," Helen said, settling herself on the bench and fanning her face ineffectually with a beermat.

"About Penny?"

"Penny's books, actually. I was talking to a mate of mine, Kes, who brokers co-production deals, and I asked her what she was working on and she told me she's putting something together on Penny's books. Some transatlantic deal to do a TV series. Serious players, too. Galaxy Pictures in the States and an independent over here called Primetime, who've got it slotted in with the BBC."

Lindsay stared. "The Darkliners novels? Is that what we're talking about?"

Helen nodded. "Apparently so. We're talking a big deal here. First series will be three books, three thirty-minute episodes per book. If it takes off, they'll do all the books, then they'll do like they did with Morse—use the characters and get other writers to do the storylines."

Lindsay shook her head. "There must be some mistake. Penny hated the idea of her books being made into films or TV programmes. Producers were always pitching her and she always turned them down. She said it wasn't like she needed the money, and she didn't want to see her characters trashed on the screen. I remember she used to say, 'Any time I'm tempted, I say the magic words "V. I. Warshawski" and I waken from my enchantment.' Are you sure you got it right?"

Helen breathed heavily through her nose. "I'm sure I'm sure. I didn't realise Penny felt like that. I thought this was some routine agreement they were working out with her. From what Kes was saying, they've just got some final details to iron out, but the deal should be done and dusted within the next few weeks."

"I just can't believe Penny would agree to this," Lindsay said. "She said nothing to me about it, and I'm sure if she'd discussed it with Sophie, I'd have heard. Meredith said nothing about it either. I wonder how they persuaded Penny? It must have taken something really special to get round her objections . . ." Lindsay's voice tailed off and her eyes widened.

"Like murder?" Helen wondered.

"Like murder," Lindsay echoed. "If you kill somebody, you don't need their consent any more. Particularly when you're their literary executor."

There was silence for a moment while they both considered the implications of what Helen had learned. "That can't be right," Helen said eventually. "This isn't something that's just been cobbled together over the last couple of days. Kes's company must have been in negotiation for months."

"Would Penny have had to know that?"

Helen pondered. "Not necessarily, I suppose. Authors tend to get involved in negotiations if they want to write the script themselves or if they want to have a fair bit of input into the end product. But some of them just want to take the money and run, in which case they leave it up to their agents to do the business and they never actually meet the people who are planning to make the film."

"So what you're saying—let me get this straight—is that Penny's agent could have been working out the terms of this deal without Penny ever having had to meet the other parties? And that's normal?" Lindsay asked, feeling slightly like Alice in Wonderland.

"Penny might not even have known there were negotiations going on. Quite often, agents just don't mention negotiations to their client authors till they're a long way down the road. TV and film companies are always scouting around for stuff. Out of every hundred approaches an agent gets from a film company, they might actually sign five options. And out of every hundred option contracts that get signed, maybe five get made. With those kind of odds, you can see why agents let things move quite a long way down the road before they mention them to authors. Otherwise their phone lines would be permanently clogged with clients demanding to know what the latest was on the deal and how soon they were going to be able to buy the house with the swimming pool. And then nobody would ever get any work done."

"It also makes the agents look good," Lindsay said.

"How do you work that one out?"

Lindsay shrugged. "If the only time you hear from your agent is when she's calling to tell you about the great deal she's got to offer, you don't know how many approaches she's had and fucked up, do you?"

"How did you get this cynical?" Helen demanded, full of mock outrage.

"I hung around with you at a crucial age. What kind of money are we talking about, by the way?"

"For the options, say five grand a book, and there's how many books?"

"Twenty-six, twenty-seven, something like that."

Helen's eyes swivelled up at an angle as she did the mental arithmetic. "About £130,000? Then for each one that gets made, say fifty grand. For the first series, we'd be talking options for the lot, plus rights for six—call it £450,000. And these are not high end figures, by the way. For US and UK rights, you could easily be talking double that."

Lindsay whistled softly. "So we could be looking at a million-pound scenario where your mate Kes made Penny's agent an opening offer she couldn't refuse. Catriona Polson—that's the agent—knows how Penny feels about TV and film deals, but she decides that this is too good to miss. She figures that she'll go with it and see if she can talk it up into a deal that's so wonderful that even Penny will abandon all her artistic principles and bite their hands off. How does that sound?"

"So far, so good. I like it. Nothing makes me happier than the sight of one of life's Ms Ten Per Cents getting stitched up," Helen said enthusiastically.

"Only problem is, Penny throws her hands up in horror and says she'd rather eat razor blades than betray her readers and her masterworks in such a tawdry, money-grubbing way. And bearing in mind that agents usually charge more for TV and film deals, Catriona sees the thick end of 150 grand flying out of the window," Lindsay theorised.

"Whereas, with Penny dead . . ." Helen interjected.

"The deal is even sweeter. She can probably screw more money on the notoriety basis, plus she's got the added bonus of increased sales on the books that are currently out there. When I saw her, she said that she'd be crazy to kill Penny for a short-term gain when Penny alive would write more books. But if there's TV in the pipeline, that means she'd get long-term benefit anyway, because all the books would be reissued as TV tie-ins. And Catriona Polson's a really big woman. She'd have no trouble grabbing Penny and stabbing her in the neck." Lindsay finished her beer in a single swallow, suddenly feeling dry-mouthed. "Same again?"

When she returned with fresh drinks, Helen was looking sheepish. "Spit it out," Lindsay sighed.

"You just made out a great case against the agent. It's a good motive. And it's just about credible that the agent would use the murder method in the book as a kind of poetic justice, almost to make herself feel like it wasn't real, just something in a book. Only you can't tell the police about it, can you?"

"I'm not with you. Why not?"

Helen swallowed a gulp of beer and said, "You told me Meredith is Penny's residuary legatee, yeah? Well, if it plays as a motive for the agent, it works as an even better motive for

Meredith. About ten times better, in fact. You need something
more solid before you pass this info on to the bizzies."

Lindsay closed her eyes and cursed silently. Helen was
absolutely right. If Catriona had told Penny about the talks, the
chances are that Meredith would know it was a possibility. Even
if she hadn't, if Helen had heard it on the grapevine it was entirely
possible that Meredith had too, Lindsay thought, remembering
with a lurch that Meredith's best friend from college worked in
Los Angeles, writing machine code to produce computerised
special effects for Hollywood. And there would be plenty of
special effects in any films of the Darkliners novels. It would
be almost impossible for Meredith to establish her ignorance.
Proving a negative was always the hardest thing in any investigation, Lindsay knew from her long journalistic experience.
"I can't think about this any more today," she said. "I need to
sleep on it. Maybe when I wake up tomorrow, my subconscious
will have had the chance to work out where I go for proof."

"You're probably right," Helen said. "And I know just how
to help you put it right out of your mind."

Warning bells rang like a smoke alarm in Lindsay's head.
"Oh, yeah?" she said warily.

"Yeah. You can advise me on my little problem."

Lindsay groaned and raised her hands as if to fend off a
blow. "I already gave you the only advice I know. Dig the dirt,
then dish it."

"Can't you do the digging for me?" Helen asked plaintively.
"I don't have your experience. I'm just a simple TV producer. I
don't even know where to start."

"And you think I do?" Lindsay said, amused in spite of
herself by Helen's attempts at pathos. "I know nothing about
this woman. I don't know her surname, her age, what she looks
like, where she lives, what she drives or what kind of clothes
she wears. I don't know who her friends are, what she does on
her days off or anybody she's ever shagged. If anybody's going

to get something on Stella, don't you think you're a bit better equipped?"

Helen shook her head. "Her surname is Piper and she's thirty-two." She rummaged in her bag and came out with an A3 brochure promoting Watergaw Films. She flicked it open to the back cover. There, beneath Helen and Guy, was a head-and-shoulders shot of Stella Piper. Straight dark hair cut close to her head, liquid brown eyes accentuated with eyeliner and mascara, a pert, upturned nose and a rosebud mouth.

"She looks like Bambi," Lindsay said.

"Knowing her, it wouldn't have been the hunters who shot her mother," Helen said darkly. "She drives a metallic green Fiat Punto and she lives in some trendy warehouse conversion on the canal behind King's Cross station when she's not round Guy's flat in Stoke Newington. She wears that skin-tight fashion that looks great on Kate Moss and would make you and me look like sausages that need to go on a diet. As for friends, I shouldn't think she's got any."

"Fine, but I still don't know where to start digging," Lindsay insisted firmly.

"You could start by following her."

"Helen, I haven't even got a car," Lindsay protested.

"That's no problem. We use a hire firm just round the corner when we need some extra wheels. I'll take you round there and sort you out with something right now." She finished her beer in one swallow and looked expectantly at Lindsay.

Lindsay closed her eyes and sighed. In the long years of their friendship, Helen had only ever asked for Lindsay's help once before. It had seemed straightforward that time too, but it had led Lindsay into a confrontation with a murderer that had forced her into the hardest decision she'd ever taken and had altered the course of her life irrevocably. It wasn't an experience she'd willingly repeat. But even putting the most pessimistic of glosses on Helen's present request, it was hard to see how it could get her into the kind of trouble she'd been trying to avoid ever since that bitter tragedy in Glasgow.

She opened her eyes and shook her head with an air of fatalism. "I have a horrible feeling that I'm going to regret this," she said, picking up her glass and following Helen's example. "Let's go and get me a set of wheels."

11

Lindsay fiddled with the radio tuning buttons again. She'd been parked across the street from the industrial unit that housed Watergaw Films for the best part of an hour. So far, she'd grown irritated with one presenter's attempts at controversiality, bored with a magazine programme that seemed to cater for the prurience of people without a life of their own, and infuriated to discover a play she'd been listening to was the first of three episodes of a serial. Now she'd never know why Prunella had taken the Old English sheepdog to the archbishop's consecration. Giving up on talk radio, she settled for a station that played oldies with minimal chatter between records.

It was at times like this that she missed smoking. It was one of the few pastimes observers could indulge on a stakeout without having to take their eyes off the target. And of course, Lindsay realised with a shock, surveillance was something she had only ever done as a smoker. Since she'd quit, she'd been doing the kind of respectable job that didn't involve spying on complete strangers. It wasn't something she'd missed, especially on a baking afternoon in a car with no air conditioning. Already her whole body felt slick with sweat. Wondering why she'd let herself be talked into this, Lindsay rooted in her backpack for a tissue and wiped the perspiration from her palms again.

Just after four, the metal-sheathed side door opened and a woman appeared wearing a short, sleeveless dress and low-heeled Greek sandals with thongs that criss-crossed half-way up her calves. She was so short that it should have looked absurd, but slender enough for it to seem sexy. She had a boxy leather bag slung across her body and she carried a small holdall that looked virtually empty. As she turned to check that the door had closed behind her, Lindsay caught a momentary glimpse of her face. "Bambi," she said aloud, turning the key in the ignition of the anonymous hatchback Helen had hired for her.

Stella crossed the car park, walking more briskly than Lindsay would have cared to in that heat. When she came level with a metallic green car, she slipped into the driver's door. She reversed out of her space and drove straight towards Lindsay. At the gate, Stella turned left and headed towards the tube station. Lindsay was caught facing the wrong direction and had to pull round hastily, amazed at the bus driver who let her out with a courteous wave. Maybe some things in London had changed for the better after all.

At the traffic lights by the station, Lindsay was two cars behind Stella. As they swung across into Greenland Road, one car peeled off towards Kentish Town, leaving only one as a barrier. "Perfect," Lindsay muttered as they swung right into Bayham Street. The narrow roads were hot and dusty, choked with cars and delivery vans, motorbike couriers dicing with death as they slalomed through in the canyons between tall houses grimed with a century of metropolitan pollution. Stella clearly knew where she was going, zigzagging through back streets whose bleakness was unrelieved by the afternoon sun, weaving a course that took her behind St Pancras and King's Cross stations, past dozens of struggling small businesses crammed under cheap flats.

A couple of times, it had been touch and go staying close to Stella through traffic that was heavier than Lindsay remembered it being when she had lived in the city. But she'd always managed to keep her in sight at the junctions where crucial decisions were taken. Once they'd cleared the Angel, they picked up speed on City Road, where the traffic was lighter and houses gave way to tall warehouses, old buildings where light industry had lodged since the bricks were first laid, offices nudged in among them down side streets. When they hit the big roundabout by Old Street tube, Lindsay was forced to sit on Stella's back bumper as the van between them peeled off into the middle lane. A quick left and a half right brought Lindsay on to unknown territory. All she knew was that she was heading in the general direction of the City, though she suspected they were going to skirt its eastern edge rather than penetrate the canyons of commerce themselves. Wherever they were headed, it wasn't home.

She wasn't happy with being slap bang in the middle of Stella's rear-view mirror, but she was torn between fear of losing her in unfamiliar streets and fear of being spotted as a tail. The decision was suddenly taken from her when a Porsche shrieked out of a side street, cutting in between her and Stella without even a wave of gratitude. "Pillock," Lindsay muttered, but her heart wasn't in it.

They carried on in the same direction, past streets she'd only ever heard of. Whitechapel Road from the Monopoly board. Cable Street, scene of the anti-Fascist riots of the thirties. Just when Lindsay was convinced the next junction must bring them hard up against the Thames, Stella swung left into a wide street. The Porsche roared off to the right, leaving Lindsay a gap to make up. As she turned, she saw the green car a few hundred yards down the road turning right into a narrow street. Swearing, Lindsay shot down to the turning and swung the car across the oncoming traffic in a blare of horns. She was in time to see Stella turn again. When she made it to the junction, Stella was gone, the green car somewhere in a maze of narrow streets. "Shit, shit, shit!" Lindsay yelled, smacking her hand hard against the steering wheel.

She pulled in to the kerb while she considered. If Stella had spotted her and deliberately shaken her off, there was no chance of catching her now. She'd be back on the main road and miles away within minutes. But she'd shown no signs of trying to shake off pursuit, so the odds were that she'd turned off the arterial road because she was near her destination. Logically, Lindsay decided, if she drove around the nearby streets, she'd come upon the Fiat.

As she drove slowly through the twisting narrow corridors of Wapping, she remembered the one and only time she had been here before. It had been a Saturday night, so cold her breath had puffed in clouds before her. She'd been on foot, one of hundreds of journalists and print workers who had come to demonstrate against the mass sackings of their colleagues by Rupert Murdoch's News International to make way for cheap new technology and the de-skilling of their craft. They'd come to protest but had ended up fleeing through the streets, driven ahead of mounted police gung-ho as Cossacks and with as much concern for those they pursued. The clatter of hoofs, the swish of police batons through the air, the screams of terror and the plumes of steamy breath from the horses' nostrils were still lodged in Lindsay's brain, erupting occasionally as nightmares. Somewhere in the mêlée, Lindsay had become separated from her lover, Cordelia. They hadn't found each other until they'd both arrived home in the middle of the night. Terrified of losing each other in a more permanent way, they'd never gone back on that particular picket line.

Cruising that same patch in broad daylight was a different experience, even though the sun failed to penetrate as far as the pavement in quite a few streets. There was nothing threatening on this warm summer afternoon. Lindsay sighed. It was hard to imagine she was going to get instant access to the skeletons in Stella's cupboard by driving round Wapping in the sun. About to give up, Lindsay made one last turn into a street that was more of an alley, curving like a scimitar and dead-ending by the ornamental canal. Tucked in a vanway between warehouses was the green Punto.

Lindsay felt a mixture of irritation and satisfaction. If she'd lost Stella, she could have gone back to Helen empty-handed but virtuous. Now she was nailed to her tail for another sticky journey, more likely than not. She turned her car round and backed into a space right at the end of the cul-de-sac. It was on double yellows, but she couldn't imagine a traffic warden coming all the way down there on the off chance in heat like this.

She looked across at the building whose vanway held the Fiat. There was nothing to indicate who the tenants were or what they did. It was simply a blank box in dirty red brick with windows that indicated four floors above the ground-floor level, which had no windows at all. Time to take a chance, Lindsay decided. She got out of the car, leaving it unlocked in case she needed to make a quick getaway, and walked purposefully across the street. The building had a side entrance, a pair of heavy wooden doors at the top of three shallow concrete steps. Lindsay tugged the brass handles, relieved when one opened and admitted her into a small foyer. Ahead were more double doors, this time steel and reinforced glass. By an entryphone was a bank of etched metal plaques. *Dessins Domingo* was the tenant of the top floor. Underneath them were Bronzed Bodies—Sculptures, and Media Masters, followed by Heavenly Dolls, Stationary Cycles plc and Gorton Engineering.

Lindsay made a quick note of the names, though she felt fairly sure she wouldn't be far wrong if she looked for Stella Piper at Media Masters. The only question was what Media Masters did, and what Stella was doing there. She walked back to the car and moved it to the street where the cul-de-sac emerged, finding a handy space facing in the direction Stella would logically take to get back to civilisation as Lindsay knew it. She settled down for another wait. This time, she didn't have to hang around long. Within ten minutes, the Punto appeared at the junction and shot off into the Wapping labyrinth.

Once they were back on the main road, the route could not have been more simple. Tower Hill down to the Embankment, round the choked artery of Trafalgar Square and up Charing Cross Road, where the traffic was moving so slowly Lindsay could read the promotional posters in the bookshop windows. There were a couple of times when she thought she'd lost Stella at traffic lights, but the rush-hour traffic was so sluggish, she caught up on the next change. At Cambridge Circus, Stella slipped left into Shaftesbury Avenue, then turned right into the pulsating heart of Soho café society. She dog-legged her way through the streets until they reached a backwater where the flesh trade had not yet been ousted by fashion. Stella had slowed down to a crawl, obviously looking for a parking place. Behind Lindsay, a car pulled out and swung round a corner. Quickly, she reversed into the available space and jumped out in time to see Stella losing patience and bumping her car on to the pavement further down the street. She got out and headed back up the street in Lindsay's direction. Lindsay walked casually towards Stella on the opposite pavement, glad of the weather as an excuse for wraparound sunglasses that let her stare without being spotted.

Before she drew level with Lindsay, Stella turned into a shop. Instantly, Lindsay sprinted across the street and followed her in, realising belatedly she had just walked into a sex shop. Videos for sale covered one wall, magazines another. Two cabinets in the middle of the floor held sex toys. A swift glance revealed dildos of proportions no one but a hard-core masochist could desire. With an inward shudder, Lindsay drifted towards the counter where Stella was standing, lips pursed in impatience, arms folded and one sandalled foot tapping. Behind the counter was a youth so spectacularly lacking in physical charm that it was hardly surprising he'd chosen to work in a place that recognised the importance of fantasy. He had a phone clamped to one scarlet ear. The other stood out at ninety degrees to his shaven head. The tattooed fingers holding the phone read "shag." In your dreams, Lindsay thought derisively. Neither of them showed the slightest interest in Lindsay as she pretended to browse the videos.

"He's not answering," he said in a thickly adenoidal voice.

"I told him I was coming in this afternoon," Stella said peevishly.

"He never said."

"He must have told you where he was going."

"He never. He just said he had some business to sort." He replaced the phone under the counter. "D'you wanna come back later?"

"Not especially, no. Did your precious boss say when he'd be back?"

The youth shrugged nervously, one finger creeping reflexively towards a nostril. "He never tells me nothing. We're open till ten, though."

"I know you're open till ten," Stella said through gritted teeth. Lindsay had often read the expression, but she'd never seen anyone perform it before now. It was impressive, she had to admit. Stella hefted the holdall on to the counter. Where it had been almost empty before, it was now bulging, square corners pushing the fabric out in several places. "Have you got a box?" she demanded.

The youth looked as if gorm had followed couth out of his life a long time ago. "A box?" he echoed.

"A cardboard box? Big enough to hold the tapes I've got in here? I'll leave them for Keith, but I don't want to leave my bag behind, *capisce?*"

"Yeah, right." The youth disappeared through a bead curtain. Stella drummed her fingers on the counter top. Lindsay moved casually behind her to the opposite wall and started looking at magazines. Out of the corner of her eye, she could still see Stella. The youth emerged with a box about twice the size of the holdall. "This do?"

Stella didn't even bother to answer. She simply unzipped the bag and transferred about a dozen video tapes into the box. "When Keith shows his face, tell him Stella was here as promised. There's twelve samples in there. Six different films, each cut in two versions—one for America, one for Europe. Tell him to call me with his orders before Monday. Have you got that?" He nodded. "Repeat it back to me," she commanded.

"Stella came with the samples. Half a dozen films, American and European versions. Orders before Monday."

"You forgot the crucial bit," she snarled. "Tell him I get seriously pissed off with men who stand me up." She zipped the bag up again and stormed out. Lindsay couldn't see any point in following Stella any further. There was no need for overkill. Why bother hunting for a rifle when you already had an Exocet missile, Lindsay wondered.

She abandoned her pretence of studying the repulsive magazines and walked out of the shop. She felt like she needed a shower and a change of clothes, least of all because of the heat. But most of all, she needed a drink. Before she could do that, though, she had one more task to perform.

Glancing up and down the street, she saw a pair of telephone boxes on the corner. She walked up there and shut herself into one, seeing to her surprise that, like American pay phones, it took credit cards as well as money. "Nice one," she said appreciatively, swiping her card through the slot and calling directory inquiries. A voice worryingly like that of Margaret Thatcher gave her the number of Media Masters and she keyed it in. "Media Masters, Julie-Anne speaking," a woman's voice chirruped.

Time to play a hunch. "Hey," Lindsay said, going for Californian. "My name is Catherine Parvenu and I'm an independent film-maker out of Los Angeles. Now, I'm in town for a few days, and I need some video facilities. Can you tell me, do you have editing suites for hire?"

"Well, yes, we do, but I'm afraid they're fully booked until early next week. I can put you on standby, if you like, but I can't make any promises."

"Gee, that's a pity. I really need something right away. Never mind, I've got a couple other numbers I can call. Tell me, do you also do video copying?"

"We do, madam. Single and multiple copies, US and UK format, overnight express facilities available."

"And do you have spare capacity this week? I'm looking for fifty copies of a one hour VHS, US format. Can you do that?"

"One moment, madam, let me check the diary . . . Yes, we can accommodate you. When will the master be available?"

"I'll have to get back to you on that. Thanks a lot, Julie-Anne, I'll be back to you tomorrow, okay?"

"We'll look forward to hearing from you."

"You have a nice day now." Lindsay intoned the West Coast mantra without obvious irony.

Now she'd confirmed her guess at what Media Masters did, she really needed that drink. Leaving the car where it was, she headed off into the heart of Soho and soon found a café bar where women who were enough like her for it to feel like home sat round a horseshoe-shaped bar drinking beer out of long-necked bottles. She ordered a Rolling Rock and savoured the moment's anticipation before the first swallow. She twirled the bottle, expecting to read through the drops of condensation the legend "Brewed in the glass-lined tanks of Old Latrobe." Instead, she discovered it was brewed in the tradition of Old Latrobe somewhere in the south of England. She sighed so hard the woman next to her asked what was wrong.

"You know that saying, 'You can never go home any more'?" she asked. The woman nodded, looking a little bemused. "Well, I think I just found out how true it is."

12

The memory banks of career waiters never ceased to amaze Lindsay. It must have been at least seven years since she'd eaten in the little family *trattoria* in Camden, but the waiter who had always flirted with her and Cordelia greeted her as if it had been only seven days. "*Bella signorina, come sta?*" he'd asked automatically, sweeping a deep bow in front of her that revealed his hair was starting to thin round the crown.

The exchange continued as it always had. She was fine, how was he? He was so-so, but what was the point of complaining, the government always got in. He ushered her to a familiar table at the back in a corner. The same bad paintings of Sorrento still hung in their identical positions. The walls had acquired some Italia '90 memorabilia, but apart from that everything was the same. Without being asked, the waiter brought Lindsay a Peroni while she studied the menu. It was as if the door to the restaurant was a time slip. When the door opened next, Lindsay half expected to see Cordelia glide in. It was both a relief and a disappointment when Helen swept in instead.

She plonked herself down and mouthed, "Gin and tonic," at the waiter. "God, what a day," she sighed.

"It's not going to get any better, trust me on that," Lindsay said. The waiter placed a sweating glass in front of Helen. "I couldn't believe it when you suggested meeting here. I'd no idea it was still going. I imagined it would have turned into some terrible pizza parlour. I felt really dislocated when you said the name—this was one of the places I always came with Cordelia. It was our private secret. Like we thought we were the only people who knew about it. We never had dinner with anybody else here. So I didn't expect you to know about it. Illogical, I know, but . . ."

Helen snorted. "You think I could work five minutes" walk away and not know about the best Italian restaurant in north London? Do me a favour! You ready to order? I need the prospect of something solid in me before I can bear to hear any more bad news."

While they waited for their meal, Lindsay outlined her afternoon discoveries to Helen, who looked more and more glum with every passing sentence. Even the arrival of a lasagne that looked rich enough to have its own Swiss bank account couldn't relieve her gloom. As Lindsay virtuously wolfed her tuna and bean salad, Helen said disconsolately, "It's a bit of a double-edged sword, isn't it? We've found the skeleton in Stella's cupboard, but if I expose her I'm bound to bring Watergaw's reputation down with her." She banged the end of her fork angrily on the table, attracting glances from the handful of other diners. "I can't bear it," she raged. "We built this company up from nothing, we've started to get a really good name in the business for delivering what we promise, and now this bitch is using us to make scummy little porno films. How dare she? It's so outrageous that if it had come from anybody except you, I wouldn't have believed a word of it. It's not just that she's exploiting the knickers off me and the company, it's the fact that she's involved in the skin trade. It goes diametrically against everything Watergaw is supposed to stand for." Her eyes sparkled with anger. "I don't suppose there's any chance that her nasty little racket doesn't involve the company?" she asked, faint hope in her voice.

Lindsay stretched out her free arm and squeezed Helen's hand. "It's always a possibility, but I wouldn't hold out too much hope. But I thought the best thing to do was to get as clear a picture of what's gone on as we possibly can. That's why I suggested we got together tonight, so we can map out a plan of campaign."

"You've got an idea?" Helen said eagerly.

"Nothing specific. We've got to try and uncover how long it's been going on, how involved Guy is, and, if we can, how seedy these films are. We also need to establish what the involvement of Watergaw is in what she's been up to. It might be that there's a way to manipulate the information so you can get her out of the door and out of the business. But we won't know until we've had a good trawl through her computer and her filing cabinets. Which is why I suggested meeting on this side of town."

"You want to do it tonight?" Helen asked.

"How soon can you finish your lasagne?"

"I want to kill her," Helen growled. On the TV screen in Stella's office, a slightly built woman was fellating one man while another entered her from the rear. It was the fifth of a couple of dozen video tapes they'd found in the bottom drawer of Stella's filing cabinet. They'd sampled brief sections of each, their disgust and anger mounting with every one. "I want to kill her with my bare hands," Helen continued. She'd been delivering variations on the same theme ever since they'd turned their attentions from paperwork and computer files to the videos. "She's even used the sets from one of Watergaw's drama productions, the cheap bitch. Turn it off, Linds, I'm going to be sick if I watch any more of these."

Lindsay pressed the "stop" button with an overwhelming sense of relief. "We probably should check the others, make sure they're all the same sort of thing."

"You do it if you feel you have to. I'm going to get some mineral water from my office to try and take the taste away." Helen walked out and Lindsay slotted the next film into the player. She wound it on a fair way, then hit the "play" button. The screen filled with a close-up of a woman masturbating. Behind her in the corridor she heard a set of footsteps. "Did you bring me some?" she asked.

"Who the fuck are you?"

Lindsay whirled round, dropping the remote control, and stared open-mouthed at Stella. She stood in the doorway, a tall man with cropped pepper and salt hair behind her. Stella advanced a step. "What the fuck are you doing in my office? You're a burglar!"

Regaining her composure, Lindsay shrugged. "So call the cops. Go on, give them a bell." She pushed the phone towards Stella. "You must be Stella. And you, I presume, are Guy."

Guy pushed past Stella and loomed above Lindsay, so close she could have identified the stone in his nose stud if she'd been interested. "And who the hell are you?"

From behind them all, Helen's voice came, cold as the ice that clinked in the jug she carried. "She's with me. She's a friend. It's a concept you won't be familiar with, Guy."

He flinched at her tone as much as her words. "Whoever she is, she's got no business in here."

"He's right," Stella butted in, finding outrage from somewhere. "She's been going through my stuff. Look, there's papers everywhere. And she's been in my filing cabinet. Those tapes were locked in there. She's broken in!"

"No, she hasn't," Helen said wearily. "Who do you think has the master keys to all the office furniture, dumbshit? You think I trust my staff not to lose the keys to their desks and storage cupboards? You've never had any idea, have you, Stella?" She managed to make the name sound like an obscenity.

"You're out of order, Helen," Stella said. "You've got no right to be doing this. What's the matter with you? Don't you trust your business partners?"

"I don't trust pornographers," Helen said. "You do something that exploitative on a routine basis and you forget where the lines get drawn in real life. I wouldn't trust you if your hands were nailed to the wall. Which frankly would be too good for you and I'd resent spending the money on redecoration afterwards. How dare you do what you've been doing?"

Stella looked at Guy, who was hiding his discomfort in the business of lighting a cigarette. "So what's the charge, Helen? Me and Guy like to watch porn? It's a criminal offence to keep a few horny films for our personal pleasure? I didn't realise you dykes were so puritanical."

"This isn't about watching blue movies. It's about making them," Helen said flatly.

Stella laughed. "What is she on?" she demanded. "Whatever it is, I don't fucking want any. Helen, where do you get this strange idea that I've been making pornographic films?"

Helen looked as if she was on the point of realising her ambition to kill Stella. "You were too tight, Stella. You were too keen on making a profit. You used the sets we built for *Home Movies* to make your scummy skin flicks. You didn't even attempt to disguise them."

Stella's hands clenched into fists and Guy sucked in smoke like it was oxygen. Lindsay decided it was time she butted in to lower the temperature before Helen did something they'd both regret. "You film on site and do the editing in the suite here," she said, her voice clinically matter of fact. "Then you take the edited film over to Media Masters and they make you video versions in US and UK formats. You take the samples to your outlet—*It's Personal* in Robb Street in Soho—and they place their order."

"That's where I've seen you before," Stella interrupted angrily. "You were in the shop. You've been following me!" Her voice climbed in volume and pitch as she made her accusation and she pushed Guy out of the way. "I'll have you, bitch. Fucking dyke. Just wait, I'll have you."

"Will that be before you come out of the nick or after?" Lindsay asked sweetly.

Stella laughed in her face. "I'm not going to jail. That's not on the agenda. You can't hand me over to the cops, because this is all being done under your precious friend Helen's umbrella. I go down and I take my partners with me."

"Wait a minute," Guy said nervously.

"It's all right, Guy," Stella said, reaching out and patting his arm as she would have done a dog. "I don't think Helen's friend wants to come and visit her in Holloway."

"I don't think that will be necessary," Lindsay said, relaxing as she played her trump card. "We didn't just look in the bottom drawer. We've been right through your filing cabinet and your computer files. Pretty stupid to use Blue as your password when you're making pornography, don't you think?"

Guy looked as if he wanted to be sick. His eyes were everywhere except on Helen and Stella. "Listen, I'm sure we can sort this out . . ." His voice trailed off as he realised no one cared what he thought.

"Shut up, Guy," Helen said savagely. "Listen to some sense for a change."

Stella cocked her head to one side and put her hands on her hips. "Okay, smartarse. Tell us what it is you think you know."

Lindsay perched on the corner of the desk and spoke as dispassionately as she could manage. "We know all about Shooting Star Investments. We know that since it started with virtually no assets except an interest-free loan of £500,000 from an unspecified source, it has built into a considerable earner. In the space of a mere eight months, it has made profits of around £450,000 from the sale of video films produced by Shooting Star Investments."

"There's nothing wrong with that," Stella said, refusing to give an inch. "There isn't a court in the land that's going to penalise me for being a successful businesswoman. And there isn't a police force in the land that will prosecute Shooting Star for those videos. I'm not a fool. We might have sailed close to the wind, but none of the films we made is anything like hard core enough to interest the Vice Squad."

"Who said anything about the Vice Squad?" Lindsay asked, a threatening edge slipping past her control and into her voice. "I'm talking about the Fraud Squad."

For the first time, Stella's defiance took a dent. She looked momentarily uncertain, glancing at Guy, who was too busy lighting a fresh cigarette off the end of the previous one to notice. "You're full of shit," she said, but her eyes told a different story to her words.

"I'm not the bullshitter in this room. As we say where I come from, Stell, the ball's on the slates. The party's over. I've read the paperwork." Lindsay turned to a neat pile of papers behind her on the desk. As she went through them, she slapped each document down hard on the desk in front of Stella. "Exhibit number one. Helen's submission to the EU for funding for a three-part drama about asylum seekers. Exhibit number two. A letter from the EU revealing the application has been successful and enclosing a cheque for the cash. Exhibit number three. A forged letter purporting to be from the EU to Helen explaining her application has been unsuccessful in this round of funding awards but it will be reconsidered in the next bidding sequence when it stands a strong chance, and that she need not resubmit her application. Exhibit number four. A bank statement showing the deposit of the identical sum of money in the account of Shooting Star two weeks after the date on the authentic EU letter."

"A real shit's trick," Helen said.

Stella closed her eyes and breathed heavily through her nose. "I'm really fucked off about this," she said. "You have no idea how fucked off I am."

"We were going to put the money back, Helen," Guy said, moving a couple of steps closer to her and spreading his hands in a supplicatory gesture. "As soon as we'd generated enough profit, we were going to replace the money with another faked letter saying the money had come from a fresh allocation of funding.

It's a licence to print money, Helen. With the profits Shooting Star generates, we can make all the films we want about things that really matter. Like Stella said, it's not as if we're doing hardcore stuff. And if we weren't doing it someone else would be."

Helen's upper lip twitched in contempt. "Any minute now you'll be telling me you were only obeying orders. How can you think I'd ever want to make a film with you again? Less than six weeks ago, we were sitting in my office trying to put together a proposal for a film about the evils of sex tourism. Where's your brain gone, Guy?"

"Helen, don't get worked up . . ."

"Don't get worked up!" she yelled. "Don't get worked up?"

"He's right," Stella said with an exasperated sigh. "Look, Helen, you get your EU money, you get to make your films, everything goes on exactly like it did before. There's no reason why not."

Helen stared at Stella, for once in her life beyond speech. Lindsay jumped in. "I don't think that's going to be possible, Stella. I don't think Helen would feel comfortable with that."

"I don't want to be in the same hemisphere as you, never mind the same company," Helen snarled. "I'm leaving this partnership and I'm taking my grant money with me and I'm going to set up my own company that is totally vermin-free, even if I have to get Rentokil to vet every member of staff."

"That's not what we want, Helen," Stella said calmly. "Your expertise and your street cred is really important to the company. If you were that dispensable, don't you think we'd have dumped you ages ago? If you go, you go without a penny. The legal battles to dissolve the partnership against our wishes will take years and every penny you've got."

It was Lindsay's turn to look thunderstruck. "I don't think you appreciate the position you're in," she said incredulously. "We've got you bang to rights. All we have to do to end your career is to call the Fraud Squad and show how you expropriated the money to start Shooting Star with no intention of paying it back."

Suddenly, Stella jumped forward and grabbed the documents off the desk. Lindsay snatched at them, but Stella danced across to the corner behind Guy, waving the papers. "No evidence, no case," she said, grinning crazily. She grabbed Guy's lighter, spun the wheel and let the flame dance along the bottom of the pages. The papers caught and yellow flames started to lick their way up the paper.

With a scream of rage, Helen threw the jug of water she was still carrying across the room at Stella. She raised one arm to fend it off and the jug tipped, then tumbled, cascading down Stella and the papers. The flames died, leaving the papers charred and sodden. Stella laughed. "You don't stop me that easily," she said, grasping the soggy paper and tearing it into irregular pieces. "Get the vids, Guy."

Showing more *savoir faire* than he'd managed so far, Guy swept the videos off the desk into the wastepaper bin, which he clutched to his chest. Helen leapt at him, clawing his arms with her nails, but he clung on grimly to his burden. Lindsay stepped up behind Helen and grabbed her, pulling her back.

"Leave it, Helen," she said.

"But they're destroying the evidence," she said, her voice teetering on the edge of a sob.

"And we can't stop them. Two on two, nobody with a weapon, it's just going to degenerate into a rammy. She's determined to destroy it, we're not going to stop her, and the cops aren't going to get here in time. Come on, Helen, don't give her the satisfaction."

All the fight suddenly went from Helen and she subsided into Lindsay's arms. "Sensible move," Stella said approvingly. "By morning, there won't be anything left to tie us to the blue films or to the missing grant. In fact, if you do call in the cops, the only thing they'll be able to investigate is the misappropriation of the EU grant. And let's face it, Helen, the person who could rip that money off easier than anyone else is the person it was intended for. All you had to do was tell me and Guy that the EU had blown you out, and you could have pocketed the readies no trouble. But for me to do that . . . Well, it'd be complicated, wouldn't it?"

"Let's get out of here, Helen," Lindsay said, steering Helen towards the door. Somehow they made it out of the building without giving way to the fury that bubbled inside them both. Out in the car park, Helen turned back and stared up at the lighted skylight above Stella's office.

"I can't believe we were so stupid," she said bitterly. "We let them get away with it."

"We were scuppered as soon as they found us in there," Lindsay said, furiously kicking the tyre of Stella's Fiat. "You'd only ever have nailed her with the element of surprise on your side."

"I just can't believe Guy was involved with her seedy, scummy little scheme."

"When sex walks into a relationship, sense walks out," Lindsay said, squatting down by Stella's car with her Swiss Army knife in hand. She uncapped the valve on the nearest tyre and opened it up with the tip of the blade, taking childish satisfaction in the hiss of escaping air. Methodically she worked round the wheels, letting the air out of each tyre while Helen paced the car park, ranting.

"Let's go," Lindsay said when she'd finished. "I'm sorry it didn't work out the way you wanted."

"It's worse than when we started. At least then I didn't know what her dark secret was. Now I'm implicated."

"I let you down."

Helen shook her head. "No. It's my fault. I underestimated the bitch. Now I'm completely boxed into a corner. I want out and I want revenge, but what can I do?"

"Yeah, well, it's not over till the fat lady sings," Lindsay said grimly. "There's got to be a way to screw them like they've screwed you. And I'm the very person to find it."

13

Lindsay drove back in silence, replaying the confrontation like a tape loop. Somehow, there had to be a way for Helen to get what she wanted out of the mess Lindsay had helped create. She was operating on automatic pilot, her eyes focussed on the tail lights of Helen's car in front. At junctions where the car had to come to a halt, her mind seemed to go into free fall, the street and the traffic dissolving into the vile and vivid images she'd absorbed from Stella and Guy's videos. They had only seen short bursts, but it seemed to have saturated her visual cortex, becoming the wallpaper on which everything else was superimposed. Take away the outside world and all that was left were the writhing bodies and her impotent anger.

She was reunited with Helen on the doorstep. "A stiff gin and a bath, that's what I need," Helen said wearily as she fumbled her key into the lock.

"A Scotch and a shower for me," Lindsay said, following her indoors. "At least you've got a shoulder to cry on."

The living room appeared to be empty, though Lindsay wasn't prepared to commit herself. As far as she could tell, there might be a tribe of pygmies living among the detritus. Tonight, though, she was too tired to care. They went through to the kitchen in search of drink and found Kirsten and Meredith either side of a bottle of red wine on the kitchen table. Kirsten looked up expectantly, but seeing their faces contented herself with a quiet, "Oh dear."

"'Oh dear' doesn't even scratch the surface," Helen said wearily. She walked round the table so she could see Meredith. "We haven't met, have we?"

"This is Meredith," Kirsten and Lindsay said in ragged chorus.

Meredith smiled. It looked tentative as a first rehearsal. "You must be Helen," she said. "I'm sorry to invade your personal space like this, but I really needed to talk with Lindsay and I didn't want to wait till she checked in tomorrow morning. This has been kind of a difficult week, I guess you know."

Impulsively, Helen stepped forward and hugged Meredith. "You're all right here," she said. "It must be a complete bastard, what you're going through." She stood back. "You're welcome here any time, whether Lindsay's here or not. You need a bit of company, just get yourself round here. Okay?"

Looking slightly stunned, Meredith nodded. "I thought you English were supposed to be reserved and standoffish?" she asked with a more relaxed smile.

"She's not English, she's from Liverpool," Kirsten remarked drily.

"A far-off country of which we know little," Lindsay added.

"Very funny. Come on, K, let's leave Lindsay and Meredith to talk down here. I need the biggest gin in the Home Counties and someone to wash my back while I slag off that scheming cow Stella and gutless Guy the porn king."

"Porn king?" Kirsten said faintly.

"I'll tell you all about it," Helen promised, sliding a bottle of eighteen-year-old Macallan towards Lindsay and half filling a tumbler with gin. She tossed in a couple of lumps of ice, a slice of lemon and a token splash of tonic, then shooed Kirsten out of the door.

"That is one helluva woman," Meredith said.

Pouring herself a good two fingers of the golden liquid, Lindsay nodded. "Sophie's ex. You see what I have to live up to? Ebullient. Irrepressible. Generous to a fault. And right now, possessed of a rage that would make the Eumenides look a teeny bit cross." She took a bottle of still mineral water from the fridge and carefully added about the same again to her glass. Then she swirled the liquid round, watching the sobs of spirit subside down the glass. "How have you been?" she asked, settling down at the table, taking in Meredith's improved appearance. She looked as if she'd had a decent night's sleep, and her hair was washed and pulled back in a loose pigtail.

Meredith shrugged. "Up and down. I can go for whole chunks of time on automatic pilot, getting through the day. Then it comes at me out of left field, no warning. It's like I hear her voice, or I half see her out of the corner of my eye. I get a whiff of her perfume. Or some memory ambushes me. I went to the local bakery today to buy some bread, and the baker was coming through with a tray of freshly baked cinnamon Danish and I just burst into tears. Penny loved his Danish, she'd send me down there every morning to pick some up for breakfast whenever we were in London together. I felt so stupid. I mean, how can you get emotional about a tray of Danish?" Even the recollection was enough to make Meredith's voice tremble and her eyes grow damp.

Lindsay swished a mouthful of Scotch round her mouth, making her taste-buds snap into wakefulness and her gums tingle. She swallowed and said, "The last thing Frances ever gave me was a jar of quails' eggs. I still have them, lurking at the back of the fridge. The oldest quails' eggs in the world. It's not rational, but if Sophie ever threw them away I'd probably take a kitchen knife to her, and she knows it. We're a good pair, you and me. I have a sentimental attachment to quails' eggs and you cry at Danish pastries. We'd better not have a day out in Harrods food hall, eh?"

"I guess." Meredith gave a watery smile. "Did I tell you, my employers have shown a novel way of expressing their sympathies?"

"No. What have they done?"

"They fired me. Apparently, I no longer meet their criteria on security. They seem more concerned that I'm a lesbian than they are about me being a suspect in a homicide inquiry."

"That's terrible," Lindsay protested. "They know your partner's been murdered and they phone you up to sack you?"

"Fax, actually. I don't even get to go in and empty my desk and say goodbye to my team." Meredith sighed. "I suppose I should look on the bright side. I mean, it kind of ruins my so-called motive for murder, doesn't it? If I'm supposed to have killed her to preserve my in-the-closet status, you'd think I'd have had the sense to realise that I'd be outed by the investigation."

"It's outrageous," Lindsay said. "Can't you sue them?"

Meredith shrugged. "I don't think so. And why would I want to prolong my connection with them by one single minute? A week ago, it would have been the end of the world to lose my job. Now? It's no big deal. I can get another job. I can't get another Penny." For a moment, they both sat silent, reflecting. Then Meredith straightened up in her chair. "Enough moping. How's your investigation going? Have you made any progress?"

"Not as much as I'd have liked," Lindsay admitted. "I found out a few interesting things. First, and this is probably the most significant thing from your point of view, there's no closed circle of knowledge about the murder method. Penny and Baz had an animated discussion about it on the editorial floor, overheard by everybody who was close by at the time. Every one of them probably told at least one other person, and chances are it was all over the publishing world by teatime. Second, whoever killed her probably hadn't been a regular visitor to the flat because he or she didn't know the procedures for locking up. Third, did you know about the film and TV deal that Catriona's been working on?"

Meredith frowned. "A TV deal? With Penny?" She sounded as thunderstruck as Lindsay had felt when she'd heard Helen's news.

"Straight up. Galaxy Pictures in a co-production with the BBC via an independent UK production company. Three Darkliners books in nine episodes planned initially, with more if they get the audience figures. I'm told the deal's near completion."

Meredith shook her head. "Somebody's feeding you a line. You know what Penny thought about adaptations. She said it was like hiring cannibals as babysitters. They might promise to be good, but you couldn't be sure what they'd get up to as soon as your back was turned."

"You know that, I know that. But the industry gossip says different. I guess we have to work on the premise that Catriona Polson still hadn't told Penny what was on offer."

Meredith shook her head in amazement. "No wonder she wanted to get me out of the way in a police cell," she said. "I mean, I know that as literary executor, she can do pretty much what she wants in terms of deal-making, but I'm not going to sit on my hands and let her push this through. Even if it's a *fait accompli*, I can still make sure the world knows that Catriona Polson is taking the grossest advantage of Penny's death."

Lindsay rolled her glass between her hands and gazed into the amber glow. "Do you think it's a motive for murder, though?"

Meredith stopped short and stared. "You think she might have killed Penny?"

Lindsay shrugged. "She's a strong possibility. A lot depends on her personal and corporate financial situation, which I know absolutely nothing about. But if she's strapped for cash, or if she's just looking to get rich quick, then she's got motive. And she's big enough to have overcome Penny if there had been any struggle."

Meredith dropped her face into her hands and rubbed the skin round her eyes. "I suppose so," she said, her voice muffled. She looked up. "You know, I can imagine how the passion between lovers leads to killing in the heat of the moment. And I can imagine the casual violence between strangers erupting into murder, because the person you're fighting is a stranger, not a real person with emotions and dreams and a family and a life. What I cannot grasp is what drives a person to kill someone who is a friend or a business associate. It's not a relationship that should contain the kind of passion that leads to murder. But at the same time, it's a killing that means you're involved in the aftermath. I really do not understand it."

"Me neither, but it happens." Lindsay swallowed another rich mouthful of whisky and continued. "Catriona's definitely a contender. She's the only person so far with a known motive."

"Apart, supposedly, from me," Meredith said bitterly.

Lindsay ignored the comment and carried on. "We shouldn't lose sight of Baz, though."

"Baz, her editor?" Meredith said, looking startled. "There's another one?"

"No, no, I was just a little surprised, that's all. I hadn't really considered her. I mean, thinking about what you were saying about Catriona, surely Baz is a little on the small side to struggle successfully with Penny?"

"Maybe there wasn't a struggle. Hey, what are you doing?" she demanded, outraged, while Meredith took a cigarette out of a packet on the table that Lindsay had assumed belonged to Kirsten.

"I'm smoking," Meredith said out of the side of her mouth as she lit up. "I know, I know. But I need it right now. I can stop again when all of this is behind me. Don't make me feel any worse than I already do, Lindsay," she pleaded with a crooked smile.

"I'd probably be doing the same thing in your shoes," Lindsay said sadly. "Anyway, as I was saying, if I could only pin down a motive, Baz would be my favourite suspect rather than Catriona."

"Why so?" Meredith asked, her voice sharp.

"Something happened between her and Penny that changed their relationship. I don't know what it was yet, but it was obviously something pretty important. They went from being easy together, enjoying each other's company, to being stiff and formal on this last trip. There's no evidence of any similar rift with Catriona. Plus Baz is really uncomfortable talking about Penny."

"Of course she is," Meredith protested. "She's in shock. She's grieving. They'd known each other a long time. They were friends."

"Not any more they weren't. When Penny died, they were awkward and distant with each other. They had a row in the middle of the editorial floor about the very murder method that Penny used in the book."

"What do you mean, a row?" Meredith demanded.

"Baz said it was a ridiculous, impractical way of killing someone, but Penny was adamant that it should stay in."

"And you think Penny invited Baz round to give her a demonstration of how well it would work?" Meredith asked sarcastically. "Use some logic here, Lindsay. That argument says to me that if Baz was going to kill Penny, this is the one method she absolutely wouldn't use because she believed it wouldn't work."

"Unless it was a double bluff," Lindsay countered. "Because she backed down, Baz did, and she never backed down with her authors. Maybe she was thinking ahead and already setting up a defence for herself."

"She's not like that," Meredith protested angrily. "I know this woman. If she was going to kill anyone, that's not the way she'd behave."

There was a sudden silence. Lindsay looked at Meredith, a strange suspicion growing as she stared at her friend sullenly smoking. She could almost hear crackling inside her head as connections slipped into place. "It was Baz," she said slowly. "Your fling. It was with Baz."

"You're out of your mind," Meredith blustered, too quick to convince.

"It was Baz, I'm right. You slept with Baz the last time you were in London. That's why you wouldn't tell Penny who you had your fling with. Because it was Baz and it would poison their professional relationship."

"This is bullshit," Meredith tried. She had more chance of stopping a runaway train with one hand.

"But Baz felt awkward with Penny, knowing why you two had split up. And Penny, who as we both know, was very sensitive to atmosphere, twigged there was something wrong. And she put two and two together, and that's why she wanted to get into Baz's office that night. It was Baz, wasn't it?" Lindsay demanded, slamming her drink on the table. The remaining whisky seemed to rise and fall in a pillar, spilling only a few drops as it settled down.

"You've got no grounds for saying that," Meredith said.

Seeing she was about to capitulate, Lindsay kept up the pressure, her voice rising inexorably. "You dragged me over here to sort this mess out for you. I can understand you not levelling with your lawyer, because it looks bad that the prime suspect's last lover was not the victim but one of the other suspects. But you should have levelled with me, Meredith!"

Meredith ground out her cigarette and pushed herself away from the table, the chair legs shrieking a protest as she half turned away from Lindsay. "It was a one-off, for both of us. Her lover was visiting her family in Ireland. We were both lonely and feeling sorry for ourselves. She was just as keen as I was that nobody should find out we'd slept together. She had a lot to lose, after all—her lover as well as her professional relationship with Penny. And that brought her a lot of kudos there at Monarch. She cares too much about what people think of her professionally to fuck around with that."

"I think Penny guessed," Lindsay said flatly. It was neither her place nor her inclination to condemn. Fidelity wasn't hard between her and Sophie. But she had no feelings of selfrighteousness on that count. She knew how easy it was to slip out of that habit when a relationship was on a rocky road where reassurance had become a rarity.

"She didn't say anything directly to Baz," Meredith said.

"Penny wouldn't have. Not without evidence. And that's what she was looking for in Baz's desk and her computer. She bribed one of the staff at Monarch to smuggle her in after everyone had gone home for the day. She was looking for some piece of evidence to confirm her suspicions. I think she found it."

Meredith swung back to face Lindsay, reaching again for the cigarettes. "Baz wouldn't have left anything incriminating in her desk."

"No? What about e-mail?"

Meredith's grey eyes widened in shock. "Ah, shit," she said softly. "Yes, there would be an e-mail trail a yard wide."

"Still think Penny didn't know?"

Meredith sighed a stream of smoke. "I guess it's possible she found out. Depends if Baz has her files well protected or not."

Meredith's words snagged Lindsay's memory. She'd completely forgotten about Penny's missing computer. Clearly, investigating murder and jet lag didn't go together. "Speaking of computer files, do you know where Penny's laptop is?"

"Her laptop? Isn't it in the flat?"

"No. The power lead is still plugged into the wall, but there's no computer. Do you happen to know if the police took it?"

Meredith shook her head. "They haven't got it. I know because I got my solicitor to ask if they had taken anything of Penny's from the flat. I wanted to know if they had the answing-machine tape, right? And it turns out that all they took away was the answering-machine tape." Meredith's expression was wry.

"This is weird. Not only is the computer itself missing, but there isn't a single floppy in the place, not even a box of blanks. And there isn't a single copy of the manuscript lying around either. What was in *Heart of Glass* that's so dynamite?"

"You think someone killed her to prevent the book being finished?" Meredith's tone reflected Lindsay's own incredulity that a novel could provoke such passion.

"I know it's bizarre, but it's looking a lot like it. The only way we're going to know for sure is if we can track down a copy, and I haven't the first clue how we're going to do that."

They sat in silence until Meredith reached the end of her cigarette. "She was always paranoid about back-ups. She always backed up on to floppies at the end of the working day. She kept one set in the house and another tucked into the back of her personal organiser. And the third set she took down to Half Moon Bay once a week," she said slowly.

"What? She never left them with us."

Meredith shook her head. "I know. She used to drop them off with her best friend from high school, Carolyn Coogan. She and her husband, John, both teach math up in Pacifica. They live on the other side of the highway from you, about a mile south. She'd drive down one evening a week, or sometimes in the small hours of the morning. If she was late, she'd leave them in the mailbox."

"Couldn't she just have posted them?"

"By US Mail? Puh-lease! Penny wouldn't trust her disks to them, but she wanted a set somewhere they'd be safe if the house burned down, and where she could have easy access to them if it became necessary. So she'd bring them down herself."

"That explains why she used to drop in unannounced so often. She always said she'd just come down for a walk by the ocean. She'd borrow the dog and off they'd go, then she'd sit down for a beer afterwards," Lindsay said. "Obviously she can't have been doing that while she was over here. Do you think she'd have made alternative arrangements in England? Maybe left the disks with somebody she knew in London?"

Meredith shrugged. "It's possible. I'd say it's more than likely. But I don't know how we find out."

"If need be, we go through every single person in her address book," Lindsay said grimly.

"Oh, great," Meredith sighed. "Lindsay, I think you're going to have to handle that one by yourself. I'm not ready to talk to all those people yet."

"Well, let's hope it doesn't come to that. Oh, one other thing."

"What?"

"This murder by exploding beer bottle. It's really off the wall. Where did she get the idea for that?"

"You ever notice her scar? On her left forearm, about two inches long? Well, years ago, before she knew me or you guys, she was on holiday in Austria and it was a real hot summer like this one. She had some bottles of this wheat beer sitting on the kitchen table, waiting to go into the fridge once there was room for them. She accidentally knocked against the table, the bottles rocked back and forth, and one of them exploded. She said it was like a bomb going off. Glass everywhere. And one chunk of glass embedded itself in her arm. I guess she should have had the cut stitched, but she didn't want to go to hospital in a strange country, so her girlfriend closed it with surgical tape. That's why she had such a noticeable scar. She always said one day she was going to use it in a book."

"And when she did, it looks like it killed her."

Meredith looked at Lindsay while she automatically lit a third cigarette. "So what are we going to do about it?"

14

Sophie Hartley had just settled her patient on the examining table when the summons came. Rita Hernandez was an illegal immigrant who had escaped from El Salvador in search of the American dream. Instead, she'd ended up working a street corner in the Mission with a pimp who thought wearing a condom was a denial of machismo. Now she was HIV positive and six months pregnant and she wasn't convinced that the Grafton Clinic was a safe place to be. Sophie had finally persuaded her she wasn't going to turn her in to the authorities, so a nurse telling Sophie she had a transatlantic call was the last thing she needed right then. "*Momento, por favor, señorita*," she said in her English-accented Spanish, giving Rita a calming pat on the ankle. "Stay with her, would you?" she asked the nurse, then headed for the reception area.

"Line two," the receptionist mouthed at her between responding to waiting patients.

Sophie picked up the phone. "This had better be good," she said impatiently.

"I love you too," the familiar voice said. "Sorry to hit you at work, but it's the time difference. I hoped I could pitch you into doing me a favour this evening when you get off work, then you'd be able to call me back in the morning our time with the results."

"What kind of a favour?" Sophie said guardedly, running a hand through her hair in the familiar gesture of affectionate frustration that Lindsay tended to produce in her.

"Penny was so paranoid she used to drive down to Half Moon Bay every week with a spare set of back-up disks. She used to leave them with—"

"Carolyn Coogan, her best friend from high school," Sophie finished for her. "They live on Palisades Drive."

"How did you know that?" Lindsay demanded.

"There are a lot of miles of shore around the Bay Area. I once asked Penny if she had some sentimental attachment to Half Moon Bay, given how often she used to drop in on us. She said there was nothing sentimental about it, purely practical."

"You never told me," Lindsay said.

"Just one of my hundreds of dark secrets," Sophie teased. "You want me to go and see Carolyn?"

"Penny's laptop has gone missing. There are no back-up disks anywhere in the flat, and nobody's got a copy of her manuscript. I was thinking maybe she'd stashed another set somewhere, with somebody like Carolyn. And if so, whether she mentioned it to her. I know it's a long shot, but it would save me wasting tomorrow trying to track down everybody Penny knew over here. I'd really appreciate it," Lindsay added, injecting a dose of pathos into her voice.

"I'll see what I can do," Sophie said repressively.

"So you won't want to know who Meredith had her fling with," Lindsay said tantalisingly.

Sophie groaned. "Make it quick. I have a patient waiting."

"Baz Burton. Penny's editor."

"No!"

"Would I lie to you?"

"Not and live. I want chapter and verse on this, Lindsay, but not now. Call me tomorrow, okay? Love you."

"Love you too," Lindsay said to dead air.

Radio stations all smelt the same, Lindsay had realised in recent years. It didn't matter how old or new the studios were. A blind person who had once sampled the ambience would have it indelibly stamped in their olfactory banks forever. It was an indefinable smell: a history of cigarette smoke now abolished but present like a ghost; a faint whiff of nervous sweat, the decaying molecules of the pheromones still lingering; the unmistakable tang produced by hot coffee in plastic or polystyrene; and dust. The office where Kirsten was working had the radio smell, even though it was in a sixties building behind Broadcasting House which seemed to be occupied almost entirely by teenagers.

Lindsay was sitting on the tiled windowsill, feet on a chair, head tilted back and hanging out of the metal window-frame in a vain attempt to get some air in her lungs that hadn't already been breathed by half the population of London. Kirsten sat at a cluttered desk swigging some designer fruit drink from the bottle while sweat ran down either side of her nose as she talked into the phone. ". . . that's right, you remember! Well, I'm sort of looking at an idea that might make a piece for one of the media magazine programmes . . . Yeah, that's the sort of thing. I was wondering, you know. We still keep hearing about authors getting swag bags of money—Jeffrey Archer getting millions for his backlist, Martin Amis getting half a mill for a two-book deal. Plus, with the end of the Net Book Agreement, what seems to be happening is that bottom of the list authors, the unpromotables, they're getting the bullet, leaving the marketplace to the ones who can reasonably claim to be worth half-decent advances, yeah?" Kirsten paused in her flow, obviously listening to the voice on the other end. It was the third call she'd made so far.

At breakfast, Lindsay had moved in for the kill. She'd tried to talk to Sophie, but she'd only reached their answering machine, which informed her that Sophie had been called in to an emergency and that Lindsay should ring her around six in the morning, California time. Rather than kick her heels until early afternoon, she'd hit on the bright idea of using Kirsten's contacts to dig up background on Catriona Polson. She'd been perfectly prepared to do the research herself, but Kirsten was adamant that she wanted to help out. Lindsay wasn't sure if it was because she'd had the chance to get to know Meredith the previous evening, or because Helen had warned her not to let Lindsay close enough to her contacts to upset them. Either way, it relieved her of the tension of telling lies convincingly to strangers. Looking at Kirsten grafting away there, she wasn't sorry she'd been forced to abdicate the responsibility.

"Yeah, right," Kirsten resumed, blowing out a cloud of smoke from the forbidden cigarette she'd just lit. "Anyway, it seemed to me that the people who must really be coining it in off of this are not the authors, who after all, let's face it, have probably spent years in abject penury to write that one special book. And it's not even the publishers, given the balancing act they're all playing at just now with the ending of the Net Book Agreement and getting to grips with electronic publishing. No, the people who must really be raking it in are the agents . . ." Kirsten made a face, casting her eyes upwards and holding the phone away from her ear so Lindsay could hear the yakkety-yak coming from the receiver.

"Yeah, yeah, yeah, Clive, but think about it for a minute. All their crap authors get dispublished . . . yeah, I said dispublished, it's the new Americanism for what happens when your publisher tells you to get a life that doesn't include book signings. So you've got these literary agencies, right, with all their dead weight dropping off their client lists, and let's not forget that these are the authors who take up a disproportionate amount of time compared to the actual cash they bring in. So what they're left with . . ." Kirsten leaned back in her chair and mopped her face with a crumpled tissue.

"That's *exactly* what I'm saying. So you get someone like Catriona Polson coming along and not only swallowing up an old, established firm like Paul Firestone but also moving into the kind of naff but flash offices that Saatchi and Saatchi wouldn't sniff at. So I thought we could maybe look at these super-agents, and of course, I thought, Clive's the man. So take somebody like Catriona Polson. How did she go from a three-woman operation in Holborn to head honcho of Polson and Firestone?" Kirsten listened for a moment, then abruptly tipped forward and started scribbling on a scratch pad by the phone, dumping her cigarette in the flower vase on the desk. Now Lindsay knew how the carnations had died. She watched Kirsten take notes, interjecting the occasional, "Yeah," or, "Well, *there's* a surprise." In spite of the sweat and the pressure, she couldn't help feeling a faint pang of nostalgia for the journalistic trade she'd left behind her. Moments like this, when the adrenaline was pumping and there was the unmistakable sense of a hunch paying off, were simply not available in teaching.

Eventually, Kirsten's writing hand started to slow and she shifted in her seat, reaching into her desk drawer for another cigarette. "Clive, I owe you one," she sighed through a cloud of smoke, then replaced the handset. Kirsten grinned up at Lindsay, who found herself wondering just how it was that Helen managed to attract stunning women who also possessed brains and a sense of humour. Sophie and Kirsten were the two who had lasted longest, but they were far from the only ones. "Bingo," Kirsten growled happily.

"You going to tell me or do I have to hang you out of the window by the ankles and threaten to drop you?" Lindsay asked, sliding off the windowsill and into the chair.

"Sounds like fun, but I haven't got time for all that sophisticated foreplay," Kirsten said. "I'll cut to the chase."

"I was right, then? There is something dodgy at Polson and Firestone?"

"Well, not dodgy so much as stretched. When she 'discovered' Penny, she was literally a one-woman show. It was Penny's success that created her business and brought other writers beating a path to her door. Her business grew and she took on a couple of assistants, but she needed to expand, and the lesson everybody learned in the eighties was that the quickest way to do that was to swallow somebody else, preferably somebody bigger than you."

"The reverse takeover?"

"Sort of. Only in this case, Catriona Polson was the company that was making the money. The Firestone Agency was struggling, to be honest. They had quite a few talented people on the staff, but Paul Firestone had lost his edge and morale was crap. They lost a couple of their bigger names and soon as they started to slide, Catriona pounced. According to my buddy Clive, who works for *Bookselling News*, Paul Firestone hadn't entirely lost his marbles. He negotiated a deal on the sale of his agency that concluded with a balloon payment after three years, the amount to be dependent on Polson and Firestone's turnover. On a sliding scale that increased geometrically once profits hit a certain target." Kirsten paused expectantly.

"Wasn't that kind of betting against her own success?" Lindsay asked.

"Yes and no," Kirsten said. "Under normal circumstances, no literary agency would hope to generate the kind of profits in a single year that would have caused problems for Polson."

Lindsay grinned. "Why do I have the feeling you're about to outline a set of circumstances so far off the normal curve that our instruments have no way of measuring it?"

"Because you're psychic?"

"It's not a phenomenon I'm noted for. So what were these exceptional circumstances?"

Kirsten leaned back in her chair and stared up at the ceiling. "After Martin Amis got his half-million-pound advance, literary novelists woke up to the fact that they might have a bit of clout. When Milos Petrović won last year's Booker Prize, he decided that he more than deserved what Martin had already achieved, but his current agent couldn't get the deal up above

£350,000. Meanwhile, Polson's personal assistant was bonking a chap called Jeremy Dunstan, who's head honcho of a new literary imprint that one of the populist houses is trying to get off the ground. And Polson hears pillow talk that Jeremy is about to go out with a wallet full of dosh to pull in a couple of prime catches so that agents and authors will get their heads round the idea that his list is serious business, not some loss leader to make his company look like they're not dragging their knuckles on the bottom of the cave. With me so far?" she asked, tipping herself forward to extinguish her cigarette.

"Fascinated," Lindsay said, heavy on the irony. "I had no idea the world of gentlemen publishers had spun into the orbit of the eighties. So what happened next? As if I couldn't guess."

"Polson poached Petrovič and got him half a million to head up Jeremy's list. His previous agent was chewing the carpet, but there was nothing he could do. Petrovič paid him the commission on the £350,000 he'd negotiated already, as per his contract, and Polson got the reputation. And in this business, where reputation goes, authors follow, sure as seagulls follow the sardine boat. The end result being that Polson had to pay Paul Firestone a massive chunk of dosh about three months ago and now her cash flow is plunging through the floor. The business owes money to its landlord, its authors, and Polson's taken out a second mortgage on her house." Kirsten smiled sweetly. "Looks like the Darkliners film deal was her lifebelt."

Lindsay stood up and wiped the sweat from her upper lip. "Does Helen know about your killer instinct?"

Kirsten grinned like a barracuda. "What else do you think she sees in me? I'm just glad I could help you out. You're a bit of a legend in our house, you know. Radical feminism's answer to Miss Marple."

"I wish," Lindsay said wryly. "If I was ever radical, it's ancient history now. If I'm the answer, somebody's asking the wrong question."

The climb to Catriona Polson's office hadn't got any easier since Lindsay had last scaled the heights. Nor had the stairwell become any more appealing. It was hardly surprising, given what she now knew about the agent's finances. If you were looking at losing the roof over your head, paying a cleaner wasn't going to be high on the list of priorities.

The receptionist hadn't become any more welcoming, either. "You can't see Ms Polson without an appointment," she announced as soon as recognition sparked in her eyes.

"That what you say to Milos Petrović, is it?" Lindsay said conversationally.

"Anyway, you lied about not being a journalist," the receptionist continued.

Lindsay shrugged. "I never said I wasn't a journalist. You assumed I wasn't. However, if you'd looked at that card with half a brain, you'd have seen it was at least eight years out of date. Nation Newspapers moved to Docklands back in '88. And London phone numbers have changed a bit since then, too."

"She won't see you, you know. There's no point in me even trying."

Lindsay had always hated gatekeepers who, powerless in their own right, jealously guarded access to the source. If there was one thing she valued about her years as a journalist, it was the selection of methods it had shown her to get past the dragons at the gates. Taking out her notebook, she scribbled, "Give me one good reason why I shouldn't tell the police about the Darkliners film deal. V. I. Warshawski." She tore the page off, folded it half and said, "I think you might find that will change her mind. And don't even think about not showing it to Ms Polson. I can guarantee that that would seriously upset her." She placed the note on the receptionist's keyboard.

She glowered at Lindsay, then picked up the paper and dialled a number on her switchboard. Picking up the handset as the number rang out, she said, "Trish, there's a note here for Catriona. Can you come and get it? I can't leave reception right now." She gave Lindsay a malicious little smirk.

"I'm really not going to steal the art," Lindsay said, settling into one of the enveloping leather sofas. She leaned back and gazed into the middle distance, affecting not to notice the dumpy gopher who emerged from the tall office door, snatched up the note and disappeared again. Within five minutes, the gopher returned and muttered something to the receptionist, who scowled, gestured with a pen and said, "That's her."

The other woman came over and said, "Catriona will see you now."

As she followed, Lindsay winked at her antagonist. "Aren't you glad we didn't take a bet on it?" she asked, enjoying the pink fury of the receptionist's face.

Lindsay was escorted to the same conference room and left to her own devices for the best part of ten minutes. When Catriona Polson finally entered, she found Lindsay sitting staring at the portrait of Penny Varnavides. "I can't get used to the idea of not seeing her again," Polson said.

"Really? Don't you worry she might come back to haunt you once Galaxy Pictures have fucked over her books?" Lindsay said, hoping she sounded as offensive as she intended.

"I don't think either of those things is going to happen," the agent said icily, folding her long body into one of the chairs. "Look, I really don't want to get into a ruck with you. The only reason I agreed to see you was in the hope that we could strike me off your ridiculous suspect list for good and all. I had no motive for Penny Varnavides' death. Yes, it would have been a blow if she had turned down what is a very attractive TV deal, but it would have been a long way from the end of the world."

Lindsay snorted with a mockery of laughter. "Oh, yeah? When your company's so strapped for cash you've had to take out a second mortgage on your home?"

Polson tilted her head on one side. "You really have done your homework, haven't you? And two weeks ago, you're right, the thought of losing the Darkliners TV deal would have rendered me near suicidal, if not homicidal. And then a deal we thought was dead rose from the grave. A Hollywood producer called to say they'd finally got the green light for a film adaptation of someone else's work. And that means even more in financial terms to this agency than the Varnavides deal."

Lindsay's stomach seemed to hollow as the agent's words sank in. "You expect me to believe that?" she tried, knowing it was a last-gasp bluff.

"I've got a file of signed contracts and faxes that demonstrate the truth of what I'm saying," she said, not unsympathetically. "I'm not prepared to show you, since I have no conviction that you would treat it confidentially. But I'm perfectly prepared to show it to the police, should you be inclined to make yourself look foolish by involving them."

Lindsay took a deep breath and stood up. "I seem to have wasted your time as well as my own," she said, unable to keep an edge of bitterness out of her voice.

Polson gave her a look of shrewd appraisal. "I wouldn't beat yourself up too much. I know you blame me for telling the police about Meredith, but I was upset. I don't know Meredith very well, and it seemed to me she had a motive. I applaud what you're trying to do and if I can help, I will. I'm sorry I was so unhelpful before."

If she'd wanted to make Lindsay feel worse, she couldn't have found a better way to do it. "Mmm," she mumbled, looking everywhere but at Penny's picture or her agent. "Okay."

"There are more motives than money," Catriona said. "There's reputation for a start. Maybe *Heart of Glass* trashed somebody who lives by their name."

Lindsay found a self-pitying smile from somewhere. "Like an agent, you mean?"

"It's about an editor."

15

Back on the street in the suffocating late morning heat, Lindsay walked through the sweating tourist crowds towards Leicester Square, pondering Catriona Polson's final suggestion. Whatever Meredith felt about Baz, she was going to have to have another confrontation with the editor. But Lindsay needed all the ammunition she could lay her hands on before then, and since *Heart of Glass* might contain some of the answers, it seemed sensible to wait until she'd spoken to Sophie and discovered whether there were any extant copies that the killer hadn't taken.

Sensible had never been her strong suit, but for once she was able to possess her soul in patience, since she had something else on her mind that was sufficiently interesting to occupy her. She emerged into Leicester Square and waited for an empty phone box. The one she ended up in smelt of sour milk and strong aftershave, its windows papered with postcards advertising the services of an assortment of prostitutes. Lindsay found it as sexually alluring as the inspection pit of a garage. Trying to ignore the pathetic faces whose photographs stared down at her in a parody of desire from several of the cards, she called Helen. "I've got an idea," she said. "Can you meet me for lunch?"

"I can't really go out, I've got a million and six things to do and I'm expecting a phone call from New York that I don't want to miss. Why don't you come here?" Helen said. "Those two gobshites are out filming today, so you won't have any embarrassing encounters. I'll order in some sandwiches and we can have a picnic in my office, okay?"

"Perfect," Lindsay said. "See you around one."

Her next call was to Eleanor Purdey, a fellow alumna of her Oxford college. Although they'd both read English, Ellie had abandoned literature for the law, joining a large commercial firm just as the eighties had started to boom. Now she was a full equity partner, a profitable role since her company had avoided the worst excesses of the recession by moving neatly into rescue packages for companies facing financial and fiscal disaster. They'd never been close at university, but when they'd met a few years later at a party Lindsay had attended with her barrister lover, they'd discovered they were both gay. Coupled with their St Mary's connection, it had been enough to forge a bond. In spite of their widely differing political perspectives, Lindsay and Ellie had always stayed in touch. In Lindsay's journalist days, Ellie had been a valuable insider contact. For Ellie, Lindsay suspected, she had provided a tad of street cred in a lesbian scene where establishment professionals like Ellie were mistrusted and often excluded.

Once she'd made it past Ellie's secretary and they'd exchanged greetings and agreed to meet for a drink in a day or two, Lindsay got straight to the point. She outlined an idea that had dawned on her as a possible answer to Helen's problems and was gratified to hear Ellie confirm what she'd thought to be the case. Not only that, but after a couple of minutes during which Lindsay could hear the tapping of her computer keys, Ellie was able to cite cases that would give Lindsay details of how to set up her little sting. "A couple of these cases got quite extensive coverage in the press," she added. "Not the tabloids, but the *Telegraph* and the *Financial Times*. The *Economist* ran something as well, I seem to remember. If you can get Internet access, you can look it all up for yourself." She gave Lindsay the necessary details, which she scribbled down in her notebook.

"I owe you one," Lindsay said, after she'd double-checked she'd got all the dots and slashes in the right places on the Internet addresses Ellie had provided.

"And not for the first time. Give my love to Sophie when you speak to her."

"Will do. Oh, and Ellie? Will you be at home this evening?"

Ellie made no attempt to hide her sigh. "Exploit-a-friend not done enough for one day?"

"Sorry, but no. I might need some practical assistance if what I'm planning comes off. Just by phone . . ."

"I'll be here till around eight, then I'm going straight home to sit on my balcony with a very sexy futures trader and an ice-cold bottle of Chardonnay. So you can take your chances," Ellie said, sounding amused.

Armed with the information from Ellie, Lindsay headed back across the square towards Charing Cross Road, stopping at a computer supplies shop to buy a few blank floppies. She cut through side streets until she found Cyberia, the Internet café she had read about but never visited before. A few pounds bought her an hour's access to cyberspace and an icy Diet Coke, and she settled down at one of the table-top terminals to check out the sources Ellie had suggested to her.

It didn't take long to unravel the web that took her to the heart of the information she needed, since America was still only waking up and there wasn't too much traffic on the Net. Her initial idea had come from a distant memory she'd dredged up of a court case she'd heard referred to on the BBC World Service. With Ellie's guidance and a little manipulation, she could see how it might be possible to use the bare bones of the case to construct a sting that would cut the feet from under Stella and Guy far more effectively than the Obscene Publications Squad could ever have managed.

She downloaded the relevant files on to her blank disks and closed down her terminal with twenty minutes to spare, which she passed on to a grateful youth who'd been hanging around looking wistfully at her and her fellow netheads. A quick glance at her watch told her she'd better get a move on, so she walked back to Leicester Square tube and endured the stifling and stale wind of the Northern Line tunnels until a train groaned into the station to jolt her to Camden Town.

Helen closed the door of her office behind Lindsay, who caught the look of surprise on her secretary's face. "It's not that I don't trust her," Helen said defensively, seeing Lindsay's raised eyebrows. "It's just that I don't actually trust anybody in here as of last night. Isn't that the pits? As if it's not bad enough that they've done what they've done, they've got me so paranoid I think everybody's in it with them. Toerags." As she spoke, she unwrapped a series of soft ciabatta rolls with a variety of fillings. They looked like a row of mismatched children's slippers arranged on a plate.

"Serious sandwiches," Lindsay commented, settling herself in the canvas director's chair facing Helen.

"They probably go through the books as stationery supplies," Helen said sourly, opening a small executive fridge and taking out a couple of bottles of alcoholic lemonade and uncapping them. "So what's new?"

"I had this idea of how we can screw Stella and Guy," Lindsay said simply. A wide grin split Helen's face. "Now I remember why I like you so much," she said.

"What you do here at Watergaw, you work quite closely with ethnic minority groups, am I right?"

"That's supposed to be our brief, yeah. Couldn't you tell from the women in those delightful films we saw last night?" Helen asked savagely, grabbing a sandwich and biting into it as if it were Stella's head she was snapping off.

"So would I be right in thinking that means you film abroad from time to time?"

Helen nodded, managing to look puzzled even with a mouthful of sandwich.

"Is there anywhere that Guy and Stella have been on a joint project, relatively recently?"

Helen swallowed, her brow furrowing. "The most recent trip they did was for a series of Channel Four documentaries. We had this idea of going back with immigrants from the subcontinent to the villages they left thirty years ago. We wanted to see how the villages had changed, and we thought it would be interesting to do it through the eyes of the villagers who had stayed and those who had left. *Thirty/Three*, I called it. It was my idea, but I couldn't fit the filming timetable in with other stuff I already had booked in. It's always the same in this game, feast or famine. I've either got three projects all demanding my attention or else I'm running around like a headless chicken doing a rain dance, trying to raise funding from anywhere to make the next film."

"So Guy and Stella had to make the films for *Thirty/Three* without you?"

"That's right. Why d'you want to know? Are you on to something?"

"In a minute. Which country were they in?" Lindsay asked through a mouthful of cream cheese and sun-dried tomatoes.

"India, Pakistan and Bangladesh. We made one film in each of the three of them," Helen explained. "We took three families back, original immigrants and their kids, so that we could compare and contrast the achievements and expectations of both groups, as well as the straightforward lifestyle stuff. It wasn't a particularly cheap or easy set of films to make. It's never simple when you're juggling that many people with their own separate agendas, but they got some good stuff."

"Were you involved in the project at all after the early stages?" Lindsay asked.

"Are you kidding? I was in the middle of making a six-half-hour drama series for children's TV about racist bullying.

I hardly had enough brain cells to spare for going to the toilet. I just told them to bugger off and come back with enough film for three forty-minute slots."

"Perfect," Lindsay breathed.

"Linds, I know I can be a bit slow sometimes, but I'm obviously missing something here. Why does it matter where Stella and Guy were filming and whether I was there or not?"

"Kickbacks," Lindsay said.

Helen managed to look both worried and suspicious. "What about kickbacks?"

"You know and I know that to operate any kind of business in certain developing countries, you need to pay nearly as much in backhanders as you do in legitimate fees."

"More sometimes," Helen interrupted gloomily. "If I live to be a hundred, I will never ever film in Sierra Leone again. But I don't see what that's got to do with stitching up that pair of gobshites."

"You will, Oscar, you will. Okay, so we've got a scenario where Guy and Stella are off on their Asian tour, handing out kickbacks right, left and centre. Which, of course, is against the law over here and therefore not a legitimate company expense."

"Yeah, but hang on a minute," Helen protested. "Every company that works in places like that has to pay kickbacks and bribes. You disguise it in the books. You make it look like something else. Guy told me once the accounts were done on the Asian trip, it would all look kosher. Just like everything we've ever done abroad in the past. You're not going to get him for paying kickbacks."

"I know that," Lindsay said, calmly finishing her sandwich and mopping her lips with a paper napkin. Then she beamed at Helen. "What we *are* going to nail them for is defrauding the VAT and the Inland Revenue."

For a moment, Helen was speechless. But only for a moment. "Do what?" she said weakly.

"Defrauding the VAT and the tax. If you disguise the kickbacks and bribes as something else in the books, you're acting fraudulently. Inevitably, you're making false declarations to the Inland Revenue and to Customs and Excise. It doesn't matter that everybody does it—when it's reported to them, they take action all the same. Guy and Stella are not going to know what hit them. You can mess with the law, but you never mess with the VATman and the taxman. Or woman. When I was a freelance, I remember one of the first things my accountant ever told me was never get clever with the VAT. 'Take out a second mortgage if you have to,' he told me, 'but always pay the VATman.'"

"You're out of your mind," Helen said weakly.

"No, I'm not. Customs and Excise have more powers than the police. They can kick your door down in the middle of the night without a warrant. They can kick your mother's door down in the middle of the night without a warrant if they have reasonable grounds for suspecting you've hidden your second set of books in her linen cupboard. They can freeze your bank accounts and make you a social leper faster than appearing on a daytime game show can."

"I know all that," Helen interrupted. "But you seem to be forgetting something here. I'm one of the partners in this company. They go down, I go down."

Lindsay shook her head. "That's the beauty of it." She smiled. "Trust me. What time is this place empty tonight?"

Helen shook her head. "I've no idea. Stella and Guy'll be coming back here after they've done their filming and they'll probably hang around to take a look at what they've got. There's no knowing how late they'll be working. Whatever dirty deeds you've got up your sleeve, do they have to be done at night?"

Lindsay grimaced. "It'd be easier if I can get a straight run of a few hours when I can be sure there won't be anyone else around."

"Will it wait until tomorrow? Only, they've got a night shoot and there's no way they'll be back here before two or three in the morning. There'll only be me here after about half past six."

Lindsay winked. "Let's make it seven tomorrow, then."

"But . . ." Helen said.

"Like I said, trust me. By this time the day after tomorrow, they'll be done up like a pair of kippers and you'll be smelling of roses."

"Oh, yeah?" Helen said dubiously.

"Yeah. One thing I will need is superuser clearance for your computer network. Can you get that for me? Your systems manager should be able to give you the codes, no trouble."

"Superuser?"

"The systems manager will know what you mean, honestly. Now, can I use your phone? I have to speak to my stitching-up consultant. Oh, yeah, and then I need to speak to Sophie. If your phone bill will stand it."

"She was a creature of habit," Sophie said. "Just because she couldn't get round to Half Moon Bay didn't mean she felt she had to change her usual routine."

Lindsay leaned back in Stella's executive leather desk chair, a sharp contrast with Helen's rather battered cloth seat. Helen had shunted her down the corridor because her New York call had come through just as Lindsay had finished making arrangements with Ellie to postpone her consultation till the following evening. Now Lindsay had privacy for her call to Sophie. "I can't believe she trusted the post," Lindsay said. "She wouldn't even trust them to deliver a package from San Francisco. That's why she used to bring the back-ups down to Half Moon Bay in person, according to Meredith."

"She didn't. But she did trust courier service," Sophie said.

Lindsay gave a low whistle. "She wasn't afraid to spend her money, was she? Transatlantic courier, eh?"

"In fairness, she didn't go for the expensive overnight service. She just sent them by regular courier, five or six days, especially if the weekend got in the way."

"So when did the last lot arrive?" Lindsay asked eagerly.

"Six days ago."

"Have you got them?" Lindsay demanded.

"I managed to persuade Carolyn to let me make copies of them," Sophie told her. "I also took copies of the previous disks Penny had sent since she arrived in England. The first disk has *Heart of Glass* from the beginning to Chapter 12, the second from the beginning to Chapter 15 and the last one goes up to Chapter 18. There seem to be about twelve pages to a chapter. But bear in mind, these chapters must have been completed about a week before Penny died. They may not be current enough to be any help to your investigation," Sophie cautioned.

"Have you looked at them?"

"I spent most of the night with a very awkward delivery," Sophie protested.

"I'm sorry, I'm sorry, I'm just a bit keyed up over this," Lindsay apologised. "What's the best way for you to get them to me? Express courier?"

Sophie chuckled. "You're still a Luddite at heart, aren't you? I thought you were supposed to have embraced the new technology now?"

"Eh?"

"If you pick up your e-mail, you'll find them all there. In the few odd moments of calm during the night, I put the files into a format I could transmit, and sent you a bunch of massive e-mails."

"Hellfire!" Lindsay exclaimed. "You are a fucking genius, Doc! Oh, God, now I've got to get right across town to Helen's, I don't have my laptop with me and she's got a different network provider for her Internet connection and I don't know how to use the software and I've got to read up on all the stuff Ellie pointed me at . . ." She stopped gibbering and subsided into thought.

"Carolyn reckoned there could be another delivery in the pipeline, if Penny was sticking to her usual weekly cycle. She was due to have sent another disk off the day she was killed," Sophie said.

"Yeah, yeah," Lindsay said, too distracted to take in what Sophie was saying. "That's terrific. Soph, you're the berries. The absolute berries. Listen, I'm going to have to run. I've got to pick up my laptop and start ploughing through this stuff, plus Helen's got a hell of a situation going on here that I'm trying to help her out with, so I'm going to have to steam off. I'll call you, okay? I love you."

"I love you too. Take care," Sophie said. But she was already speaking to herself.

16

Lindsay rubbed her eyes and drew the curtain a few inches further across her bedroom window to keep the sun at a distance. In vain she'd searched for a lead that would connect her computer to Helen's printer, so instead of printing out the long files of text that Sophie had sent her so she could read them on paper, she was forced to struggle with a laptop screen that was perfectly adequate for normal use, but never meant for long hours of close scrutiny.

It wasn't just having to read the novel on screen that was causing her problems. If she'd been able to print out the three versions of the book she would have been able to lay them alongside each other and make a page-by-page comparison. But even with the split-screen facility her word-processing software allowed, she could only compare two versions at a time. She had decided to work through it chapter by chapter, first comparing the original version with the second, then the second with the third.

It was heavy going, even with the work of a writer as talented as Penny Varnavides had undoubtedly been. Lindsay, who had read most of the Darkliners series, at first out of loyalty and later pleasure, was astonished by the maturity and depth of the writing. If Penny had had work of this calibre in her, it was no wonder she was frustrated by the scope of teenage fantasy. The only marvel was that it had taken her so long to develop the confidence to break out of the comfort zone and stretch herself.

Lindsay wriggled around, trying to find a more comfortable position on the bed. She knew she was welcome to set herself up either at the kitchen table or in Helen and Kirsten's home office, but she wanted neither to be in their way when they got home nor to have the distraction of their inevitable interest. So she had holed up in her room with a bunch of grapes from a stall by the tube station and a six-pack of Rolling Rock. The beers were cooling in a basin filled with the bag of ice she'd bought at the small supermarket at the corner of Helen's road. After five hours of staring into the screen, she was starting to wonder if she should be applying the ice to her gritty eyes.

It wasn't as if she was coming up with anything that pointed the finger of suspicion at anyone she knew about. *Heart of Glass* was the terrifying story of two serial killers, one deliberate, the other accidental. The central character was a mystery novelist who realised that every time he created a particular murderous scenario, it was reflected almost immediately in real life. As an experiment, he deliberately wrote a book where his despised older brother, thinly disguised, died in a murder made to look like a freak accident with an exploding beer bottle. Just as Penny herself had died. Within weeks, his brother was dead, by almost identical means.

With this gruesome proof of his gift, the writer set about killing off everyone he had ever disliked. Judging from Penny's novel, he'd devoted a lot of energy over the years to hatred. In parallel with his remote-controlled homicidal spree ran the story of a surgeon who had developed his surgical skills in the bedrooms of his victims as efficiently as he had in the operating theatre. He had been killing successfully for years, escaping detection by never murdering in the same city twice. An international serial killer, he'd earned frequent flyer miles for murder.

The connection between the two men was the surgeon's wife, who was also the writer's editor. The final ingredient in the heady stew was the wife's lover, a charismatic congressman about to mount a presidential campaign.

Knowing that Penny used elements of her friends, acquaintances and professional contacts in the construction of her characters, Lindsay tried to match the characters in the book to people she knew in Penny's life, to see if any clues lay there. But Penny was too skilled in her craft to have left an obvious trail leading back to her immediate circle. Even where parallels seemed possible, there were no correlations that struck Lindsay. The editor was nothing like Baz, being a weak character swept along by events, unable to control her life. Nothing like the woman Meredith had described, a woman capable of seizing the opportunity for infidelity, then taking steps to make certain it didn't disrupt the relationship at the heart of her professional life.

There didn't even seem to be any signposts in the changes Penny had made between the drafts. There was a certain amount of linguistic tinkering, some reorganisation of material, rearranging the order in which certain sections appeared. But there was no structural rewriting that went to the heart of the book. However Penny had fiddled superficially, her central storyline had driven forward with the impetus of an arrow flying from a bow.

By the time she had reached the end of the final chapter, it was after midnight and Lindsay was no nearer an answer. Whatever Penny's killer had feared from the pages of *Heart of Glass*, it was far too subtle to strike her.

"You're never going to believe this," Sophie said, the excitement in her voice travelling easily across ocean and continent.

"Mmm," Lindsay grunted, forcing her eyebrows upwards in a vain attempt to get her eyes to stay open. It was quarter past seven in the morning, but it felt like the middle of the night.

Seeing her plight, Kirsten thrust a mug of pitch-coloured coffee in front of her. Lindsay took a scalding sip and felt synapses snap to attention all through her brain. "Believe what?" she asked, sounding like a reasonable approximation of a human being.

"Penny's latest draft. *Heart of Glass*. The package arrived by courier today and Carolyn called me right away, at work. She knew you'd want to see it. Penny actually sent it the day she died. Three new chapters plus the very last revisions she ever made to the text." There seemed to be an exclamation mark hanging in the air at the end of each of Sophie's sentences.

"And?"

"I skimmed it. I knew you'd want chapter and verse on any substantial changes as soon as possible."

"I didn't realise you'd read the earlier drafts," Lindsay muttered.

"I dipped in and out of it whenever I could get a spare moment," Sophie said. "Darling, she'd made a lot of changes in this draft. The surgeon's wife—the editor? She's had a complete personality change. You know how she was passive and weak in the first drafts? Well, she's not any more. She's been turned into a strong, scheming bitch. A real sexual adventurer. Now it's her who seduces the politician, not the other way round. And it's clear she's not a victim any more. In fact, it looks like Penny was shaping up to turning her into a killer—I think the twist she was aiming for is that the novelist isn't really capable of causing death by remote control, but his editor goes out and makes his books come true, partly as a publicity stunt and partly because she enjoys it."

By now thoroughly awake, Lindsay drew her breath in sharply. "Now that's what I call a significant change. Tell me, Soph. Has Penny changed the physical description of the wife at all?"

"Funny you should say that," Sophie said. "In the first draft, she's described as slightly built with mousy blonde hair, pale skin."

"Human wallpaper," Lindsay interjected. The coffee was starting to do its stuff.

"Right. But the description this time is quite different. Hang on, I printed it out . . . 'Her hair was hennaed a dark, glossy auburn, cut like Mia Farrow's in her waif period. It contrasted with dark eyebrows and eyes the colour of Hershey's Kisses, and served to emphasise chubby cheeks that reminded Carradine of a squirrel storing a lucky find of nuts for later. Somehow, he wouldn't have been surprised to discover her body pierced in places that would make most women wince.'"

"King hell," Lindsay said.

"I take it that means something to you?" Sophie asked.

"With a description like that, you could pick Baz Burton out of any line-up," Lindsay said. "You think there's any doubt that Penny knew about Baz and Meredith's night of passion?"

Sophie chuckled at Lindsay's ironic tone. "Is the Pope a Catholic? Remind me never to cross a writer. If what you're saying is right, the character would have been instantly recognisable to everybody at Monarch as Baz."

"Not to mention the rest of the publishing world. And not just in London. What do you think they'd be gossiping about at the Frankfurt Book Fair, if not the way that Penny Varnavides had extracted her revenge against her former editor? Make no mistake, sending a message like that to Baz is the longest sacking note in history," Lindsay pointed out as Helen barged into the kitchen.

"What is this, Pinkerton's Detectives, we never sleep?" she demanded loudly enough for Sophie to hear her in California.

"Tell Helen to shut up, we're talking serious murder motives," Sophie said.

Lindsay relayed the message and Helen poked her tongue out at the phone. Kirsten shook her head in amusement and gestured at the oven with her thumb. "Get on with your call then, Sherlock," Helen mock-grumbled, taking warm pastries out of the oven.

"It is a motive," Lindsay said. "No two ways about it."

"It's horrible to think of Penny dying for something so petty," Sophie said soberly.

There was a long silence as they both recalled what lay behind the excitement of the hunt. Then Lindsay said, "I need to see this stuff soon as."

"I know," Sophie acknowledged. "But I'm up to my eyes. I've had to come back into the clinic."

"The joys of high-risk deliveries?"

"Yeah. I had to come back into the city after I'd picked up the disk from Carolyn. I don't know how soon I'll have the chance to reformat these text files and e-mail them to you."

Lindsay groaned. "Oh, God." Both Helen and Kirsten looked up momentarily from their morning paper and Danish, decided it was nothing serious and carried on, ignoring Lindsay's histrionics.

"I'm doing my best, Lindsay," Sophie said, sounding hurt.

"I know, I know, I wasn't having a go," Lindsay said apologetically. "It's just so frustrating."

"I promise you'll have them by the end of the day," Sophie said.

"That's terrific, honestly. That's fine," Lindsay reassured her. Then she sighed. "I really miss you, you know. Helen and Kirsten have been great, but it's not like having you around."

"It won't be long till I'm back in Britain too. Don't forget, we already had our flights booked for next week."

"I know. I just wish I didn't have to do without you that long. You're always telling me I'm not fit to be let out on my own."

"You need some back-up, huh?"

Lindsay grinned. "That's right. I need someone to cover my back when I'm dealing with these heavy people. Violent types like publishers."

"Joking apart, you be careful. At the risk of sounding like the last line before the commercial break in *Murder, She Wrote*, there's a killer out there, and I don't want you to be the next victim."

"Don't worry," Lindsay said. "With what you've told me this morning, I think I've got a pretty good idea who killed Penny. And I'm not about to confront her up a dark alley. I don't think that even Baz Burton has the bottle to jump me in an open-plan office in front of the entire office staff of Monarch Press."

"I don't suppose there's any point in me suggesting you hold off on this confrontation till you've had the chance to read the revised text for yourself? So you can quote chapter and verse at Baz?"

"Absolutely correct. What would be the point in that, unless you're winding me up and telling me stories?"

Sophie sighed. "Promise me you'll be careful?"

"I promise I'll still be in one piece when you get here," Lindsay said.

"So let me speak to Helen now," Sophie said. "I love you."

"Love you too," Lindsay said, waving the phone at Helen, who grabbed it and had a short conversation with Sophie which was remarkable for its monosyllabic quality. Lindsay had never seen anyone but Sophie reduce Helen's dialogue so drastically, and it appeared the old gift hadn't left her. After a series of grunts, "yeahs" and "no problems," Helen hung up.

"So," she said to Lindsay. "Are we on for tonight? The big sting? Or are you going to be too busy catching murderers?"

"Trust me, I'm a doctor," Lindsay said.

Helen snorted. "It'd take more than an American PhD to make me trust you, kiddo."

Lindsay stood up, pretending to be on her dignity. "It'll all be done and dusted by seven. Then you and I will be ready to roll."

Impatiently, Lindsay drummed her fingers on the arm of the chair she was reluctantly occupying at Monarch Press. Seeing her scowl, Lauren leaned forward across the reception desk and said confidentially, "She won't be long now. The editorial meeting never lasts past eleven. Danny's always got too much on to waste time letting them rabbit. He only allows the editors five minutes max to pitch any of their titles."

Lindsay pursed her lips and glared at her watch again, as if that would make the time pass more quickly. She couldn't even use the minutes constructively to see if Lauren's brain contained anything else worth picking since the reception area was never empty for more than a minute at a time. The longer she had to wait, the more her conviction of Baz's guilt grew. No matter that the meeting Baz was in was a routine weekly session, Lindsay couldn't prevent herself feeling Baz had made herself deliberately unavailable to spite her. Illogical and paranoid, she knew, but the feeling still wouldn't depart. She flipped open the front pocket of her backpack again and checked that her microcassette recorder was in voice-activated mode. She wasn't taking the risk that Baz would confess something she'd later try to deny.

Finally, as the minute hand crawled towards the hour, a young woman appeared, looking harassed. "You're waiting to see Baz, right?" she greeted Lindsay. Without waiting for an answer, she gestured impatiently to the door. Lindsay got to her feet and forced herself to follow the woman through the editorial floor at a measured pace rather than the trot that would have matched her mood.

Baz was sitting behind her desk shuffling papers when Lindsay walked in. She glanced up. "Hi. Siddown, yeah?" she said as she finished reading the top sheet and scribbled what might have been a signature across the bottom of it. Then she looked up, her face still a painful scarlet from too much sun. "I've spoken to Meredith," she said bluntly.

"Good. That's one less awkward conversation for us to have," Lindsay said, her voice the only chilly thing in the partitioned space.

"So what brings you back here?"

"Your boss asked if I could track down a copy of *Heart of Glass*," Lindsay said, avoiding the guest's chair and perching on the edge of a credenza stacked with manuscripts that ran along one wall, forcing Baz to turn awkwardly in her chair to maintain eye contact.

"You've managed to find it?" Baz asked cautiously. "Where was it?"

"Penny always deposited a set of back-up disks with friends for safekeeping. It wasn't hard to find out where they were and to get a copy. You don't seem as excited as I expected." Lindsay crossed her legs at the ankles and leaned back on her arms.

"I'm just relieved," Baz said, a note of defensiveness creeping in. "I've got a lot riding on this book."

"Oh, I know you have. A damn sight more than a bloody big hole in your catalogue."

Baz shifted in her chair, almost imperceptibly altering her position to close herself off from Lindsay's probing stare. "You're going to have to explain that. I'm not quite sure what you're getting at."

Lindsay snorted with sardonic laughter. "Was that meant to be a subtle attempt to find out which draft I've got? If so, there was no need for the subtlety. I'll happily tell you, Baz. I've got the lot. I've got three early drafts, going as far as Chapter 18." Lindsay paused, gauging Baz's watchful stare. She thought she saw relief there, but couldn't be sure.

"How soon can you let us have a copy?" Baz asked, fiddling obsessively with the pen she'd used to sign the document.

"That's going to be up to Meredith and Catriona Polson," Lindsay replied. "Oh, and probably the police as well."

"Why should it have anything to do with the police?" Baz asked, her busy fingers freezing, the pen stationary in mid-turn.

"I've also got the final draft." Lindsay stared steadily at Baz. "The one I wouldn't want anyone to see if I was in your shoes. The one that gives you a motive for wanting Penny Varnavides dead." Her words cut through the humid air like the hiss of a thrown knife.

Baz's mouth twisted into the kind of smile that's normally only seen in distorting fairground mirrors. "Come on," she said in an attempt at jokey contempt. "You can't be seriously suggesting that a rewrite Penny did in the heat of anger would give me a motive for *murder*?"

Lindsay's grim smile would have worried a shark. "One," she said, ticking off her points on her fingers, "*Heart of Glass* as rewritten represents total humiliation for you, personally and professionally. Two, Penny and you could never have worked together again, which scuppers your brilliant career. Three, your girlfriend's going to be more than a little baffled as to why your formerly fabulous relationship with your most successful author has turned so sour, and I'm sure Penny would have been more than happy to enlighten her. Will that do for starters?"

Baz's eyes narrowed perceptibly, but when she spoke her voice struggled for lightness. "This is madness. Look, whatever Penny may or may not have done in some intermediate draft, I was her editor and the final shape of the book depends on me as much as on her. I have the authority to demand that she change back to what was, after all, the book outlined in her synopsis, the book I had commissioned."

"Oh, sure! If it came to a showdown between what Penny wanted and what you wanted, obviously Danny King's going to side with you," Lindsay said sarcastically. "Come on, Baz. Let's get real here. Penny wasn't exactly Ms Nobody submitting her first novel. If it was a case of losing Penny or losing you, I can't imagine Danny having to agonise for more than ten seconds."

Lindsay didn't think it was possible for anyone to have a higher colour than the editor had already, but she was proved wrong as Baz darkened almost to purple. "It wouldn't ever have come to that. Penny reacted the way she did because she was hurt and angry and that was the easiest way to get back at me. But she wasn't a fool. She was planning on coming out when this book was published. If she'd gone with the draft you're talking about, then someone would have sussed that we'd fallen out and, eventually, why. The last thing she would have wanted was that kind of tabloid notoriety. If you knew her half as well as you claim to, you'd know what I'm saying is the truth," she added defiantly.

Rather than give Lindsay pause for thought, Baz's words served only to add fuel to the flames of her conviction. "Maybe so. But it doesn't alter the fact that enough people would have seen that draft to humiliate you in the business, and jeopardise your relationship with your lover. And you can't tell me Penny Varnavides would ever have worked with you again after the way you wrecked her relationship with Meredith!"

"What the hell is going on in here?" a male voice interjected.

Lindsay turned to see Danny King in the doorway looking baffled. Baz wiped her sweating upper lip with the back of her hand and said bitterly, "Glasgow's answer to Emma Victor here is accusing me of murdering Penny."

Danny King threw back his handsome head in a guffaw of laughter. "You mean you haven't told her about your alibi?" he gasped.

17

Thunderstruck, Lindsay's head swung from Danny to Baz and back to Danny again like a nodding dog on a car parcel shelf. "Alibi?" she said faintly, clinging to the hope that life would imitate crime fiction, where alibis, like rules, were made to be broken.

"Obviously not," Danny chuckled. "Go on, Baz, put her out of her misery."

Baz's tight-lipped smile was closer to a sneer. "I was taking part in a panel of agents and publishers at a literary festival in Colchester at the time Penny died," she said smugly. "I travelled down by car with Elizabeth Root. She's an agent, her office is a few minutes' walk from here. We had a drink together, then did the panel—which, incidentally, was broadcast live by Oyster FM. All four of us on the panel went for a meal afterwards, and I didn't get back to London until nearly midnight. As I explained to the police the following day," she added with a vicious little smirk.

Danny moved into the office and laid a friendly arm across Lindsay's shoulder. "So you see, I'm afraid you're barking up the wrong tree with Baz. Whoever killed Penny, it was nothing to do with Monarch Press."

Lindsay edged away from Danny's arm, making the excuse of standing up and moving towards the door. "Just because Baz seems to be off the hook, it doesn't mean Monarch is in the clear," she said in an attempt at a defiant face-saver.

Danny opened his mouth but before he could say anything, Baz butted in. "She's got the book," she said urgently.

He looked astonished. "You managed to track it down?" he said. "But that's . . . that's amazing. Wonderful. How soon can you let us have it?"

"It's not up to me to let you have anything," Lindsay said stubbornly. "It's up to Meredith. She inherits everything from Penny. She might not want you to have it."

"She's got to, I'm afraid," Danny King said, his patronising tone setting Lindsay's hackles on full-scale bullshit alert. "Penny signed a contract. She'd been paid the first chunk of a very substantial advance. The biggest we've ever paid, as a matter of fact. That manuscript belongs to us."

Lindsay shook her head. "Not if Meredith decides to repay the advance," she pointed out as she sailed out of the office, head held high.

The satisfaction of her parting shot lasted for as long as it took her to cross the rapt editorial floor and reach the street. Never had she been more grateful to breathe the fumid air of a steamy London morning. Without hesitating or allowing herself to think about what she'd just experienced, Lindsay strode across the supermarket car park and into their blissfully air-conditioned cafeteria, where she found a quiet corner to drink her mineral water and regroup.

She had been so certain that Baz had killed Penny. Ever since Sophie had passed on the information about the changes to the latest draft, she'd been running the film in her head of Penny inviting Baz to her flat, maybe even for a showdown over Meredith; of Baz arriving with her bottles of wheat beer; then of the murderous attack that had left Penny bleeding to death somewhere as prosaic as an Islington kitchen.

But she'd been wrong. Completely, utterly wrong. Her first serious suspect, Catriona Polson, had been stripped of motive.

Now Baz Burton had been revealed as devoid of opportunity. Of the limited group of suspects she'd started with, only Meredith remained. And since she'd known from the start that while Meredith might have killed Penny in a moment of passion, so carefully staged a crime was beyond her, Lindsay was left with no one in the frame.

There was nothing for her to do now except admit to Meredith that she was utterly defeated by the mystery of Penny's death. With a sigh that turned heads at nearby tables, Lindsay acknowledged to herself that she had failed not only Meredith but also Penny. Although her mind knew it for an over-reaction, her heart comprehended it as a betrayal of a friendship that had often sustained Lindsay when she needed it most. To admit that failure to Meredith of all people would be one of the hardest things she had ever faced. Leaving most of her drink untouched, Lindsay walked out into the sunshine and headed for the tube station.

She caught Meredith coming back from buying the newspapers. "At least they've lost interest in me right now. Kinda late, though," Meredith had said as they went up in the lift. She had visibly lost weight even in the short time since Lindsay had last seen her. Her eyes lurked at the bottom of darkly shadowed sockets and her cheekbones seemed on the point of bursting through her taut skin.

"When did you eat last?" Lindsay had asked while she watched Meredith make them coffee.

"I went out for a pizza last night," Meredith said. "I managed to get some down. But it's hard to eat. I feel like I've got a rock lodged in my throat." Lindsay's heart went out to her, and she reached out impulsively to hug her friend. But this time, Meredith's grief didn't burst forth like an undammed stream. She sighed deeply, but her hand mirrored Lindsay's, each stroking the other's back in mutual sympathy. "When you love somebody and you commit yourself to sharing her life, you can't help imagining what it would be like if she died," she said softly. "Only nothing you imagine ever prepares you for the reality."

"I know," was all Lindsay could manage. They held on to each other until the urgent spluttering of the coffee pot forced them apart. Then, sitting with Meredith in the stuffy gloom of the flat, Lindsay reviewed what she had done in the previous couple of days. "I've hit a dead end," Lindsay confessed finally. "I really don't have any idea what to pursue."

Meredith nodded sadly. "I guess it was a long shot, bringing you over here. But don't think I don't appreciate it. There is one other thing you could do for me, though," she added, almost as an afterthought.

"Sure, if I can."

"Leave me a copy of *Heart of Glass*. I think it would be good for me to see the last thing she was working on. I also need to decide if it's possible for another person to finish what she'd started."

Lindsay rooted in her backpack and came up with the floppy disks on which she'd made back-up copies of the files Sophie had e-mailed to her. "There you go," she said, passing them across. "I've not got the final draft yet, but I should have it some time this evening. Are you online here?"

Meredith gestured with her thumb towards a repro Regency table where a laptop sat incongruously. "Sure. Did you want to e-mail it to me? You've got my address, yeah?"

"Soon as I've got it, I'll shunt it on to you."

"Who knows?" Meredith said wistfully. "There might be something there that'll give us a clue. Maybe even point you in a fresh direction."

Lindsay shrugged. "I wouldn't hold out too much hope. But if there is anything there, you can rest assured I'll be on to it like a rat up a drain." She finished her coffee and got to her feet. "I've got to go now, Meredith. I've got a bit of business to sort out for Helen. But I'll be in touch."

Out in the sunshine again, Lindsay sought out the shade of the plane trees that lined the street. She could escape the merciless heat, but there was no escaping the overwhelming guilt she felt at her failure to exonerate Meredith. She'd blown any attempt to place the blame for Penny's death at someone else's door; she hadn't even managed to come up with any concrete evidence that would clear her friend. And her ridiculous antics with Derek Knight meant she didn't dare to return to Islington to question the neighbours on the off chance that someone had seen something that would cast doubt on the police's seeming conviction that in Meredith they had found the killer.

No matter how she cut it, she couldn't see any way forward. To someone as stubborn as Lindsay, it was a bitter blow. But she was no quitter. If she couldn't go forward, maybe she could go backwards. As soon as Sophie managed to snatch a moment to send her Penny's final draft, Lindsay decided, it was time to start working in a completely different direction.

Just after seven, Lindsay faced Helen across Stella's desk, the terminal in front of her switched on, with Lindsay logged in as a superuser. "Okay," she said. "This is how it goes. Companies like Watergaw need to pay kickbacks and bribes if they're going to operate in certain countries. Traditionally, the Inland Revenue have taken the view that, while payments like these aren't strictly tax-deductible, if they go through the balance sheet as commissions paid to third parties, they'll turn a blind eye and allow the company to offset them against their profits. However, a couple of years ago they announced they weren't going to allow that any more. In practice, nothing has changed, it's just that the Revenue have taken a position that means they keep their hands clean. And every now and again, they'll do somebody, just to keep everybody else on their toes."

"Yeah, yeah, I know all that," Helen said impatiently. "I still don't see how you're going to use it to nail Guy and Stella. We're a minnow compared to the multinationals that get away with it every day of the week."

"Bear with me," Lindsay said. "This is where it starts to get interesting. There are two separate issues that make it possible to create a scenario that looks very unpleasant for Guy and Stella. First, you have to consider why the tax authorities have been prepared to look the other way. Why do you think that might be?"

Helen shrugged. "Because the companies involved go out there to make a tasty profit? And if the taxman stopped them paying bribes, their nice healthy profits wouldn't be there to be taxed in the first place?"

"More or less. Traditionally, it's been the manufacturing and service sectors that have benefited from this selective blindness. That's because the Revenue are perfectly well aware that if our companies don't win contracts, they go to our competitors in Europe and America and, increasingly, on the Pacific Rim. So not only do we lose taxable profits, we ultimately lose more jobs. Which is not something this government can afford."

Helen nodded, on familiar ground. "Even if it means turning us into the Taiwan of Europe, outside the Social Chapter and without a single employment right among us."

"So in those terms, technically what you've been doing at Watergaw falls into a grey area. It's not the kind of fraud that gets the taxman too excited. It's not like some companies, where they set up a dummy outfit in a tax haven and pay the commissions through that," Lindsay added.

"What's wrong with that?"

"In itself, nothing. But in practice, what usually happens is that for every ten dollars that goes out in bribes, a couple go into a separate numbered bank account for the company's directors. So they can pay themselves a tasty tax-free bonus for being clever enough to bribe their clients."

Helen shook her head. "You know, the sheer deviousness of financial crooks never ceases to amaze me. But this still doesn't explain how you're going to drop Guy and Stella in it."

Lindsay sighed. It wasn't as if she really understood all the ins and outs herself, only the bare bones on which Ellie had put sufficient flesh for her to understand what she had to do. Explaining it to Helen was turning out to be more difficult than she had anticipated. Still, it was good experience for getting it straight in her own mind before she tried to put the theory into practise. "Watergaw isn't a manufacturer, in the sense of making something for export. It's not a service company in the sense of earning money for Britain by selling insurance or financial services abroad. The bribes you've paid have been handed over to make your filming run smoothly, yeah?"

"Of course. You'd never believe some of the things you have to hand out the readies for. I've paid people to muzzle their goats so they wouldn't bleat at a crucial moment, I've paid yobs to let actors walk down their street without them mooning in the background, I've paid traffic cops not to give parking tickets to film units. I once bought fried-chicken dinners for an entire African village and laid on the coaches to take them to and from the fast-food stall." Helen leaned back in her chair with the air of a woman who has only just opened the doors on her stock of anecdotes.

"Exactly," Lindsay said hastily. "And what would happen if you hadn't paid those bribes?"

Helen frowned. "We wouldn't have got the films made."

"And would people have lost their jobs if you hadn't been able to make those films?"

"Well, probably, if we'd gone out there and then not been in a position to film."

"But if you'd known in advance that you'd be penalised for paying kickbacks, you'd have been crazy to contemplate making those films, right?"

Helen frowned, unable to see where Lindsay was heading. "Right. So we'd have made other films instead. Films set over here. Or in developed countries where the bribe culture is more or less dead."

"My point exactly," Lindsay said triumphantly. "For manufacturers, the paying of bribes is a *necessary* business expense or else they go to the wall. For you, it's a luxury. You could conceivably make other films that would equally ensure your continued success. So if someone grassed you up to the taxman, you'd be a perfect case to use to trumpet to the world that this government is encouraging the Inland Revenue to clamp down on corruption."

Helen looked gobsmacked. "You are fucking wicked," she said admiringly.

"You've only heard the half of it. Customs and Excise have never really gone along with the Revenue on this one. Their view has always been that if there's anything in the VAT accounts that looks dodgy, they'll come down like a ton of bricks. Mostly, foreign kickbacks don't have any impact on the amount of VAT a company's due to pay. But there are circumstances where they do—like if you've disguised a bribe as a payment for goods or services and you've paid it to a company with a UK subsidiary. Would there be anything like that in these accounts?"

"Oh, yeah," Helen said eagerly. "I can show you, if you like." She pulled the monitor towards her so she could see the screen. Lindsay passed the keyboard across and Helen moved expertly through a set of accounts till she found what she was looking for. "We keep the accounts for each project totally separate," she said as she moved the cursor down a list of payments. "This is *Thirty/Three*, Guy and Stella's little honeymoon on the subcontinent. There, that's what I'm looking for. Canopus Islamabad." She double clicked on the file. A window popped open detailing dates and amounts of payments. "We hire our lighting from them. We pay them in the UK, with a hefty slice on top of the actual hiring charge."

"Perfect," Lindsay said softly. "Now I need you to show me the way round your accounts software."

"You're not going to alter them, are you?" Helen asked, looking aghast.

"Nothing that crude," Lindsay said. "I just want to get familiar with the ins and outs of what was paid, when it was paid and who got the cash. Then I can get to work."

"So what are you going to do?" Helen nagged.

"I'm going to plant some files in Stella's personal desk. And some in Guy's. I can't tell you the details, because I don't know what they are yet."

"Are you sure you know what you're doing?" Helen asked, worry replacing fury for the first time since Lindsay had revealed Stella and Guy's racket to her.

"Sort of. Where I don't, I know a woman who does. And she's only a phone call away. Helen, you've got to trust me on this. Unless you've got any better ideas, I'm your best chance of getting that pair out of your life for good."

Helen fiddled with a strand of hair, a strangely coy gesture from a woman normally so up front she made Roseanne look demure. "I just don't want you getting in too deep," she said.

"I think I can look after myself," Lindsay said gruffly. "Now, are you going to show me how this bloody software works, or do I have to work it out for myself?"

An hour later, Helen reluctantly left. She had given Lindsay a swift tutorial in both the accounts and the word-processing packages that Watergaw used as standard on their network of computers. Then Lindsay had insisted she go home. "It's better you don't see how I do this," she said. "That way you can't let anything slip."

Left to her own devices, Lindsay spent a couple of hours gaining a thorough grasp of the payments that had been made as part of the production budget of *Thirty/Three*, taking notes

as she went. Then, exploiting her superuser status, she changed
the computer's internal date stamp so that it read a few days after
Stella had joined the company. Next she entered Guy's private
directory and created a memo, dated to correspond with the
new internal date on the computer. The long document outlined
for Stella's benefit a series of fraudulent practices which "Guy"
explained were standard. It also contained a caveat warning
Stella not to discuss these procedures with Helen. "*Our partner,*"
Lindsay typed, "*has rather old-fashioned views on fiscal matters. I
have tried in the past to explain to her how the real world works, but
her response hasn't encouraged me. However, she doesn't have enough
experience of commercial matters to unravel the accounts I prepare for
her. When we set up the company, I promised her faithfully I would
be fiscally prudent, and she took that to mean I'd stick to the letter of
the law. You've no idea how liberating it is to be working with someone
like you, who understands the realities. It's a jungle out there, and we
need to use whatever weapons come to hand so we can survive. Besides,
everybody rips off the taxman and the VATman. It's the national sport.*"

Then, changing the internal date to the following day, she
moved to Stella's personal desk and produced a second memo,
acknowledging Guy's to her and suggesting a couple of dodgy
wrinkles of her own. Next, she changed the computer's date
to that of a couple of weeks after the end of filming on *Thirty/
Three.* With constant reference to her notes, she constructed a
long memo purporting to come from Stella to Guy, explaining in
detail the subterfuges she had employed to disguise the crooked
payments. It finished with a contemptuous reference to Helen,
looking forward to a time when she and Guy could dump her
from the partnership. Finally, after changing the internal date on
the computer to the correct one, she printed out all three memos.

It took a little longer to make them look appropriately
aged. A coffee mug ring here, a smudge of cigarette ash there.
Here a curl at the corner, there a crease. Her *pièce de résistance,*
Lindsay felt, was to copy a doodle she saw replicated a dozen
times on Stella's scratch pad, a five-pointed star with the central

pentagon inked in. Then she put Guy's into Stella's desk drawer, towards the bottom of the pile of papers in there. She walked down the dim corridor to Guy's office, where she deposited the fake memos from Stella among a stack of papers in a deep tray marked "To be filed when hell freezes over."

Back at the computer, she used the system's in-built retrieval system to recapture the forged EU letter about Helen's grant which Stella had deleted the previous evening in her and Guy's attempts to cover their tracks. Like most people, she had once thought deleting something was enough to erase it from the system forever. Thanks to Meredith's teaching, Lindsay now knew different.

Finally, she made a lengthy call. Just after midnight, Lindsay put the phone down. She had run the final details past Ellie, and been assured that what she had put in place was the perfect frame that would cheerfully convince any investigator from Customs and Excise or the Inland Revenue. One of the knock-on effects of new technology that usually worried her was how easy it had become to frame the innocent. It made a pleasant change to exploit it against the guilty. She stretched her back, thrusting her arms into the air and yawning like a basking lioness. The sooner she got back to a routine where she could run and work out, the better she'd feel.

She switched off the computer and gathered her papers together, making sure she had left only the materials she wanted the investigators to unearth all by themselves. Then she let herself out of Stella's office and headed for the exit. There, she consulted the note Helen had given her and set the alarm as she opened the door to the car park. As Watergaw's door closed behind her with a sharp click, Lindsay was uneasily aware of how dark the car park was. She could have sworn she'd previously noticed security lights mounted on the side of the building, angled to shine across the car park, but now the only light came from the distant streetlights, reduced even further by the bulk of the Watergaw building.

Swallowing her apprehension, Lindsay walked boldly along the side of the building to the place where she'd left her car. Suddenly she was aware of glass crunching under her feet and she stooped to look more closely. As she registered the broken glass of the security lights, she heard the soft footfall of running trainers on asphalt. Startled, Lindsay jumped up and swung round to face the direction of the sound. As she turned, she saw outlined against the pale orange of the sodium streetlights the unmistakable shape of a baseball bat. It was heading straight towards her as if she was the pitcher's finest curve ball.

18

Using the momentum she'd gained straightening up from her crouch, Lindsay pushed off from the ground and veered out of the way of the bat, stumbling backwards as her assailant continued towards her, drawn forward by the follow-through of that first vicious swipe. Her feet scrabbled against the asphalt of the car park, the grip of leather sandals puny in comparison with her attacker's trainers. She could make out only the vague outline of a medium-sized frame with a head sleek as a seal, but that was enough to see that already the shoulders were tensing to lift the bat in a second back-swing, aimed straight at her head.

With no time even to think, Lindsay acted on pure instinct. As he swung the bat from above his left shoulder, she leapt forward and to the side, so that she undercut the arc of the blow. Then, hitting the ground running, suddenly she was past him, sprinting for the street with a turn of speed she had no idea she possessed. Faster than she'd ever run along the beach at Half Moon Bay, she headed across the car park at the angle that would bring her to the street most quickly.

Her blood thudding in her ears and her own breathing sounding loud as a steam engine to her heightened senses, Lindsay pounded the asphalt, aiming for the light. So obsessed was she with reaching the relative safety of a street with traffic and other human beings that she completely failed to register the low wall that bordered Watergaw's unit until it was too late. Like a badly prepared showjumper, she tried to adjust her stride to take the wall, but mistimed it completely.

The sandal on her trailing leg caught the top of the foot-high wall, catapulting Lindsay into a scrappy somersault. She flew over the pavement, landing in an awkward sprawl a yard into the road. White light bathed her as a taxi's brakes screeched in a screaming swerve, bringing it to a juddering halt in a stutter of diesel engine mere inches from where she lay groaning in the road.

The taxi driver jumped out and ran round to the front of the cab, his "What the fuck?" strangled at birth when Lindsay lifted a face that was a Janus mask half blood, half green-tinged flesh. "Jesus Christ," he gasped instead.

Lindsay pushed herself on to her knees, then, using the cab's radiator as a prop, to her feet. Casting a desperate glance behind her that seemed surprisingly agonising, she stuttered, "A bloke. With a baseball bat. Chasing me."

"I can't see nobody, love," the cabbie said. "Whoever he was, he must have legged it when he saw you flying through the air with the greatest of ease. He's gone, love. You're all right." He reached out a hand. "Well, when I say all right . . . maybe we should get you to hospital."

Lindsay shook her head. Again pain shot along her jaw. But she couldn't work out why. She must have scraped her face on the asphalt when she hit the ground. Bruises and a nasty graze, that's what it would be. "I'm just a bit bruised. Nothing broken. I'll be fine," she said, her voice clear with the disengaged calm of deep shock.

The cabbie put a firm arm round her shoulder. "Hospital, love. You can't see what I can see. You must have hit a bit of broken glass in the road. Look, you can see it shining there. A broken milk bottle, it looks like. Whatever, that face of yours is gonna need more than an Elastoplast, believe me."

Lindsay frowned, bewildered. What was he talking about? She put her hand up to the side of her neck that seemed to be causing her most pain. There was something warm and wet all over her jawline. Along the bone, it didn't feel like skin. It felt like raw meat. And it hurt. As she took her hand away and saw it was covered in blood, she started to shake. It began as a slight quiver, but by the time the cabbie had virtually carried her into the back of his taxi, she was shaking from top to toe like someone on the edge of hypothermia, her teeth chattering and her hands twitching.

All the way to the Royal Free's casualty department, the cabbie talked reassuringly to her. He talked about his wife and his two teenage daughters, about their forthcoming holiday in Turkey, about his hobby, angling, and how it wasn't a hardship to work nights on account of the rubbish they put on the telly. And all Lindsay could think about was how near she'd come to something far worse than whatever it was that had happened to her.

By the time they reached the hospital, the worst of the shakes were behind her and she could just about manage to climb out of the taxi unaided. The cabbie took a clean, soft handkerchief out of a satchel on the floor by the driver's seat and folded it into a long pad. "You just hold that against it," he said, sounding nervous as he demonstrated what he meant. "It'll stop the flow of blood." Numb now, she did as she was told. He helped her out and led her into the reception area, where a man who looked less healthy than she felt started to take her details. When she turned to thank her rescuer, he was gone.

"I didn't even pay the fare," she said vaguely to the receptionist, who looked blankly at her and said, "GP?"

Unable to bear the complication of explaining that she lived in America, Lindsay gave the name of the woman who had been her doctor seven years before, when she'd lived with Cordelia in Highbury. It seemed to satisfy the receptionist. It clearly wasn't his job to care why she was giving an address in

west London and a GP in north London. Telling her to take a
seat, the receptionist turned back to stare at his computer screen.

Feeling more disorientated than jet lag had ever left her,
Lindsay walked slowly towards a bank of pay phones on the far
wall. Her legs felt out of her control, as if her knees had been
replaced with some flexible rubbery solid which left her out of
touch with her feet. Every step was tentative, in case the place
where her knees used to be suddenly rebelled and deposited her
in a crumpled, helpless heap on the floor. But she made it to the
phone without incident.

By some miracle, she still had her backpack. Awkward fingers fumbled some change out of her wallet and she punched in
Helen's number. It rang five or six times without reply, then the
answering machine clicked in. Lindsay leaned against the wall
and waited for Helen to stop giving her instructions. She couldn't
understand why no one was picking up the phone. She knew it
was late, but there was an extension in the bedroom, right next
to Helen's bed. They couldn't sleep through this, could they?

The machine beeped and Lindsay said, "Helen? Kirsten? Is
anybody there? Can you pick up? It's Lindsay? Hello? . . ." She
waited for a moment, but no one answered. She sighed. "Bit
of a problem. Um . . . I'm at the Royal Free. In casualty. Had a
bit of an accident. Nothing to worry about, but if you get this
message, can you come? I'll . . . I'll speak to you later," she ended
up, unable to think straight.

She replaced the receiver and wobbled over to the nearest
vacant chair. She slumped into it and looked around vaguely.
There seemed to be a lot of people here, considering it was nearly
one in the morning. They mostly looked stunned with pain
or indifference, especially those who were only accompanying
someone more obviously damaged. Lindsay closed her eyes and
sighed. Where could Helen and Kirsten be? Helen hadn't said
anything about plans for the evening, and she'd have been too
desperate to hear Lindsay's report on her mission to consider
going out on the spur of the moment. She couldn't believe they'd

turned off the phones and gone to bed either. Helen's eagerness to hear that Stella and Guy had been stitched up would never have allowed her to go to sleep. Besides, Helen would be conscious of the possibility that things might go wrong. She wouldn't leave Lindsay hanging on the telephone needing help.

It was a mystery, but right then it seemed to Lindsay about as intractable as Penny Varnavides' murder. Before she could worry about it too much, she felt a hand on her shoulder. She opened her eyes to see a nurse's uniform containing a stocky redhead who looked about twelve years old. "I'm the triage nurse," she chirped cheerily in a harsh Belfast brogue. "If you'd like to come through to a cubicle, I can assess your injuries there."

Lindsay got to her feet and followed the nurse past the reception desk and into a curtained cubicle. "Up we get," the nurse said, helping her on to an examination table and gently removing hand and handkerchief pad from Lindsay's now throbbing jaw. "My, we have been in the wars, haven't we? That's some mess you've got yourself into there. Never mind, we'll soon have you cleaned up and good as new." Lindsay could see why the woman had become a nurse; with that degree of insensitive exuberance, she wouldn't dare work with the able-bodied and expect to live.

The next hour was a blur. No, she hadn't lost consciousness. No, her shoulder and knee didn't hurt any more than she'd expect from grazed skin. Yes, she could see how many fingers the doctor was holding up. No, she wasn't allergic to penicillin. Eventually, a soft-voiced Asian man with cool, gentle hands cleaned up her face, stitched the long cut that sliced up the line of her jaw, reassured her that the scar would be virtually invisible and fetched her a cup of tea. As she struggled to swallow it without losing half out of the side of her mouth that felt numb, Lindsay heard a familiar voice.

"I told you, soft lad, we're the nearest she's got to family, that's why she phoned us to come and get her. How else do you think we knew to come here?" Helen announced. A man's voice mumbled something in response. "Cubicle three? Right, come on, girls."

"Girls?" thought Lindsay, vaguely wondering who else Helen had in tow. She didn't have to wonder for long. The curtain parted and Lindsay had her second shock in the space of a couple of hours. "Sophie?" she said, not entirely certain whether she was hallucinating. "Is it really you?"

Sophie crossed the cubicle in two strides and gripped Lindsay's shoulders, her expression a mixture of relief and affectionate exasperation. "What am I going to do with you? I turn my back for five minutes, and look at you!"

Lindsay felt her eyes film over with tears. "This is a nice surprise," she said, her voice shaky. "You'll have to forgive me if I don't kiss you just yet."

Sophie crouched down and stared intently at her lover's battered face. "Whoever stitched you did a good job. You'll not have much of a scar."

Lindsay dropped her head so it rested on Sophie's shoulder. "I'm so pleased to see you," she said. "How come you're here?"

"I managed to get away from work a few days early. The housesitter was delirious to swap her parents for Mutton this soon. Changing the flights was slightly more difficult. But I missed you, and besides, I didn't like the idea of you chasing a killer on your own. Looks as if I was right to be worried, doesn't it?"

"I don't think it was anything to do with Penny," Lindsay sighed. "Can we get out of here now? You know how much I like hospitals."

"Sure," Sophie said, gently stroking Lindsay's head.

"Oh, my God, look at the state of you. This is all my fault! What happened? Was it Guy or was it Stella?" Helen demanded, unable to contain herself a moment longer.

"Later, Helen," Sophie said. She kissed the top of Lindsay's head and tenderly extricated herself from her lover's embrace. "Go and find someone in authority, tell them we're taking her home."

Before Helen could leave, a white-coated doctor whom Lindsay had a dim recollection of seeing earlier appeared at Kirsten's shoulder. "What's going on here?" he demanded. "This patient has had a head injury. The last thing she needs is crowds of people around her. I could hear the shouting half-way down the corridor." Helen had the grace to look embarrassed.

"Doctor," Sophie said. "The very person I wanted to see. We're taking Ms Gordon home now."

"Oh, no, you're not," he said obstinately. "Ms Gordon is my patient and we're keeping her in overnight for observation. It's standard procedure in cases of head trauma."

Sophie ran a hand through her silver curls. "I'm a doctor myself. I know what the symptoms of concussion look like, I know the procedures. I'm prepared to take responsibility for her." She pulled her wallet out of the back pocket of her jeans and gave him a card that announced she was Dr Sophie Hartley, consultant obstetrician and gynaecologist of the Grafton Clinic, San Francisco. He looked slightly dazed as he read it, then looked at this tall woman wearing a T-shirt that read "Netheads do IT better." Sophie grinned disarmingly. "So, we'll be leaving shortly," she said with all the authority of half a dozen years as a consultant.

"But I've managed to get her a bed," the hospital doctor protested. "Have you any idea how hard that is these days?"

"Looking at the patient, I'm sure you've done a really good job," Sophie said, reassuring without patronising. "Look at it this way—now you know there's a bed available for one of your other patients."

He muttered something under his breath, then said, "On your head be it."

Within ten minutes, Lindsay and Sophie were settled in the back of Helen's car, with Kirsten driving so Helen could turn round in her seat and demand information. "So what happened?" she asked again.

"Helen," Sophie warned. "Not now."

"No, it's okay," Lindsay said. Either Sophie's arrival or the hospital tea seemed to have revived her. Apart from the ache in her shoulder and leg and twinges penetrating the local anaesthetic in her face, she felt almost alert. "My brain seems to have reconnected with the rest of me."

"See?" Helen said triumphantly. "Call yourself a doctor, Hartley?"

Sophie smiled. "You have your medical adviser's permission to tell her to shut up any time you want," she told Lindsay, pulling her closer. "To be honest, I'm curious myself. Helen met me at Heathrow and told me you were working alone at her office, where nothing bad could possibly happen. The next thing I know is you look like Mike Tyson's speed bag."

"Watch who you're calling a bag," Lindsay said. "The short answer is that I don't really know what happened. I'd done everything I had to do at Watergaw, so I set the alarm and locked up. The security lights weren't on, so it was really dark. I was walking to my car and I stood on some glass. I bent down to see if I could see what it was, then I heard these footsteps running behind me. I jumped up and turned round just in time to get out of the way of some maniac with a baseball bat. I managed to dodge him, but I was concentrating so hard on getting away that I didn't see the wall until it was too late." For Sophie's benefit, she added, "There's this little wall runs along the frontage of Watergaw, and I took a header over it. Unfortunately, I came down on a bit of broken glass. Hence the duelling scar."

"It sounds like you would have come off a lot worse if you'd stuck around," Kirsten commented.

"Trust a journalist to look on the bright side," Helen said. "So, did you see who it was doing the Joe DiMaggio impersonation? Was it Guy? Or even Stella?"

Lindsay sighed. "I don't think it was Stella. I couldn't see much except a silhouette, and it looked like a male body shape. I don't think he was as tall as Guy, but I couldn't swear to it.

I think he was wearing a stocking over his head as well. I was giving it some thought back in the hospital. At first I couldn't work out why his head was such a neat shape, then I realised what he must have done."

"It must have been Guy," Helen said. "He knows me well enough to realise I wouldn't just lie down and die after what he's done to me. He'll have left that bitch Stella in charge of the night shoot, and he'll have come back to stake out the offices. The bastard!"

"It certainly sounds a possibility," Sophie said. "But what about your murder investigation? Isn't it possible that someone connected with that has been tailing you, waiting for an opportunity to strike?"

Lindsay sighed. "It's not very likely, given that I seem to have hit a brick wall. Unless there's something in Penny's last draft to point me in a different direction, I'm stuck. I can no more prove Meredith innocent than I can show someone else is guilty. Helen's probably right. Most likely it was Guy."

"You've got to go to the police," Helen said firmly.

"No way. That's the very last thing I should do," Lindsay said wearily.

"You can't let him away with this," Kirsten chipped in as she braked for a pedestrian crossing. "He could try again, and next time he might really hurt somebody."

"It's not worth it. He didn't actually hit me. All this," she said, fluttering her fingers in the direction of her face, "was incidental. I doubt he'd even get a custodial sentence. No, the revenge I've got lined up for Guy and Stella is going to hurt them a lot more than a something or nothing charge in a magistrates' court. And to make it work, the last thing we want to be doing is explaining why I was in Watergaw's car park the wrong side of midnight."

"This sounds devious," Sophie commented.

"You haven't heard the half of it," Helen said ominously.

"And you don't want to, either," Kirsten chipped in. "I had it over dinner and then all the way to Heathrow. Believe me, Sophie, this is one case where ignorance is bliss."

"I'll tell you later, Soph. Suffice it to say, Guy turned out to be a real shyster, so I've been fitting him up good style," Lindsay said. "But I need to brief you now, Helen. If you go into my backpack, you'll find a document wallet with three printed memos in it." As Sophie passed the bag over and Helen unzipped it, Lindsay continued. "First thing in the morning, you go to your local VAT office and request an interview with an investigator. Failing that, you want the inspector who deals with Watergaw. You tell him you had been told that one of your staff had been using your computer to run their own business on the side, so you were doing a file audit. While you were in there, you found these memos in the private desks of your business partners."

Helen was skimming the documents as she listened. "Jesus!" she exploded. "This is dynamite. You don't take prisoners, do you?"

"And that was presumably written before your colleague tried to cave her head in," Sophie said drily. "Probably just as well. If she was framing him now, she'd not be satisfied with anything less than serial murder."

"Never mind all that," Lindsay said. "The important thing is that you stress that you knew nothing about all of this, and you want them hammered because you don't want your company destroyed. I know it's casting against type, but for once play the dumb broad," she added wryly.

"Oh, God," Helen groaned. "I should have known better."

"That," said Sophie, "is what they all say."

19

At first when she woke, Lindsay couldn't figure out where she was. She knew she wasn't at home, remembered she was staying with Helen, but the silence disorientated her. She couldn't recall ever waking into quiet in Helen's home. If it wasn't the radio, it was music, the volume pumped up till it threatened to explode. But there was nothing. Just the distant hum of traffic on Fulham Palace Road and the chatter of city sparrows from the open sash window. That and the pounding of her head, a throb so intense it seemed audible.

Something else was wrong, she realised, still not moving. She was alone. Her memory of the night before was trickling back from behind the barrier of drugged sleep and she knew she shouldn't have been waking alone. Sophie! Sophie was in England. She had been there with her when the hospital painkillers had finally carried her over into what felt like a coma. But where was she now?

Lindsay rolled over, making the mistake of turning on to the side where a row of stitches held her face together. "Shit," she exploded, squirming swiftly up the bed and into a sitting position. Sophie, sitting by the window in a basket chair, looked up from the book she was reading.

"If it hadn't been for the snoring, I'd have started to think you'd died," she said. "How are you feeling?"

Lindsay's face twitched as another worm of pain snaked down her jaw. "My face feels like it's wired for electric shock treatment and my body thinks it's been hit by a bus. My brain seems to have been connected to a bass drum machine and while I was sleeping, somebody stuffed my mouth with cotton wool, then left a dead reptile there for long enough to make my mouth taste of decaying lizard. Apart from that, I feel terrific," she grumbled.

Sophie smiled sympathetically, closing her book and crossing to the door. "I'll get you some coffee and a couple of painkillers."

"Great. But just some paracetamol or aspirin, not those industrial-strength ones the hospital gave me. I've decided I want to put the zombie lifestyle on hold until I'm actually dead."

"Wise move."

"What time is it anyway?" Lindsay asked, looking around vainly for her watch.

"You broke the glass on your watch when you did your swallow dive into the asphalt. It's ten to twelve," Sophie said on her way out.

"Ten to twelve? As in lunchtime? It can't be! You mean I slept through Helen greeting the world with Radio Four?"

"I made her leave the radio off," Sophie shouted from the stairs.

"I have died and gone to heaven," Lindsay said faintly. Kirsten could only get the radio turned off in the kitchen, but Sophie could still pitch Helen into starting the day without it altogether. If she'd had a suspicious mind, Lindsay would have wondered if there was still unfinished business between them. But six years with someone as dependable as Sophie had restored Lindsay's fractured trust in human nature. Helen's radio silence, she felt sure, was more to do with concern for her health than a desire to creep into Sophie's good books.

While she waited for Sophie to return, Lindsay shifted across the bed so she could see herself in the wardrobe mirror. Her right cheek was a patchwork of purple and blue-black bruising and brownish scabbed grazes, with her stitched scar running like a line of black thread up her jaw from the angle under her ear to a point level with the corner of her mouth. The bruising continued on her shoulder and down her right arm as far as the elbow, which sported an ugly scrape that still looked red and raw. As Sophie came back, Lindsay said, "Really, you have to wonder if I'd have been better off with the baseball bat."

"Not if you've ever worked a shift in casualty, you don't," Sophie said drily, depositing a mug of coffee on the bedside table and handing Lindsay two paracetamols and a glass of water. "Believe me, if that bat had connected, you wouldn't be lying here. You'd still be in the Royal Free. Either that or in a drawer in the mortuary."

"I don't think he was trying to kill me," Lindsay objected. "He gave up too easily. I think it was a warning."

"So you think Helen's right? That it was Guy?" Sophie asked.

"Who else? I've dead-ended on the murder inquiry, so I'm no threat to Penny's killer."

"But does the killer know that?" Sophie mused.

"If the killer is anybody I've met over the last few days, then they've seen me floundering around making a complete arse of myself," Lindsay said bitterly, then winced at the effort of swallowing the painkillers. "They're not going to feel threatened, they're going to be laughing their socks off. I've accused one person whose motive crumbled faster than an Oxo cube and another who had an alibi with thousands of witnesses. Well, hundreds. It was *local* radio, after all."

Sophie gave a conciliatory shrug. "Just a thought. So that leaves Guy. Funny, he never seemed like the violent type."

"People do ridiculous things when they feel threatened."

"Yeah, but . . ." Sophie frowned. "I thought they'd seen you and Helen off with your tails between your legs." She sat on the bed beside Lindsay, resting an arm on her lover's unhurt shoulder.

Lindsay cautiously drank some coffee. She closed her eyes as the rich flavour burst on her tongue and savoured the sensation of its warmth coursing down her throat. "Heaven," she murmured appreciatively. Then she opened her eyes and said, "Guy's known Helen a long time. He knows she's not the sort to give in easily. I wouldn't be at all surprised if he'd decided to keep an eye on us. It would also explain where he disappeared to when I got away. He didn't follow me to the street; the taxi driver said he couldn't see anybody. But Guy could easily have slipped back inside the Watergaw building. He'd have keys and he knows the alarm code."

"I suppose you're right. It is the logical answer," Sophie sighed.

Lindsay drained her coffee cup and presented it to Sophie. "I wouldn't mind another cup," she said, looking up from under her eyebrows.

"Cut out the pathos and you might just get lucky."

Lindsay forgot herself enough to smile, gasping as the pain kicked in again. "Just get me some more coffee, or I'll find somebody that knows how patients should really be treated," she growled.

Sophie chuckled. "Did they give you a charm bypass before I arrived last night? Okay, more coffee it is."

As she got off the bed, Lindsay said, "Be a pal and pass me my laptop. It's over there on the chest of drawers. And if you could dig out Penny's last disks, then I can get stuck into the stuff she was working on when she died."

Sophie shook her head. "No way. Not today, Lindsay. You need to rest and recover. Doctor's orders. Believe me, you'll know exactly what I mean as soon as you get up to go to the loo. You'll have legs like rubber and muscles that are stiffer than a sergeant-major's salute."

Lindsay scowled. "Look, I know my body's cream-crackered, but my brain is working just fine. I'm not an invalid.

It's not exactly going to strain me to hit the 'page down' key every few minutes, is it?"

Sophie smiled. Lindsay's irrepressible determination was one of the things she loved about her partner, but there were times when it slid inexorably into stubbornness. This looked like being one of them. Sophie walked across to the chest of drawers and picked up the laptop. Turning back, she noticed a look of triumph on Lindsay's face. "I meant what I said," Sophie told her, walking out of the room with the laptop under her arm. Ignoring the howl of frustrated fury behind her, she carried on downstairs and put it in one of the kitchen cupboards before pouring another cup out of the pot.

"I don't believe you just did that," Lindsay said, outraged, the moment Sophie walked back into the room. "I do not believe you just did that."

"One day is not going to make a blind bit of difference. If the cops were going to charge Meredith, they'd have done it by now," Sophie said mildly, holding out the fresh coffee. "Believe me, you'll feel so much better for it tomorrow, the day won't have been wasted."

"Huh," Lindsay snorted, grudgingly taking the mug. "So what am I supposed to do? Play I-Spy with you?"

"Relax. Read a book. Have a bath. Watch some TV."

"Boring." Sulky as a teenager, Lindsay glowered at Sophie.

"Okay. So tell me about the investigation, all the things you didn't go into over the phone. Two heads are supposed to be better than one."

"I thought I was supposed to be having a day off?" Lindsay grumbled. Sophie just stared her down. Eventually, Lindsay relented. "All right, sit down and I'll tell you all about it."

She'd got as far as Lauren's tale of being bribed by Penny to get into Monarch's offices when the phone rang. Sophie rolled off the bed and raced out of the room, calling, "It's probably Helen. She said she'd check in to see how you were."

At first, Lindsay could hear only a distant mumble from Sophie, then her voice grew clearer as she mounted the stairs, still talking into the cordless phone. ". . . quite a battering, so she's not in a fit state to do much . . . Yes, I appreciate that, and I know she'll want to know what's happened . . ." Sophie walked into the bedroom and held the phone out. "It's Meredith's solicitor. The police have taken her in for further questioning."

Lindsay grabbed the phone. "Hello? Ms Cusack?"

"Ms Gordon. I'm sorry to hear about your injuries. No permanent damage, I trust?" Geri Cusack asked, her creamy voice as rich as a pint of Guinness on a winter night.

"I suspect I'll have to forget the modelling career," Lindsay said drily. "But never mind me. What's this about Meredith?"

"The police hung on to her this morning when she reported in under the terms of her bail. I've just had them on the phone. I'm on my way there now." That explained the background noises on the line. She was talking on a car phone, Lindsay realised.

"Why have they pulled her in?" she asked.

"According to the custody sergeant, they've got a new witness. Danny King, the boss of Monarch Press?"

"A witness to what?" Lindsay demanded.

"It's something and nothing. He's given a statement saying he saw Meredith hanging around outside their premises the last time Penny was visiting. I'm sure it's nothing, but they're clutching at straws. Is there anything you've come up with I should know about?"

"As of now, I've got zilch," Lindsay said, her bitter tone revealing exactly who she blamed for that. "But hang on a minute," she added, puzzled. "How come it's taken till now for King to come forward with this statement?"

"I don't know. I agree it's odd." The line started crackling, the static like emery board on fingernails. "I'll tell you what," she shouted. "I'll call you back after I've spoken with Meredith."

"Thanks," Lindsay said. But the line was already dead, their conversation abruptly terminated. She looked up at Sophie and gave a lopsided smile. "What was that you said about one day not making any difference?"

"I have this funny feeling we're going to have to forget about the day off," Sophie sighed. "I'll get the laptop."

"Can't we print this stuff out?" Sophie complained after an hour of looking over Lindsay's shoulder at the laptop's tiny screen.

"I haven't got a lead that connects into Helen's printer," Lindsay explained.

"So let's just stick the floppy into Helen's PC and print from that."

Lindsay guffawed derisively. "Helen's PC came out of the ark. She hasn't upgraded since before you two split up."

Sophie groaned. "Wrong size of floppy disk?"

"Got it in one. We're stuck with the migraine master here."

With a sigh that made the mattress quiver, Sophie read on. "It's very different from the first draft."

"Mmm. It's better, too. More hard-edged, more economical with the language. I just can't get over how good it is," Lindsay said without taking her eyes from the screen. "One thing's for sure. Whoever tries to finish this has got a hell of a job on their hands."

They carried on reading in silence, Sophie swept away by her first close read of *Heart of Glass*, Lindsay marvelling at the improvements that fury and heartbreak had brought to her friend's novel. They were disturbed twice, once by Helen inquiring after Lindsay's health and revealing that, as she spoke, VAT inspectors were going through every piece of paper in Guy and Stella's office, every file in the computer, and Watergaw's accounts. "They're going to have to explain where that EU grant went as well," she said gleefully. "One of the inspectors stuck his head round the door half an hour ago to ask me about it. It turns out Stella was so sure of herself that she didn't erase the text of the forged letter from her personal section of the computer."

"I like it," Lindsay said, glad something she'd attempted had worked out. She didn't get long to bask in her success. Only minutes later, Geri Cusack had called back. Lindsay asked her to hold on while Sophie picked up the extension.

"Okay," she said when she heard the click and the line quality changed subtly, "here's the meat. They're holding Meredith while they 'develop their lines of inquiry' following Danny King's revelations. Apparently there's a supermarket opposite Monarch's offices and King's office overlooks it. He says he saw Meredith hanging around the car park, looking as if she was trying not to be conspicuous. She'd sit in one spot for a bit, then move and lean against a car, then move somewhere else again. This was when Penny made her last visit to Monarch."

Lindsay clenched her eyes shut. "This does not sound pretty," she said. "But how come it's taken him the best part of a week to 'remember' this?"

"He claims he didn't know it was Meredith," Geri said evenly.

"He didn't know it was Meredith? He's been publishing Penny for ten years and he didn't know Meredith?" Lindsay demanded. "Shit, I know they were in the closet, but I can't believe he never met Meredith. Baz knew her. How come Danny didn't?"

Geri sighed. "Meredith confirms she never actually met Danny. A couple of times, they were both at parties to celebrate Penny's books, but Meredith always kept a low profile."

"Even so, her pictures were all over the newspapers after her arrest. I don't see how he can have missed that," Lindsay protested.

"He says he only realised this morning. He claims Penny's editor was putting together the programme for a memorial service, and they were going through her photographs of Penny to choose which one they'd put on the front. Among the photographs was one of Meredith and Penny together. Danny immediately recognised the woman in the car park, he says." Geri's voice was crisp, the warmth gone like a winter's day when the sun sets.

"You don't believe him either," Lindsay said flatly.

"I can't think why he would lie," she replied obliquely.

"To protect the killer?" Lindsay said.

"Or if he is the killer," Sophie chipped in. "Maybe it's nothing that dramatic," Geri said.

"Maybe he just wants to keep the pot boiling so Penny Varnavides and Monarch Press stay in the news? You've met him—do you think he's capable of being that venal?"

Lindsay thought for a moment. Then she said, "He's a wide boy. I'd say it's more likely than him taking a risk to protect somebody. How long can they hang on to her before they have to charge her?"

"Murder's a serious arrestable offence," Geri said. "So they have an automatic thirty-six hours. But if they need an extension, I suspect they won't have too much trouble finding a friendly magistrate to grant it. Fugitive risk and all that. Look, I have to go now. If there's any development, I'll be sure and let you know."

"Thanks," Lindsay said dully. She heard the double click as Geri and Sophie both hung up. Lindsay ran a hand through unwashed hair that was already standing up in a halo of spikes round her head. She felt impotent, trapped as much by her inability to think of something to do as by her physical incapacity.

Sophie appeared in the doorway. "It doesn't sound good," she said glumly.

"So we'd better get on with *Heart of Glass*."

"It doesn't seem to be taking us much further forward," Sophie sighed, coming back to squat on the bed beside Lindsay.

"I know, but what else is there?" With a profound sigh, Lindsay picked up the laptop and started to read again.

It was early evening by the time they'd finished the revised draft of Penny's final work. And nothing had leapt out at either

Lindsay or Sophie to suggest motive or identity for her killer. Sophie stretched, thrusting her shoulders back and arching her spine, a soft groan escaping from her lips.

"See, I told you staying in bed was unhealthy," Lindsay teased. "Look at the state of you."

"I blame the airline seats," Sophie said, dotting a kiss on Lindsay's undamaged cheek and getting up. "I'm going downstairs to start some dinner for us all. Helen and Kirsten should be home in a couple of hours or so. You fancy pasta with a Provençale daube?"

"I fancy you, but my face hurts too much. Not to mention the crucial damage to upper arm and elbow . . ." Lindsay smiled sadly.

"Not the pathos again, please, spare me the pathos! Do you fancy coming downstairs now?"

"In a bit," Lindsay said. "There are some other files on here that I want to have a look at. Look, these ones that end. LET. They're probably letters. And these other ones. God knows what they are. Probably nothing to do with anything, but you never know. I might as well finish while I'm stuck here."

"Glutton for punishment," Sophie said, rumpling her lover's hair and pulling a face. "Perhaps a bath wouldn't be a bad idea later. Blood, sweat and tears is not a great recipe for hair care." She went downstairs and investigated cupboards, fridge and vegetable rack. Half an hour later, she was about to deglaze the caramelized onions with balsamic vinegar when she heard Lindsay's voice shouting urgently.

Hurrying to the bottom of the stairs, Sophie called, "What is it?"

"I said, I think I've found it," Lindsay yelled.

20

Lindsay pointed to the screen. "Look there," she said, indicating with the cursor what she wanted Sophie to pay attention to. "It wasn't the manuscript of *Heart of Glass* that the killer was after. It was the notes for the next one. 'Structure: five sections, alternate POV between Sam McQueen and Martha Denny: *The Invisible Man, The High Cost of Living, The Ghost Road, The Information, Crime and Punishment*,'" she read out. "One of the few pieces of paper left in the flat had those titles written on it. I thought it was a reading list when I first saw it, but she was obviously starting to think about a new novel. She was going to call each of the sections after a book."

Sophie nodded. "Yeah, so far so clear. But what's that got to do with Penny's death?"

Lindsay scrolled down further. "*Outline,*" Sophie read over her shoulder. "*Chicago??? NYC??? Sam McQueen: early thirties, Irish/Italian, third-generation respectable face of the Mob, has legitimate front business—???magazine publishing??? Hits on a way of cleaning up the lives of serious criminals. He turns his publishing house into a money laundry. Step one—makes Mob figures respectable; hires them as commissioning editors on huge salary. Every month, the company pays their salaries into offshore accounts, then the money comes back into their US-based accounts from the offshore bank. But what really happens is Sam's firm pays the money into an account in Sam's name offshore. And the 'employees' bring in their own dirty money from offshore into their domestic bank account, thus making dirty money look clean. Not only that, but they are legitimized in the eyes of the government—they pay taxes, they have Social Security numbers, they pay insurance, and they earn hugely inflated salaries because they are shit-hot editors—ho, ho, ho!"*

"My God," Sophie breathed. "That's bloody clever."

"You're not kidding. It gets better, though," Lindsay said drily, flicking the "page down" key to bring up a fresh screen.

"In order to pay these non-productive, fake employees, the company has to have a much higher turnover. They pretend to produce fake magazines, which are sent to outlets that are Mob fronts. Outlet claims to have sold, say, 100 copies of computer magazine per week, thus legitimately putting an extra $500 through their till. They pay Sam's company for the magazine at wholesale, say $250 a week. And so Sam has, on paper, a string of highly profitable magazines with a team of commissioning editors. Only nothing is real."

Sophie looked up and grinned admiringly. "That is wicked," she said. "That is so clever. Where on earth did Penny get an idea like that? I never heard her show any interest in that kind of scam, did you? She was always much more interested in the psychology and sociology of lawbreaking than the mechanics."

"Read on," Lindsay said, gesturing towards the screen. Sophie scrolled down and carried on reading. *"Sam's a keen yachtsman, likes racing yachts. One weekend, he's sailing and he meets a woman who's crewing on the yacht he's helming. Martha Denny. Twenty-nine, undercover Treasury agent working on anti-racketeering crackdown. She's infiltrated Sam's social world to try and gather information on Mob-related activities. He thinks she's a photographer, and he falls for her. Soon, they're lovers—Martha battles with conscience as government agent, but figures he's clean, his company is clearly legit. Then odd things start happening. He gets his magazines to commission her to take pics, so she's around the office a lot. She notices a lot of calls come in for people who are never there; messages get taken, and*

presumably passed on, but she never meets the guys attached to those
names. Then she finds out they all supposedly work on the mysterious
tenth floor—in a nine-story building???

"Martha's torn between love and duty. (Watch out—bit of a cliché?
Or is that just men?) Sam realising early on that she's got suspicions, but
he loves her too much to want to lose her, so at first he finds justifications
and then has to cope with idea of ??Martha dead?? or ??himself dead??
if his Mob connections find out he's harboring a viper in their midst.

"Resolution???"

Sophie took a deep breath and exhaled slowly. "Powerful
stuff," she said. "I mean, it's a great story by any standards, but
when you know what Penny could have done with it . . . it makes
her death seem so much more tragic. I know that's a terrible
thing to say, like saying some people's deaths are more significant
than others, but that's how I feel about Penny." She buried her
face in her hands, feeling the prickle of tears in her eyes.

Lindsay pushed the laptop to one side and put her arm
round her partner's shoulders, hugging her as close as her painful body would allow. "You're right to feel like that. Penny
was special. Most of us, if we make a difference to the lives
of the people we care about, we're doing well. But Penny
made a difference in a lot of people's lives, thousands of them
strangers. She'll go on doing that for a lot of people, but all
the books she still had to write won't get written now, and
we're all poorer for it."

Sophie leaned against Lindsay and smiled sadly. "I'm really
going to miss her. You know how it is with couples you spend a
lot of time with—you tend to pair off crosswise as well. I always
felt you were closer to Meredith than I was, and I was closer to
Penny. I talked about things with Penny that I didn't discuss
with many people."

Lindsay sighed. "You're right. I loved Penny, but she could
do my head in sometimes. When she got into her New Age
meaning of life stuff, it was time for me to go and hug a PC.
Or sneak off to Burger King with Meredith." They sat together

in companionable silence for a moment, each busy with their own memories.

Then Sophie remembered what she'd come upstairs for. "You said this was it, the message that explained why Penny had to die. I don't understand. Are you saying it was a Mafia hit?"

"There's more than one kind of organised crime," she said. "Look at all the clues in the text. Who published Penny's novels? Monarch Press, owned by Danny King. Doesn't that sound a lot like Sam McQueen?"

"That's a bit thin," Sophie protested.

"Is it? Let's not forget that Danny King is one genera-tion away from the old-fashioned East End, where organised crime flourished. It didn't die just because they put the Krays behind bars. It's still going on. The gangland families are just as powerful as they ever were. More so, probably. They've spread out into Essex and branched out into drugs, but they're still basically the same mobs who have run London since Jack the Ripper was pulling the wings off flies. Just say, for the sake of argument, that Danny didn't use his pools winnings to set up Monarch—what if he used dirty money from friends of the family to get the business up and running and turning a legitimate profit?"

Sophie looked sceptical. "Isn't this all a bit far-fetched, Lindsay? We're talking a London publishing house, not a New York casino."

"You think publishers can't be crooks too?"

"Not like this, no. It sounds like a bad gangster movie script."

"This isn't a gangster movie, it's a hi-tech thriller," Lindsay replied, her voice bitter and sharp. "One of those ones where somebody gets burned because they pick up too many pieces of the jigsaw by accident and suddenly they're looking at the whole picture. That's what happened to Penny."

"But how? Penny wasn't an undercover FBI agent. She was just an ordinary writer."

"She was an observer," Lindsay pointed out. "Penny was shrewd and sharp when it came to watching people. That's why her psychology was always so spot on, why her characters felt so real. Think about it. All those afternoons she spent at the mall or the bowling alley, hanging out, watching the teenagers, listening to them, absorbing everything about their culture. And she had that uncanny skill for identifying what was a nine-day wonder and what was a genuine trend that would still have resonance for her readers five or ten years down the road. You mean to tell me that if the jigsaw pieces were there for the grabbing, Penny wouldn't have gone for them with both hands?"

Sophie disentangled herself from Lindsay's encircling arm and got up, fanning herself with her hand. "Nothing personal, I was just overheating. I can't believe this weather, it's hotter than at home." She sat down by the open window, trying to convince herself there was a breeze. "So what were these jigsaw pieces you reckon Penny picked up on?"

"The phone messages. When I read that in her synopsis, I knew exactly what she meant. I didn't really register it at the time, but both times I've been at Monarch, Lauren the receptionist has dealt with phone calls a bit strangely. Some are totally routine—'Hold the line, I'll see if she's free,' 'Hold the line, I'll put you through to her secretary,' that sort of thing. But there were others where she said straight off, 'I'm sorry, he's not here, can I take a message?' Not, 'Let me see if he's available.' Or, 'He'll be in later, can I get him to call you?' Or, 'Would you like to speak to his secretary?' Just a flat offer to take a message. But if Danny King's operating a ghost-employee scam, that would be exactly what would happen!" Lindsay's voice was excited, her eyes sparkling for the first time since Sophie had arrived in the UK.

Sophie frowned. "Okay, I grant you it makes a certain kind of sense if you reason it backwards. But how did Penny get from noticing a peculiarity in the receptionist's phone habits to working out the whole ghost-employee scam? I mean, you heard the same thing and it meant nothing suspicious to you until you understood what was really going on."

Lindsay shrugged, then glanced at the bedside clock. "I don't know the answer to that. But I know a woman who might. And with a bit of luck, I might just catch her."

Sophie looked around the café with a critical eye. "A bit gloomy, isn't it? You'd think she'd be glad of the chance to get a bit of sunshine on her day off." Judging by the absence of other lunchtime patrons, everyone else was doing just that.

Lindsay shook her head. "She doesn't want to risk being seen with me. Even on a Saturday. Lauren has the same relationship to Monarch as a flea has to a cat, which means she doesn't want to risk losing her meal ticket, though she's not averse to a nibble elsewhere as long as the price is right."

"One look at you and she might think twice about opening her mouth," Sophie commented, gesturing at her own cheek to illustrate her point.

Another night had spread Lindsay's bruises up and across her face to engulf her eye as well as her cheek and jaw. Time had rendered them more lurid shades of blue, with green and yellow making an appearance round the edges. The scabs covering her grazes had darkened, looking like mud that had been flicked over her skin and allowed to dry there. Under Sophie's gentle bathing, the dried blood had been cleaned from the long hairline cut along her jaw, leaving it looking far less serious than it had done the day before. The pain had subsided to a gentle throb, the ache dulled by the paracetamol Lindsay was still swallowing at four-hourly intervals. "I'll just have to tell her the truth," she said wryly.

"Let's hope she shows up," Sophie said.

"Yeah. Before the cops decide they've got enough circumstantial evidence to charge Meredith," Lindsay said glumly. "They're not going to wait forever, and they obviously think they know who did it. Which means nobody except us is look-ing for the real killer. Who thinks he's got away with it." As she spoke, she saw Lauren walk in, and waved at the receptionist. "Over here," she called.

Lauren walked towards them. When she saw Lindsay's face, her double take was almost comical. Her face fell like a failed soufflé and her step faltered. Cautiously, she approached. "What the fuck happened to you?" she said wonderingly. "You look like you just went ten rounds with Freddy Krueger. I don't think I wanna be here." She took a step backwards.

"I had an accident," Lindsay said hastily. "It's the truth. I took a header over a wall I didn't know was there and landed on top of a broken bottle. Nobody's had a go at me."

"She's telling the truth," Sophie butted in. "I'm a doctor and believe me, her injuries are consistent with that explanation. Look at those grazes—you don't get skin damage like that in a straightforward beating."

Lauren scowled. "Who the hell are you anyway?" she demanded of Sophie, then rounded on Lindsay. "I'm taking a risk, coming here to talk to you. What d'you want to bring a stranger along with you for?"

Lindsay sighed. "Sophie is my girlfriend. She also happens to be a doctor, and on both counts she wasn't about to let me out of the door by myself this morning. It's okay, Lauren, you can trust her. Sophie was Penny's best friend back in California."

Lauren looked uncertainly from one to the other. Some-thing in Sophie's steady eyes calmed her and she sat down abruptly. "You going to get me something to drink, then?"

"I'll go," Sophie said, taking details of what everyone wanted.

While she collected drinks and food, Lauren said, "You better be making this worth my while. Baz was having a right go about you yesterday, taking the piss something shocking. About how you was accusing her of murder, then Danny walks in and points out that she was doing a live radio show when it happened. And Baz says to me that if you turn up again looking for her, I'm to show you the door. So this better be good."

Lindsay nodded calmly. "I hear what you're saying. You'll be well looked after, I promise you. First off, I've got a couple of questions, but if you don't mind, I'd rather wait till Sophie comes back."

Lauren's eyebrows flicked upwards in bored exasperation. Her response was to take out her cigarettes and light up. "What do you need her for?" she asked petulantly.

"Because my brain's still cabbaged from all the painkillers the hospital shoved into me when I did my swallow dive on to the asphalt. Chances are I won't remember all the things I need to know. Okay?" Lindsay said mildly.

"I suppose." Lauren smoked furiously, her lips pursed between inhalations. When Sophie rejoined them with mineral water and sandwiches, she ostentatiously crushed out her cigarette. "So how much are you offering me?" she demanded, all empty belligerence.

"How does two and a half sound?" Lindsay said. "That's a final offer, by the way. Non-negotiable."

"Two hundred and fifty?" Lauren squeaked, impressed in spite of herself. Then suspicion kicked in. "What d'you want me to do that's worth that kind of money? I ain't putting myself at risk here."

"Pretty much the same as you did for Penny. Let us in the building today and we'll drop the keys off with you later."

"There'll be people there. Working."

"On a Saturday?" Lindsay sounded incredulous.

"You've got no idea. Workaholics, some of them. Brown noses, the rest of them. Think just because Danny sometimes drops in on a Saturday that they'll get Brownie points if he sees them at their desk. Saddos."

"So what time do they leave?" Sophie asked.

"Look, what are you going to do in there? I'm not going along with anything criminal, like trashing the place." Lauren's voice was apprehensive underneath a superficial bravado.

"Nobody will even know we've been in there," Lindsay promised. "All I want to do is exactly what Penny did. There's something I need to check out for myself, just like she did."

Lauren picked up one of the sandwiches and tore into it as if she hadn't seen food for a week. "How do I know you're telling me the truth?" she said through a mouthful of sandwich.

Lindsay shrugged as Sophie leaned forward, pinning Lauren with her eyes. "You have to trust us, Lauren. Lindsay told me how fond you were of Penny. Well, so was I. She was my best friend. I know we're asking you to take a big risk, but we're not asking for fun. This is as serious as it ever gets, Lauren. This is about my best friend's death, and I am absolutely determined to find out what really happened to her. Now, if you want to help, I'd be delighted to accept your assistance. But if it's too much to ask, that's okay too. We'll just have to find another way of getting at what we need."

Lauren gave up trying to outstare Sophie and mumbled, "All right. But this is the last time I take any chances, okay?"

Sophie reached out and touched Lauren's shoulder. "Thanks."

"Cash, mind," Lauren said gruffly. "Up front."

Lindsay took out an envelope and pushed it across the table. Lauren paused for a moment, her eyes going from one to the other in a flickering gaze. Then she snatched up the envelope and ripped it open, revealing five new fifty-pound notes. Glancing quickly round her to make sure no one was watching, she held them up to the light to check metal strip and watermark. "Oh, yeah," Lindsay said with a tinge of sarcasm, "I really look like a big-time forger."

Lauren gave a sunny grin. "All I know, you could be Al Capone. Right now, I couldn't care less. Be outside the office at half past five. They'll all have gone by then. I'll let you in."

She grabbed her bag and stuffed the envelope in an inside zipped pocket. Then, picking up the remains of her sandwich, she pushed back from the table, about to leave.

"Wait a minute," Lindsay said. "One or two questions, remember?"

Again the "Oh, God" upward flick of the eyebrows, accompanied by the heavy sigh of the hard done by. "All right, then, what do you want to know?"

"The couple of times I've been in reception, I've noticed you taking messages for people without checking if they were in. Is that a regular thing?"

Lauren frowned. "Yeah. I've got a list of about a dozen blokes. They never come in the office, but I get messages for them regular."

"What do you do with the messages?" Lindsay asked. The hair on the back of her neck seemed to be standing on end and, in spite of the stuffy heat inside the café, she felt a chill inside. So much hung on Lauren's answer.

"I pass them on to Danny's secretary. When I started working on reception, I asked who they all were and she said they were business associates of Danny's. She said they were consultants who didn't have offices with secretaries of their own and it was convenient for them to be able to leave messages here. I thought they must be a right bunch of tossers if they couldn't spring for a mobile phone or voice mail or something."

Lindsay let out the breath she hadn't been aware of holding. "Thanks, Lauren," she said softly. "We'll see you tonight."

She nodded and gathered up her bag, pausing to light a cigarette. "Funny you should ask about the messages," she said conversationally. "Penny wondered the very same thing."

21

Lindsay popped the last mouthful of strawberry tart in her mouth and carefully mopped her lips with the paper napkin. The movement of her jaw while eating still gave her twinges of pain, but she'd never been able to resist strawberry tarts, and those she'd found in California just weren't the same. Sophie was watching her with an air of bemused affection. "I don't know how you can think about eating when the next thing on the agenda is burglary," she said.

"S'easy," Lindsay said, swallowing her mouthful of cake. "Besides, it's not burglary. No breaking, no intent to steal or rape or commit GBH on the premises. It's not even criminal trespass."

"You sure they haven't changed the law since you last covered the criminal courts?" Sophie said dubiously.

"They have changed the law. That's the current status. Which you would know if you actually read the *Guardian Weekly* instead of using it to put under Mutton's food bowl. That dog knows more about current British politics than you do." Suddenly, Lindsay leaned forward and pointed across the car park to the front door of Monarch Press. "Fuck! That's our man," she said, indicating Danny King, who had just left his office with a tall man in shirtsleeves and suit trousers who carried a square sample case in one hand and a briefcase in the other. Danny was empty-handed, dressed in baggy cream-coloured trousers and a flowing dark blue long-sleeved shirt.

"The one who doesn't look like a sales rep?" Sophie asked.

"Got it in one. Oh, shit, they're headed this way!" Lindsay exclaimed, shrinking back from the window, as if that would render her invisible. For a taut moment, she was on the point of taking flight. Then the two men paused by a dark saloon.

"It's okay, they're only going to their car," Sophie said, relief spreading across her face. The man in the collar and tie dumped his bags in the boot, then climbed into the driving seat, while Danny strolled further down the car park and climbed behind the wheel of a silver Mercedes convertible.

"Nice wheels," Lindsay enthused as Danny shot out of his slot and headed for the exit. "Shame about how he paid for them."

"We don't know that for sure," Sophie said.

"We soon will." Lindsay checked her watch. "Nearly five now, and anybody left will be out like greased lightning now Danny's gone and there's no one left to impress. I don't know about you, but I fancy another strawberry tart." Sophie pulled a face. "Hey," Lindsay said. "The night is young. My blood sugar needs all the help it can get. Like you said, it's a tough business, burglary."

Forty minutes later, they stood inside the reception area of Monarch Press. Lauren had hustled them through the front door faster than a Royal aide helping the boss escape the paparazzi. Then she'd handed over a bunch of keys and a sheet of paper that provided Lindsay and Sophie with the instructions for setting the intruder alarms when they left, and Lauren's address so they could return the keys later.

"The list?" Lindsay demanded.

Lauren reached behind her desk and grabbed a scruffy sheet of A4 paper with a list of names. She thrust it at Sophie and, before they had a chance to ask her any more questions, was off.

The vertical blinds that lined the windows of the publishing house let in more than enough light for the two women to see where they were going and what they were doing. "His office is upstairs," Lindsay whispered, handing Sophie some latex gloves and wrestling her hands into her own pair.

"Why are we whispering?" Sophie hissed, efficiently covering her hands.

"Because burglars always whisper?" Lindsay said in her normal voice as she picked a way through the open-plan office to the stairs.

"I thought we weren't burglars?"

"So sue me. I can't believe I'm doing this for the second time in the same week. Raiding offices, poking around in other people's data."

Sophie shrugged. "Synchronicity. You probably wouldn't have thought of this approach if you hadn't already been messing around with somebody else's computer. But let's face it, you dropped lucky with Guy and Stella. Do you really think we're going to find proof that Danny's running a ghost-jobs scam?" she said sceptically. "Wouldn't a sensible man have destroyed all the evidence after Penny confronted him?"

"Professional criminals are convinced they're smarter than the police. They know they're never going to get caught. So they hang on to all sorts of incriminating stuff. Besides, Danny King can't get rid of the evidence without explaining to the tax people why it is his company has suddenly shed half its editorial staff when on paper they're the ones generating his profits."

"Good point," Sophie acknowledged.

They emerged in a corridor at the top of the stairs. On the first floor at Monarch Press, democracy and openness yielded place to hierarchy and privacy—or secrecy, depending on where the observer was standing. Lindsay was in no doubt which word she'd have chosen.

They walked to the far end of the corridor and started working their way back towards the stairs. The end room was a boardroom that ran the full depth of the building, its centrepiece a vast antique oval table that must have used most of a mahogany tree. "There's always something, isn't there," Lindsay muttered. "All these supposedly radical, right-on companies, they always have an Achilles' heel of good old greedy capitalist materialism lurking somewhere. Now why do I not believe that table's one of Danny's family heirlooms?"

"Because you're a twisted old cynic. Now come on, never mind the self-righteousness. We've got more important things to think about," Sophie said, chivvying Lindsay out of the doorway and towards the next office, whose door revealed it belonged to the Sales Director. Opposite that was the Marketing Director, then Publicity, opposite Accounts. Finally, they came to an office with no nameplate on its door. "I guess this is it," Sophie said, turning the door handle.

They stepped into a small office with a modern desk and the usual array of electronic equipment. A buttoned damask Victorian *chaise longue* ran along one wall, beneath a framed photograph of Danny with a jeroboam of champagne surrounded by his staff under a banner that announced "Monarch's Ten Year Reign." This was clearly a reception area that doubled as his secretary's office. A second door led off it at right angles to the corridor. Lindsay opened it to reveal another room that ran the full depth of the mews.

One end of the room was arranged as a meeting space, with four grey leather sofas surrounding a glass and polished-granite coffee table. At the other end, two desks sat in an L-shape. The one facing out into the room was empty. The other held a computer. Between them was a black steel shelving unit that contained TV, video and a Bang and Olufsen stereo that had probably cost as much as the average family car. A run of low-level black filing cabinets occupied the back wall below the window.

"Toss you for it," Lindsay said, fishing a coin out of the pocket of her baggies. "Call?"

Sophie groaned. "Whatever I say, I just know I'm going to end up with the filing cabinets. Heads."

Lindsay tossed the coin, caught it, slapped it on to the back of her left hand and revealed it with a flourish. "Tails it is. I'll take the computer, you take the filing cabinets. Hang on, I'll get you a copy of the names on Lauren's list." She disappeared back into the secretary's office, where, rather than wait for the photocopier to warm up, she slipped the sheet of paper through the fax machine. Giving the original to Sophie, she laid the flimsy fax paper on the desk next to her and switched on the computer.

"These are locked," Sophie said, rattling the first drawer fruitlessly.

"Try these," Lindsay said calmly, pulling a bunch of small keys out of the desk drawer to her right. "Arrogant little shit deserves to be burgled."

While Sophie searched for the correct key for the cabinet, Lindsay found her way around Monarch's computer software. It wasn't hard; they ran a network of PCs, an expanded version of systems Lindsay had worked on both in her university department and in small magazines where she'd contributed articles. It didn't take her long to find the personnel directory, where a database held files on all their employees. "Yes," she said softly, a sense of triumph surging through her.

"Got somewhere?" Sophie said, her voice muffled from kneeling on the floor with her head bent over a filing drawer.

"I think so. Look for personnel dossiers, see if they compare with what's in here." Now that she was faced with the answer she'd been desperately searching for, Lindsay was almost superstitiously reluctant to start checking the individual files of the men on Lauren's list. Instead, she typed in a search request for Baz's file. Just for comparison purposes, she told herself.

The file listed Baz's title—Editorial Director (Fiction)—her work station number—026—her salary, date of birth, home address and telephone number, the names and job titles of staff she was responsible for, her starting date with the company and details of her pension fund contributions. Unable to resist, Lindsay called up Danny King's file. Publisher, work station 101, plus all the other details. What looked like an extremely expensive address in Holland Park. Plus a very healthy and generous pension. Now she had an idea what a file should look like, she typed in the first name on Lauren's list.

Paddy Brown was allegedly the Foreign Rights Acquisition Director at work station 201. He earned three times what Baz was paid, though he lived in what sounded like a block of flats in Bethnal Green. Like Danny, his pension arrangements looked well cushioned. The picture was similar for Bill Candy, the Translation Rights Director (work station 202), Paul Edwards, the Senior Commissioning Director (work station 203), Brian Hedges, the Promotions Controller (work station 204) and the other names on the list.

"It's just like Penny laid out for us," Lindsay said. "Look, he's even put the equivalent of an extra floor on the building." Sophie stood up and looked over Lindsay's shoulder. "That's what she meant with that cryptic note about the tenth floor of a nine-storey building. All the ground-floor staff have work stations beginning with zero, and everybody on the first floor begins with one. But all the shady staff's work stations begin with a two. That way, if there was ever a snap raid, all Danny King would have to say is that those members of staff work from home, or they have a roving commission or whatever."

Sophie slapped a pair of files on the desk. "Compare these. Legitimate employee files have copies of all the correspondence from when they applied for a job and were interviewed and had their references called in. Ghost personnel just have a letter of appointment. Bit of a giveaway, isn't it?"

Although she was eager for evidence to support her case, Lindsay was determined not to jump to conclusions again. "I don't know . . ." she said. "Couldn't he just say he head-hunted them?"

"I suppose so. That would save him having to forge letters and references. So does any of this actually prove anything?" Sophie asked.

"Taken on its own, none of it means much. But if we took this to the police, along with Penny's synopsis, plus Danny King coming forward at the last gasp to make a false statement about Meredith . . . well, it all adds up. It hangs together. This ghost-employment con couldn't stand up to any serious scrutiny, especially if he's supplementing it with a ghost-publication scam. As soon as the cops start looking at it seriously, the whole house of cards is going to collapse."

"And this is what Penny uncovered," Sophie said dully.

"I think so. The phone calls made her suspicious, especially when she found out about Lauren's little list. My guess is that her main motive for getting into the computers here was to check out Baz's files, to see if there was any solid evidence for her suspicion that Baz was the one that Meredith had had her disastrous little fling with. But when she was actually faced with the prospect of uncovering the truth, she bottled it."

"So she took a look at the mystery men in Danny's files as a way of putting off what she knew she had to do," Sophie said. "That would be just like her. She hated unpleasantness. She'd have done anything she could think of to postpone actually having to face up to the proof that she'd been betrayed twice over."

Lindsay took a floppy disk out of her bag and slotted it into the computer, keying in instructions for it to copy the files in the personnel database. "I think that's the way it happened. She had a devious mind, did Penny. She'd have realised right away there was something seriously dodgy going on. Even if she didn't work it all out at the time, she learned enough to figure it out later."

Sophie turned back to the filing cabinets and started pulling out the files that corresponded to the list. For a few moments the only sound was the rattling of file drawers and the mechanical groans of the disk drive. Then Sophie said, "But how did Danny find out she knew what was going on?"

Lindsay took the floppy out of the drive and zipped it into the back pocket of her organiser. She shrugged. "I don't know for sure, but I think it went something like this. Penny, as Meredith found out to her cost, is a woman to whom honesty and integrity were paramount. The issue between her and Meredith splitting up wasn't infidelity, it was breach of trust. And Penny was ruthless, even though it cost her the woman she really loved. Agreed?"

"Oh, absolutely," Sophie said. "She wasn't a forgiving woman. She was absolute for truth and it made her judgemental. It was the side of Penny I liked least. You think she confronted him with what she suspected?"

"I'd put money on it. Remember that curious incident the day before she died? When she came to Monarch supposedly for a meeting with Baz, only Baz was out having lunch with somebody else and Penny kicked off? It wasn't like Penny to stand on her dignity like that. I reckon she was engineering an opportunity to get Danny on his own. And knowing Penny, she probably laid it out for him over the starters." Lindsay slipped into a Californian accent. "'I know what you're doing here, Danny Boy. I know about the ghost jobs. I know so much about it, I'm going to put it at the heart of my next novel. And then people will ask where I got the idea from. They'll especially wonder if I change publishers at around the same time. Time you cleaned up your act, pal. Exorcise the ghosts or lose me.'"

Sophie looked wide-eyed at Lindsay, rocked by the accuracy of her impersonation. "Jesus! You gave me gooseflesh!"

Lindsay slid out of the chair and gave Sophie a hug. "I'm sorry, I didn't mean to upset you."

Sophie smudged a kiss across the top of Lindsay's ear. "It was just a bit creepy. As if there aren't enough ghosts in here already," she added with a nervous laugh, brandishing the files she'd extracted. "We should photocopy these, so we can take them to the police, right?"

"Wrong."

The voice came from behind the door. Deep, tight and angry. The two women swung round in time to see Danny King step out into the office. Lindsay's eyes swept over him, then swung irresistibly back to his right hand. Dull blue steel, just like in the movies. She didn't know what kind it was, but staring down the business end, the gun looked bigger than anything Clint Eastwood had ever relied on to make his day. The shock of it hurt her stomach and made her bladder burn. Years of journalism and messing with murder investigations had never taken her quite so close to her own mortality. It wasn't a place she liked. Instinctively, she moved closer to Sophie.

"Get away from each other," Danny said. His cold control was almost more frightening than the black hole of the gun barrel. Without even considering the alternative, Lindsay obeyed, moving away from Sophie at the same moment as Sophie separated herself with a sidestep. That left Sophie in the inside corner of the L of the desks, with Lindsay a foot beyond the empty executive expanse that had stood between her and Danny.

Lindsay forced her eyes away from the gun to look at Danny's face. His expression was set, his jaw clenched so tight the muscles bunched under his ears. His creamy pale skin was flushed along the cheekbones, like two badly applied smears of a blusher designed for someone else's skin tones. His eyes glinted in the evening light like dark sapphires, hard and terrifying as the gun barrel. They carried about the same promise of compassion. "It's over, Danny," Lindsay said.

"I don't hear no fat lady singing," he grated contemptuously, his veneer of cultured civilisation stripped away to reveal a savage gangster bent on survival. "You're the ones that are over."

"Killing us doesn't solve anything. It's just two more bodies for the police to investigate. This racket of yours—how many lives is it worth? Sooner or later, the trail's going to lead back to your door," Lindsay said defiantly, praying her voice wouldn't crack or her bladder give up.

Danny made a sound like a dog coughing. Lindsay translated it as a harsh laugh. "What fucking planet are you on? Do you have any idea of the people you've been messing with? This is not some cosy fucking TV series where the villain folds up in a heap and you get to be heroes. This is reality, and this is where you get to be dead."

"There are people who know we were coming here tonight," Sophie interjected, her voice low and calm. It didn't stop the sweat of fear running down Lindsay's armpits.

"I don't give a monkey's fuck if the Commissioner of the Metropolitan Police knows you're here," Danny said, taking a couple of steps forward. "The people I deal with, I don't have to give a toss about stuff like that. You don't understand a fucking thing, do you? Just like your stupid fucking friend Penny. She thought she could threaten me and my operation with her Goody Two Shoes mentality. None of you have the faintest idea of how the world works." He ran his free hand over his sweating forehead. But the gun didn't even waver.

"How does the world work, Danny?" Sophie cut in, sounding as relaxed as a chat-show host asking him about his latest book.

"Money buys everything. Including love. And death. And it ain't love I'm offering tonight."

22

Danny took another couple of steps closer to them, his eyes moving calmly from one to the other, making sure they knew he was watching them. "So what happens now?" Lindsay demanded.

"I make a phone call, we wait for a little while and then it's 'Saturday night and I ain't got no body' time, ladies," Danny said sarcastically. He reached into the hip pocket of his fashionably crumpled linen trousers and pulled out a slim mobile, flipped it open and keyed in a number with his thumb. It looked like it wasn't the first time he'd used the technique. Lindsay wondered if he made a habit of holding a gun on people while he phoned his friends. Was this how it had been for Penny, the gunpoint hostage, then the setting up of the scene for murder made to look like accident?

A moment for the phone to connect, then Danny spoke, never taking his eyes off them. "It's Danny. I've got a waste disposal problem at the office. Two loads. I want a team round, soon as . . . Yeah, it'll have to be moved before it can be dealt with . . . See you." He closed the phone, a smile thin as a filleting knife slicing across his face. "Sorted," he said contemptuously.

"Let's hope you make a better job of us than you did of Penny," Lindsay said. In some strange way, hearing Danny transmit the order for her death had lifted the fear. It was inevitable now, there was nothing left to lose. It wouldn't take long for the hired guns to arrive and once they were there she and Sophie were good as dead. If there was ever going to be any hope, it was now.

"Oh, I think that went off all right, actually," he drawled, his urbanity restored now he was convinced everything was under control.

"The freak accident line didn't hold for long, did it?"

A quick, careless shrug of the eyebrows. "Accident, murder, what does it matter what the filth think? I could have had her shot or stabbed or strangled or battered to death. I know specialists, men who know what they're about. Professionals. But I thought, since it was costing me, I might as well get an earner out of it. So I took one of my boys along to her flat. She thought I'd come to talk terms. She never knew what hit her. But I had some great publicity for the new book. Which I figured she owed me, since I wasn't going to be getting any more books from her." As he preened himself, his wariness was slowly receding, forced back by a tide of complacency. Lindsay wasn't the only one to notice it.

"It was a clever idea," Sophie said. "Utilitarian."

"I hate waste," he said. "But I can't think of any way of making a shilling out of you two. Shame, really."

"Another reason to avoid killing us," Sophie said, still managing to sound as calm as a midsummer pond.

He snorted derisively. "Don't give me that bollocks. I told you, this isn't like the telly. You don't get to talk me out of it. You're going to die. If you're a Catholic, I'm sorry, you're going to have to manage without the last rites."

"Without these files, we haven't got a shred of proof," Sophie said. "The cops are never going to take us seriously. They'll realise Lindsay's a friend of Meredith, that she's grasping at straws to make it look like somebody else was responsible for Penny's death. All they're going to see is the money. Why would a millionaire publisher kill the goose that lays the golden eggs?

Legitimate businessmen don't do things like that, not even ones who have a bit of a murky past."

"You must think I'm a real punter if you think that bullshit cuts any ice," Danny said, his eyes on Sophie. "Anyway, if you didn't get any joy with the cops, you're just as likely to shop me to the taxman. Which is just as dangerous and probably more expensive in the long run."

Sophie shrugged. "All you have to do is send out redundancy notices and close the racket down." She inclined her head towards the chair behind her. "All right if I sit down? I've got a bad back, I can't stand for long. If I'm going to die, the least you can do is let me do it in comfort."

Danny eyed Sophie suspiciously, then took a couple of steps forward to check there was no trick, nothing dangerous in reach once she was sitting at the desk. Lindsay instantly recognised the only opportunity she was likely to get. As he nodded and said, "Okay," she gathered her strength in a crouch and launched herself through the air at Danny.

She was slower than she anticipated, muscles still suffering from being crushed against asphalt. Worse, Danny was faster than she'd thought possible. He swivelled on the balls of his feet, his gun arm straightening without a jerk, his finger squeezing the trigger. A flash, a boom, the smell of cordite and her shoulder felt like it had hit a brick wall at something approaching the land speed record. The impact spun her round in a half-circle, but her momentum carried her crashing forward in an unintended shoulder charge.

They collided and crashed to the floor, Lindsay realising as she landed on top of him that only one of the screaming voices was hers. Beneath her, Danny gagged, trying to squeeze some air back into lungs that felt paralysed. The gun barked once, twice as Lindsay lay on top of him, incapable of struggle, beyond even wrestling for the weapon.

When they went down, Sophie threw herself across the desk, screeching like an express train, then crouched, panting, trying to stay away from the lines of fire as Danny's gun arm thrashed pointlessly around. Her eyes raked the room for any kind of weapon. But nothing suggested itself as a potential cosh.

Necessity mothered invention. Like a crab, she scuttled round the desk and ripped cables out of the back of the computer monitor, not caring that her fingers throbbed from the violence of her actions. All she could think about was Lindsay and the grunts and sobs coming from behind her.

The monitor came free in seconds that felt like weeks. Sophie slipped both forearms under it and lifted it clear of the desk. She turned to see Danny thrashing under Lindsay, his breath recovered. He was trying to free his gun arm enough to bring the barrel round to where he could blow a bloody tunnel through Lindsay's brain. She was incapable of stopping him, her body a dead weight leaking blood all over Danny's silk shirt and antique silk rug.

"Fuck you," Sophie roared, standing over him. His panicked eyes rolled up in his head and he saw her standing there like a time-slipped Greek goddess of vengeance.

"No!" he yelled, his voice outraged, his face a mask of astonishment that anyone could have the upper hand over him.

Sophie dropped the monitor.

Sophie crouched over Lindsay, a 9mm Glock sticking out of the waistband of her jeans. She was packing the hole in Lindsay's shoulder with the rags of the silk shirt she'd ripped from Danny King's unconscious body. She'd checked him for vital signs once she'd made sure Lindsay wasn't bleeding from an artery. He was unconscious, though not deeply so. She'd ripped his office phone from the wall and used the cable to tie his hands and feet behind his back in a vicious ligature that would guarantee he came round with excruciating cramps. It was, she had decided, the very least he deserved.

It was a long time since she'd worked in a casualty department, and even then she'd only ever seen one gunshot wound. It was a failure of experience that worried her, leaving her uncertain as to how life-threatening Lindsay's injury might be. She could gauge something from the blood loss, but when it came to assessing the actual extent of the injury or the degree of shock involved in such a wound, Sophie reckoned she might as well be a riveter as a doctor. She avoided mentioning that to Lindsay, settling instead for telling her that she was going to be okay, that Sophie would get her out of here and to a hospital just as soon as she had stopped her bleeding to death. She knew that even *in extremis*, Lindsay would appreciate the drama of that expression.

Lindsay lay still, curiously aware of the texture of the short silk fibres of the rug against the skin of her uninjured hand and arm. She felt strangely distanced from her pain, being more conscious of the shallowness of her breathing and the fat blobs of sweat running down her forehead and cheeks. The whole upper left quadrant of her body felt so strange, so alien, it might as well have belonged to someone else for all the connection she could make between it and her past experience. "I love you," she said, aware of Sophie's hands moving over her body. It came out as a croak, but Sophie understood.

"You're going to be all right," she said gently. "I love you too. Even if you are a complete headbanger."

"Alive," Lindsay croaked.

"Yeah, you're right. Better a live headbanger than a dead sensible head. Don't talk now, darling, save your strength. You'll need it if we're going to get out of here before the execution squad arrive." Sophie wiped the sweat from Lindsay's face with a crumpled tissue, then stood up. "I'm going to see if I can find a trolley or something that I can wheel you out of here on," she said.

"No," Lindsay grunted, forcing herself on to one elbow. "Not time. For that. I can. Walk. If you just. Help me."

Sighing in exasperation at her partner's refusal to accept defeat, Sophie crouched beside her and pushed her into a sitting position. Then she slung Lindsay's good arm round her shoulder, held on to her wrist with both hands and tried to straighten up. It was a backbreaking job which Sophie would never have managed if the lie she'd told Danny about her back had been the truth. Lindsay's feet scrabbled uselessly under her as Sophie dragged her upright. Finally, they stood together in the middle of the room, Lindsay listing into Sophie, swaying slightly, but managing to keep her feet. The door seemed a very long way away.

"Okay," Sophie said. "One step at a time." They managed a jerky movement in the right direction, then a stumble, a stuttering correction and, after what seemed an eternity, a few coordinated steps.

They had almost reached the door when the constipated quacking of a man's voice coming through a loud-hailer split the quiet of the mews. "Armed police. The building is surrounded. Come to the front door and throw out your weapons. I repeat, armed police. Come to the front door and throw out your weapons."

The voice stopped them in their tracks. "Oh, shit," Lindsay mumbled.

"At least it's better than King's thugs," Sophie said. "Come on, let's get you through into the secretary's office." She edged sideways through the door, supporting Lindsay as she staggered through behind her. "Sit down a minute," Sophie said, easing Lindsay on to the chaise. "I'm going to call for an ambulance. I don't know if they'll have one, and you need to get to hospital as soon as possible."

"Fine," Lindsay groaned weakly as she slumped against the back rest. The initial physical blow to her system was deepening into a more profound state of shock, her mind a place where thought was as much of an effort as movement was for her body. Things were starting to look fuzzy round the edges of her vision. The focus of her world had narrowed till all she was aware of was the growing shriek of pain in her shoulder battling with the almost overwhelming desire to slide into sleep. Dimly, she heard Sophie speak. But the urgency in her voice was lost to Lindsay, as were her words. "Soph . . ." she mumbled, her voice tailing off as unconsciousness absolved her from the necessity of decision or action.

"Oh, shit," Sophie cursed, watching helplessly as Lindsay crumpled before her eyes. "Ambulance? I'm a doctor. Two injured at . . . you've got the location? Fine. One just gone unconscious, GSW to the left shoulder, considerable blood loss. One unconscious, single blow to the head. How soon?" She compressed her lips at the estimate of seven to ten minutes, then realised it would probably take her that long to get Lindsay downstairs.

She replaced the phone and hoisted Lindsay over her shoulder in a fireman's lift. It wasn't the most sensible way to carry someone with a gunshot wound to the shoulder, but Sophie didn't have a lot of choice. There was no way she was leaving Lindsay upstairs with Danny King, unconscious or not. Besides, she knew how important first impressions were to the police, and she wanted a clear separation in their minds right from the start between the two of them and King. It was going to be hard enough to convince them she and Lindsay were telling the truth, given the flimsiness of their evidence and the undoubted weight a corrupt system would place on the word of a rich and successful businessman. "And he probably supports the Tory Party," Sophie complained to her unconscious burden as she staggered down the stairs one at a time.

At the bottom, she paused for breath. The loud-hailer invaded her ears again. "Armed police. You are surrounded. Give up your weapons and nobody will get hurt. Throw your weapons out of the front door and show yourselves. I repeat, you are surrounded."

"Yeah, fine, we get the message," Sophie panted, bracing herself and heading across the open-plan office, grateful for the blinds that hid her from the police marksmen she had no doubt would be in place, fingers on triggers, nerves strung tight as a fishing line with a shark on the other end. She prayed nobody would be too eager tonight.

After what felt like half a lifetime, Sophie was across the office and into the reception area. The muscles in her thighs were trembling, but she wasn't going to open the door until she knew the ambulance was there. Legs apart, free arm straight against the wall, she stood sweating for a full minute that stretched her patience near breaking point. Then she heard the swoop of an ambulance siren, growing closer, then abruptly silenced, like someone clamping a hand over a child's mouth.

Dry-mouthed with apprehension, Sophie cracked the door open a couple of inches. "Don't shoot!" she yelled, reaching behind her to pull the gun free. She tossed it out underarm, giving it a flick of the wrist to carry it well away from her. The gun clattered on the road, then there was silence.

"I'm coming out," she yelled. "We're the victims here, understand? I've got a wounded woman here. We're the victims!"

"Come out slowly, with your hands raised," the megaphone voice quacked.

Sophie curled her free arm under Lindsay's legs and let her slide down from her shoulder until she carried her in both arms across the front of her body. Then she slowly staggered out into the street, blinking the tears from her eyes. "Get the paramedics," she shouted. "Somebody get the paramedics."

EPILOGUE

The light in the seat-belt sign died with an electronic bong. Lindsay waggled her fingers at the window and said, "Goodbye and good riddance."

"You didn't enjoy your holiday?" Sophie asked.

"Two trips to hospital? Scarred for life in two separate places? Temperatures higher than California and not a room that has air conditioning from London to Loch Fyne? All the guns in America and I have to come to London to get shot?" Lindsay demanded, her voice rising to a squeak.

"We had a nice time in Scotland," Sophie reminded her.

"You had a nice time in Scotland," Lindsay said darkly, shifting in her seat to make her bandaged shoulder more comfortable. "I had my mother acting like I'd been brought home to die and my father taking the piss out of me every night. And then when we did get up to Torridon, you wouldn't let me up any decent hills in case I wasn't recovered enough."

Sophie shook her head, grinning. "I don't think I was unreasonable to put my foot down about a Munro that involved an eight-mile hike just to get to the bottom of the mountain, followed by a 3,000-foot climb and another eight-mile hike back to the car."

"Well," Lindsay grumbled. "I've never done Maol Chean Dearg. And now I probably never will."

"Maybe we could have a trip up there when the taxpayers pay for us to come back and testify against Danny King."

Lindsay brightened up at the thought. It was the least she felt they deserved after the long hours—in her case, excruciatingly painful hours of police interviews and making statements. After all that, King still hadn't been charged with Penny's murder. As a holding measure, they'd kept him in on attempted murder against Lindsay, conspiracy to murder and illegal possession of firearms. It was fortunate that the police had arrived when they did, alerted by a supermarket security guard who'd heard gunshots, still a rare enough occurrence in London to bring the police within minutes. Any later and King's sidekicks would have got in to destroy the evidence.

Lindsay had hit it off with the officer in charge of the murder inquiry, who had instinctively recognised a kindred pig-headed spirit. Privately, she had told them that they were never going to have more than a purely circumstantial case against King on Penny's murder and that it was up to the Crown Prosecution Service to decide whether they should go for it.

"Spineless tossers," she'd confided over a cup of tea in the police canteen. "I've tried to argue that the attempt on you only makes sense if you allow the previous murder, but they want more. They always bloody want more. Even against a toerag like Danny King. Trouble is, you put a toerag in an Armani suit and he looks like the frigging lawyers. It's the same as hostages starting to identify with their kidnappers. Suddenly all the briefs forget they're supposed to be on the side of the scruffy coppers and they come out in sympathy with the scrote in the suit."

She'd sounded a lot more cheerful a few days later when she'd tracked them down by phone at Lindsay's parents' house. "Your friend's neighbour. I think you met him? A Mr Knight?"

Lindsay cleared her throat. "Might have done," she said cautiously.

"I thought, what about putting Danny Boy in a line-up? Last resort, you know? His brief starts screaming, which makes us think it's definitely going to be a good idea. So we bring in Mr Knight and bugger me if he doesn't pick him out straight away. He remembers him because of his car. A Mercedes convertible. He noticed it because the arrogant little shit had parked it right outside our Mr Knight's house and he was just pulling away when our witness arrived home from work. Can you believe the conceit of the man? He thinks he's come so far from the East End that he's invincible. And our Mr Knight never thought to mention it because he didn't look like he was in a hurry and he didn't have any blood on him that he could see. Well, of course he didn't, did he? He's a professional. He knew he was going there to take part in a very bloody murder—he'd either have stripped or worn disposable overalls.

"Then our prize witness says, well, we can't blame him, can we? I mean, murderers don't drive around in top of the range Mercs like hospital consultants, do they?

"Soon as Danny Boy realises he's been fingered, he starts shitting it. He knows he's in the frame for murder. So he decides it's time to get out from under. He does nothing more than give us his sidekick, the thug who actually did the killing. King was just there to get him in and give the instructions about the stage setting. Can you believe it?

"Once he started talking, we couldn't get him to stop. His brief was practically in tears. We even found out you had a second lucky escape. You was attacked the night before, wasn't you? It wasn't some accidental trip over a wall that sliced your face up, was it? It was one of Danny King's little thugs, hired to scare you off."

Lindsay couldn't prevent a dry laugh spilling down the line. "Is that what he told you? Somebody's been winding him up. Yes, somebody tried to put my lights out with a baseball bat, but he didn't connect, so I legged it. That's when I really did trip over a wall. So if Danny got told I'd been cut, somebody ripped him off."

"Couldn't happen to a nicer bloke," the policewoman had said. "Arrogant, vain, stupid as well. He doesn't even realise that he still gets charged with murder even though it wasn't him who did the actual killing. Joint enterprise, it's called. We've got him, nailed down at all four corners. Not even the CPS can walk away from it now."

They'd celebrated that night, a double celebration since Helen had also called to announce that Guy and Stella would be facing charges of fraud and false accounting. "I owe you," she'd said. "You gave me my professional life back."

"You mean that?" Lindsay said.

"Of course I mean it. Why? What do you want?" Instant nervousness at the other end of the phone.

Lindsay let her stew for a few moments, then said, "I can't think of anything off the top of my head . . ." Helen had exploded with laughter. It was a sound that cheered Lindsay even more than putting Penny's murderer behind bars. She wondered if she'd ever hear Meredith laugh like that again.

Meredith had left for San Francisco a few days before, her life in pieces. If it had been hard to contemplate life without Penny as a lover, it was impossible to imagine it without her very existence. Losing her job had been the final blow, a knockback whose impact had only really hit in the days since King's arrest, when the imperative of finding Penny's killer had been answered. The night before she'd left, she'd told Lindsay she wasn't going to make any decisions about her life for at least six months, displaying a strength and good sense that Lindsay envied.

The cabin steward's inquiry about drinks roused Lindsay from her preoccupation. "To hell with sensible," she said. "I'll have a Scotch."

When she'd taken her first sip, Sophie said gingerly, "There's something we need to talk about."

Lindsay turned her head and stared, a worm of worried fear stirring in her gut. Had she finally pushed Sophie too far? Was this the kind of trouble that altered lives beyond recognition?

"No more murders? That's not a problem, I promise." Recognising her apprehension, Sophie reached out and squeezed her hand. "That would be nice, but that's not it. After we came back to London, while you were giving the cops the statement about your attack, I had coffee with somebody I used to work with in Glasgow. She's doing similar work to what I've been doing in San Francisco, and their consultant is leaving in the New Year to go to Australia. She's been asked to sound me out to see if I'd consider applying. What do you think?"

Lindsay looked aghast. "British winters?"

"Proper curries."

"No air conditioning?"

"Decent TV."

"No sea?"

"Great theatre."

Lindsay frowned. There had to be something that would clinch the argument against leaving California. Then her face cleared and she smiled triumphantly. "Quarantine," she said firmly. "Six months behind bars. You couldn't do that to Mutton."

It was Sophie's turn to look horrified. Then she nodded slowly, conceding defeat. "I am reminded," she said, "of the joke about Jesus and the woman taken in adultery."

"The joke about . . . ?"

"Jesus stops the crowd stoning her and says, 'Let the person among you who is without sin throw the first stone.' And this little old lady pushes her way through the mob, picks up this massive boulder and throws it at the adulterous woman. Crash, bang, wallop, she's dead. And Jesus turns to the old dear and says, 'Sometimes, mother, you really piss me off.'"

HOSTAGE
TO MURDER

ACKNOWLEDGEMENTS

I had no plans to write another Lindsay Gordon novel until the British Council invited me to Russia. But I fell in love with the country and wanted to share my delight. Among those who contributed to the Russian end of this book are Kate Griffin, my minder, who showed me the ropes and found the Diet Coke; Volodya Volovik, who shared his affection for his adopted city of St Petersburg; Seamus Murphy, whose enthusiasm took me places I'd never otherwise have seen; Irina Savelieva, who interpreted the dark and dangerous for me; Varya Gornestaeva, without whom none of it would ever have happened; Gavrilov and Shatalov, for the encouragement and the good company; Marna Gowan, who exploited her contacts shamelessly; Maxim Shvedov, for all the St Petersburg sailing info; and Stephen Dewar, who explained the intricacies of Russian customs and immigration. To all of you, thanks for being such generous companions.

Leslie Hills, who has forgotten more than I know about story structure, helped me hone the plot. Thanks for seeing me through the dark night of the soul and for always travelling off limits with me.

Thanks too to Lisanne Radice, who always believed in Lindsay.

In memory of Gina Weissand (1946–2001),
who was everything a friend should be.
You blessed us all, babe, and we miss you.

He that hath wife and children hath given hostages
to fortune.

"Of Marriage and the Single Life"
Francis Bacon

PART I

1

A murder of crows swore at each other in the trees that lined the banks of the River Kelvin. A freezing drizzle from a low sky bleached the landscape to grey. Nothing, Lindsay thought, could be further from California. The only thing in common with the home she'd left three months before was the rhythm of her feet as she ran her daily two miles.

On mornings like this, Lindsay found it hard to remember that she'd once loved this city. When she'd come back to Scotland after university and journalism training, she'd thought Glasgow was paradise. She had money in her pocket, she was young, free and single and the city had just begun the process of reinvigoration that had, by the millennium, made it one of the most exciting cities in Britain. Now, fifteen years later, there was no denying it was a good place to live. The cultural life was vibrant. The restaurants were cosmopolitan and covered the whole range from cheap and cheerful to glamorous and gourmet. There were plenty of beautiful places to live, and more green spaces than most cities could boast. Some of the finest countryside in the world was within an hour's drive.

And all she could think of was how much she wanted to be somewhere else. Seven happy and successful years in California had left her feeling that this long narrow land was no longer full of possibilities for her. Partly, it was the weather, she thought, wiping the cold mixture of sweat and rain from her face. Who wouldn't long for sunshine and the Pacific surf on a morning like this?

Partly, it was that she missed her dog. Mutton had always accompanied her on her runs, his black tail wagging eagerly whenever she walked downstairs in her jogging clothes. But she couldn't contemplate putting him in quarantine kennels for six months, so he'd been handed over to some friends in the Bay Area who'd guaranteed him a happy life. He'd probably forgotten her already.

But mostly it was not having anything meaningful to do with her days. Lindsay would never have described herself as someone who was defined by her job, but now that she had none, she had come to realise how much of her identity had been bound up in what she did for a living. Without some sort of employment, she felt cast adrift. When people asked, "And what do you do?" she had no answer. There were few things she hated more than the sense of powerlessness that provoked in her.

In California, Lindsay had had a response, one she felt proud of, one she knew carried a degree of respect. She'd reluctantly abandoned her post lecturing in journalism at Santa Cruz to come back to Scotland because her lover Sophie had been offered the chair of obstetrics at Glasgow University. Lindsay had protested that she didn't have anything to go back for, but Sophie had managed to convince her she was mistaken. "You'll walk into a teaching job in Scotland," she'd said. "And if it takes a while, you can always go back to freelance journalism. You know you were one of the best."

And so she had stifled her doubts for Sophie's sake. After all, it wasn't her lover's fault that Lindsay had reached the age of thirty-nine without a clearly defined career plan. But now she was confronted by the cold reality of unemployment, she wished she'd done more to persuade Sophie to stay in California. She'd looked around for teaching work, but vocational journalism training wasn't nearly as widespread in Scotland as it was in the US. She'd managed to secure some part-time lecturing at Strathclyde University, filling in for someone on maternity leave, but it was dead-end work with no prospects. And the idea of going back to the overcrowded world of freelance journalism with a contacts book that was years out of date held no appeal.

So her days had shrunk to this. Pounding the walkway by the river. Reading the papers. Shopping for dinner. Arranging to meet old acquaintances for drinks and discovering how much distance there was between them. Waiting for Sophie to come home and bring her despatches from the world of work. Lindsay knew she couldn't go on like this indefinitely. It was poisoning her soul, and it wasn't doing her relationship with Sophie much good either.

She reached the point where she had to turn off the walkway and head up the steep hill to the Botanic Gardens, the halfway point on her circuit. Head down, she powered up the slope, too wrapped up in her thoughts to pay heed to her surroundings. As she rounded a blind bend, she realised she was about to cannon into someone walking down the hill. She swerved, but simultaneously the other woman sidestepped in the same direction. They crashed into each other and Lindsay stumbled, smacking into a tree and falling to one knee, her ankle twisting under her. "Shit," she gasped.

"Oh God, I'm sorry," the other woman said.

"My own fault," Lindsay growled, pushing herself upright, then wincing as she tried to take her weight on the damaged ankle. "Jesus," she hissed, leaning forward to probe the joint with her fingers.

"You've not broken it or anything?" The woman frowned solicitously.

"Sprained, I think." She drew in her breath sharply when she touched the tender heart of the injury.

"Have you far to go? Only, I live just the other side of the river. My car's there. I could drive you?"

It was a tempting offer. Lindsay didn't fancy hiking a mile on a damaged ankle. She looked up, taking in her nemesis turned Good Samaritan. She saw a woman in her late twenties with an angular face and short blonde hair cut to fashionable effect. Her eyes were slate blue, her eyebrows a pair of dark circumflex accents above them. She was dressed out of Gap and carried a leather knapsack over one shoulder. She didn't look like an axe murderer. "Okay," Lindsay said. "Thanks."

The response wasn't what she expected. Instead of the offer of an arm to help her down the hill and across the bridge, the woman looked taken aback, her eyes widening and her lips parting. "You're Lindsay Gordon," she said, bemused.

"Do I know you?" Lindsay leaned against the tree, wondering if she'd taken a blow to the head she hadn't registered at the time.

The blonde grinned. "We met about ten years ago. You came to the university GaySoc to talk about gays and the media. A bunch of us went out for a drink afterwards."

Lindsay strained at the locked gates of memory. "Edinburgh University?" she hazarded.

"That's right. You remember?"

"I remember doing the talk."

The blonde gave a rueful pout. "But you don't remember me. Well, that's hardly surprising. I was just a gawky wee fresher who was too overawed to open her mouth. But, hey, this is terrible. Me standing here reminiscing while you're suffering like this." Now she extended her arm. "Lean on me. I'm Rory, by the way. Rory McLaren."

Lindsay took the proffered arm and began to limp gingerly down the slope. "I'm amazed you recognised me all these years later," she said. The least she could do was make conversation, even though she felt more like swearing with every step.

Rory chuckled. "Oh, you were pretty impressive. You're part of the reason I ended up doing what I do."

"Which is?"

"I'm a journo."

"Oh well, never mind," Lindsay said, attempting a levity she didn't feel. The last thing she needed right now was some bright and bouncy kid still jam-packed with idealism making her feel even more old and decrepit than she already did.

"No, I love it," Rory assured her.

"How do you manage that?" They had reached the bottom of the hill and were making their way across the bridge. Moving on the flat was easier, but Lindsay was glad she'd taken up Rory's offer, even if the conversation was depressing her.

"It's a long story."

Lindsay looked up at the climb that would take them back to street level. "It's a big hill."

"Right enough," Rory said. "Well, I started off on the local paper in Paisley, which wasn't exactly a barrel of laughs, but at least they trained me. I got a couple of lucky breaks with big stories that I sold on to the nationals, and I ended up with a staff job on the *Standard*."

Lindsay snorted. "Working on the *Standard* makes you happy? God, things must have changed since my day."

"No, no, I'm not there any more."

"So where are you now?" Even in her state of discomfort, Lindsay noticed that Rory seemed faintly embarrassed.

"Well, see, that's the long-story bit."

"Take my mind off the pain and cut to the chase."

"I came up on the lottery."

"Jammy," Lindsay said.

"Aye. But not totally jammy. I didn't get the whole six numbers, just the five plus the bonus ball. But that was enough. I figured that if I invested the lot, it would earn enough in interest to keep a roof over my head. So I jacked the job in and now I'm freelance."

"And that's your idea of fun? Out there in the dog-eat-dog world?" Lindsay tried not to sound as sceptical as she felt. She'd been a freelance herself and knew only too well how tough it was to stay ahead of the pack.

"I figured what I needed was an angle. And I remembered something you said back at that talk at the GaySoc."

"This is surreal," Lindsay said. The word felt entirely inadequate to encompass the situation.

"I know. Wild, isn't it? I can't believe this is really you."

"Me neither. So what did I say that was so significant it came back to you all those years later?"

"You were talking about the ghetto mentality. How people think gays are completely different, completely separate from them. But we're not. We've got more in common with the straight universe than we have dividing us. And I thought, gays and lesbians don't just have gay and lesbian lives. They've got jobs. They've got families. They've got stories to tell. But most folk in our world have no reason to trust journalists. So I thought, what if I set myself up as the journalist that the gay community *can* trust? What a great way to get stories to come to me." Rory's voice was passionate now, her excitement obvious.

"And that's what you did?"

"Right. I've been at it over a year now, and I've had some fabulous exclusives. I mostly do investigative stuff, but I'll turn my hand to anything. And I'm making a good living."

They were almost out of the woods and on to the street. But although she desperately wanted to get the weight off her ankle, Lindsay didn't want this conversation to end. For the first time since she'd got back from California, she was hearing someone talk about her field with something other than apathy or cynicism. "So how did you get started?"

Rory pulled open the gate that led out from the riverbank on to the quiet backwater of Botanic Crescent. "That's my flat, on the corner there. I could fill you in over a coffee."

"Are you sure I'm not keeping you from anything?"

"God, no. Have you any idea how amazing it is for me to be talking to you? It'd have to be a bloody good story to make me miss a chance like this."

They crossed the road. Rory keyed a number into the security door of a red sandstone tenement and ushered Lindsay into a spotless tiled close. They made their way up one flight of worn stone stairs, then Rory unlocked the tall double doors that led into her first-floor flat. "Excuse the mess," she said, leading the way into the big dining kitchen at the back of the flat.

There was no false modesty behind Rory's words. It was, as she had said, a mess. A cat sprawled on a kitchen worktop by the window, while another lay curled on one of several piles of newspapers and magazines stacked on the floor. The tinfoil containers from the previous night's curry sat on another worktop alongside three empty bottles of Beck's, while the sink was piled with dirty plates and mugs. Lindsay grinned. "Live alone, do you?"

"That obvious, is it?" Rory picked a dressing gown off one of the chairs. "Grab a seat. Do you want some ice for that ankle? I've got a gel pack in the freezer."

"That'd be good." Lindsay lowered herself into the chair. In front of her was that morning's *Herald*, the cryptic crossword already completed with only a couple of jottings in the margin.

Rory rummaged in a freezer that looked like the Arctic winter, but emerged triumphant with a virulent turquoise oblong. "There we go." She handed it to Lindsay and crossed to the kettle. "Coffee, right?"

"Is it instant?"

Rory turned, her eyebrows raised in a teasing question. "What if it is?"

"I'll have tea."

"I was only bothering you. It's proper coffee. I get Mit from an Italian café in town."

She busied herself with beans and grinder. When the noise subsided, Lindsay said, "You were going to tell me how you got started."

"So I was." Rory poured the just-boiled water on the grounds she'd spooned into a cafetiere. "I decided I needed to be visible. So I had a word with the guy who owns Café Virginia. You know Café Virginia? In the Merchant City, down by the Italian Quarter?"

Lindsay nodded. It hadn't been a gay venue when she'd lived in the city. It had been a bad pub that sold worse food, called something stupidly suggestive like Pussy Galore. But she was aware that it had been reincarnated as the city's premiere gay and lesbian café bar, although she hadn't paid it a visit yet. Sophie hadn't had much time for hitting the nightlife; she'd been too busy getting her feet under the operating table. Most of the socialising they'd done had been at dinner parties or in restaurants. Another sign of ageing, Lindsay had already decided. "I know where you mean," she said.

"I told him my idea, and we did a deal. Three-month trial basis. He'd let me use one of the booths in the back bar as a kind of office. And I'd do bits and pieces of PR for him. So I wander down there most mornings and set up shop in the bar. Pick up the papers on the way, take my laptop and my mobile and get to work."

"And people actually bring you stories?"

Rory poured out the coffee and brought two mugs across to the table. She sat down opposite Lindsay and met her questioning gaze. "Amazingly enough, they do. It was a bit slow to start with. Just the odd gossipy wee bit that made a few pars in the tabloids. But then one of the lunchtime regulars who works in the City Chambers dropped me a juicy tale about some very dodgy dealing in the leisure department. I got a splash and spread in the *Herald*, and I was away. People soon realised I could be trusted to protect my sources, so everybody with an axe to grind came leaping out of the woodwork. Absolute bonanza." She grinned. It was hard not to be seduced by her delight.

"I'm impressed," Lindsay said. "And it's not a bad cup of coffee, either."

"So what are you doing back in Glasgow? Last I heard about you was when you got involved in Union Jack's murder at the

Journalists" Union conference. The word was that you were living in California, that you'd given up the game for teaching. How come you're back in Glasgow?"

Lindsay stared into her coffee. "Good question."

"Has it got an answer?" There was a long silence, then Rory continued. "Sorry, I can't help myself. I'm a nosy wee shite."

"It's a good quality in a journalist."

"Aye, but it's not exactly an asset in the social skills department," Rory said ruefully. "Which would maybe be why, as you rightly pointed out, I live alone."

"I came back for love," Lindsay said. The kid had worked hard for an answer. It seemed a reasonable exchange for a decent cup of coffee and some pain relief.

Rory ran a hand through her hair. "God, what a dyke answer. Why do we ever do anything demented? Love."

"You think it's demented to come back to Glasgow?"

Rory pulled a rueful face. "Me and my big mouth. I mean, for all I know, California's not what it's cracked up to be. So, what are you doing with yourself now?"

Lindsay shook her head. "Not a lot. Mostly waiting for the love object to come home from the high-powered world of obstetrics and gynaecology."

"You don't fancy getting back into deadline city, then?"

Lindsay leaned back in her seat, trying to ease her T-shirt away from her shoulder blades now that the sweat had dried and stuck it to her skin. "I've no contacts. I've not written a news story in seven years. I don't even know the name of my local MSP, never mind who's running Celtic and Rangers. It'd be like starting all over again as a trainee reporter on the local weekly."

Rory gave her a speculative look. "Not necessarily," she said slowly.

"Meaning what?" Lindsay couldn't even be bothered to be intrigued.

"Meaning, you could always come and work with me."

2

Morning rain on the Falls Road, grey sky only half a shade lighter than gunmetal: a comparison that still came too easy to too many people in Belfast. Ceasefires, peace deals, referendums and still it caught people by surprise that the disasters on the news were happening some other place.

A black taxi pulled up outside a betting shop on a street corner. These days, sometimes a black taxi was just a taxi. This one wasn't. This one was bringing Patrick Coughlan to work. To his official work. When he went about his unofficial work, the last thing he wanted to be seen in was IRA trademark wheels. In the days when he went about his unofficial work rather more frequently than of late, he had always gone under his own steam, in any one of a dozen nondescript vehicles. Of course the security services had almost certainly known Patrick Coughlan was a senior member of the IRA Army Council, but they'd never been able to catch him at it. He was a careful as well as a solid citizen.

The cab idled for a full minute by the kerb while Patrick scrutinised the street. If someone had asked what he was looking for, he'd have been hard pressed to answer. He only knew when it wasn't there. Satisfied, he stepped out of the cab and across the pavement. A man in his early fifties, obviously once very handsome, his features now blurred with slightly too much weight and high living, his walk betrayed a sense of purpose. His hair was a glossy chestnut, suspiciously so at the temples for a man who had lived his particular life. In spite of the laughter lines that surrounded them, his eyes were dark, shrewd and never still.

He pulled open the door on a gust of stale air and stepped inside. To the uninformed eye, just a busy Belfast betting shop, nothing to differentiate it from any other. Odds were chalked up on whiteboards, sporting papers pinned to the walls, tiled floor pocked with cigarette burns. The clientele looked like the unemployed, the unemployable and the retired. Every one of them was male. The staff were working hard behind metal grilles, but not so hard that they didn't all glance up at the opening of the door. The smoke of the day's cigarettes already hung heavy in the air, even though it was barely eleven.

Patrick crossed the room like the lord of the manor, nodding affably, waving a proprietary greeting to several regulars. They returned the greeting deferentially, one actually tugging the greasy brim of a tweed cap. It had never struck anyone as odd that so avowed a Republican should behave quite so much like an English patrician.

Patrick continued across the room towards a door set in the wall by the end of the counter. One of the staff automatically slid a hand beneath the counter and the sound of a buzzer followed. Without breaking stride, Patrick pushed through the door and into a dim corridor with stairs at the far end.

A door in the wall opened and a young woman with hair like a black version of Ronald McDonald and skin the blue white of skimmed milk stuck her head round it. "Sammy McGuire was on earlier. He said would you give him a call."

"I will, Theresa." Patrick continued down the corridor and up the stairs.

It would be hard to imagine how the office he walked into could have been more different from the seediness downstairs.

The floor was parquet—the real thing, not those pre-glued packs from the DIY superstore—with a silver grey Bokhara occupying what space wasn't taken up by a Regency desk that looked almost too much for its slender legs. The chair behind it was padded leather, the filing cabinets that lined the wall old mahogany buffed to a soft sheen. Two paintings on the wall, both copies, one of a Degas and one of a Stubbs, both featuring horses. The only thing that let the room down was the view of the Falls Road.

He'd thought of having the window bricked up and replacing it with another Degas. But it didn't do to let people think you weren't keeping an eye on them. Information had always been a commodity in Belfast; and if you didn't yet have the information, it was almost as important to make it look as if there was no reason why you shouldn't. So the window stayed.

Patrick lowered himself gingerly into the chair, a martyr to his back as well as his country. Settled, he reached for the phone and pushed a single button on the speed dialler.

"Sammy?" Patrick said.

"Patrick. How're ye?"

"Well, Sammy. And yourself?"

"Ah well, no complaints, you know?"

"And the family?" The rituals had to be observed.

"They're all doing fine. Geraldine's got herself a nice wee job with the Housing Corporation."

"Good for her. She'll do well there, so she will. So, Sammy, what can I do for you?"

"Well, Patrick, it might be that I can do something for you."

Patrick opened the humidor on his desk and selected a King Edward half-Corona. "Is that so, Sammy?" he said, tucking the phone into his neck while he lit the cigar.

"Have you still an interest in Bernadette Dooley?"

Patrick clenched the phone in his fist. Only a lifetime of dissimulation allowed him to sound unruffled. "Now there's a name I've not heard in years," he said genially. But his heart was jittering in his chest, the surge of memory flashing a slideshow of images across his mind's eye.

"Only, when she went missing, I seem to remember you were pretty keen to find out where she'd gone."

"I'm always concerned about my employees, Sammy. You know that."

"Oh aye," Sammy said hastily. "I know that, Patrick. But I didn't know if you were still interested?"

He couldn't maintain the pretence of disinterest any longer. "Where is she, Sammy?"

Patrick heard the sound of a cheap lighter clicking. "I was in Glasgow last weekend—a cousin of the wife's wedding. Anyway, I went into a supermarket to get some drinks in, and I saw Bernadette. Not to speak to, like, but it was definitely her, Patrick." Sammy spoke rapidly.

"Was she working there?"

"No, no, she was walking out with her shopping. I was at the checkout, in the middle of paying, there was nothing I could do . . ."

"What supermarket would that be, now?" Patrick said, as if it were a matter of supreme indifference.

"I'm not sure of the name of it, like, but it's right at the top of Byres Road. Behind the Grosvenor Hotel. That's where the wedding was, you see. I didn't know if you were still interested, but I thought, no harm in letting your man know."

"I appreciate that, Sammy. There's a twenty-pound bet for you in the shop next time you're passing." It would cost him nothing. Sammy McGuire was one of life's losers. "Take care now."

Patrick terminated the connection. He leaned back in his chair and stared at the Degas, two frown lines between his eyebrows. Few people had ever touched his heart; Bernadette Dooley had been the only one of those who had ever dared to betray him. Even now, the thought of what he had lost when she had disappeared gave him physical pain. For seven years, he'd dreamed of finding her again, convinced that their paths would have to cross sooner or later. Not a day had passed without consciousness of what had gone when she had vanished from his life. At last, he had a chance to regain the peace of mind she had stolen from him. He flicked the intercom. "Theresa, Sammy McGuire's due a twenty on the house. He'll be by later on."

Then he hit the speed dialler again. The other end answered on the second ring, if silence could be called answering. "Michael?" Patrick said softly.

"No, it's Kevin."

Patrick stifled a sigh. The way it worked, you had to find a place for the stupid ones because it was bad politics to turn them away. So you put one thick one on every team and hoped the others would keep him out of trouble. Funny, it always was a him that was the thicko. You could get away with it without too many problems usually, because one dummy in a cell of four or five wasn't too much of a liability. But in a team of two . . . it might be a different story. Patrick hoped not, for all sorts of reasons. "Put Michael on," he said wearily.

A long moment of silence, then Michael's hard voice cut through the ether. "Patrick," he said.

"Come in. I've got something for you." Patrick put the phone down. Only then did he realise his cigar had gone out.

The headlights turned into the drive. Lindsay checked that it was Sophie's car and reached for the phone. "Carry out, please," she said when it was answered. By the time the front door closed, she was listening to the invariable, "Twenty-five minutes, Mrs Gordon." She twisted round on the window seat so she was half-facing the door. She heard Sophie's briefcase hit the floor, heard the snick of the cloakroom door shutting, then her partner's voice.

"I'm home," Sophie called. Her shoes clicked on the wooden flooring as she turned into the kitchen. "Lindsay?" She sounded puzzled.

"I'm through here."

Sophie appeared in the doorway, still elegant after a day's work in a tailored suit and plain silk shirt. She had the grace not to ask why Lindsay wasn't in the kitchen as usual, putting the finishing touches to dinner. "Hi, darling," she said, the smile reaching her tired eyes. Then she took in the bandaged ankle propped on a cushion and raised her eyebrows, concern on her face. "What on earth have you been doing to yourself?"

"It's just a sprain."

Sophie crossed the room and perched by Lindsay's foot, her hand drawn irresistibly to the neatly wrapped crepe bandage that swaddled the injured ankle. "Suddenly you're the doctor?"

"I'm the one with the sports injuries experience." Lindsay grinned. "Trust me, it's a sprain."

"What happened?" Sophie tenderly stroked Lindsay's leg.

"I wasn't paying attention. I was running up the hill to the Botanics and I crashed into somebody."

Sophie shook her head, indulgent amusement on her face. "So how much havoc did you create?"

"None. She was absolutely fine. She ended up driving me home."

"Lucky for you her car was there."

Lindsay shrugged. "She lives across the river. It was easier to give in and hobble there than to risk doing myself serious damage by walking all the way home."

"Still, it was nice of her to take the trouble." Sophie began gently massaging the relaxed curve of Lindsay's calf.

Lindsay leaned back against the folded wooden shutter. "Aye, it was. And then she propositioned me."

Sophie's hand froze and her eyes widened. "She what?"

Lindsay struggled to maintain a straight face. "She made me the kind of offer you're not supposed to be able to refuse, especially when it comes from a cute blonde baby dyke."

"I hope this is your idea of a joke," Sophie said, her voice a dark warning.

"No joke. She asked me if I wanted to come and work with her."

Sophie cocked her head to one side, not sure how much her lover was playing with her. "She offered you a job? On the basis of crashing into you and watching you sprain your ankle? She's looking for a bull in a china shop?"

"On the basis that I am still apparently a legend in my own lunchtime and she's got a very healthy freelance journalism business that could use another pair of hands." Lindsay let her face relax, her eyes sparkling with the delight of having wound Sophie up.

Sophie gave Lindsay's knee a gentle punch. "Bastard," she said. "You had me going for a minute there." She ran a hand through her silvered curls. "I don't believe you," she sighed. "Only you could manage to turn a jogging accident into a job opportunity. But how did she know you were a journalist? Is she someone you used to work with?"

"No. She was barely in the game by the time we left for California." Lindsay quickly ran through the details of the encounter with Rory that she'd been polishing into an anecdote all afternoon. "And so," she concluded, "I said I'd think about it."

"What's to think about?" Sophie said. "It doesn't have to be forever. If something else you really fancy comes up, you can always move on. Idleness makes you miserable, and it's not like you're snowed under with prospects."

Lindsay pulled a face. "Thanks for reminding me," she said frostily.

"I didn't mean it like that. I just meant that it sounds like what Rory's doing would be right up your street. Chasing the kind of stories that interest you. Working with a community you can feel part of."

Lindsay drew her leg away from Sophie and swung round to face the living room. "Never mind that I'd be working for somebody ten years younger than me. Never mind that she only offered it because she felt sorry for me. Never mind that it feels like back-tracking to where I was fifteen years ago."

Sophie got to her feet and moved to turn on the lamps. "It doesn't sound like she felt sorry for you. It sounds like she was blown away by the chance of working with one of her heroes. Anyway, from what you've said, you wouldn't be working *for* Rory, you'd be working with her."

"And who do you think is going to get first dibs on the stories? They'd be coming from her contacts, not mine. Coming on the basis of her reputation, not mine. I'd end up with the scraps from the table. The stories that don't interest her. The down-page dross."

Sophie leaned on the mantelpiece, casting a speculative look at her lover. "It might start off like that. But it wouldn't be long before the word went out that Lindsay Gordon was back in town. You'd soon be pulling in your own stories. Where's your fight gone, Lindsay? You've always had a good conceit of yourself. It's not like you to indulge in self-pity."

For a long moment, Lindsay said nothing. Finally, she took a deep breath. "Maybe I've been sitting in your shadow for too long."

Sophie's face registered shock. But before she could say anything, the doorbell rang.

"That'll be the takeaway," Lindsay said. "I hope you don't mind, but I didn't feel up to standing around cooking."

Sophie frowned. "Of course I don't mind. Why would I mind, for God's sake?"

"Because you'll be paying for it. You'd better go and answer the door. If we wait for me to stagger out there, it'll be cold by the time we get to eat it." She pushed herself upright and began to limp towards the kitchen, using whatever furniture was available as a prop.

By the time Sophie returned with a carrier bag full of Indian food, Lindsay had managed to put plates and cutlery on the kitchen table. Sophie dumped the takeaway on the table and headed for the fridge. "You want a beer?"

"Please." Lindsay busied herself with unpacking the foil containers and tossing the lids into the empty bag. When Sophie returned with a couple of bottles of Sam Adams Boston Lager, Lindsay looked up. "I'm sorry. That was out of order."

Sophie sat down and helped herself to pilau rice. "Is that how you feel? That you're living in my shadow?" Her voice betrayed the anxiety Lindsay's words had provoked.

Lindsay worried at a piece of naan bread. "It's not that. Not exactly. It's more that I feel I've been drifting. No direction of my own. It's like the teaching job in Santa Cruz. I'd never have moved into teaching journalism if I'd stayed in the UK, but we went to the US for your career, and I had to find something to do."

"But I thought you enjoyed it?"

"I did. But that was pure luck. It wasn't because I had a burning desire to teach. And if I'd hated it, I'd still have had to stick with it, because there was bugger all else I could do." Lindsay reached for the bottle and took a swig of beer. "And now, here we are, back in Scotland because of your career, and I'm still no nearer figuring out what I want to be when I grow up."

Sophie opened her mouth to say something but Lindsay silenced her with a raised finger. "Don't get me wrong. I'm not saying that's your fault. Nobody is more pleased than me that everything's going so well for you. I know what it means to you and how hard you've worked for it. But it doesn't make it any easier for me. And you being so keen for me to hitch my wagon to Rory's star—that feels like you being desperate for me to take up any kind of stopgap that'll keep me from going out of my head with boredom and frustration. I don't want another stopgap, Soph, I want to feel passionate about something. The way you do."

Sophie looked down at her plate and nodded. "I understand that," she said. "But you used to feel passionate about journalism.

When I first knew you, ages before we got together, you really cared about what you were doing. You really believed you could make a difference."

Lindsay gave a bark of ironic laughter. "Yeah, well, we all thought we could change the world back then. I soon got that knocked out of me."

They ate for a few minutes in silence. Then Sophie reached out and covered Lindsay's hand with her own. "Why don't you give it a try? It sounds as though Rory's way of working is light years away from the daily grind that turned you into a cynic. It can't hurt to put your toe in the water. Besides, when the gods drop such an amazing piece of serendipity in your lap, it seems to me it would be tempting fate to thumb your nose at it."

Lindsay tried to swallow her mouthful of bhuna lamb, but it seemed to have lodged in her throat. She'd never had sufficient defence against Sophie's kindness. Her partner had never once complained about being the sole breadwinner since they'd returned from California, and Lindsay knew she genuinely harboured no resentment about it. All Sophie wanted was for Lindsay to feel as happy and as fulfilled in whatever she chose to do as she was herself. She hadn't applied any pressure, simply offered encouragement. The least Lindsay could do was kick her pride into touch and take a chance on Rory McLaren. "You're right," she said. "Heaven knows, I can't afford to fly in the face of serendipity. And besides, I've got nothing to lose, have I?"

3

Lindsay squirmed around in bed, trying to get comfortable. The weight of the duvet made her ankle ache, distracting her from the Denise Mina novel she was trying to read. "Can you bring me a couple of ibuprofen when you come through?" she called to Sophie, who seemed to be taking forever in the bathroom.

When she finally emerged and slipped into bed beside Lindsay, Sophie seemed unusually quiet. Lindsay swallowed the pills and put her book down. "Is something bothering you?" she said. "You've hardly said a word since dinner. Are you having second thoughts about me working with Rory?"

Sophie looked surprised. "No, not at all. Why should I?"

"No reason. But I couldn't think why else you'd gone so quiet."

Sophie sighed. "There's something we need to talk about. I was going to bring it up earlier, but we were talking about your future and it just didn't seem like the right moment."

Lindsay eased herself on to her side and put an arm round Sophie's waist. "That sounds ominous. I'll never sleep now, you know. You'd better tell me what's on your mind."

Sophie lay back and stared at the ceiling, one hand on Lindsay's encircling arm. "It's the baby thing."

Lindsay felt a pit opening in her stomach. Sophie's desire for a child had been an intermittent bone of contention between them for the past couple of years. Whenever Sophie had tried to discuss it, Lindsay had either stonewalled or blanked it. She might not have much of a life plan, but she knew for certain that parenthood wasn't part of it. So she'd worked on the principle that, if she ignored it, Sophie would eventually get the message and it would all go away. And inevitably, the attrition of time would render it academic. But since they'd come back to Scotland the subject had surfaced more regularly. Every few days, Sophie had raised the topic and Lindsay had tried to sidestep it. "You know how I feel about that," she said.

"Yes. I know how you feel about that. But I don't think you have the faintest idea how I feel about it. Lindsay, it's all I think about," Sophie said, anguish unmistakable in her voice. "Everywhere I go, all I seem to see are pregnant women and women pushing babies in prams. I'm so envious it makes me feel violent. I can't even get away from it at work, because it's what I deal with all day, every day." Sophie blinked hard, and Lindsay couldn't avoid seeing the sparkle of tears in her eyes. "Lindsay, I'm desperate. I'm nearly forty. Time's running out for me. Already, the chances are that I'm not going to be able to conceive without some sort of clinical intervention. And there isn't a fertility clinic in the whole of Scotland that will treat lesbian couples. Not even privately. If I'm going to have any possibility of a baby, I need to start doing something about it now."

"Look, you're broody, that's all. It'll pass. It always has before," Lindsay said wretchedly.

"No. You're wrong. It never passed. Sure, I stopped talking about it, but that was only because you were so negative about the whole thing, it felt like pushing a boulder uphill. Just because I stopped talking about it doesn't mean it wasn't always there, constantly nagging away at me. If I don't have a child, there's going to be a hole in my life that nothing else will fill."

Lindsay drew her arm away and rolled on to her back. "You're saying I'm not enough for you. That what we have isn't good enough."

Sophie shuffled on to her side and reached for Lindsay's hand. "That's not what I'm saying. I love you like I've never loved anyone else. I want to spend the rest of my life with you. But this need in me—it's different. It's a kind of desperation. If you've never felt it, you can't know what it's like. If you could walk for five minutes inside my skin, you'd maybe comprehend how this is consuming me. I need to try, Lindsay. And I need to try now."

Lindsay squeezed her eyes shut. *Please, let this not be happening*, she thought. "I don't want a child." She spoke slowly and deliberately.

"You'd make a great parent."

"That's not the issue. The issue is that I don't want to."

"But I need to."

Lindsay jerked upright, oblivious to the stab of pain in her ankle. "So what are you saying? You're going to go ahead anyway? Regardless of how I feel?"

Sophie turned away. Her voice was shaky with tears. She feared she was driving Lindsay further from her with everything she said, but she couldn't keep the churn of emotions secret any longer. "Lindsay, if I have to lose you to have the chance of a child, then I'll do it. This is not about choice, it's about compulsion. This isn't some whim, some spur of the moment desire for a designer accessory. It feels like life and death to me."

Her words shook Lindsay like a physical blow. She pulled her knees up to her chest, gripping them tightly with her hands. She knew her lover well enough to realise that this was no empty ultimatum. Sophie didn't play games like that. And she was sufficiently resolute to carry out her stated intention.

This was the moment Lindsay had always dreaded, ever since the issue of motherhood had first raised its head between them. Her life had been bound to Sophie's for so long, she couldn't imagine what it would be without her. She didn't even want to try. But if she didn't give in, that would be exactly what she would have to face. "I can't believe you're making me choose between losing you or having a child with you," she choked out.

"I can't either," Sophie said. Her chest hurt, as if she was being physically rent in two. "Surely that alone tells you how powerless I feel? I'm in the grip of something I've got no control over, and it's killing me. But I've got to try, Lindsay. I've got to."

"I've got no choice either then, have I?" Lindsay said bitterly.

There was a long silence. Finally Sophie said, "You have got a choice. You can stay with me and try to make a family with me and our child. Or you can choose to walk away."

Lindsay snorted. "Some choice. At least you've got a chance of getting something you want out of this. I don't. Either I lose you, which would break my heart, or I have to be a parent to a child I don't want. This is emotional blackmail, Sophie."

"You think I don't know that? You think I want to behave like this?" Sophie turned to face Lindsay, tracks of moisture glistening on her cheeks. "You think I like myself like this?"

Lindsay tried to stay resolute, to keep her eyes on the opposite wall. But it was more than she could manage. She slid down the bed and reached for Sophie. "You know I can't leave you," she mumbled into Sophie's hair.

"And you know I don't want you to. What would be the point in having a baby without you there to share it with?"

For a long time, they clung to each other, their tears salt against each other's skin. Then Lindsay leaned back. It was going to be a long night; time they made a start on what had to be said. "So. What's your next step?" she asked, resignation heavy in her voice.

Café Virginia was suffering its daily identity crisis in the hiatus between the after-work drinkers and the evening players. The music had shifted into more hard-core dance, making conversation difficult, and there was a strange mixture of outfits on display, from business suits to T-shirts that clung to nipples and exposed midriffs.

The quietest place in the bar was the corner booth where Rory McLaren ran her business and held court. Nobody else ever sat in the booth, mostly because of the foot-high scarlet neon sign that said "Reserved." Rory had wanted it to say "Gonnae Fuck Off?" but Cathy the bar manager had vetoed it on the grounds that it would be too big for the table. Rory was hammering out the finishing touches to a memo on a story proposal for the *Herald* feature pages, occasionally pausing to sip at her bottle of Rolling Rock. She looked up, sensing company heading her way, and saw a sharp-suited Asian woman with gleaming hair in a shoulder length bob weaving her way through the tables towards her.

Sandra Singh flopped on to the bench seat opposite Rory, dumping raincoat, handbag and briefcase beside her. "That jerk Murray," she spat.

"Thought as much," Rory said, giving Sandra the quick once-over. "Love the earrings."

"A wee shop in Cambridge. I'm going to kill him, I swear to God. Three weeks hammering out the new format and then this morning it's, 'the network disnae like it.' I tell you, some days I wish I'd never left newspapers." She raked in her handbag and came out with a packet of Marlboro Red and a matchbook from last night's restaurant.

"You don't mean that." Rory leaned out of the booth and waved to the bar, holding up two fingers.

Sandra's grin was even sharper than her suit. "You're right, I don't." She sighed. "I just wish I did. So, any news?"

"You could say that. Looks like I might have got myself a partner."

Sandra snorted smoke. "As in, you got laid?"

Rory's attempt at dignity wouldn't have fooled a drunken child of two. "Sandra, there's more to life than sex."

Sandra's laugh attracted every woman in the place. "You didn't get laid, then."

"I'm talking business here, fool."

Sandra nodded acknowledgement to the barmaid, who placed two sweating bottles in front of them. "You serious? I thought the whole point of this was being a one-man band?"

"I thought so, yeah. But this one's really special."

Sandra took a long swallow of her beer. "So you're planning on getting laid?"

Rory shook her head in affectionate exasperation. "No. Focus your mind above the waist for once, would you? I'm not looking for a shag, I'm looking to build a business. Listen, do you remember me telling you years back about Lindsay Gordon?"

Sandra frowned. "Lindsay . . . ? Oh, wait a minute. The great lesbian icon hack. The one that turned you on to the beautiful game. This would be that Lindsay Gordon?"

"One and the same. Well, you'll never guess what happened. You couldn't write this, people would say, 'Yeah, right, and then the Pope said abortion was fine by him.' But this is the absolute, no messing, God's honest truth." Rory gave Sandra the full version of her meeting with Lindsay, punctuated by her friend's regular interruptions.

"That's wild," Sandra finally said. "So she said she'd think about it?"

"That was just for show. You could tell she's gagging to get back in harness."

"You wish." Sandra finished her cigarette and her beer. "Sorry, babe. I'm out of here. In fact, I never was in here. Got a date with a beautiful boy from Radio Clyde." She stood up, gathering her universe. She leaned across the table and kissed Rory on the cheek. "See you, darlin'."

On her way out, she passed a baby dyke, black leather waist-coat over white T-shirt, black jeans, dyed-black cropped hair, bottle of Rolling Rock in her hand. "She's all yours," Sandra told her, patting her on the arm. The baby dyke flushed scarlet and edged towards the booth.

"I got you a drink, Rory," she said, a nervous smile twitching at the corners of her mouth.

"Thanks. You want to sit down?"

The kid squirmed into the seat Sandra had left. "You pay folk for stories, eh?" she scrambled out.

"Depends. What's your name?"

"I'm Kola. Wi' a K. Ma pal Ginger says you gien her a fifty for something she told you last year."

Rory nodded. Ginger had tipped her the wink about a candidate for the Scottish parliament with a sideline in cigarette smuggling. She'd got a splash in the *Herald* and follow-ups in all the dailies the next day. "I remember. How's Ginger doing? I've not seen her about the place for a while."

"She's went tae London. She got taken on by BHS. The clothes are shite, and so's the money, but she's having a ball. So will you pay me for a story?"

"Let me hear what you've got and I'll tell you what it's worth. Okay?"

Kola thought about it. It was a bit more complicated than buying a drink or scoring some E, so it took a minute or two. "How do I know you won't just write it anyway?"

"You don't. You have to trust me. But you know I didn't let Ginger down."

Kola nodded, her face clearing, relieved at having the decision made for her. "Right. Okay. It's about Madonna."

Rory fought to keep her face straight. Whatever was coming, she didn't think it was going to keep the cats in Whiskas for life. "Madonna? We're talking the singer, not the one with the statues in the cathedral?"

It was beyond Kola, who frowned. "Aye, the singer. Her and that Guy Ritchie, they're gonnae buy a big house out in Drymen."

Stranger things have happened, Rory thought. *4, 6, 11, 24, 39 and the bonus ball is 47.* At least Drymen was the right sort of territory for someone like Madonna. Big houses, country estates, high walls and gamekeepers with shotguns. "In Drymen?" she echoed.

"You don't believe me, do you?" Kola accused her with the tired hurt of someone used to being taken for a liar.

"It's a bit . . . surprising," Rory said. "Gonnae tell me where you heard this?"

"It's right enough," Kola said defensively. "The folk that work for her have been on the phone to an estate agent out there."

"You're going to have to tell me how you know that, Kola," Rory said, suddenly wondering if the baby dyke might not be as daft as she looked.

Kola sighed in exasperation. "I'm shagging his wife."

4

People would cross the road if they saw Michael Conroy walking towards them. Whether they knew him by sight or by repute or not at all, they instinctively knew better than to block this man's piece of the pavement. His eyes were the greenish amber of a bird of prey; his narrow face involuntarily called up memories of a wood-axe. He looked precisely what he was. Dangerous and mean. To Patrick Coughlan, this limited his usefulness. He'd never have dreamed of sending Michael undercover unless the aim was to scare the shit out of everybody he came into contact with.

Michael didn't mind. His idea of being a soldier wasn't pretending to be a librarian in north London or working on a building site in Derby while other people did the dirty work. He liked what he'd spent the past fifteen years doing. Ceasefire didn't suit him and he knew it.

He sat in the chair facing Patrick, his eyes calm and watchful. Dressed in an olive green combat jacket and blue jeans, he would have fitted in perfectly with any group of squaddies in a bar anywhere. Entirely self-contained, he cleaned his nails with the blade of a penknife, an absent-minded habit that he was unaware was marked down on the file MI5 had held on him for some years.

Kevin O'Donohue was the gopher. A thin, wiry grey-hound, he fetched and carried without the wit to question what or why. Loyal to the point of stupidity, he was reliable only in the sense that he didn't have enough brains to act on his own initiative. He did what he was told, and mostly he did it well enough. Michael tolerated him for his sister's sake. Siobhan got Kevin's share of intelligence in the genetic share-out. It wasn't imbecility that had got her caught in the aftermath of the Dock-lands bomb. Just bad luck. Michael hadn't seen her for three years, but he'd kept his word and made sure Kevin was sorted. Kevin, of course, had no idea of this pact.

Kevin looked like a harmless rodent, which was appropriate enough. Coarse auburn hair badly cut so it emphasized the jut of his forehead, the sort of freckles that looked like a nasty rash and the fashion sense of Man at Millett's told any casual encounter all they needed to know. He fidgeted in his chair, nervous in the presence of Patrick, who always made him feel like he was about to make his first confession all over again.

"I've a wee job for you," Patrick said. "It's what you might call private enterprise. You'll need to keep your mouths shut, but you'll be well looked after."

Michael nodded. "Whatever you say, Patrick."

"It's a matter of finding somebody I have an interest in." Patrick pushed a photograph across the desk. Michael leaned forward and picked it up. He gave it the hard stare, then off-handed it to Kevin.

"She used to work downstairs," Michael said, his voice as uninterested as if he'd been asked the time.

"That's right. She did a disappearing act six, seven years ago with something that belongs to me. I've had the word out in a quiet sort of a way, and now I've got intelligence that she's in Glasgow."

"And you'd like us to find her for you." It wasn't a question.

"D'you have an address, then?" Kevin asked.

Patrick ignored him. "She was seen at the weekend in a supermarket at the top of Byers Road. Behind the Grosvenor

Hotel. It's the only lead I've got. Obviously she's not going to be using her own name, so there's no point in looking in the phone book or the voter's roll."

Michael folded his knife shut. "We'll manage," he said.

Patrick opened his desk drawer and took out a brown envelope. "I don't want you using any of our people over there, so you'll need a float. Theresa's got tickets downstairs for tonight's ferry."

"What about a car?" Michael asked.

Patrick raised one finger and smiled approvingly. "There's a British driving licence in the envelope. You can use it to hire a car if you need one."

Michael pocketed the envelope without looking at the contents. "Daily calls?"

"At least. You've got a clean mobile, haven't you?"

Michael's grin would have put Red Riding Hood's wolf to shame. "Clean, not cloned," he said.

"Any questions?" Patrick asked, his voice a silky challenge.

"What are we supposed to do when we find her?" Kevin asked, oblivious.

"Whatever Patrick tells us," Michael sighed. He got to his feet. "I'll be in touch," he said.

Patrick inclined his head. "I can't wait." If they'd seen the look in his eyes, anyone with any sense would have already left town.

Lindsay stared out of the window of the cab, taking in nothing of the late-morning bustle of Great Western Road. Normally, she'd have used the Clockwork Orange, Glasgow's underground system, to go into the city centre, but her ankle was stiff and swollen and today she cared more about comfort than being environmentally friendly.

It had been a long night. They'd talked for more than an hour after Sophie's bombshell, and it hadn't got any better from Lindsay's point of view. The revelation that had shocked her most of all was that Sophie had already identified a possible donor, had approached him and had secured his agreement. Fraser Tomlinson was a researcher in Sophie's department, a gay man in a steady relationship. He and his boyfriend Peter had been to the house for dinner, and Lindsay had found them pleasant company. According to Sophie, Fraser was HIV negative, his family medical history gave no grounds for serious concern and he had no desire to play any role in the life of any child that might result from the donation of his sperm. It was so cut and dried, it had left Lindsay lost for words.

"And when were you thinking of starting?" she'd managed at last.

"I'm due to ovulate in a couple of days' time," Sophie had said. "The best chance is to bracket the ovulation. I was planning to have the first go tomorrow night, then again two nights later."

Lindsay swallowed hard. "I can see why you wanted to bring it up now." Involuntarily, she moved so her body no longer touched Sophie's.

"I'm sorry to spring it on you like this. But we've talked and talked and got nowhere. I realised that we were never going to get anywhere unless I did something about it. Lindsay . . ." Sophie's voice was a plea. "Every time I bleed, it feels like a lost opportunity. I can't afford to wait. I've done the blood tests. So far, my hormone levels are okay. But every month that goes past takes me nearer the point where they're not going to be okay any longer. I've got a donor now, I'm not prepared to hang on until you come round to feeling positive about this."

"Fine. So we do it tomorrow night. What's the drill? Is there an etiquette here? Our place or theirs?"

"Fraser and Peter will come round here. What I hoped was that you would be here for me."

"You want *me* to do the thing with the turkey baster?"

"It won't be a turkey baster, for God's sake. It'll be a sterile syringe." Sophie reached for Lindsay's hand. "Please, Lindsay. I need you now more than I ever did."

Lindsay, who had always found it impossible to hold out against Sophie for any length of time, let her hand be held. "Fine. Whatever. Now, can I go to sleep?"

The end of the conversation had not led directly to sleep. Lindsay had lain awake long after Sophie's breathing became deep and regular. There was a hollow feeling in her stomach, a nameless grief that ached insistently. Something had shifted inside her tonight with the knowledge that she could never give Sophie enough to satisfy her. She had thought their life together was good, their relationship solid. Now, it felt as if her house was built on sand. Maybe it was true that she hadn't been hearing Sophie. But it was equally true that Sophie hadn't been hearing her.

She'd mooched around the house after Sophie had left for work, unable to settle to anything. She couldn't be bothered answering the morning's e-mails. She was impatient with the newspapers and their flood of irrelevancies. Finally, stir crazy, she'd decided to pay a visit to Café Virginia. Perhaps Rory McLaren had something to offer that would make her feel better about herself. But first, she had a couple of phone calls to make. Lindsay might have been out of the game for a long time. But she still knew one or two of the faces that counted. She wasn't going to hitch her wagon to Rory McLaren's star until she had confirmed that the world's estimate of the young freelance bore some relationship to Rory's own pitch. In her early years as a national newspaper journalist, she'd wasted too much time chasing the fantasies of freelances keen to make an easy buck to take any of the breed at their word.

On the other side of the city centre, Rory was swanning into the offices of the *Scottish Daily Standard*. The security men didn't care that she'd stopped working there six months before. They figured she'd had a better motive to blow the place up when she was on the staff than she ever could have as a freelance. She took the lift up to the editorial floor and walked into one of the side offices off the features area.

Giles Graham, lifestyle editor and secretly agony aunt of the *Standard*, was stretched out on his sofa, reading the pained letters of his correspondents and eating very low-fat cottage cheese and chives from the tub with a plastic spoon. Rory could never figure out how a man who managed such fastidious elegance in every other area of his life that he could be taken for a gay man still managed such disgusting eating habits.

"That's revolting," she said, crossing the room to sit in the swivel chair behind a worryingly tidy desk.

"I know. You'd think people would have the good sense not to go exploring their gay side with their brother-in-law, but they never learn," he drawled in the English-accented speech of the privately educated Scot. He put his lunch down on the coffee table and carefully gathered the letters together before sitting up and brushing down his immaculate navy linen shirt for invisible crumbs. "How delightful to see you, Rory. Are we having social intercourse or is there a sordid financial motive behind your visit?"

"You want social intercourse? Okay. How's Julia?"

Giles smiled fondly. His wife was the Member of the European Parliament for Central West Scotland. Julia's frequent absences, he maintained, were what rendered her capable of putting up with him. "She's on a jolly in Oslo."

"That's a contradiction in terms," Rory observed. "Give her my love next time you pass in the night." She leaned back in the chair and hitched her Gap-clad legs on to the desk. "I've got a very good tip for you, babe."

Giles groaned. "Why not copy? Why do I have to do all the work?"

"Because it's not my kind of story. I do investigative journalism, remember? Stories like this are the reason I quit working for the newsdesk."

"That and the thick end of a hundred and fifty grand," Giles said cynically.

"The lottery was the means, not the reason, as well you know. Now, do you want this story, or do you want me to toddle round to the *Sun*?"

Giles stretched his arms along the back of the sofa, languid as a trout stream on an August afternoon. "As if," he said. "So tell me what you know."

"Madonna's people are having hush-hush talks with estate agents about her buying a property on Loch Lomond. In the Drymen area."

Giles raised one eyebrow.

"Don't do that, you look like Roger Moore in a bad Bond movie," Rory complained. "It's straight up. I got it from the horse's mouth. Well, the groom's best mate's mouth. But I know for a fact that Struther Wilson have been approached, and if they've had the word, so have other people."

"If it's true, it's not a bad little tale," Giles said cautiously.

"It's me you're talking to, Giles. When you stand it up, it's a guaranteed splash and you know it."

His smile conceded. "How much are you looking for?"

"A generous tip fee. I've got to split it with my source. I'll leave the details to your sense of propriety."

Giles pushed his dark blond hair back from his forehead. "Very trusting."

"Hey, I know you're the only person under this roof who knows the meaning of the word." Rory dropped her feet to the floor and stood up. "I'll leave you to it. Some of us have got work to do."

He snorted. "Cappuccinos to drink, more like. By the way, Sandra tells me you think you're in with a chance with some woman you bumped into in the Botanics."

Rory shook her head. "If you guys worked as hard at getting stories as you do at spreading gossip, I'd be out of a job. Let me know how you get on with Madonna."

Before he could reply, Rory was out the door. She had more than cappuccino on her mind, but that was none of Giles's business. She still couldn't quite believe in her encounter with Lindsay; it felt too good to be true. Her freelance business had begun to generate more work than she could handle alone, but she hadn't wanted to share with just anyone. She'd always been a loner, hiding her self-sufficiency behind a mask of easy charm, letting few people see the vulnerability and damage behind the façade. Sandra was one of a handful who had been allowed past the barrier of her public face, but Sandra was too much in love with the buzz of television to consider giving it up for the slog of freelancing. And there was nobody else that Rory had ever seriously considered working with.

But something had sparked between her and Lindsay Gordon, and it was something more than hero worship. They'd made an instant connection, and Rory still felt faintly baffled by the speed with which she'd offered Lindsay a share in her closely guarded world. She had no conviction that Lindsay would take up the invitation without more work on her part; her self-belief couldn't quite carry her that far. So somehow Rory was going to have to figure out how to entice her in.

Lindsay dipped another crispy chip into the bowl of relish and turned another page of the paper. She'd been waiting over an hour for Rory, but it hadn't been a problem. Somehow, the restlessness that had afflicted her earlier had dissipated in the congenial atmosphere of Café Virginia. And besides, she'd made good use of the time.

She'd limped in, her eyes roving round the bar area, taking in the décor that somehow managed to be stylish without being impersonal. Trance music played, not loud enough to make conversation uncomfortable. A handful of patrons sat on high stools at tables built on to the square pillars that supported the ceiling. A few glanced up as she walked in, but nobody gave her a second look as she made her way to the zinc-topped counter. Behind the bar, a woman with cropped black hair was stocking cold cabinets with bottled beers. As Lindsay approached, she turned and stood up. "What can I get you?" she asked.

"I'll take a cappuccino."

The barmaid nodded and moved to the gleaming coffee machine. While she fiddled purposefully with taps and spigots, Lindsay continued to scan the place. The bar area occupied the front of the café, but beyond she could see a bigger room. Wooden booths lined the back wall, but the rest of the space was occupied with round metal tables and Italian-style chairs with slender chrome legs. At two of the tables, lone women sat with coffee cups, cigarettes and newspapers.

Lindsay paid for her drink, then said, "I'm looking for Rory McLaren."

The barmaid smiled. "The Scarlet Pimpernel of the Merchant City." It came out with the smoothness of a familiar line. "She's no' been in yet."

"She's got a regular table, right?"

The barmaid leaned on the counter and pointed through to the back room. "Furthest booth at the end. She expecting you?"

Lindsay shrugged. "I suppose that depends on how confident she is of her pulling power."

The smile widened to a grin. "She'll be expecting you, then. Go away through. Mind you, there's no telling when she'll show up. If she's not in first thing, it could be quite a while."

"That's okay, I'm not in any hurry."

"Aye well, all good things come to those who wait."

"Will you have one with me while I'm waiting?"

The barmaid raised her eyebrows. "Aye, all right. I'll have a Diet Irn-Bru, if it's all right with you." She reached into the chill cabinet and pulled out a can, popping the top and taking a swig.

"Do you mind telling me your name? Only, I reckon there's a fair chance I'm going to be in here quite a bit, and, 'Hey, you,' isn't really my style."

"Oh God, not another smooth operator," the barmaid sighed, raising her eyes to the ceiling.

Lindsay grinned. "Truly, that wasn't a line. I might be doing a bit of work with Rory and, from what she's told me, this is where it all happens." She shrugged. "I prefer to be on friendly terms, that's all."

"What sort of work?"

"I used to be a journalist. And Rory seems to think I could be again." Lindsay's self-deprecating shrug was perfectly calculated.

"She can be very persuasive."

"So I've heard. But you need to be in this game. So humour me that I can still cut the mustard and tell me your name."

The barmaid grinned. She had a tiny diamond inlaid in her left canine. It added shock value to the smile. "I'm Annie," she said.

"And I'm Lindsay." She looked around. "Rory tells me she keeps pretty busy. Plenty stories coming in all the time."

Annie nodded. "Everybody knows her in here. You'd be amazed the things she picks up just hanging out. It was slow at the start, but these days she's always got something on the go. Mind you, I'm surprised she's thinking about working with somebody else."

"How so?"

"No disrespect, but Rory's no, exactly what you'd call a team player. She likes her own company too much. Half the baby dykes in here are in love with her, but she never takes advantage. See Rory? She figures out what she wants and goes for it, and hell mend the hindmost. And people see that, and they trust her because of it."

"So you'd recommend working with her?"

"You could do a lot worse." Annie took a long swallow of her drink and put the can down behind the counter as another customer approached.

"I'll let you get on," Lindsay said, sliding off her bar stool and making her way through to Rory's booth. She smiled at the "Reserved" sign on the table, eased herself on to the padded bench seat and stared at the pile of morning papers neatly stacked against the wall. Her morning's research had been productive, and Annie's responses had confirmed her half-made decision.

The first journalist she'd spoken to had been a former colleague on the *Standard*. Gus was now news editor for BBC Radio Scotland and, although their relationship had been closer to that of sparring partners than friends, he'd seemed pleased enough to hear from her.

Gus didn't like Rory. He thought she was a chancer who pushed the very limits with her stories and who didn't care whose toes she trampled on when she was on the chase. But then, Gus had never liked women, least of all dykes. If that was the worst he could find to say about Rory, Lindsay reckoned her potential workmate was probably almost as good as she'd said she was.

Lindsay's second call was to Mary Salmond. They'd both been active in the Journalists' Union at the same time, and Mary was now women's editor of the *Reporter*. She'd sounded positively delighted to hear Lindsay's voice and immediately insisted they have lunch together to catch up. Lindsay reluctantly agreed; she'd always found Mary far too Edinburgh earnest for her taste. But she wanted information, and she'd have to pay for it.

Mary had gushed at the mention of Rory's name. "She's done awfully well since she went freelance," she said. "Awfully well indeed. She's done the odd piece for me, always her own ideas, and her copy's a joy. She writes to length, she pitches it at the right level for my readers and she's got the knack of getting doors to open for her."

"What's she like personally?"

"I wouldn't say I knew her that well. She seems very private, never really gives much away. She's not one of those freelances who's always trying to freeload in the pub, you know the kind?"

Lindsay knew the kind. "But you like her?"

"Oh yes, I like her fine. She's very pally with Giles Graham. You know Giles? Such a sweetie. If Giles likes her, she must have something going for her; I've always thought he's an awfully good judge of character. I've seen her about with Sandra Singh as well. You won't know Sandra, she's a factual programmes producer at STV, after your time. Does that help?"

It had helped. Lindsay had instinctively liked Rory, but she was too shrewd an operator herself to trust her future to someone she knew nothing about. Now she knew enough to take a chance. She picked the top paper off the pile and began browsing. After an hour, she ordered a burger and fries. The burger turned out to be a very poor relation of what she was accustomed to in California, but the chips were glorious—fat chunks of real potato, golden brown and crunchy, the way she liked them and had seldom found them in America. *That would be how I stayed so slim over there*, she thought. She decided she'd give Rory till she'd finished her lunch, then she'd leave her a note and go. It really didn't do to seem too keen, after all.

A shadow crossed the page she was reading and Lindsay looked up to see Rory standing before her, laptop slung over one shoulder, a delighted grin on her face. "Couldn't stay away, huh?" Rory asked, sliding into the seat opposite Lindsay.

"Well, I could hardly go running, could I?"

Rory winced. "How is the ankle?"

"Sore. But not as swollen as it was. A week or so and it'll be back to normal."

"That's the official clinical view from the resident medic?"

Lindsay snorted. "Given Sophie's area of expertise, she'd take one look at a swollen ankle and probably tell me I was suffering from pre-eclampsia."

Annie arrived carrying a couple of cappuccinos. "There youse go. You want something to eat, Rory?"

"I'll take a plate of stovies, Annie."

The barmaid nodded and left them to it.

"Three cappuccinos in one day. I'll be jazzed till bedtime at this rate," Lindsay said.

"Would you rather have something else? Only, Annie said that's what you were on." Rory looked momentarily anxious.

She's trying to make an impression, Lindsay thought wryly. "No, that's fine. I suspect I'm going to have to have my wits about me to deal with you anyway."

"So, you've decided to take me up on my suggestion?" Rory kept her eyes on her coffee, but Lindsay could sense the eagerness underlying the question.

"I'm giving it serious consideration. But if it's going to stand any chance of working, we've got to be up front with each other." Rory's head came up as she registered the seriousness of Lindsay's tone. The banter was over, and it was time to get down to business.

"Point taken. So, what do you want to know?"

Lindsay sucked some foam off her cappuccino and wiped her top lip clean. "My big reservation is that, initially, stories would only be coming my way on the basis of your reputation. Which obviously means you get first pick of whatever lands on the table. I have no idea what that means for me. If I'm just going to be running around doing the dross that doesn't interest you or that you think isn't worth your time and attention, then, frankly, I'm not interested."

Rory looked wounded. "No, that's not how I see it at all. See, the thing is, I already get more stuff coming to me than I can deal with. I end up selling stuff on as tips that I'd rather work myself, but if I'm in the middle of something big and I get a lead on a story that's time-sensitive, I have to let it go. The way I see it, when a story comes in, whichever one of us is free to take it runs with it. Anyway, the reputation you've got, you'll be pulling stories in yourself in no time."

Lindsay's eyebrows shot up. "The reputation I've got? Come on, Rory, I'm hardly a household name."

"I've just been in at the *Standard*, passing a tip on to Giles Graham. He remembers exactly who you are. And you didn't even work together. Your by-line will sell stories that I'd struggle to place. Lindsay, I'm not handing out charity here. You'd be doing me a favour by coming in with me."

Lindsay gave Rory a long, considering look. Sure, the kid was probably a bit starry-eyed about her, imagining a past crammed with glory days and 22-point by-lines. But surely that had to be better than trying single-handed to carve out a niche among the sceptical new faces that were running the newsdesks and magazine supplements these days?

It wasn't the hardest decision of her life. "Okay. Let's give it a go. A month's trial, and at the end of it, either of us can walk away if it's not working out."

Rory punched the air. "Yes! That's brilliant, Lindsay. Hey, you won't regret this, you know."

I sincerely hope not, Lindsay thought. But she stifled her remaining reservations and extended a hand across the table. "Nor will you," she said.

"So, when do we start?"

5

Kevin followed Michael out into the street and sniffed the air like a dog in a new wood. "So this is Glasgow," he said. "It's not that different, is it?" There was a note of disappointment in his voice.

Michael said nothing. He simply turned left and set off towards the bus stop he'd been told he'd find a couple of streets away. He carried his heavy holdall as lightly as if it held nothing more substantial than an evening newspaper. At the bus stop, he came to a halt, dropped his bag at his feet and lit a cigarette.

"Where is it we're going again?" Kevin asked.

"A bed and breakfast," Michael said. "Argyle Street."

"So what's the plan?"

"We'll take a wee look round the pubs near where she was spotted."

Kevin's face lit up at the prospect. "Sounds good to me, Michael."

A bus drew up and the two men boarded. It was almost empty and they had the rear area to themselves.

"We won't be drinking, Kevin. This is an operation, not a holiday," Michael said. His tone of voice would have signalled to anyone else that this wasn't a subject for debate.

Not to Kevin. He gave the cunning smile of the truly stupid. "But we'll need to fit in, Michael. We'll stick out like a sore thumb if we go in and just order a couple of cokes."

"That's why we won't be going in and ordering any cokes, Kevin," Michael snarled. "You'll be going up to the bar and asking for change for the cigarette machine. Or a box of matches. Meanwhile, I'll be taking a good look around. If I see her, we'll be stopping for a glass of stout. And we'll be making it last."

Crestfallen, Kevin slumped in his seat, watching the unfamiliar city roll past the windows. He knew he was supposed to like Michael, for his sister's sake, but he was a moody bastard to work with and no mistake.

By closing time, Michael's mood had blackened to a pitch where even Kevin realised silence was the best option. They'd explored pubs ranging from raucous student bars with loud insistent music to more traditional pubs where old men nursed their pints with the tenderness of new mothers. Michael had cast an apparently negligent but actually sharp look over hundreds of women, none of them Bernadette Dooley.

They walked back through streets shared with drinkers heading home, the air aromatic with curry and fish suppers, to the scruffy B&B where they were inconspicuous among the transient workers and DSS claimants who made it their home. All the way back, a scowl deepened the crease between Michael's eyebrows. Kevin had lost count of the number of pubs they'd scouted out, but his pockets were bulging with boxes of matches and loose change. And not so much as a glass of stout had passed his lips.

Michael broke the silence as they turned on to Argyle Street. "We'll do a school in the morning."

"Eh?"

"Patrick says she has a child. A child has to go to school. We'll stake out the nearest primary to the supermarket."

"I don't remember anything being said about a child," Kevin complained.

"I checked in when we got here. You were in the toilet. Patrick said he'd forgotten to mention she has a child."

"I never knew that. From before, like. When she was working in the shop."

Michael made a kissing sound of exasperation. "She didn't have it then. Whoever it was who spotted her in the supermarket told Patrick she had a child with her."

"Maybe it's not old enough to be at the school," Kevin pointed out, proud of himself for coming up with the argument. "I mean, it's not seven years since she left."

Michael flashed a look of surprise at Kevin. It was always a shock when he said something that wouldn't be self-evident to a three-year-old. "Maybe not. But apart from hanging around the supermarket, we've got nothing else to go at. Like Patrick said, she'll not be on the voter's roll or in the phone book, not if she's got any sense. So we'll check out the primary schools on the map and we'll be there first thing."

Kevin saw the prospect of a decent night's sleep rapidly receding. "Right you are," he sighed. "The school it is."

Kevin wasn't the only one who reckoned sleep might be elusive. Lindsay had had one of the worst evenings in living memory, and the turmoil of emotions raging through her didn't feel as if they were going to subside any time soon. Part of her wished she'd taken Rory up on her suggestion of a celebratory meal out to cement their new partnership and to hell with the consequences. But she knew that, being who she was, that would always have been impossible. She couldn't be sure whether it was cowardice, love, good manners or fear that meant she had to go home and participate in the insemination she dreaded; all she knew was that she couldn't bring herself to do otherwise.

She'd returned via the greengrocer in Hyndland who seemed somehow always to have the freshest vegetables in town. Sprue asparagus, a selection of wild mushrooms, fresh strawberries, peaches and raspberries. She'd remembered Fraser's boyfriend was vegetarian, and while deep down she longed to serve them all congealed Kentucky Fried Chicken, her need to see the world well fed wouldn't allow it. It was a mark of pride to Lindsay that when people ate in her kitchen, they ate memorably and well. So she'd take the time and trouble to produce grilled asparagus, wild mushroom risotto garnished with parmesan and rocket, and a fresh fruit salad. If she'd liked them better, she'd have made a meringue shell for a pavlova, but her soul wasn't feeling that generous.

She'd thought that Sophie would be home early for once, but her lover only just made it through the door ahead of their guests. "Trying to avoid talking about it?" Lindsay had said sourly when Sophie finally walked into the kitchen and came up behind her to kiss her on the neck.

"No," Sophie replied evenly, refusing to be drawn. "I was called in on an emergency consult at the Western. You'll be pleased to hear we saved the baby and the mother, though it was touch and go with the mum."

Guilt-tripped, Lindsay said nothing, taking out her spleen on the parmesan, producing a pile of extravagant curls.

The rest of the evening hadn't gone any better. Fraser and Peter had clearly already been to the pub before they arrived, drowning their apprehensions in whisky, to judge by the smell on their breath as they leaned forward in turn to plant air kisses on Lindsay's cheeks. "So, what's the drill?" Fraser had demanded with an air of forced gaiety. "Is there some ceremony to the Goddess, or do we run straight through to the spare room and have a wank?"

Lindsay closed her eyes momentarily, biting down hard to keep her mouth firmly shut. "Don't be daft," Sophie said, her voice more affectionate than Lindsay could ever have managed in the circumstances. "We'll eat first. Lindsay's cooked us a lovely meal. And then . . ."

"He can provide his specimen, eh?" Peter chipped in, his ferret smile disturbingly predatory. Lindsay was glad Sophie had asked Fraser to be their donor; at least he looked like a human being, not an escapee from a vivisection lab. Sophie's chosen donor would be a good match for her, Lindsay thought dispassionately as she poured wine for everyone. Like her lover, Fraser was above average height, especially for a Scot, and he had the same trim build. His hair and eye colour were close to Sophie's and, like her, he had good facial bone structure.

Lindsay supposed it made sense to have a donor who resembled Sophie so closely. It increased the chances of any baby that resulted resembling its mother. But she couldn't help feeling an irrational pang of exclusion that Sophie had never even bothered to ask if she'd like them to find a donor who was a match for her, so that there would be at least a chance that any child would look like an amalgam of both of them, rather than be so clearly Sophie's child.

The dinner conversation had been gruesome. When the two men had eaten with them previously it had been an easy and comfortable evening. But what lay ahead sat like a ponderous elephant in the middle of the dinner table, impossible to ignore yet equally unfit for discussion according to any rules of decorum.

Fed up of the dismal attempts at small talk that kept running aground, Lindsay finally said, "You don't want to be a parent, then, Fraser?"

Fraser looked startled. "Well, not in the sense of day-to-day involvement, no. Though I like the idea that my genetic material will continue after I've gone."

Selfish bastard, Lindsay thought. She wondered why he thought his genes were so special they deserved to be preserved, but realised this wasn't a line of conversation that would endear her to Sophie. "So you're not going to be popping round to take the wean to the football? Or the Scottish country dancing," she added as an afterthought, remembering that Peter had revealed that he and Fraser had first met at a gay and lesbian ceilidh—the sort of event she would have slit her throat rather than attend. Lindsay had grown up in the Highlands and knew what ceilidhs were supposed to be like. She thought Peter and Fraser would last about ten minutes, tops, at any village dance she'd ever attended.

Fraser smiled uncertainly, unsure if he was really hearing hostility. "I'm happy to let you and Sophie bring up the child without any interference from me," he said cautiously. "I don't mind it knowing I'm the other half of its genetic make-up when it's older, but I'm not planning on being a father in any active way."

Lindsay smiled. Out of the corner of her eye, she could see Sophie suddenly look apprehensive. "Let's hope he doesn't decide when he's thirteen that he'd rather live with the other half of his genetic make-up, then," she said.

"Lindsay, do stop trying to frighten Fraser," Sophie said. Her voice was light, but the look she gave Lindsay would have melted the snows of Kilimanjaro. "Now, would anyone like any more fruit salad?"

Fraser and Peter exchanged a swift glance "Maybe we should just cut to the chase, Sophie," Fraser said.

"I'll show you to the spare room," Sophie said, ushering them out of the dining room and throwing a warning look over her shoulder at Lindsay. When she returned a few minutes later, she found Lindsay clattering the dirty plates into the dishwasher.

"Are you deliberately trying to fuck this up for me? Or are you behaving inappropriately because you're nervous?" Sophie demanded.

"Neither. I was simply trying to make sure we all knew what the ground rules were." Lindsay closed the machine forcefully.

"But I told you that last night. You knew I'd already been through it all with Fraser."

Lindsay tipped the remains of the fruit salad into a plastic container and headed for the fridge. "I wanted to hear it from the horse's mouth." She leaned against the worktop, her arms folded across her chest. "I'm sorry, Sophie, but it's hard for me to take your word for things when I know how desperately you want this.

You'd tell me black was white if you thought it would prevent me standing in the way of you chasing this particular dream. So I don't think it was out of order for me to ask Fraser what I did."

Sophie's grey eyes blazed anger. "I don't suppose you stopped to think that it made us look like anything but the close and confiding couple?"

Lindsay shrugged. "Maybe Fraser will just figure that I'm cautious. Which is a sensible thing to be."

Sophie ran her hands through her hair. "Jesus. I'm supposed to be in a relaxed and receptive state for insemination and look at me. Wound up like a fucking spring, thanks to you."

Her partner's anguish worked on Lindsay as no rational argument could have done. She put her arms round Sophie and murmured, "Oh Christ, I'm sorry. Come on, let's get you sorted."

Sophie led the way through to their bedroom. Somehow, she'd found the time to lay out a sterile plastic syringe by the side of the bed. "What's the drill?" Lindsay asked grimly.

"Peter will bring the sperm through in a glass. It starts to thicken once it leaves the man's body, so we have to keep it at blood heat for about ten to fifteen minutes so it'll liquefy again."

"Too much information," Lindsay muttered.

"The best way to do that is to put the glass between your breasts."

"*My* breasts? What's wrong with yours?" Lindsay demanded.

"I'll be lying on my back with a pillow under my hips, Lindsay," Sophie said impatiently as she began to undress.

"Great," Lindsay muttered. "Then what?"

"You take it up into the syringe and inject it as far up my vagina as you can get."

"And that's it?"

Sophie, by now stripped down to her underwear, had the grace to look embarrassed. "Not quite. There's strong anecdotal evidence that an orgasm around the time the sperm is introduced increases the chances of success."

Lindsay looked appalled. "You're not suggesting we . . . ?" Then she suddenly saw the funny side and burst out laughing. The release of the tension that had them both clenched in its grip brought them together again like a stretched elastic band snapping back into shape. "I really don't think I can do it," Lindsay spluttered.

Sophie finished undressing, slipping quickly beneath the duvet. "I don't think I could keep a straight face now. Probably better if I do it myself."

Lindsay closed her eyes and rubbed her eyelids with thumb and forefinger. "I think that might be best," she said, shaking her head incredulously, a final snigger escaping her lips.

Before she could say more, there was a tentative tap at the door. "All ready, girls," Peter sang out from the hall.

Lindsay opened up and stared down in disbelief at the glass being proffered to her. A large gob of off-white mucus clung to the bottom of the Edinburgh crystal, as viscous and slimy as phlegm. Wordlessly, she took it and closed the door. "You gave him one of my whisky tumblers," she said plaintively. "How can I ever drink out of them again?"

Sophie snorted with laughter. "That bloody dishwasher's about as hot as an autoclave. Trust me, you're not going to catch anything."

"It's not a matter of hygiene, it's a matter of taste. And I'm not talking flavour," Lindsay growled, thrusting the glass down the front of her shirt to nestle in her bra between still firm breasts. "Oh God, the smell," she moaned as the sharp tang of the sperm invaded her nostrils. "It's like municipal swimming pools. Jesus, I really thought being a dyke meant I'd never have to deal with this gunge again. This is so disgusting, Sophie."

"You think I don't know that? Listen, you're not the one facing the prospect of having it inside you."

Lindsay gave a savage grin. "It's not too late to change your mind."

"Very funny. Come and give me a cuddle, please?"

Gingerly, careful of her cargo, Lindsay edged alongside Sophie. With her free hand, she stroked Sophie's hair, letting her lips brush against the top of her head. "I don't think I've ever felt less sexual," Sophie said, her voice wavering on the edge of tears as she struggled for arousal.

You and me both, Lindsay thought grimly. But she kept her thoughts to herself and dropped her head to Sophie's breast, gently nuzzling her nipple. She licked it harder, sucking it into her mouth and tonguing it firmly. She was rewarded, as she knew she would be, with a soft moan and the arching of Sophie's spine.

Then suddenly it was all action. Lindsay had to pull away to draw the sperm into the syringe. Placing her hand over Sophie's, she slid the barrel into her lover's vagina as far as it would go, then depressed the plunger. There was a desperation in Sophie's cries as she came almost simultaneously. When Lindsay dared look up, she saw tears tracking down Sophie's cheeks. She knew her own eyes were pricking almost to overflowing.

Their reasons, she knew, were dangerously different.

Lindsay leaned against Sophie's bent legs, her cheek against Sophie's knee. As soon as was decently possible, she pulled away. "I'm going to see if the guys need a drink," she said. Anything to get out of there and find a moment to get her face in order.

Now, two hours later, Lindsay was staring out of the living-room window to the moonlit playing fields across the road and the tawdry glitter of the city lights beyond. She had shared a large malt with Fraser and Peter then seen them out. She'd made a cup of herbal tea for Sophie, whose body had overnight become a temple worshipping very different gods from before. She'd climbed into bed as she suspected she was expected to do and had faked sleep. Once she'd been certain that Sophie's deep and regular breathing wasn't feigned, she'd slipped out of bed, poured herself another Caol Ila and sat on the window seat wondering how much of her future lay within these walls, and how much within the walls of the Café Virginia.

6

A few miles away, Rory McLaren was also pondering Lindsay's future, though not in quite the same terms as the subject of her plotting. She swigged greedily from a bottle of water and let herself slide down the wall she was leaning against until she was hunkered down level with Sandra. Sweat streaked their faces and bodies as they grinned inanely at each other in the chilling-out space in the basement of E-scape, their favourite dance club, which occupied a former warehouse where Garnethill merged into Cowcaddens.

They'd split a tab of ecstasy earlier in the evening, they'd danced like dervishes and now they were both starting the gradual descent to the point where sleep might be possible at some time in the not too distant future. But for now they were content to let the gentle throb of the ambient track ease them down gently.

"What're you thinking?" Sandra said after a few minutes.

"How useful Lindsay's going to be."

"That would be in a work context?"

Rory giggled softly. "I was thinking about work. But you never know . . ."

Sandra groaned. "Stick to the work. Useful how?"

"Well, take Keillor. I've got the tip, I've hardened it up pretty well, but I need some solid evidence. But Keillor knows me, so I've got no chance of scamming him. He's never seen Lindsay, though. Maybe between us we can figure out how to have him over and she can do the sharp end."

Sandra's mouth curled up in a feline smile. "Oh yes, I like it. Nail the wee slug to the floor."

"I'll talk to her about it in the morning."

"It's already the morning."

"Only technically." Rory hugged herself and scrunched her face up in an expression of amused cunning. "A couple of real buzzes like creepy Keillor and she'll be so hooked. Which will be nice."

Sandra chugged on her own bottle of mineral water. "Uh oh."

"I mean it'll be nice to have somebody around to work with. I never thought I'd miss the newsroom—and I don't, not really. But it does get lonely sometimes. Everybody in the bar is a potential source, so I can't afford to let them be my friends. I spend most days not really talking to anybody unless you or Giles stop by. Lindsay . . . now, there's somebody I can talk to. Nice woman. Very nice woman."

"She's also a happily married woman, Rory. Tell me you're not going to crash through her life like an express train on speed," she sighed.

Rory shook her head vigorously, droplets of moisture scattering from her sweat-darkened hair. "Hey, she's a grown-up. She can make her own choices. I don't force myself on anyone."

Sandra snorted. "Little Miss Butter-wouldn't-melt. Rory, just for once, walk away from it. You know you don't do relationships. You're the emotional equivalent of a hit-and-run driver. You never get hurt yourself, you just leave a trail of wreckage in your rear-view mirror."

Rory pulled a face. "Yeah, well. When the only relationship you've ever seen close up was as fucked as my mum and dad's was, you'd be mental to think it was as easy as falling in love. Dive in, dive deep and then climb back out and dry off before you catch a cold, that's what works for me. But if it makes you any happier, I promise not to make a move on Lindsay. Okay?"

Sandra put an arm round her friend and hugged her close. "It's not about making me happy. It's about you making yourself happy."

"Which I do, with lots of girlies." Rory's smile was wry. "Only, never for very long."

"Well, remember that if Lindsay starts looking like Mount Everest."

"Eh?"

"You don't have to climb it just because it's there. You'll have more fun in the long run working with her."

"Sandra, are you sure you're not Jewish?"

Sandra gave her an affectionate punch in the ribs. "Fuck off, Rory. C'mon, let's go and have a last dance and see if I can pick myself up some wee boy who wants to be initiated into the secret world of the older woman."

Rory chuckled as she got to her feet. "And you've got the nerve to talk about me."

Sandra rumpled Rory's damp hair. "Difference is, I can do the serious thing just as well as I do the playing." She pushed past and made for the stairs leading to the main dance floor, entirely missing the momentary flash of sadness and longing that crossed Rory's face.

The raw cold ate into Kevin's bones. Michael seemed oblivious to the weather, as affected by the penetrating damp as were the concrete and glass of the primary school they were watching. The school was near the Botanic Gardens, in a quiet side street lined with tall sandstone tenements, which posed something of a problem for them. There was no convenient bus shelter or phone box to use as a surveillance point. Nor was there a handy café with windows overlooking the school entrance. And in these days of paedophile paranoia, nothing would provoke a call to the police faster than two men standing on a street corner scrutinizing the children arriving at a primary school.

If it had been up to Kevin, they would have gone back to bed after their preliminary reconnaissance at half past seven had demonstrated how apparently impossible was the task facing them. But this was the school nearest the supermarket where Bernadette Dooley had been spotted, so they had to start here, Michael decreed. And besides, he had spent long enough on the front line to have honed his improvisational skills. As they had walked up Byres Road towards the school, he'd noticed two youths by the Underground entrance handing out copies of a free newspaper to the commuters hurrying into the station. When he realised how exposed the school was from a surveillance point of view, he'd remembered the newspaper distributors.

He'd marched Kevin back down to the station and gone into a huddle with the youths. A threatening look from his amber eyes would probably have been enough to achieve his goal, but Michael didn't want to be fixed in anyone's memory as a bad lad. Not just yet, anyway. So a couple of tenners were swapped for two bundles of freesheets and they walked back to the school, where they took up position at either side of the gates, handing out the paper to teachers and parents as they arrived.

Nobody gave them a second look.

"Won't she recognise you?" Kevin had asked as they'd walked back.

In reply, Michael had taken a pair of glasses from his inside pocket. They had thick black frames and lenses tinted blue. He put them on and simultaneously let his shoulders slump. In that instant, the threat disappeared like the sun behind a cloud.

"No, right, I see what you mean," Kevin muttered.

Now, he watched how Michael scrutinised every face that approached. When the electric bell finally sounded on the dot of nine o'clock, he was satisfied that Bernadette Dooley was not among the parents who had delivered their offspring to Botanics Primary.

"So what do we do now?" Kevin asked forlornly, clutching the leftover newspapers to his chest.

"We go and see if that supermarket's got a café," Michael said. "And if it hasn't, we find someplace to watch it from. And this afternoon we find another primary school at chucking-out time." He was already striding down the street.

Two hours and forty-three minutes later, Kevin shifted in his plastic chair. "She's giving us funny looks, that woman on the till," he muttered.

Michael scowled. "You're too fucking obvious, that's why." He glanced at his watch. Three teas each and a couple of bacon butties. The worst part was not being able to smoke. *No*, Michael corrected himself. The worst part was having to work with a fucking eejit like Kevin who could no more blend into the background than a naked woman at High Mass.

"I'm not doing anything," Kevin whined.

Michael bit back a vicious response. He sipped his luke-warm tea. "Away and get me a fresh cup of tea. And when you've done that, you can go into the supermarket and buy me some bananas."

"Bananas?" Kevin frowned in puzzlement.

"They're a good source of potassium. Just do it, Kevin."

Kevin pushed himself up from the table. He strolled over to the counter, his attempt at nonchalance setting the till operator's antennae jangling. She couldn't figure out his game at all, but she was mentally rehearsing his description. When he returned with the tea, Michael said, "Fine. Now the bananas, there's a good lad. And take your time about it. Have a browse. See if there's any new flavours of Pot Noodle to get you excited." The sarcasm was wasted on Kevin, who shrugged and walked off to join the milling shoppers.

Left to himself, Michael pulled out his mobile and called Patrick. "It's me," he said as soon as they were connected. "So far, no joy."

"I didn't expect anything so soon." Patrick's voice was flat, unreadable. "Stay on it. Call me tomorrow."

The line went dead. Whatever Bernadette had taken from Patrick, it had clearly pissed the man off more than Michael would have risked lightly. He put the phone back in his pocket and continued his scrutiny of the entrance to the store. Barely taking his eyes off the harassed mothers and the slow-moving pensioners who made up most of the clientele at that time of the morning, he sugared his tea and began to drink it. This was probably a total waste of time, but they had nothing else to chase. As long as Patrick was willing to spend his money, Michael was content to watch and wait.

Time ticked inexorably past and still Kevin didn't return. He was probably memorizing the Pot Noodle flavours, Michael reckoned. Then suddenly all thoughts of Kevin disappeared. He went immobile as a lizard that knows it's been spotted and still hopes its camouflage will keep it safe.

It was her. Pushing past an elderly couple, dark hair swinging round her head in a long bob, heavy coat wrapped round her, disguising a figure that Michael remembered had always been worth noticing. Bernadette Dooley was hurrying into the supermarket, making straight for the counter that sold cigarettes, confectionery and lottery tickets.

If he leaned over in his seat, he could see her back view. She was scrabbling in her bag for her purse, pulling it out, opening it, taking out a couple of notes. She handed over the money and received a carton of 100 Silk Cut in return. Then she was turning away, pushing the cigarettes into her bag, head down, making for the door again.

Michael was on his feet. By the time she made it to the street, he was a handful of steps behind her. He glanced quickly over his shoulder. Where the fuck was Kevin? Ah, the hell with it. Bernadette was the important one. Kevin would doubtless sit in the supermarket till it closed. Either that or he'd have the sense to make his way back to where they were staying. Wouldn't he?

Bernadette turned right out of the store and headed down Byres Road. The pavements were busy enough to give him cover. With the total focus of the hunter whose oblivious prey is well upwind and living on borrowed time, Michael began stalking Bernadette Dooley.

Rory was already settled into her booth at Café Virginia when Lindsay arrived. "Hey," she greeted her, "You look worse than I do, and I was clubbing till gone three."

Lindsay squeezed out a vague smile. "I was up half the night. And not in a good way."

"Must have been something you ate, eh?"

"Must have been. So, what's doing?"

Rory pushed a manila folder across the table as Lindsay's cappuccino arrived. "Take a look at that."

Curious, Lindsay studied the contents. The first page was a memo to herself from Rory:

Tip re Keillor/Kilwinning. CCD, the multinational pharma-ceutical and agrichemical company, have a small plant on the outskirts of Kilwinning. Just over a year ago, local farmer sells biggish chunk of land to a suit from down south, who says he wants to retire and do rare-breed sheep. Few months later, planning application goes in for change of use from agricultural to light industrial. Turns out land now belongs to CCD; they want to expand in unspecified ways to extend their research. Locals convinced they're going to be poisoned with chemicals or overrun with cloned sheep. Think the local plan will keep them safe. But Chief Planning Officer David Keillor leans heavy on councillors and the change of use goes through. Source tells me that Keillor is running round in a brand-new BMW

4x4—costs about a year's salary new—and his wife has a neat wee Porsche Boxster. Source also tells me that vehicles were originally registered to CCD.

The other documents were reports of the planning committee meetings and transcriptions of Rory's interviews with the farmer who sold the land and various locals with an axe to grind.

Lindsay digested the material then looked up and said, "And?"

"Well, obviously, we need to get a look at the vehicle registration document for Keillor's Beamer."

Lindsay nodded. "Obviously. So what's been keeping you?"

The sarcasm was gentle enough for Rory to grin. "Keillor knows me. We had a wee bit of a head to head a few years ago when he was working for the city planning department. Something to do with selling off school playing fields. So there's no way I can get close enough. I thought maybe you'd have an idea how we could pull it off?"

Lindsay scooped the froth off her coffee and slowly licked it off the spoon. "How bent do you want to get?" she asked thoughtfully.

Rory scratched an eyebrow. "Run it past me."

"Do you happen to know if Strathclyde Police have changed their warrant cards in the past two years?"

Before Rory could answer, Sandra breezed up to their table. "Hiya, girls." She inclined her head towards Lindsay. "You must be Splash Gordon." She thrust a hand out. "I'm Sandra Singh. I'm supposed to be this one's best pal." Lindsay took the offered handshake with a nod.

Rory gave an exasperated little smile. "Lindsay, meet Sandra. Sandra is a factual programmes producer/director up the road at STV. She hates her boss, she likes boys that are barely old enough to shave and she thinks that, since my mammy's dead, she should poke her nose into my business all the time."

Lindsay moved up the bench to make room for Sandra. "Good to meet you. It's nice to know there's somewhere I can go to get the dirt if I need an edge."

Sandra shook her head at the available seat. "I'm not stopping. I was passing and I thought I'd say hello. You girls plotting?"

Lindsay said, "Yes," at the precise moment Rory said, "No."

"I'll take that as a yes, and leave you to it. Catch you later." With a wave of her slender fingers, Sandra was off.

Rory raised her eyes heavenwards. "Something else."

"Clearly. So, do you have an answer?"

Rory looked momentarily bewildered. "An answer?"

"Warrant cards."

"Right. Eh, not as far as I know. Why?"

"I think this comes into the category of what you don't know can't hurt you. Have you got an address for Keillor? There isn't one in the file."

Rory dug around in her backpack and produced a battered filofax. She rummaged inside and finally unearthed a torn scrap of paper. She tore a sheet out of the notebook on the table and scribbled down an address in Milngavie. "You sure you don't want to talk it through?" she said almost wistfully as she handed it over.

"I'm sure. If it all goes horribly wrong, at least you'll be able to put your hand on your heart and say it was nothing to do with you."

"Well, damn," Rory said. "Haven't you figured out yet that I like trouble?"

"All the more reason not to tell you what I've got in mind," Lindsay said drily. "I can get into enough trouble for both of us, all by myself."

Rory grinned. "Oh good. You know, I think we're going to be pure dead brilliant together."

Lindsay's smile didn't make it to her eyes. It wasn't so long ago that she would have said the same thing about her and Sophie. Now, she really wasn't sure any more.

7

Bernie Gourlay took the washing out of the tumble drier and began to fold it. She noticed that one of Jack's school sweatshirts had begun to split at the shoulder seam and put it to one side to sew up later. She often heard mothers complaining about the things they had to do for their kids, but she'd never once felt like that. She knew what a miracle he was, and she counted it a privilege to be able to take care of the details of his life. She'd been conscious ever since he'd been placed in her arms that his dependency on her would wane consistently as he grew older, and she'd determined then that she would enjoy every moment, every phase of his development, but that she'd let go when she had to.

She was, she thought, the luckiest person she knew. She'd escaped from a life that was difficult and anxious, and, although the journey hadn't been without its ups and downs, now she'd achieved something she'd never have believed possible. Happiness. Jack was growing strong and healthy, a cheerful child whose face never seemed crossed with shadows. And she had Tam. Big, daft, lovely Tam who had swept her off her feet and never minded that Jack was another man's son, nor that she was incapable of having more children by him. Tam, who had bought this beautiful big garden flat for them to live in, who saw to it that none of them ever went without, who worked hard to take care of them all but who never let his business interfere with enjoying his family to the full.

Bernie glanced at the clock. Ten minutes before she had to leave and pick up Jack from school. Tam sometimes dropped him off in the mornings, but she always made sure she was there in plenty of time to pick him up. She couldn't bear the thought of him standing at the school gates, worry at her lateness puckering his face and darkening his china blue eyes. Soon enough, he'd be begging her to let him walk home with his pals, but for now he was still pleased to see her when the bell went.

The electronic chirrup of the phone disturbed her cheerful thoughts. *Probably Tam*, she thought, reaching for the handset. It was seldom that a day passed without him calling just to say hello. Four years married, and he was still a big soft romantic at heart.

But the voice that insinuated its way into her brain wasn't Tam's. It was a voice she'd often prayed she would never hear again. It was a voice whose very tone was a masquerade, disguising the viciousness behind it with a beguiling softness. Bernie wasn't beguiled. She was terrified. She felt as if a block of ice was dissolving in her stomach, sending cold trickles through her whole body. She clung to the phone, mesmerized, unable to put it down even after the line went dead.

Staggering slightly, she collapsed into a kitchen chair. Tears pricked her eyes and her dry lips trembled. Eventually, she got to her feet, still shaky. Although she had prayed she'd never have to put it into action, she had a contingency plan in place. She took a well-worn leather address book from a kitchen drawer and looked up an unfamiliar number. She keyed it into the phone and waited for the international connection. When the phone was answered, she gave the name of the person she desperately needed to talk to. Another pause. Then Bernie closed her eyes with relief. "It's Bernadette," she said. *Please God, let this work.*

Late the following afternoon, Lindsay drove out through the south side of the city towards the prosperous suburb of Milngavie. She never failed to be struck by the contrasts in Glasgow, even between areas that superficially seemed to have much in common. The average income in Milngavie was probably only marginally above that in the smart part of the West End where she and Sophie lived. But, culturally, it felt like a different world. The West End had traditionally been more genteel, drawing its residents from the academics at the university and the medical staff at the city's hospitals. Now, it had added media, IT professionals and the arts to the mix, making it a place where Lindsay felt as at home as she was ever going to be.

But Milngavie had always felt more culturally barren. The money here came from retail empires, from accountants, from people who preferred Andrew Lloyd Webber to Mozart or the Manic Street Preachers. The difference was obvious to her even in the architecture. This was the land of bungalows and detached houses, where to inhabit a semi was somehow to have failed. There was nothing here to compare with the grandeur of the red sandstone tenements of Hyndland or the imposing houses of Kelvinside. Lindsay knew she was indulging her prejudices with such facile thoughts, but she didn't care. From everything she'd read about David Keillor, she'd have been astonished to find him living anywhere else.

She turned into the quiet side street where Keillor lived and cruised slowly down till she spotted his house. It was a two-storey detached property in a decent-sized garden, a double garage tacked on to one side. The brilliant white harling that covered the house looked as if it had recently been repainted, and the double glazing was the expensive sort that mimicked traditional sash windows. It didn't look as if Keillor was strapped for cash. She parked a little way past the entrance to his drive and settled back to wait.

She'd borrowed Sophie's car for the afternoon, knowing that the anonymous saloon her lover drove was more appropriate

for what she had in mind than the classic MGB roadster she'd
bought on her return to the UK. Sophie had teased her about
having a mid-life crisis, but Lindsay had pointed out that she had
always driven classic cars and because she'd previously owned
an MGB she knew enough to carry out her own maintenance.
Since she couldn't hope to do that with a modern car crammed
with electronics, she was effectively choosing the budget option,
she'd argued. Sophie had just laughed and kissed her.

If she has a baby, I'll have to ditch the MGB, Lindsay thought
sourly. She knew Sophie well enough to realise that no child of
hers would be allowed on the narrow bench seat in the rear of
the 1974 sports car lest it fly into the air and disappear from the
rear-view mirror, bouncing down the motorway. Her life would
have to change in far more profound ways, she knew that. But
today what rankled was the potential loss of her car. She knew
she was being childish, but she was the only person who knew
that, so it didn't count.

Lindsay forced herself to stop thinking about the baby and
concentrate instead on what she had to do. She dug into her
jacket pocket and took out the small black leather wallet with
the Strathclyde Police crest on it. A couple of years before,
she'd been instrumental in saving an American friend, Meredith
Miller, from facing a murder charge. A few weeks later, the fake
warrant card had arrived in the post, along with a brief note:
"You're better than the real thing. I thought this might amuse
you. Thanks, Meredith." She'd never imagined using it; but
then she'd never imagined being a journalist again, particularly
not in Scotland.

She adjusted her rear-view mirror so she could see approaching traffic and settled down for a wait. She didn't expect it to be
too long. Officials like David Keillor left the office on time. It
was only their minions who had to stay late to deal with their
workloads. With luck, he'd be home very soon. She wanted to
hit him as soon as he got out of the car, catch him on the back
foot before he could settle in to his normal evening routine.

Lindsay had guessed right. A mere twenty minutes after she'd arrived, a black 4x4 BMW rolled into sight. As the electronically operated gates opened to allow the car to enter, she was on the pavement, walking briskly on to the herringbone brick of Keillor's driveway. His face swung towards her, a look of suspicious surprise narrowing his eyes.

Lindsay smiled disarmingly and walked right up to the driver's door. The window sank down a few inches. "What are you doing? This is private property," Keillor snapped. He had the well-groomed appearance of a man who knows the importance of first impressions. His dark hair was cut short, the shape sharp and well-defined. His skin was lightly bronzed, his eyebrows neatly trimmed. He smelled of mint.

Lindsay produced the warrant card and held it open long enough for him to see her photograph but not much else. "DC Lindsay, Strathclyde Police. You're Mr Keillor? Mr David Keillor?"

His frown deepened. "Of course I am. Who else would be driving my car into my drive? What's this about?" He began to open the door, forcing Lindsay to step backwards.

"I wanted to ask you a few questions regarding an inquiry we're conducting."

Keillor tutted as he climbed out of the car. He was surprisingly short, making his exit from the high vehicle comically awkward. "You'd better come in, then."

Lindsay followed him round to the front door and into the hallway. "In here," he said, ushering her into the dining room. A gleaming oval table was surrounded by six matching chairs. An antique sideboard stood against one wall, crystal glassware and silver sparkling in the late afternoon light from the bay window. Keillor gestured to a chair but remained standing as Lindsay sat down. "So what's this all about?" he demanded again.

Lindsay found his arrogance surprising. Most people, confronted by a police officer, were at the very least apprehensive, in her experience. Everybody felt a twinge of guilt about something; either that or a twinge of fear that something terrible had happened to someone they loved. But Keillor's self-confidence seemed impossible to dent. This was a man who was very sure he was untouchable. It would be a pleasure to rock that self-satisfaction to its foundations.

"We're investigating a serious incident that happened late last night in Giffnock. A hit and run. The elderly gentleman who was knocked down is quite poorly in hospital. We have a witness who saw the vehicle. The description he gave us corresponds to your car, as do a couple of the letters of the registration. So, I've come along to ask you one or two questions and have a wee look at your vehicle. If you don't mind."

Keillor shook his head. "Look all you like. But this is a waste of time. I was at home yesterday evening. We had friends round for dinner. They left around half past eleven then my wife and I went to bed. The car wasn't out of the garage all night. So, whoever your witness saw, it wasn't me. Or my car."

Lindsay nodded, taking her notebook out of her bag. "Then you won't mind giving me the names of your dinner guests?"

Keillor sighed impatiently. "For Christ's sake."

"We do have to take these things seriously, sir. If it had been you or your wife who'd been run over, you'd want us to do our job. The names?"

"Charles Wayne and his wife Sarah."

"And where might I contact Mr and Mrs Wayne?"

"He's the managing director of CCD Scotland," Keillor said, as if this were a fact any child should have known.

Lindsay couldn't believe her luck. Things couldn't have worked out better if she'd planned it. Whatever happened now, she could place the MD of the pharmaceutical company in David Keillor's dining room. She wished she'd bothered to tape the conversation. Time away from the sharp end had definitely laid a layer of rust over her skills. "So I could get him at his work?"

"I imagine so. Now, is that everything?"

"Just for the record, could I check your vehicle documents? Your insurance and your log book? And I'll need to take a look at the car."

"Why? This is nothing to do with me."

Lindsay shrugged. "It's procedure, sir. If you wouldn't mind getting the documents, I can be checking your vehicle. Save time that way." She got to her feet and smiled.

"Oh, all right." Keillor showed her out and returned indoors.

Lindsay made a pretence of studying the front nearside wing of the big BMW, crouching down to peer at the bumper. She was straightening up when Keillor re-emerged with a plastic folder in his hand. "Looks all clear to me, sir," she said.

"Of course it does," he said impatiently. "How many times do I have to tell you? Whoever knocked down your old man in Giffnock, it wasn't me and it wasn't my car." He thrust the folder at her. "There you are."

Lindsay opened the folder. She glanced at the insurance certificate then looked at the vehicle registration. She forced herself not to smile in triumph. There was all the evidence she needed. The previous owner of the BMW was there in black and white: CCD (Scotland). *Gotcha*, she thought. "That all seems to be in order." She handed the paperwork back to Keillor. "I'm sorry to have troubled you. I'll have to speak to Mr Wayne. Purely a formality, obviously. But we have to go through the motions."

At last, Keillor smiled. "I appreciate that, officer. But I'm a very busy man. I haven't got time to waste."

"In that case, I won't occupy you any longer." Lindsay nodded a farewell and headed back down the drive. She found it hard to keep a spring out of her step. Somehow, she'd managed to forget the galvanizing buzz that hit at the moment when a difficult story suddenly cracked open. If Rory McLaren had done nothing else, she had reminded Lindsay of the sheer delight of using her skills to bring down someone else's nasty little castles in the air.

First thing in the morning, she'd make the innocuous call to Charles Wayne. And this time, she'd tape it. Okay, it wasn't strictly speaking her story. And they'd have to put it out under Rory's by-line to protect Lindsay from any comeback on her illegal scam. Probably best to leave it a week or so, just to be on the safe side.

But she'd done it. She'd copper-bottomed the story. Splash Gordon was back. And it felt so good.

The high lasted as far as the Western Infirmary, where she'd arranged to pick up Sophie. Her lover stood by the outpatients entrance, deep in conversation with Fraser. Lindsay closed her eyes momentarily. *How could I have forgotten it's the second attempt tonight?* she wondered bitterly. *How could I have imagined I was going to be allowed to have a life?*

A couple of miles away, Bernie Gourlay let herself into the house. She'd walked Jack round to a friend's place for a birthday party, and she had a couple of hours to herself before Tam would pick him up on the way home. Normally, she'd indulge herself in a long bath, heavily scented with essential oils, a gin and tonic and a glossy magazine. But relaxation was beyond her now. Fear gnawed at her, its sharp teeth cutting into her peace of mind and ripping it to shreds.

With a deep sigh, she dropped her handbag on the hall table and walked through to the kitchen. She knew at once that something was wrong, chill damp air hitting her where warmth should have been. Her eyes darted round the room and terror gripped her chest in a physical constriction. The window by the back door was shattered, the glass crunched into fragments on the tiled floor. And on the kitchen table, clear when she had left, was a sheet of paper.

On automatic pilot, Bernie crossed the room. She gazed down and read, in thick black capitals, NO HIDING PLACE, BERNIE. She gave a faint whimper of anguish and crumpled into the nearest chair. Dear God, he could put his hand on her any time he chose. Her breathing was fast and shallow as dread coursed through her. What was she going to do?

"Get a grip," she admonished herself, trying to draw herself upright. Somehow, she had to keep this from Jack and Tam. She had to protect them from what she knew. Numb, Bernie pushed herself to her feet. Things to do. There were things to do. She found the Yellow Pages and looked for emergency glaziers. It didn't matter if the man was still here when Tam got back. She could make up some story about slipping on the floor and losing her grip on a tin which had smashed the glass. First, find a glazier. Then clear up the broken glass. Burn the note. Make everything normal again.

It was, she knew, a losing battle. Nothing was ever going to be normal again. But she had to try.

8

The school playground was deserted. By the gates, a man leaned against the wall. If it hadn't been for his air of relaxed nonchalance, the sense of entitlement that seemed to emanate from him, he'd have looked worryingly out of place in his stylish Italian suit and glossily polished loafers. His dark hair was cut short, apart from a heavy, side-swept fringe that fell just above his eyebrows. Without his beak of a nose, he'd have been handsome in a heavy-lidded Southern European way. He carried a smart briefcase and a plastic bag with the logo of a computer shop on the side. His eyes scanned the street constantly, but without disturbing his appearance of self-containment.

The shrilling of the interval bell rang out from the school building and a stream of chattering, liberated children began to emerge. The man calmly pushed himself off from the wall and walked through the gates, his attitude suddenly intent. His eyes lit on a dark-haired six-year-old, careering round in a game of tig with half a dozen others. The man headed straight for him.

As he approached, the boy caught sight of him and stopped dead, his face uncertain. The man walked up to him and dropped into a crouch, meeting him eye to eye. "Ciao, Giaco," he said, his eyes crinkling in a smile.

Jack Gourlay said nothing. He broke eye contact and looked at the ground.

"Didn't your mamma tell you I was coming today?"

Jack shook his head. The man held the bag open and showed it to Jack. While he peered into it, the man looked swiftly around, to check if he'd been spotted. Seeing nothing to worry him, he said, "Look, Giaco. It's for you. A Nintendo. For taking on holiday. You're coming on holiday with me. Today."

The boy shook his head. "I can't."

"You can't? Who says you can't come on holiday with your papa?"

"I've not got my jammies or anything."

"We'll buy anything you need. Come on, Giaco, it's an adventure. I thought you liked adventures? It's been so long since we had fun together. I really missed you." He dropped bag and briefcase and put his hands on the boy's shoulders. "You miss me too?" he asked softly.

"Yeah, I suppose," Jack said, still not meeting his eyes.

"So now we make up for lost time, Okay?"

"I better tell Jimmy."

It was, the man recognised, capitulation. "Who's Jimmy?"

"Jimmy Doran. He's my pal. The one over there with the ginger hair. He'll wonder what's happened to me if I don't tell him."

"Okay. Tell him you've had to go off with your dad. But be quick. We've got a plane to catch."

Jack's face lit up. The prospect of a plane journey clearly dispelled any lingering doubts he had about entrusting himself to Bruno Cavadino.

It had been a toss-up whether Lindsay would call Charles Wayne from home or wait till she arrived at the Café Virginia. If she did it from home, she could present Rory with a *fait accompli*, all the loose ends tied up in a neat wee parcel, Charles Wayne on tape admitting he'd had dinner with David Keillor as the glittery silver bow on top. But if she did it from the flat, she'd have to contend with Sophie, who was working from home that morning with her feet up on the window seat, presumably to minimize sudden movements that might dislodge any potential embryo. Sophie certainly wouldn't approve of the co-parent of her potential offspring committing an arrestable offence under the family roof. On the other hand, Lindsay didn't really want Rory eavesdropping on her impersonation of a police officer either.

In the end, she compromised. On her way to the Hillhead underground station, she took a detour down Ashton Lane and slipped into Bean Scene. Armed with a large cappuccino, she huddled into the furthest corner, jacked the mobile into her mini-disk recorder and called the main CCD switchboard. After a little preliminary jockeying with a secretary then a personal assistant, she was finally put through to the great man himself. His voice was a light tenor, its strangulated vowels testifying to its owner's origins somewhere around the Thames Estuary.

"Mr Wayne? This is DC Lindsay, Strathclyde Police. I'm sorry to bother you. I wondered if you could help me with a wee inquiry."

"Of course, of course." Wayne sounded both enthusiastic and unctuous. "Anything to assist the police. We like to foster good relations here at CCD."

I bet you do, she thought. "I've got a witness statement from Mr David Keillor that says you spent the evening before last dining at his house. Would that be correct?"

"Spot on, Detective. A lovely evening it was too. But why are you interested in my social engagements?" Now there was a note of caution.

"I'm trying to eliminate Mr Keillor from an inquiry into a road traffic accident. Could you tell me what time it was when you and your lady wife left the Keillors?"

"Let me see . . . I paid off the babysitter just before midnight, so we must have left there somewhere between half past eleven and twenty to twelve."

"And Mr Keillor was with you all evening?"

Wayne chuckled. "Naturally. David's always a very good host."

"Thank you very much, Mr Wayne. I'm sorry to have taken up your time."

"No problem. Glad to be of help."

Lindsay pressed the "stop" button on the recorder as she hung up. She plugged in the headphones and listened with satisfaction. It couldn't have been better. A little judicious editing of the conversation to eliminate any reference to her subterfuge and she was home and dry. Not only did she have Wayne's admission that he had dined with David Keillor, she had the implication in his last statement that this was far from the first time the men had met socially. It would be fun watching Keillor try to wriggle his way out of this one. A pity it would be Rory doing the showdown. But she was going to have to get used to this way of working, alien as it was to her natural instincts. She'd spent years guarding her exclusives against her rivals; it wasn't going to be easy to trade that for sharing.

Rory was already online in her booth when Lindsay arrived at Café Virginia. Rory raised one finger to indicate she was in the middle of something so Lindsay booted up her own laptop and started writing up the notes of her conversations with Keillor and Wayne. Before she could finish, Rory folded her screen down and raised her eyebrows. "Well?" she said. "How did it go?"

For one crazy moment, Lindsay thought she was referring to the previous evening's insemination. She was about to open her mouth and say, "Gruesome," when she realised the topic under discussion was the story. She outlined her progress to Rory, whose grin spread wider as she grasped the full implications of what Lindsay had established.

"You are fucking outrageous," she spluttered. "They didn't call you Splash Gordon for nothing, did they?"

"I think you'll find it was more ironic than admiring," Lindsay said, remembering the less than supportive atmosphere of the newsroom. "And I wasn't exactly on the ball. I didn't tape my little chat with Keillor."

Rory shrugged. "Irrelevant. You got Wayne on tape, which is even more damning. We're going to have to wait a couple of weeks before I hit Keillor, though. If we're really, really lucky, he won't make the connection with your thespian activities."

"We'll keep my name off the finished piece, all the same," Lindsay said firmly.

"Aye. There's time enough for glory."

"I sincerely hope so."

Bernie stood outside the school gates, chatting idly to a couple of the other waiting mothers whose children were in Jack's class. The bell sounded, the doors opened and children of all shapes, sizes and colours began to pour out of the building. After a few minutes, the stream had slowed to a trickle. The other mothers were gone, one with a chattering daughter, the other with a son interested only in the collection of football cards he'd pulled out of his pocket as soon as he'd cleared the school entrance. But still there was no sign of Jack.

She felt a strange fluttering in her stomach, a physical manifestation of an undefined fear. Now, no more children emerged. It was time to panic, she realised. Bernie walked through the gates then, as she neared the school doors, she broke into a trot.

Unnoticed by her, the man leaning against the bus stop twenty yards down the street suddenly shifted. Michael hastily put away the knife he'd been using to clean his nails and began to stroll up the street towards the school. Whatever was going on with Bernadette Dooley, it wasn't in the script. Not as he understood it, anyway. Where was the boy? What was going on?

What he couldn't see was Bernie running down the school corridor to the classroom where Mrs Anderson taught Year Two. She grabbed the lintel and swung herself into the room, her breath catching in her throat. "Where's Jack?" she demanded, her voice shrill.

Mrs Anderson, a comfortably plump woman in her mid-forties, looked puzzled. "It's Mrs Gourlay, isn't it?"

"Where's Jack?" Bernie was shouting now, not caring what the teacher thought of her. "He didn't come out when the bell went. Where is he?"

Mrs Anderson's face sagged. "I don't understand. Mr Gourlay came and fetched him at morning interval. Didn't you know?"

"Tam?" Bernie looked thunderstruck. "Tam came to the school and took Jack away?" She shook her head incredulously.

"That's what Jimmy Doran told me. When the children came back after break, Jimmy came up to my table and said Jack Gourlay had told him to tell me that he'd had to go away with his dad."

"And you thought he meant Tam." Bernie's voice had dropped to a whisper. Staggering, she collapsed into a child's chair, leaned her head on the desk and sobbed in wild, uncontrolled gasps that made her whole body shudder.

"Oh, my goodness," Mrs Anderson said, suddenly understanding that there might be valid reasons for such distress. "I'd better get the head teacher."

At that precise moment, Jack Gourlay—né Cavadino—was thirty-five thousand feet above Germany. He looked up from his Nintendo, an anxious frown on his face. "Mum won't be angry with me, will she?"

Bruno Cavadino gave his son a hug. "Why would she be angry with you? I told you, she said we could go away together."

"She's never let us go away together before," Jack said suspiciously.

"She thought you were too little to be away without her. She thought you would cry because you missed her. But I told her, he's old enough now to understand that a holiday is a holiday, not forever. You won't cry, will you?"

Jack gave a tight, apprehensive smile. "No, Papa. Can we phone her when we land?"

Bruno shook his head. "You don't want her to think you're a big baby, do you? She'll call us in a couple of days. Don't worry."

The siren call of Nintendo dragged Jack back from the conversation to his screen. Bruno looked down at him with a surge of affection that surprised him. He was a good kid. Bernie had made a decent job of bringing him up. But she'd had her chance. Now it was up to him to do his best for the boy. It wouldn't be easy, but he had plans for Jack.

Bernie was sobbing into a handkerchief while a woman police constable patted her awkwardly on the shoulder. Mrs Anderson sat at her table, fingers twisting round each other as Sergeant Meldrum took her through the events of the morning.

"I thought nothing of it, you see. I mean, obviously you don't. The boy, Jimmy Doran, he said that Jack had told him he had to go off with his dad. Naturally, I assumed he meant Mr Gourlay."

Sergeant Meldrum nodded, scribbling something in his notebook. "So, the last you saw of the boy would be when, exactly?"

"When the bell went for the morning interval. Five to eleven."

The classroom door swung open and Tam Gourlay burst in. He was a bear. Six feet and six inches of brawn, topped with a thick head of dark auburn hair and a full, neatly trimmed beard one shade lighter, he stormed into the classroom like a force of nature. Without pause, he rushed to Bernie, pushing the policewoman to one side. "Has that bastard Bruno taken him?" he demanded.

"Tam, oh, Tam, I'm so sorry," Bernie sobbed.

"Sorry? It's no' your fault you married a bastard first time round." He glared belligerently at Sergeant Meldrum. "So what the hell are youse doing to stop him? Christ knows where he'll take the boy."

"We've already circulated a description to the ports and airports, sir. We're doing everything we can," the policeman said, his tone placatory.

It didn't work. "Is that all you can say? Have you not got weans? Jesus, man, can you not see the state she's in? You've got to find the boy."

"Was Mr Cavadino ever violent during the marriage?"

"What's that got to do with anything?" Tam demanded.

"No, he wasn't," Bernie cut in.

"And has he had access to Jack since the marriage broke down?" Meldrum continued.

"He's taken him out half a dozen times when he's been in the country," Bernie said, sounding calmer now her husband was present.

"Mrs Gourlay, do you think he'd offer any kind of physical threat to Jack?"

She shook her head. "Bruno wouldn't hurt a hair on his head."

"You see my problem, sir?" Meldrum asked, his tone that of sweet reason. "The child doesn't seem to be at risk. Okay, Mr Cavadino didn't have permission for this custody visit, but he has previously returned Jack safely. We've no reason to think a crime has been committed."

"I don't believe I'm hearing this," Tam roared. "Our boy gets kidnapped and you think that's okay?"

"With respect, sir, that's not what I said."

Tam looked at the sergeant as if he wanted to hit someone and he was the best candidate. "Listen, pal," he growled, "get your finger out and get our boy back. Or else you'll wish you never joined the polis. And that, my friend, is a promise."

Lindsay poured two glasses of Pinot Grigio and took them through to the living room, where Sophie was sprawled on the sofa, a book on preparing for pregnancy open on her lap. "There you go," Lindsay said, offering Sophie a drink. "I've put the potatoes in the oven. Dinner'll be about three-quarters of an hour."

Sophie shook her head. "No wine for me, love." She patted her flat stomach. "Better safe than sorry."

Lindsay put both glasses on the end table and slid on to the sofa, lifting Sophie's feet into her lap. "Sorry, force of habit. I forgot your body's a temple now. How are you feeling?"

Sophie snorted with laughter. "Exactly the same as usual. I don't think you get symptoms within twenty-four hours of insemination. What about you? How's the ankle? You should be the one with your feet up."

"Ach, it's not too bad. It's more stiff than sore now. Do you mind if I put the local news on?" she added, reaching for the TV remote control.

"News junkie," Sophie teased her. "Of course I don't mind."

The screen came alive on a police press conference. A uniformed chief superintendent sat behind a table. Next to him, a woman with red swollen eyes looked as if she was holding herself together by sheer force of will. Her hand was held by a giant of a man with a neatly barbered mane of hair and a heavy beard. What could be seen of his face looked sullen. The sound faded up on the police officer's voice: ". . . during the morning interval. We have reason to believe that the boy has been snatched by his natural father. We're obviously concerned that Mr Cavadino will try to take Jack out of this jurisdiction, even though he has no legal right to do that. If anyone has seen the boy or his father, they should contact Strathclyde Police."

Two photographs appeared side by side on the screen. The boy grinned cheerfully at the camera with the gap-toothed smile of childhood. His resemblance to the woman was obvious. The man whose photograph appeared next to him looked unmistakably Italian, his easy smile making his face more attractive than it would have been in repose. After a moment, the camera returned to the press conference.

"Mrs Gourlay, have you a message for your former husband?" the policeman asked.

The woman took a visible breath and looked straight down the barrel of the camera. "Bruno, if you're watching this . . . I know you mean well, but Jack's safety is the most important thing in the world to me." Her voice cracked and broke and tears welled from her eyes.

The picture changed to a reporter standing outside police headquarters. "Photographs of Jack Gourlay and his father Bruno Cavadino have been circulated to ports and airports. But tonight, fears were growing that they have already left the country."

"That poor woman," Sophie said, reaching for Lindsay's hand. "She must be going through hell. I can't imagine what that must be like. Not to know where your child is or what's happening to him."

"It's despicable," Lindsay said.

"What? Putting that woman on the telly?" Sophie sounded offended.

"No, of course not. I meant that thing that couples get into when they split up, using their kids as weapons against each other. It's so bloody selfish."

"That's not going to happen to us, you know," Sophie reassured her.

"What? Breaking up or fighting over the kid?"

"Neither one. It's going to be okay, Lindsay. No, it's going to be better than okay. It's going to be wonderful."

Lindsay grunted. "If it happens."

"It's going to happen. I'm sure of it. If it doesn't work this time, we'll just try again."

"And when do you stop trying?" Lindsay couldn't help herself. "How long are you giving this?"

"As long as it takes. I thought we'd try the insemination for six months, and if that doesn't work, we can look at assisted conception."

"You mean IVF?"

Sophie nodded. "I don't want to go there, but if that's what it takes, yes."

"I thought you said lesbians couldn't get IVF treatment in Scotland," Lindsay said mutinously.

Sophie squeezed her hand. "Lindsay, I'm professor of obstetrics at Glasgow University. Trust me, I've got the contacts."

Lindsay's heart sank. She saw her future contract to a pin-prick focus on the business of conception. It wasn't a pretty picture.

9

Afternoons in the Café Virginia were subdued affairs. Solo coffee drinkers flicked through newspapers, bar staff cleared lunchtime debris and cleaned tables, Horse sang "Breathe Me" and Rory wrote copy. Lindsay was online, browsing the newspaper archives, trying to get up to speed with her native land in the third millennium. There was, she thought, something very soothing about it all. She could hardly believe how quickly her general sense of malaise at being back in Scotland had fled. If nothing else, it told her how much she needed work to give her a sense of purpose. Now, if only Sophie would give up this madness, she would be entirely content.

The calm was shattered by a new arrival. His voice carried from the front bar right through to the back booth. "I'm looking for Rory McLaren," the thunder said. Lindsay looked up to see the husband from the previous evening's police press conference waving a twenty-pound note under Annie's nose.

"Through the back, corner booth," she said, trousering the twenty without missing a beat in her stocking of the fridge.

The man mountain looked around suspiciously as he wove a path through the tables towards their corner. Why, Lindsay wondered, did straight people always think they were about to be propositioned as soon as they entered a gay establishment? Had they even looked in a mirror lately?

He stopped at the table, his eyes swivelling from one to the other. "Rory McLaren?" he asked, almost hesitant.

Rory finally looked up and said wearily, "Tam Gourlay. As in," she slipped into mimicry of a semi-hysterical radio advert, "'Gourlay's Garage, your first choice for previously owned vehicles.'"

"Very funny," Gourlay growled.

"The exposé I did on the tricks of the second-hand car trade, right?"

"Hey, nobody was happier than me to see you closing down the toerags and the cowboys," he protested.

"So what do you want with me, Mr Gourlay? Come to shop some more of your dodgy colleagues?" Rory looked back at her screen, giving off boredom like musk.

"There's somebody I want you to meet."

Rory flicked him a glance, amused and questioning.

"I've got a taxi waiting outside."

She snorted. "And that's the pitch, is it? Go off in a taxi with a strange man who associates with a bunch of people I've put out of business. Very tempting."

"I thought youse investigative reporters were supposed to be fearless?"

"Fearless isn't the same as stupid."

"Rory?" Lindsay thought she'd better intervene before Gourlay burst a blood vessel. Rory raised her eyebrows. "I don't think Mr Gourlay is here because of cowboy car dealers. I think the person he wants you to meet is his wife. Her wee boy got snatched by his natural father yesterday. Tug-of-love kidnap."

"Right," Rory said, instantly grasping the tabloid shorthand. She looked up at Gourlay, her smile apologetic. "I'm sorry for your trouble. But I don't do stories like that. I think it's a private eye you need."

Gourlay shook his big head. "Christ. I don't just want the boy found, I want the world to know about this cover-up. It's a scandal, that's what it is. But you? You're as bad as the fucking polis. Because Bruno Cavadino's a diplomat, nobody wants to know."

"A diplomat?" Lindsay interrupted, her interest pricked.

"Aye. So all we're getting is, 'There's bugger all we can do, dinnae rock the boat, be a good boy.' And all the time my wife's going off her head with worry. Who knows where the fuck the boy is now? And, apart from us, it seems like nobody cares either." His frustration was obvious.

"Rory, let's go and have a wee chat with Mrs Gourlay. This diplomatic angle, it's interesting. Could be a good piece in it," Lindsay said, sounding more casual than she felt.

Rory sighed. "Oh, all right. It's not like we're snowed under with work."

Lindsay smiled up at Gourlay. "Give us a minute to get sorted here, we'll meet you outside." She extended a hand which was enveloped in a meaty paw. "I'm Lindsay Gordon, by the way. Rory and I work together."

"Thanks," he said gruffly, then turned and walked out.

"I can't believe you think this is worth pursuing," Rory grumbled as she closed her computer down. "Tug of love, ten a penny. Hague Convention doesn't work, so what's new?"

Packing up her laptop, Lindsay said, "Abuse of diplomatic immunity. You can always get a good head of moral indignation going on that one. And this is a wee bit tastier than cultural attachés not paying their parking tickets. Look, if you don't want to come, I'll handle it."

"No, you're all right. I've done more or less all I was going to do this afternoon anyway. I might as well come along for the ride."

She doesn't quite trust me yet, Lindsay thought ruefully as she followed Rory out into the street. Tam Gourlay was leaning against a black cab, waiting for them. As they headed west past George Square, Gourlay leaned forward and frowned at Rory.

"So how come you ended up with a man's name?"

"My mother's sentimental. I was conceived in a field just north of Aberdeen."

Both Gourlay and Lindsay smiled. "Aurora Borealis. Helluva mouthful for a wee lassie," he said, reaching for his cigarettes and lighting up.

"Hey," the cab driver protested. "Can you no' read? It says no smoking."

"I've got to smoke," Gourlay said. "I've got a doctor's line. See, if I don't smoke, I lose the place and rip the heads off taxi drivers. Okay, pal?"

"It's true," Lindsay confirmed. "I've seen him. We've had him on tablets, patches, the lot. It's only the fags that keep him stable."

The taxi driver shook his head in mock disgust. "See Glasgow and die, right enough."

The living room of Tam and Bernie Gourlay's flat spoke of an unpretentious comfort. It felt lived in, with a child's toys piled into a couple of boxes in one corner, shelves that contained a mixture of popular women's fiction and sports videos, Monet's Water Lilies on the walls. When they arrived, Bernie was sitting by the bay window in the late afternoon dusk. Gourlay switched the light on as he entered, but Bernie didn't react. She continued to stare out of the window, smoking with an air of desperation.

"Bernie?" he said. "Bernie, this is Lindsay and Rory. They're going to help us find Jack. They're journalists."

At the word "journalist," Bernie's head jerked sharply towards them. "I'm sorry," she said coldly, her flat Belfast accent as strong as the day she'd left. "He's been wasting your time. Everybody's written the story already."

Rory shrugged and looked at Lindsay, who kept her expression blank. "This is our best chance," Gourlay protested. "The polis willnae help, they wankers at the Foreign Office willnae help. We need somebody in our corner that knows what they're doing. Somebody that'll no' let them get away wi' it."

"No, Tam. I said no, and I meant it. A few stories in the papers won't bother Bruno. You don't know what you're getting into here." Her red-rimmed eyes stared unblinking at him, but her hands were trembling.

"This is Glasgow, no' bloody Sicily. Christ, Bernie. I don't understand you. Do you no' want the boy back, or what?"

"Of course I do." For a moment, her façade wavered and Lindsay could see naked fear in Bernie's eyes. "But what can they do to help? We've already held a bloody press conference, for all the good that did us."

"Listen, this pair, they investigate things. They expose scandals. It's what they do. And this diplomatic immunity bullshit, that's a scandal if ever there was one."

Seeing Rory edging towards the door, Bernie said triumphantly, "See for yourself. She knows it's a waste of time. Go on, darlin', away back to the pub."

Rory shrugged. "I already told your husband what you needed was a private eye. But he insisted."

This time, there was no mistaking the look of panic in Bernie's eyes. "A private eye?" she gasped.

"They're good at finding missing persons," Rory said gently. "They've got a lot of experience. I could give you a couple of names if you like?"

Bernie's eyes widened and her mouth opened. But no words came. Lindsay watched Bernie, assessing her. Something was off key. Bernie Gourlay wasn't behaving like a desperate mother who'd move heaven and earth to get her child back. Intrigued, Lindsay said, "Of course, a private eye will want to keep everything under wraps. Personally, I think publicity's your best chance of finding out where your son is. And that's the first step to getting him back."

Bernie snatched at the chance. "You know, I think you might be right," she gabbled. "All right. I'll talk to you. But don't you ever forget, Tam Gourlay, it was you that set this ball rolling."

Gourlay looked baffled but clearly wasn't about to question her surrender. "I'll make a pot of tea," he said, backing out of the room. Rory had the good sense to settle herself in an armchair and try to blend into the background.

"So, Bernie, what exactly does Bruno do for the Italian Foreign Office?" Lindsay asked.

"He's a commercial attaché."

"And where's he stationed now?"

"The last I heard, he was in Belgrade."

"Not exactly a place you'd want your six-year-old son to be, I imagine."

Bernie said nothing. But Lindsay wasn't giving in so easily. "How would Bruno get him out of the country?"

"Jack has two passports. I've got his British one and Bruno's got his Italian one."

"Convenient for Bruno. So, how did you two meet?"

"I'd not long come over from Ireland. I was working as a waitress in a hotel in town. Bruno used to come in a few times a week. He asked me out, and we just clicked. We were married two months later." Bernie lit another cigarette.

"So what went wrong?"

"Italian men don't want wives. They want servants. Just because I was a waitress when I met him, it doesn't mean I wanted to wait on him hand, foot and finger for the rest of my days. Besides, I don't think I was smart enough to make the right sort of embassy wife." There was no mistaking the bitterness now. "So I left him. Jack was only a year old."

"That must have been tough," Lindsay sympathized.

"What would you know about tough?" Bernie demanded contemptuously. "Yes, it was tough. I hooked up with one of the women I used to work with at the hotel. I minded her kids in the evenings when she was working, and she looked after Jack during the day so I could get a job. And that's when my luck turned. Tam advertised for a receptionist, and I answered the ad. I thought I'd finally fallen on my feet. It should have occurred to me that Bruno would hate the idea of another man bringing up his son."

"So Bruno tried to get custody of Jack?" Lindsay asked.

"He tried, and he failed. I thought he'd given up the idea, but clearly I was wrong." Bernie bit her lip. Now her distress was clearer than at any time since they'd arrived. Taking advantage of it, Lindsay continued to probe for more background details on Bruno, managing to extract from Bernie that he had originally come from the Val d'Elsa area of Tuscany. But whenever she tried to get Bernie to talk about Jack, she clammed up. After half an hour, Lindsay had to concede defeat. She wasn't going to get any further with Bernie Gourlay. She promised to do everything in her power to track down Jack's whereabouts, then she and Rory made their escape.

"That was seriously weird," Rory said as they walked down the street, the red sandstone tenements stained the colour of dried blood by the early evening gloom. "You'd think she'd be desperate for help. But it was like she couldn't get us out of there fast enough."

"Yeah, I know. There's something not kosher there. Maybe our Bruno is a wee bit more dodgy than a commercial attaché. Maybe he's a spook. Or maybe he has connections." Lindsay glanced at her watch.

"What? You mean, as in, 'Respect the family'?" Rory said in a terrible impersonation of Marlon Brando.

Lindsay winced. "I know, I know, you can be Italian without being a Mafioso. But I'm curious, all the same."

"Maybe there's another reason why she's ambivalent about Jack coming home," Rory said slowly.

"How do you mean?"

"Maybe it's not all happy families in Kinghorn Drive. Maybe Tam's abusing the boy?"

Lindsay turned the idea over in her mind and dismissed it. "He's not the type," she said decisively.

"Suddenly there's a type?" Rory demanded.

"Of course not, I'm not that naïve. But Tam Gourlay is possibly the least sleazy guy I've met in years. Besides, abusers don't do *anything* to draw attention to their relationship to their victims, and Tam's hardly trying to hush things up."

Rory shrugged. "It would explain what we've just seen."

"I don't buy it. My gut says no." They walked on in silence for a few yards, approaching the corner where their routes home would naturally separate.

"Hey, you know what?" Rory said suddenly, bright as fresh paint.

"What?"

"This is your very first proper story. We should go out and celebrate. A bottle of champagne, a nice dinner. What do you say?" If she'd had a tail, she'd have been wagging it in supplication.

It was tempting. An evening with Rory would have seemed like an attractive option at the best of times. And, whatever this was, it wasn't the best of times. Almost anything would have sounded more fun than another evening discussing conception. But giving in to temptation wasn't the most sensible way to fix things between her and Sophie. "I'd love to, Rory, but I need to get back."

They'd reached the corner. "Fine," Rory said, her non-chalance obviously forced. "Another time, maybe. When you've cleared it with Sophie."

Before Lindsay could protest that she didn't need to clear her social engagements with her girlfriend, Rory had swung off down the street. Oh well, Lindsay thought as she trudged up the hill towards home. At least she had a story of her own to get her teeth into.

⊰✧⊱

Michael Conroy waited for the cover of darkness before he made his latest reconnaissance of the street where Bernadette Dooley lived with her husband. Jesus, Joseph and Mary, but the husband was a big fucker. Michael feared no man, but he liked the odds to be weighted in his favour, preferably with serious hardware. Whatever it was that Bernadette had taken from Patrick, he'd be happy if it could be recovered without a direct confrontation with the big man.

Patrick had gone very quiet when he'd reported back about Bernadette getting her name all over the papers. Michael knew his boss well enough to read the silence, to realise that Patrick was seriously unhappy, not least because Michael's direct warning had proved unproductive. He figured Patrick had maybe been planning to use threats against the boy as further leverage, so his disappearance would be a helluva spoke in your man's wheel.

All the same, it was some coincidence, the lad getting snatched just when Patrick took an interest in the mother. But coincidences happened. Michael knew that. A couple of his best friends had done long stretches inside because of coincidence. It didn't worry him.

At least, it didn't worry him nearly as much as Patrick's instructions to keep Bernadette under close surveillance. King-horn Drive, where she lived with the big fucker, was a quiet residential street. The kind of place where, even if there wasn't an official Neighbourhood Watch, there was bound to be some nosy old bitch twitching the nets day in, day out. If they tried keeping watch from a car, one of the local busybodies would be on to the police within the hour.

Where the hell else could they watch from? There wasn't a single vantage point anywhere in the street that would avoid suspicion.

The answer came on his third pass along Kinghorn Drive. A couple of doors down from the Gourlays' flat, on the opposite side of the street, a second-floor flat had a poster in the window announcing it was for sale. Peering up through the dark,

Michael could make out the absence of curtains, a sure sign of vacant possession. He'd pulled a stunt like this once before with an empty flat.

Tomorrow morning, he'd present himself at the estate agent's, clean and shaved. A film-maker looking for a location. Willing to pay top dollar for the use of an empty flat for a couple of weeks. An empty flat like that one he'd noticed on Kinghorn Drive. Surely the owner would be happy to make a few bob at no inconvenience to himself? It wasn't as if there would be any obstacle to potential viewing. At an hour's notice from the agent, the film crew could be up and away, as if they'd never been there.

Michael walked briskly back to the pub where he'd left Kevin supping Guinness. With a bit of luck, he'd be able to satisfy Patrick without taking any risks. In Michael's book, that made it a very good day indeed.

10

Even if you wanted to hide from someone on Hillhead underground station in the middle of the morning, it was too quiet for that to be a serious possibility. Not that Lindsay had any desire to hide from Rory, exactly. She just felt it would be easier to handle their relationship if they kept it within professional parameters. Sharing the same journey into work somehow felt a little outside the boundaries. But she could hardly ignore the familiar figure slouched against one of the pillars, waiting for the train. She walked up and tapped Rory on the shoulder.

Her head snapped round, eyes wide, eyebrows arching in surprise. "Oh, hiya," she said, her face lighting up when she realised she wasn't being assailed by the loony on the train or importuned by a beggar. She gave Lindsay a one-armed hug and a peck on the cheek. "How're you doing, Splash?"

"Good. You?"

Rory groaned. "Sandra turned up with a bottle of vodka and the burning desire to whinge about her boss. So I'm feeling a wee bit frayed round the edges."

"I should have come out with you after all. Saved you from yourself," Lindsay said.

Rory's reply was drowned by the arrival of the bright orange train. With its carriages smaller than most public

transport systems, it always made Lindsay feel she was travelling in Toytown. She half-expected Noddy and Big Ears to
board at Kelvinbridge, hotly pursued by the golliwogs.

Once they were sitting down, Rory repeated herself. "I
said, are you always so uxorious?"

"Is that how you see me?" Lindsay stalled.

"Well, I've only known you a few days, but you always
seem to be in a hurry to get home at the end of the day. Which
is not a criticism," she added hastily. "It's just . . . well, it's just
unusual, when you've been together as long as you two."

"Yeah, well, that would be because unusual is where we
are right now." Lindsay tried to keep her voice light. She failed.

"Hey, I'm sorry if I said the wrong thing," Rory said
anxiously.

Lindsay shook her head. "It's okay." She stared at the floor
between her feet. "If we're going to work together, I guess I
should tell you what's going on in my life. At least then you'll
know, if I'm being moody, chances are it's nothing to do with
you."

"Listen, you don't have to tell me anything you don't want
to." Impulsively, Rory reached across and squeezed Lindsay's
hand. She was entirely unprepared for the charge she felt when
Lindsay returned the pressure.

"It's entirely selfish, believe me. I need to talk to someone
about it before I go mad. And all the friends I would normally
off-load it on are either in California or London. So you get
the short straw."

"Hey, that's cool. I mean, I want us to be friends, you
know?"

"I know. But let's wait till we're sitting comfortably, eh?
Preferably with a coffee in front of us."

Twenty minutes later, they were ensconced in the back
booth. Now the moment was upon her, Lindsay felt a strange
reluctance, as if talking about what ailed her was somehow a
betrayal of Sophie. But it was too late for that. Rory was staring

at her with the patient anticipation of a child who knows it will get the biscuit if it sits still for long enough. It was time to cut to the chase. "Sophie wants a baby," she said flatly.

"Ah," Rory said.

"She's been talking about it for a while. But I kept blanking it. I thought if I just ignored it, she'd get the message and it would go away." A tired smile. "I couldn't have been more wrong."

"Would I be right in thinking you're not exactly enthusiastic about the idea of parenthood?"

Lindsay stirred the froth on her cappuccino. "That would be an understatement. I like my life. And I've never wanted a kid."

"Not easy to argue with the biological imperative, though."

"That's the trump card, isn't it? But it's hard to understand when it's not something you've ever experienced. See, I've never been possessed by anything the way this has got Sophie in her grip. It's obviously not some whim. It consumes her. She's obsessed. It's like I'm not even there in her heart, in her head. There's no room for me any more, just this overwhelming need." Lindsay sighed.

"So you're at an impasse?"

Lindsay shook her head. "No. It's gone past that. A few days ago, she announced that she'd found a donor. She's been inseminating this week."

Rory looked appalled. "You mean, she's gone ahead without your agreement?"

"Well, it's more that she backed me into a corner. The only choices I had were to stay and support her in something that I hate the idea of, or else to walk away. And I love her, Rory. I couldn't leave her. That was the gamble she took. And she won."

"That's a helluva gamble."

Lindsay shook her head. "Not really. Deep down, she knows how committed I am to her, to this relationship. At some level, she knew I'd have to give in to the emotional blackmail."

"I'm sorry, I know you love her, and I don't know the woman, but I think that's a terrible thing to do. It's really selfish, really calculating." Rory's face revealed disgust and contempt in equal measure.

"The thing is, Rory, Sophie isn't selfish. And she isn't some hard, calculating bitch out for number one. She's actually the most generous and kind person I know. She's a lot nicer than me, trust me on that. It's a measure of how much this need has hold of her that she's behaving like this, and I don't think she's proud of it. In a funny kind of way, I suspect she feels as trapped by this as I do."

Rory looked bemused. "You're being a lot more generous than I would be in your shoes. I mean, the bottom line is, she's going for the thing she wants regardless of what it means to you, to your relationship."

Lindsay took a sip of her coffee and met Rory's eye with a rueful smile. "Looks like it."

"You deserve better than that," Rory said fiercely.

Lindsay laughed. "You really don't know me very well, do you? Mostly, I feel like I don't deserve someone as honest, as loyal or as supportive as Sophie. So," she continued, her tone becoming businesslike, "now you know what it is that's doing my head in. If I lose the plot, it's probably because I'm panicking about parenthood. Okay?"

"Thanks for telling me." Rory reached across the table and laid her fingers on Lindsay's wrist. This time, she wasn't the only one who felt the electricity. "Any time you want to dump, feel free."

Looking startled, Lindsay dipped her head in acknowledgement. "Duly noted. But, for now, I need to crack on with the tug-of-love kid." She switched on her laptop, connected to the Internet and a few minutes later, jotted down the number of the Italian Embassy in Belgrade.

Rory, who was flicking through the morning papers, looked up in surprise as Lindsay launched into fluent Italian.

She waited till the call was over, then said, "How come you speak Italian so well?"

"I lived in Italy for six months a few years back."

"You were a journalist in Italy?"

Lindsay grinned. "No. I was the winter caretaker on a campsite."

Rory looked puzzled. "How come?"

"It's a long story. Some other time. The main thing is, Bruno Cavadino isn't at work and he's not due back for another three days. I'm going to have to see if I can track down any family he's got in Italy." She frowned, trying to come up with a solution to her problem. "What are you up to today?" she asked absently.

"I'm taking a contact out to lunch. He thinks he's got a story about backhanders at the submarine base at Faslane. Probably the usual load of rumour and gossip, but you never know." She looked at her watch. "In fact, I better make tracks if I'm going to get to Helensburgh in time."

Lindsay nodded. "See you when I see you, then." She waited till Rory had left, then dug her electronic organiser out of her bag and checked a number. Although she hadn't worked as a reporter in Italy, her boss had a cousin who worked for one of the dailies there. They'd met at a New Year party and bonded via their common experience at the sharp end. "*Buongiorno,*" she said when she was connected. "*Vorrei parlare con Giulia Garrafo, per piacere . . . Si, va bene . . . Giulia? C'e* Lindsay Gordon . . . Yes, I know, it's been far too long. But I'm back living in Glasgow now, so coming to Italy isn't going to be such a big deal in future." The two women caught up with each other, then, the demands of friendship satisfied, Lindsay said, "Listen, I need your help with a story I'm working on."

She outlined the background to Jack Gourlay's disappearance. "Cavadino isn't back in the office in Belgrade for another three days, so I reckon he's probably getting the boy settled in with his family. But all I know is that he grew up in the Val d'Elsa area. Any chance you can find out if he still has family there?"

"It's a long shot. But I know a good stringer near there, and I have a couple of contacts in the Foreign Ministry," Giulia said. "If I have to use the stringer, you'll pay freelance rates, yes?"

Lindsay thought for a moment. Unlike private eyes, who got paid for their work regardless of results, freelances like her and Rory only earned once they'd achieved success. Paying an Italian journalist to make inquiries on her behalf could leave them out of pocket if she couldn't make a story stand up. But she also understood the need at this point in her career of speculating to accumulate. "Yes, of course," she said, hoping it wouldn't be a long job.

"Great. Give me your number, I'll get back to you."

Lindsay ended the call feeling slightly hopeful. It was good to know she hadn't completely lost her touch. Time, she thought, for another wee chat with Tam Gourlay.

Gourlay's Garage occupied a corner site on Maryhill Road. The cars were a typical mix of sales reps' saloons and dinky hatchbacks for school and supermarket runs. "Tam's Temptation of the Week" was a three-year-old Ford Mondeo with sports wheels and a wood veneer dashboard. Lindsay wasn't tempted.

The office was a Portakabin that managed to exude an air of homely comfort. No girlie calendars or car advertising posters here, just a series of dramatic photographic prints of Highland scenery and the smell of lavender pot pourri. Lindsay suspected the ambience had more to do with the woman answering the phone than Tam. The woman, a motherly fifty-something, smiled as Lindsay entered and held up a finger, indicating she was almost finished. She put down the phone with a cheery farewell and swivelled in her chair to face Lindsay. "Good afternoon, and welcome to Gourlay's Garage. How can I help you?"

"Is Tam in?"

"Mr Gourlay? Yes, he's here. Who shall I say is calling?"

The door behind her opened and Tam's head appeared in the gap. "Oh, it's you," he said, sounding faintly disconcerted. "I thought we had a customer. Come away through." He stood back and held the door open for her.

The inner office was a tidy, businesslike domain that reeked of cigarette smoke. Tam dropped into a leather executive chair and waved Lindsay to one of the less comfortable client seats on the opposite side of a cheap metal desk. "Any news? Made any progress?" he asked.

"I've got some inquiries on the go. But I wanted to have a chat with you, clear up a few details. To be honest, your wife wasn't exactly one hundred per cent co-operative last night."

Tam looked embarrassed. "Aye. I'm sorry about that. She's kind of close to the edge the now, know what I mean?"

"She's bound to be upset. But when I've done stories like this in the past, I've always found the parents were desperate to grasp at any straw that might help to get their kid back."

Tam reached for an open packet of cigarettes and took one out. "Sure. But, take it from me, Bernie's desperate, right enough. Having said that, she's scared of what Bruno might do if the pressure goes on."

"Like what?"

"She says he might do a runner with the boy. Walk away from his job, disappear into the wide blue yonder."

Lindsay looked sceptical. "It's not very likely, is it? What would he do for money?"

"Bernie seems to think his family would see him right. And she's the one that knows the guy, right?"

If Bernie genuinely believed that too much publicity might drive her ex-husband underground, it went a long way towards explaining her hostility the previous evening, Lindsay thought. Writing a story with an unwilling interviewee wasn't a recipe for success. And it certainly didn't make for a good follow-up if it turned out to have a happy ending. Maybe she should think about a more proactive approach to the problem of Jack Gourlay's kidnapping. "Tell me something, Tam. Supposing I find out where Jack is, what were you thinking of doing about it?"

Through the haze of smoke, she thought she detected a moment's shiftiness. "Well, obviously, we'd have to go through the legal channels in whatever country he's got him in."

"So you weren't thinking about snatching him back?"

There was a long silence that Lindsay was determined not to break. "What if I was?" Tam said eventually.

"Well, it would be a bloody sight more interesting as a story than some long-drawn-out court battle," Lindsay said casually.

Tam looked at her shrewdly. "Are you saying you'd help?"

Lindsay held her hands up, palms facing him. "I never said that. But obviously you'd need help. And obviously, if you asked for help from somebody who also had something to gain from a successful operation . . . well, that would be a way of making it more secure, wouldn't it?"

"I hear what you're saying," he said slowly.

"If he's abroad, it might be difficult. And expensive."

Tam shrugged. "To hell with the expense. I'm not exactly on the breadline. I'll spend whatever it takes to get Jack back."

"That's good to know. But, first, we've got to find out where he is." Lindsay got to her feet. "I'll be in touch as soon as I hear anything."

She walked out of the Portakabin, shaking her head in wonder. What had she just signed up to? Why did she always have to jump in at the deep end? Some people couldn't live without the edge of risk in their lives. Was that what the possibility of parenthood was turning her into? Or was it that she was starting to feel that she might as well be reckless since she didn't have much left to lose? Pushing the uncomfortable thought away, she headed back to her car.

Lindsay polished off the last mouthful of her baked potato with chili and pushed the plate to one side. Working from the Café Virginia had definite advantages, she reckoned, thinking back without nostalgia to her previous life as a journalist, to canteen meals drenched in saturated fats and sandwiches gobbled on the run. She'd just opened that day's *Scotsman* when an immaculately dressed and perfectly groomed man slid into the seat opposite her. He wore an expectant expression, but, although he looked familiar, Lindsay couldn't place him at once.

Seeing her confusion, he held out his hand with an accompanying smile. "Giles Graham. Lifestyle editor of the *Standard*. Our paths crossed briefly in a past life."

"Of course," Lindsay exclaimed. "I'm sorry, it was seeing you out of context, I couldn't make the connections." She shook his hand. "Are you looking for Rory?"

"I am indeed. I was passing, and I thought I'd buy her a coffee. A small thank you for a tip she gave me that seems to be panning out rather nicely. Since she's not here, perhaps you'd let me buy you one instead?"

Lindsay shook her head. "I'm awash with the stuff. But don't let me stop you."

Giles leaned round the corner of the booth and managed to catch Annie's eye. He was, she thought, the kind of man who was accustomed to catching women's eyes, regardless of their sexual orientation. "I hear you and Rory are going to be working together," he said. "About time she had someone with a bit of sense to temper her wilder excursions."

"And you think I'm that person?" She could only think that Giles had somehow managed to avoid some of her more legendary exploits.

"Absolutely. You've been there, done that, sold the T-shirt at a charity auction. Nobody knows better than Splash Gordon the kind of trouble a journalist can get into before she loses her idealism. So it seems to me that there's no better brake on

Rory's excesses than someone who understands the dangers they can lead to."

It was, she thought, charmingly put. But before she could respond, her phone rang. "Excuse me," she said, picking it up. "Lindsay Gordon."

"*Ciao, bella.* It's Giulia."

"Wow, that was quick. I take it that means you have an answer for me?"

"*Vero.* I don't think it's the one you want to hear, however. The freelance I contacted managed to track down Cavadino's mother. The family owns a café on the road from Colle Val d'Elsa to Grosseto. He got the mother into conversation, and the kid's definitely not there. The old lady was complaining about never seeing her grandchildren, especially the one in England."

"Scotland," Lindsay corrected automatically. She sighed. "Never mind. You did your best."

"I'm not finished," Giulia protested. "My boyfriend's sister-in-law, Lucia, works in the personnel department of the Foreign Ministry. I didn't want to say anything before, in case she couldn't help, but now I can boast about it." She gave her trademark giggle, a breathy sound that always reminded Lindsay uncomfortably of Jennifer Tilly in *Bound*. "Cavadino has a sister. She is married to another diplomat, a former colleague of her brother's. Apparently, sister and brother are very close."

"And where is the sister based?" Lindsay asked eagerly.

"According to Lucia, Maria Padovani is with her husband. He's the commercial attaché at the St Petersburg consulate."

"St Petersburg? As in Russia?"

"*Vero.*"

"Why there? Isn't the embassy in Moscow?"

"Sure. But everybody has a consulate in St Petersburg. All that shipping, you know? They have to maintain a presence to look after their commercial interests. Not to mention all those sailors who get into trouble ashore."

"Of course, I wasn't thinking. So, what's the score with Maria Padovani? Is the boy there?"

"Lucia said she was checking visa status for dependants. According to the person she spoke to in the consulate, the Padovanis applied for a multi-entry diplomatic visa for their nephew soon after they arrived in Russia. They were claiming him as a dependant. Apparently the line was that his father wasn't able to look after him and he had asked them to take charge of the boy. But they don't live in the residence, so nobody really knew if the boy was there or not. Sounds like Cavadino has been planning this for a while, no?"

"He certainly set it all up well in advance," Lindsay said. "I'll have to see what I can find out about the St Petersburg end of things. Thanks a million, Giulia. I owe you."

"You can pay me in Frascati in Rome."

"It's a deal." Lindsay hung up and gave Giles an apologetic look. "Sorry about that. A story I'm working on."

"With a St Petersburg connection?" he asked. "I'm not fishing, just interested," he added hastily, seeing Lindsay's look of suspicion. "I went there last year with Julia, my wife. She's an MEP, had to go there on some fact-finding mission about Russian education and I managed to ride her coat-tails. Marvellous city."

"I've never been."

"You should go, before the Russians get the hang of mass tourism and it gets ruined."

I could end up there sooner than you imagine, she thought wryly. "I don't suppose you've got any contacts there?" she asked without much hope that serendipity would weigh in on her side.

He shook his head. "Not journalists, no. I got quite pally with a chap from the British Council. He does a lot of liaison work with the local schools and colleges, which is why we ended up spending quite a bit of time with him."

A faint glimmer of an idea flickered at the edge of Lindsay's brain. "Do you think he might be up for a bit of intrigue?"

Giles laughed. "Probably. British Council bureaucracy doesn't exactly make for an interesting life. I expect he'd be terribly grateful for a bit of excitement. Do you want me to call him?"

In reply, Lindsay handed him her phone.

"You don't mess about, do you?" he said, amused. He looked up a number on his electronic organiser then dialled it. "Hello? Is that Gareth? Gareth, it's Giles Graham here. Julia's husband. How are things with you?" He listened politely for a minute. "Oh, we're both fine," he continued. "Listen, Gareth, a colleague of mine has a need for a little clandestine information gathering in your fair city. And I wondered if you'd be willing to help her? . . . I'm not entirely sure, but I suspect it's not the sort of thing she could put through official channels . . . You would? Hang on, I'll pass you over to her."

He handed the phone to Lindsay with a wink. "I think you'll be okay there."

"Hello? Gareth, my name's Lindsay Gordon. I really appreciate you talking to me."

"No problem," he said, his Geordie accent immediately obvious. "A change is as good as a holiday round here. If I can do anything to help, I will."

"Great. This is all a bit delicate, and I don't want to drop you in it professionally, so it's probably better if I don't go into the reasons why I need this information. Are you okay with that?" Lindsay's voice was warm and persuasive, honed over years of persuading the reluctant to talk.

"I suppose so," he said dubiously. "It's not anything illegal, is it?"

"No, of course not. I just don't want to put you in an embarrassing position."

"So what is it you want to know?"

"I'm trying to track down a six-year-old boy. I think he might be in St Petersburg and, if he is, I'm sure he'll be going to school. He's a native English speaker, which I guess would narrow the options down quite a bit. I wondered if you could maybe let me have a list of places he could possibly be enrolled?"

"That's it? That's all you want to know? No problem. Let me make a couple of calls. Can you ring me back tomorrow on this number? Make it around the same time, if you can."

Lindsay punched the air and gave Giles the thumbs-up. "That's great, Gareth. I really appreciate this."

"Like I said, no problem. You tell Giles, next time he comes, he owes me a bottle of Bowmore."

Lindsay ended the call, her eyes sparkling with satisfaction. "Giles, you are a prince among men. That espresso is on me."

11

People were so gullible, Michael mused. No, on second thoughts, people were so greedy. The estate agent had been a pushover as soon as the words, "I'd pay cash, of course. No need to bother the taxman, is there?" had left his mouth. You'd think with the damage Republican bombs had done over the years that any Brit with half a brain would think twice before they rented out an empty flat to a man with an accent like his. But the magic of money worked the trick every time.

It was perfect. The view from the bay window of the living room couldn't be bettered. They could see the Gourlays' front door and they could catch glimpses of Bernadette as she moved across the living room. The only thing Michael had to worry about was whether Kevin had the attention span to keep a proper watch when it was his turn.

So far, there hadn't been much to see. The big fucker had gone off in his shiny maroon Jag at twenty to nine. Bernadette had emerged just before ten and Michael had followed at a discreet distance. She'd walked down to the supermarket and bought a chicken, a bag of spuds, a cabbage, a bottle of Scotch and 200 cigarettes. She'd moved like a zombie, he'd thought. If he'd jumped up in front of her and shouted, "Boo!" he didn't think she'd have broken stride.

On the way back, he'd caught himself wondering what the point of this was. Patrick knew where she was living. He'd given her one scare already with the note he'd had Michael leave on the kitchen table. Presumably, he was also leaning on her via the phone to get her to give up whatever it was she'd walked off with. But surely he must have realised by now that the softly-softly approach wasn't getting him anywhere? Michael couldn't understand why he hadn't been instructed to try a more direct method of persuasion.

However, the habit of obeying orders was ingrained in Michael. If Patrick was holding back, there had to be a reason. It was possible he wanted to front her up himself. Christ Almighty, Michael thought, if I'd robbed Patrick Coughlan and he showed up on my doorstep, I'd sign away everything I owned in the world to see the back of him. If that was the game plan, it was possible that the delay was because Patrick hadn't been able to get away. He wasn't simply a busy man; he was important too. Just because there was a ceasefire, that didn't mean Patrick could disappear on his own private business whenever it suited him.

All in good time, Michael had told himself as he watched Bernadette let herself into the home she probably still saw as a sanctuary. For now, he was content to wait.

Sophie had woken up feeling sick. When she passed the news on, Lindsay felt sick too. "Does that mean it's worked?" she'd asked.

"I'm not getting my hopes up," Sophie had said. "It could be psychosomatic, it could be that I ate too much of your wonderful tomato and artichoke risotto last night."

"And it could be that you're pregnant." Lindsay rolled over and sat on the edge of the bed, wondering for how much longer it would only be the two of them.

"What are you so scared of, Lindsay? Are you worried I won't love you any more when the baby comes?" Sophie squirmed across the bed and put an arm round her lover's naked back.

"I suppose that's part of it. The baby will come first with you, it's the way the biology works. But mostly, it's that I like my life the way it is. I like the choices we have. Where to live, where to go on holiday, when to go to the pictures, when to go out for dinner. We've worked hard for the right to those choices and it feels like madness to throw all that away." She got to her feet and padded across the room to get her dressing gown.

"We'll have different choices," Sophie said, her voice tinged with sadness. "We'll have a lovely life, Lindsay, I promise you."

"Yeah, but on balance, I prefer the devil I know."

Her words came back to her as she sat in Café Virginia browsing the morning papers. She hadn't seen Rory since the previous morning, and had no idea what her business partner was up to. Presumably pursuing the Faslane story, whatever it had turned out to be. She wondered if they needed to set up an agreed system for communicating what they were up to, or whether that would feel too much like keeping tabs on each other. She was fairly sure Rory would hate to feel checked up on almost as much as she would.

So, what was she doing with her much-vaunted choices today? Not a lot, came the answer. She'd spent half an hour checking out St Petersburg on the Internet, formulating ideas and discarding them as fast as she thought of them. Eventually, she'd come up with the bare bones of a plan. But she needed to know she wasn't setting herself an impossible task. Three hours till she could phone Gareth in St Petersburg, and damn all to fill them with. Lindsay needed to dig up some stories for herself, but she wasn't going to do that sitting on her backside in the café. She was about to go off in search of a newsagent that sold out-of-town weekly papers when her phone rang. She grabbed it eagerly and said, "Hello? Lindsay Gordon."

"Lindsay? It's Gareth here. I got your number off Giles, I hope you don't mind?"

"Not at all, no."

"Only, I've got that information for you, but I've got to go to a meeting this afternoon, so I thought I'd better get back to you before then."

"That's great," Lindsay said, elation swelling inside her. "What's the score?"

"There's three schools that could take an English-speaking six-year-old. I can e-mail you the details, it would be easier than trying to spell them out to you."

Lindsay's heart sank. "Three?"

"Yes. They're all fairly central, and they're all much of a muchness when it comes to the quality of teaching, as far as I can gather."

"Is there any one in particular that caters to the diplomatic community?" Lindsay asked, desperate to narrow down the search.

"I don't know about catering to the diplomatic community specifically, but there are a couple of people here with kids who send them to the international school on Konstantinogradskaya Ulitsa. I've heard that quite a few of the kids there have parents who are EU diplomats."

"That's brilliant, Gareth." She gave him her e-mail address. "I really appreciate you going to this much trouble."

"It was no trouble. I'll e-mail those details to you right away."

Lindsay hung up. She dialled a new number and waited.

"Gourlay's Garage, your first choice for previously owned vehicles—how may I help you?" She recognised the voice of Tam's receptionist.

"Can I speak to Tam, please? It's Lindsay Gordon."

The line went hollow as she was put on hold. Then Tam Gourlay's voice boomed in her ear. "Have you got some news for me?"

"I've got a pretty good idea where Jack is."

The roar of delight nearly blew the electronics in Lindsay's phone. "That's fantastic! Amazing! So where is he?"

"I think the chances are strong that he's in St Petersburg."

A moment of stunned silence followed by, "You mean, in Russia?"

"That's right."

"What the fuck's he doing in Russia?" Tam sounded genuinely bewildered.

"Bruno's sister is married to another Italian diplomat. They've had it set up officially for ages that Jack would go and live with them. I can't see any reason for that unless they were planning to look after him once Bruno had snatched him. Even if it's only for a short time, until the fuss dies down."

"Fuck. What do we do now? I mean, Russia. I don't even know how you get there. Or how long it takes."

"Well, funnily enough, I've got one or two ideas about that. It's going to be risky, and it's going to cost a lot of money—"

"I told you," Tam interrupted. "Money is not an issue here. All I want is to see Bernie happy again."

"Okay. So, this is what I'm thinking . . ." Lindsay leaned back in the booth and outlined her plan.

Two hours later, the MGB was powering up the long rise of the Rest and Be Thankful. Blessedly, there hadn't been much traffic on the Loch Lomond road and she'd made good time. With luck and a continued absence of caravans and motor homes, she'd be at her parents' house in an hour and a half. The heather was turning purple on the hills, and the familiar grandeur of the landscape made Lindsay feel at home as the city never would. She recognised her membership of the national trait of sentimentality for her native land, but she didn't care. The sense of ownership she felt driving through Argyll to the Kintyre peninsula was something that could never be taken from her.

Sophie hadn't been best pleased when she'd called to tell her she was going up to Invercross overnight. It wasn't that she minded Lindsay being away; she minded not coming with her.

"We don't see enough of your parents," she'd said plaintively. "Tell them to come down and visit soon."

Aye, right, Lindsay thought, knowing how little time her fisherman father was ever prepared to spend away from the sea. Her mother enjoyed the opportunity for shopping in the big city, but watching her father fret always spoiled Lindsay's joy in her mother's pleasure. "We'll go up for a weekend soon," she promised Sophie.

"A shame it couldn't wait till the weekend this time," Sophie said.

"You know how stories don't wait." Well, it was almost the truth.

"I know. It's good to see you enjoying yourself again, Lindsay. I'm really glad you're working with Rory." They'd left it at that, neither mentioning what was uppermost in both their minds.

Lindsay was changing down to negotiate a series of bends when the phone rang. She pulled over into a viewpoint and picked up the phone. "Hello? Lindsay Gordon."

"Hey, partner, where are you?" Rory sounded cheerful. "I just got this bizarre message from Giles saying I better catch you before you went chasing off to Russia. What's going on?"

"I'm on the A83, west of Arrochar, heading down towards Loch Fyne. Which, as far as I'm aware, is not the way to Russia."

"What are you doing there?"

"I'm on my way to Invercross, to visit my parents."

"Invercross? Where the hell is that?"

"Halfway down the Mull of Kintyre, on the west side. Where I grew up. Possibly one of the most beautiful places on the planet."

Rory snorted. "Compared to Castlemilk, almost anywhere qualifies for that description. So what's all this about Russia?"

"I think I've tracked down Jack Gourlay. It's looking likely that he's in St Petersburg."

"Wow! Bizarre. So, is Bernie going to court to get him back?"

Lindsay took a deep breath. "Not exactly."

Rory picked up on the hesitation. "Oh no. Don't tell me. Big Tam wants to play at *Where Eagles Dare*."

"Something like that. So, do you fancy a trip to Russia?"

PART II

12

The first thing Lindsay noticed about Pulkovo Airport was the cigarette smoke. Accustomed to American airports where no tobacco had burned for years, she was taken aback to see people smoking everywhere. It reinforced what had already struck her on the approach to the runway—that she was heading somewhere very foreign indeed. This wasn't a landscape she'd seen anywhere else in Europe. From the plane window, it looked like Legoland: the buildings neat, square blocks, anywhere from six to twelve storeys high, laid out in grids. Sticking up apparently at random were factory chimneys, red-and-white striped, also like something from a child's construction kit, plumes of smoke coming out of them at right angles in the stiff wind. There seemed to be nothing organic about this landscape; it was as regimented as humans could make it.

Then, as the plane dipped down, Rory pointed out a landing strip exclusively for helicopters. There were dozens of them, in various liveries. "It's a flock of petrol budgies," she exclaimed.

As the plane approached the runway, silver birch trees took over. As far as the eye could see, ghostly white trunks stood in the dimming afternoon light, their fine leaves dappled with light, the chimney stacks sticking out of them, still red and white,

still spewing out ribbons of white smoke across a sky the blue
of robin's eggs.

When the wheels touched down on the tarmac, the Russians on board applauded loudly. "Tells you all you need to know
about Aeroflot," Lindsay commented.

"Where do we go?" Rory asked anxiously as they emerged
into the terminal building. She'd admitted to being less than
intrepid when it came to "abroad," and being confronted with
signs in Cyrillic everywhere clearly wasn't helping her confidence.

"Follow the crowd," Lindsay said. "We've all got to jump
through the same hoops." They descended a flight of stairs and
found themselves in a high-ceilinged immigration hall, queues
snaking the length of the room. Lindsay headed for what looked
like the shortest line, and resigned herself to a long wait. In the
week since she'd discovered Jack Gourlay's whereabouts, she'd
set herself a crash course in figuring out Russia, and she knew
getting through immigration could take a while.

She'd thought the whole process would be nightmarish and
complicated, but the travel agent had made it all look desperately
simple. Arranging visas had taken no more than a couple of days
once they'd filled in the forms and supplied passport photographs.
The hotel booking was confirmed and the flights arranged. But
a lot of what happened now they were here would be up to her.
She'd learned the alphabet, the words for "please" and "thank
you" and the invaluable sentence, "I don't speak Russian." She'd
studied a street map of the city, got her head round the metro
system and read the *Rough Guide*.

All that had been easy compared to explaining to Sophie
why she had to go off on such a risky venture at all. Her partner
had seemed emotionally vulnerable, a state Lindsay wasn't accustomed to dealing with. Sophie was the rock in their relationship, the one who was always calm in a crisis. Lindsay was the
volatile one, impetuous and prey to insecurities. She didn't know
how to respond when Sophie accused her of abandoning her
at a crucial time. She knew she was supposed to be supportive,

she just didn't seem to be able to find the necessary vocabulary. Instead, she retreated into mutinous self-justification, which only made things worse. She wasn't sure why she was behaving so badly, and she was too scared of the answers to examine her motives too closely. When she'd left that morning, she'd found herself wondering if she could ever manage to be the person Sophie appeared to need her to be. Or if she even wanted to be.

But she couldn't think about that now. She was the pivot around whom a meticulously constructed plan had to move like clockwork. That was going to take all her concentration. She was glad Rory was there to share the load, although persuading Rory to come had been almost as hard as overcoming Sophie's objections.

"You're mad," Rory had objected when Lindsay had first run the outline of her plan past her.

"Why?"

"For one, you don't even know for sure that Jack is in St Petersburg at all."

"Cavadino wouldn't leave him with strangers, and he's due back at work any minute now. Besides, Maria and her husband have had Jack down on their list of dependants since they first arrived in Russia. Where else is he going to be?"

"That could be a red herring. He could be anywhere on the planet."

"But on balance, he's more likely to be in St Pete's," Lindsay said reasonably. "And if he's not, Tam Gourlay will be the poorer, not us. Tam's prepared to fund it, so what have we got to lose?"

"Life, liberty and the pursuit of happiness?" Rory hazarded. "Lindsay, it's like a jungle on the streets of Russia. Do you really think Jack will be running around without protection? These guys shoot anybody that gets in their road. And if the Mafia don't get us, the cops probably will. I don't want to end up in a fucking gulag for kidnapping a wee boy."

"Well, please yourself. It's a risk I'm prepared to take. If you won't come with me, I'll just have to manage without you."

Now real concern crept into Rory's voice. "Lindsay, what are you trying to prove here? What's with the recklessness? You know yourself this is an act of total lunacy. And yet you're going at it like a bull at a gate. What's going on?"

"Nothing's going on," Lindsay said gruffly, denying the questioning voices inside her own head yet again. "When I say I'll do something, I do it. And I said I'd do my best to get Jack Gourlay back. So I'm going to Russia. All right? It's my life. I can take risks with it if I want. Christ, why is it all the women in my life think it's their job to tell me what I should and shouldn't do?"

Two days of frosty silence later, Rory had plonked herself down in the booth, held her hands up in capitulation and said, "Okay. Count me in. All for one and one for all, right?"

"What changed your mind?"

"Sandra reminded me that you had been a better reporter than I will ever be and if you thought it was worth going for, you were more likely to be right than a big jessie like me."

Lindsay grinned. "Thank you, Sandra." She remembered the moment now as the line shuffled forward at reasonable speed. Ever since she'd agreed to come, Rory had been reminding Lindsay on a more or less hourly basis of the dangers that lay ahead. But, in spite of her apprehension, she was still here, at Lindsay's side.

After a twenty-minute wait, Lindsay finally handed her passport over to an unsmiling immigration official who seemed to spend forever scrutinizing her seven-day visa and entering details into his computer. At last, he stamped passport and visa and she was released into the baggage hall, where a couple of carousels grunted and wheezed under their burden of luggage. The screens that should have indicated which belt carried the bags from their flight were resolutely blank. "You stay by this one and I'll go over to the other one," Lindsay said to Rory.

Eventually, their holdalls appeared on Rory's carousel and they made their way through the green channel into a morass of people peering through the doors in an attempt to glimpse their loved ones. Lindsay pushed forward, craning her neck, trying to find their driver.

They were almost at the doors leading to the car park outside when she spotted a burly old man with a shock of silver hair resembling Boris Yeltsin's. But there the resemblance ended. This man was clear-eyed, erect and handsome, his skin the weathered tan of an outdoorsman. He spread his arms wide and shouted in a deep voice, "Lindsay! You grow more lovely with every passing year." He pulled her into a bear hug, smacking kisses on both cheeks.

Lindsay freed herself and stepped back to include Rory in the group. "Honestly, Sasha, age hasn't slowed you down, has it? Rory, meet Sasha Kuznetsov. Sasha, this is my colleague, Rory McLaren."

Sasha enveloped Rory's hands in both of his. When Lindsay had told her she had enlisted the help of one of her father's friends, she hadn't known what to expect. She'd imagined the former skipper of a Russian factory ship to be as dark and forbidding as the waters he fished, but this man was as warm and sturdy as a sunbathed rock. Something about Sasha's solidity gave her more confidence than anything she'd seen or heard since Lindsay had dragged them into this folly. "Pleased to meet you," she said, meaning it.

"The pleasure is always mine when beautiful women are concerned." He winked to emphasize the lack of threat behind his gallantry, then reached for their bags. "Welcome to Russia. Now, follow me."

He led them outside to an elderly but gleaming Peugeot. It was as warm and sticky outside as it had been inside the terminal. "Is it usually this hot at the beginning of September?" Lindsay asked as they climbed into the car.

"Not always. This year, we have a lot of sunshine. More than normal. Maybe it will be cooler in a day or two."

"Please God. I don't know if I can think straight in heat like this," Lindsay said.

"Let's hope none of us has too much thinking to do. Now, best if you relax and gather your strength. We have plans and, in the morning, we work. But for tonight I will leave you in peace to recover from plane."

"Sounds good to me," Lindsay said.

As they reached the outskirts of the city, Sasha began to point out sites of interest. "This is the Moscow Prospekt, this triumph arch was once the largest cast-iron structure in the world. Dostoevsky lived here. And here also. He lived a lot of places—I think they paid him to live in their buildings so they could put up a sign saying, 'Dostoevsky lived here' and put the rents up." He guffawed at his own joke. "Senate Square, with the bronze horseman, Peter the Great. The gold dome, that's the Cathedral of St Isaac. The Admiralty. Palace Square and the Hermitage."

The names flowed over Lindsay as she drank in the sights. She'd seldom seen anywhere so imposing. Even the apartment blocks were built on a scale to command admiration. The late afternoon sun seemed to pull all the colours out of the build-ings, emphasizing the ochres, yellows, blues, pinks, sage greens and browns of the flaking and faded stucco. The years of Soviet neglect had left St Petersburg looking raddled and decayed. But it was clear that a massive programme of restoration was under way. There was scarcely a street without signs of building work.

Rory was unusually quiet, clearly struck by her surround-ings. "I can't get over the churches," she said eventually. "Every time we turn a corner, there's another one. All those gilded domes and glamorous colours, all those gold crosses. I thought the Communists pulled all the churches down."

Sasha chuckled. "They never wasted a building. They just used them for other things. Builders' yards, carpentry workshops, even a swimming pool, that's what they turned them into. One of the finest churches in the city, they made it the Museum of Atheism. Now, the Church makes them good again."

"All they need to do now is fix the roads," Lindsay said drily as Sasha swerved to avoid yet another pothole. "I thought at first all the drivers must be drunk, then I realised they were avoiding the ruts and the holes in the road."

"It's getting better," he said as they left the grand façade of the Hermitage behind and swept across the steel grey River Neva. "Vasilievsky Ostrov," he added. "Vasily's Island, where your hotel is. Also, where I live. When Peter the Great built the city, he wanted the island to be another Venice. All the streets in the main part are in a grid. They were supposed to be canals, but it never happened. There are three big parallel avenues, and the streets that cross them are numbers. You are on the Seventh Line. Near McDonald's."

"McDonald's?" Rory echoed faintly.

He turned off the wide boulevard into a broad street. "We are here." He helped them out with their bags and walked them into the hotel. "Okay. I go. You need me, you have my number. I am near, on the Tenth Line. But I will be here in the morning at seven. There is a good restaurant up the street, Georgian restaurant." He gave Lindsay a hug and shook Rory's hand again. "We will do well. Enjoy your evening." With a wave of his big square hand, he was gone.

Checking in proved painless, since the reception staff spoke English. Within minutes, they were walking into their third-floor suite. Lindsay didn't know what she'd been expecting, but it wasn't this. The two rooms were airy and spacious, freshly decorated and furnished in contemporary style. "Amazing," Rory said, wandering through the rooms. "Hey, we've got two bathrooms. I thought it would be like some bed and breakfast in Rothesay, all 1950s furniture and no mod cons. But this is lush."

There was, Lindsay noted, a single divan in the living room of the suite. Just as well, since the bedroom contained only a double. She'd asked for twin beds, but the message had clearly got lost in translation somewhere. "Yeah, it looks like we landed on our feet with this place." She unzipped her holdall and started unpacking.

"Sasha's terrific," Rory said.

"I've known him since I was a kid. Luckily my dad and him stayed in touch after he gave up the fishing. When my dad called him and said I needed his help, he jumped at the chance to pay back a wee bit of the hospitality he's had from his Scottish friends over the years. I'd trust him with my life."

Rory snorted. "Isn't that exactly what we're doing?"

"I think it's more that we're putting him on the line. He's the one that gets left behind to face the music if it all goes sour on us. Which, by the way, it's not going to do, okay?"

Rory pulled a face and began browsing the Guests' Guide to the hotel. "Hey, there's a leaflet here about a Russian banya. It sounds a bit like a sauna. Do you fancy doing that tonight?"

"Is it not hot enough for you already?"

"I wasn't thinking about the heat, I was thinking about the experience. We're not going to have much time to do anything touristy, we should at least get a flavour of Russia." She waved the flyer under Lindsay's nose. "Look, it's not a communal thing. We could hire it for an hour. Four hundred roubles—that's only a tenner, isn't it? It would give us a chance to talk in private about what we've got to do."

Lindsay relented in the face of Rory's enthusiasm. Besides, she could use some relaxation. "Okay. Let me unpack, then I'll go downstairs and ask them to book it."

An hour later, they were standing outside an archway, exchanging anxious glances. "It doesn't look very promising," Rory said dubiously.

"It's the address the receptionist gave me," Lindsay replied, sounding more confident than she felt. She walked through the archway into a courtyard and found herself in what looked disturbingly like a scrap yard. There was an assortment of vehicles in various stages of dismemberment, a fork-lift and a pick-up truck, and a row of lock-up garages. There was nothing that looked remotely like a bath-house. A man emerged from one of the lock-ups and said something incomprehensible. Lindsay took a deep breath and said, "Banya?"

The man pointed to a rickety wooden staircase that resembled a fire escape on the point of being condemned. Somewhat apprehensively, they mounted the stairs and arrived at a door with a handwritten sign next to a doorbell. "In for a penny," Lindsay muttered and pressed the bell.

The door was opened by a young man dressed in a clinical white uniform. Lindsay uttered her one Russian sentence and he nodded. "*Angliski, da?* Is okay, I do English. I am Dimitri." He ushered them in and handed them a pair of rubber flip-flops each, then escorted them to what looked like a 1950s family living room, minus the TV. Fake wooden cladding covered the bottom half of the wall, complete with highly visible nails. The top half of the wall rejoiced in imitation stone wallpaper. There was a black leatherette sofa with a couple of tears patched with packing tape, a few hard chairs and a table holding a samovar, some teacups, teabags and sugar. This, it emerged, was the changing room. Dimitri gave them a couple of white sheets each, then disappeared.

"This is a bit wild," Rory said.

"At least you're having your post-war chic experience," Lindsay said, stripping off with her back to her business partner and wrapping herself in a sheet.

When they emerged, Dimitri was waiting. He led them down a corridor and opened a door leading into the business end of the banya. He showed them two wooden cabins—one, a Swedish-style dry sauna, the other a traditional Russian banya. There was also a plunge pool, inexplicably empty. But he pointed out a row of shower cabinets that would provide the necessary freezing-cold shock to the system.

He led them into the banya, pointed to a low wooden bench and said, "You sit here." It looked like a sauna, Lindsay thought, taking in the brazier filled with stones, and the bucket of water with a ladle. Then Dimitri revealed the difference. He poured what seemed like an absurd amount of water on the coals to activate them. The heat rose dramatically, along with the humidity. But bizarrely, there was no accompanying cloud of steam.

Dimitri left them to it, and inside a minute, the heat hit 80 degrees and the humidity 95 per cent. Within seconds, their bodies were slick with a mixture of sweat and steam. "My God," said Lindsay. "What a sensation." Her skin tingled, her face prickled and she could feel her shoulders dropping as her muscles started to relax.

"It's brilliant," Rory said, unwrapping herself to let her whole body feel the damp heat. Lindsay leaned back against the wall, allowing her sheet to fall away from her.

"Aah," Lindsay sighed. "What a good idea this was, Rory."

"Precisely what we need to get us in prime condition for breaking the law."

"Don't say that," Lindsay groaned.

"So, tomorrow we've got to find Jack, right?"

"We've got to find him *and* figure out the best way to get him on his own so Tam can move in on him."

Rory stretched luxuriously. Lindsay couldn't help noticing the line of her small breasts tapering into her ribs, the almost imperceptible swell of her stomach, the triangle of dark blonde hair between her legs. It was oddly asexual in this context, she realised. "When will Tam and your dad get here?"

"They left Helsinki at dawn yesterday. My dad reckons they should be here tomorrow evening, provided they get decent winds."

Rory shook her head. "I can't believe they're doing this. Sailing a boat from Helsinki to St Petersburg to kidnap a wee boy. Your dad must be some guy."

Lindsay nodded. "He's sound. Doesn't have much to say for himself, but he's always been there for me. Never criticizes, just accepts whatever daft thing I do. As soon as I told him why I wanted to speak to Sasha in the first place, he made me tell him the whole story. And he pointed out that my original idea of taking Jack out of the country on a train was stupid. And then he announced he had a better idea but it would only work if he came too. And that was that. *Fait accompli.*"

Rory closed her eyes and let the sweat and steam run down her face. "You don't know how lucky you are. My father is a boil on the bum of the universe. He's a drunk and a waster. I never saw the bastard from one year's end to the next till he heard about me winning the money. Now he turns up on the doorstep every few weeks, bubbling and greeting that he loves his wee lassie, and could I see my way to slipping him a few hundred quid. I tell you, I wouldn't piss on him if he was on fire, not unless I'd been drinking lighter fuel."

"I'm sorry," Lindsay said.

Rory smoothed back her dripping hair. "Don't be. I'm not. After what he did to me, he'll go to his grave without a penny of mine."

"What did he do?" It wasn't her natural curiosity that prompted Lindsay's question; it was more that she sensed Rory wanted to be pushed into revelation.

"In a minute," Rory said, pushing herself upright. "I need to cool off."

Lindsay followed her to the showers, admiring the shift of Rory's muscles as she walked. Grateful for the cold shower, she stood under the stream of water, gasping at the change in temperature, convinced she could feel her pores snapping shut.

Back in the banya, Rory ladled more water on the coals, pushing the temperature up another five degrees. "Magic," she said, returning to the bench. "So, you want to know what my piece-of-shit father did to me?"

"Only if you want to tell me."

"I came out when I was at university. Well, when I say I came out, I only came out in Edinburgh. The last people I would ever have told were my parents. I knew what his homo-phobic wee soul would make of it. And I knew it would break my mother's heart. She was a good woman, my mother. She worked double shifts as a cleaner all her days to keep him in money for beer and bookies. She took the beatings he handed out when he'd lost on the horses—and he lost plenty, believe me. But she never complained, she never spent a penny on herself; bought her clothes from charity shops so I could have the latest fashions. She always encouraged me to get an education, anything to avoid having a life like hers. But she was a devout Catholic and she'd never have been comfortable with the idea of a dyke for a daughter.

"Anyway, one night my girlfriend persuaded me to go to Glasgow for some lesbian benefit. I didn't want to go, but I let her talk me into it. We were staggering down Argyle Street, heading for the station for the last train back to Edinburgh, arms round each other, probably snogging every few yards. And my father walked out of some shitty dive where he'd been knocking back the pints and the whiskies and practically fell over us. Can you believe it? My one trip to Glasgow, and we walk smack bang into him. He was pissed, but not so pissed that he didn't understand what he was seeing. He called me all the names under the sun. And I just stood there. I didn't know what else to do."

Lindsay wanted to reach out and hug Rory, but, in the absence of clothes, it felt too intimate a gesture. "That must have been horrible," she said, settling for the inadequacy of words.

"It wouldn't have been so bad if that had been all. But he rang me the next day. He said he'd told my mother and she was broken-hearted. And, because she was a good Catholic, she wanted me never to darken her door again." Rory's face crumpled in bewilderment. "I look back at it, and I can't figure out why I believed him. Because my mother wasn't like that. She'd have been hurt, but she'd never have rejected me. I should have realised he was lying to drive a wedge between us. He'd always been jealous of the fact that she loved me more than him. But the bottom line is that I did take him at his word. So I stayed away.

"And six months later, my mother was dead. Breast cancer. She never went to the doctor till her whole system was riddled with it. And I never knew. I never got to say goodbye. And she must have died thinking I didn't give a shit." She crossed her arms across her chest. "That's what my daddy did to me."

"I can see why you hate him. Anybody would, in your shoes."

Rory screwed up her face. "I don't think I hate him. I don't want to expend that much energy on him. I despise him, but I try not to hate him. What fucks me off most, I suppose, is that I feel like he's poisoned me emotionally." She turned to look at Lindsay, a wry smile on her lips. "I'm crap at relationships. You grow up exposed to a marriage like that and you get really cynical. I don't want to turn into my mother or my father, and the best way to avoid that is to avoid getting emotionally involved."

Lindsay shook her head gently. "You don't have to turn into either of them. From where I'm sitting, it looks like you've escaped that. You're a creature of your own making, Rory. You just need to let yourself love the right person."

Rory gave a bitter laugh. "You sound like my pal Sandra. 'Wait till you meet the right woman, then it'll happen.'"

Before Lindsay could reply, there was a pounding on the door. They both grabbed their sheets as Dimitri opened the door a crack. "Time for tea," he said firmly. "Then you have Russian banya."

They looked at each other, bemused. "I thought that's what we were doing," Rory said.

"Obviously Dimitri doesn't agree."

13

Michael threw the last piece of pizza crust into the box, then methodically put the remains of his meal in a black plastic bin liner. He'd given Kevin the rest of the day off, because if he had to spend another hour listening to his mindless attempts to pick a winning horse, he'd have had to take steps to silence his sidekick permanently. Besides, there was nothing doing.

The big fucker had left in a taxi with a holdall three days ago and hadn't been seen since. He hadn't been suited up like a man going on a business trip. But what did Michael know about the way second-hand car dealers did business? Maybe they met regularly for conventions in jeans and sweatshirts and waterproof jackets. Maybe Gourlay was going off for a few days' fishing with his mates. The stress of living with a woman climbing the walls about her missing kid would drive any man to the quiet of a trout stream.

Since he'd gone, Bernie had barely left the house, other than to visit the supermarket to stock up on ready meals, whisky and fags. Patrick had sounded bored with the whole business when Michael had called in, but he wasn't for putting a stop to it. When Michael had asked if he wanted to continue, Patrick's voice had turned to steel and he'd said, "It's over when I say it's over, and not before. You'll be well looked after, Michael. I know it's not very interesting, but, when the time's right, there'll be plenty for you to do."

So he'd settled in for the evening, his miniature radio tuned to a jazz station, the lights off and the binoculars sitting on their tripod in front of him. Okay, it wasn't the most exciting job in the world. But Michael had seen more than his fair share of excitement over the years. He understood very well that there was a lot to be said for the dull. He shifted his position, getting comfortable in the camping chair he'd bought when they'd got their hands on the flat. Another night, another dollar.

Lindsay and Rory drained their teacups and exchanged a slightly apprehensive look. "What's to be scared about?" Lindsay said, going for bravado.

"Right. I mean, I went to Lesbos and lived. How bad can it be?"

They grinned in complicity and emerged into the corridor. Dimitri appeared, looking disturbingly cheerful. "You are ready?" he demanded.

"Ready for what, exactly?" Lindsay asked.

"The beating, the beating," he cried, enthusiastically waving his arms.

"You didn't tell me this was the S&M banya," Rory muttered.

"It was your idea."

"Maybe, but you're still going first."

They followed Dimitri back into the wooden cubicle, but he shooed Rory back out again. "Wait in sauna," he said. To Lindsay, he added, "Lie face down on bench. Take sheet off."

Then he disappeared. When he came back, he was wearing nothing but a towel round his waist and a felt hat that looked like a leftover prop from *Bill and Ben the Flowerpot Men*. He was also bearing two bunches of birch twigs. *Oh shit*, Lindsay thought. *I'm naked in a steam room with a nutter.*

First, Dimitri got the room hot and humid, then he started gently wafting the birch twigs over her body. This created an updraft, bathing Lindsay in moist air while simultaneously what felt like hot rain was pattering over her back. Then the birch twigs descended and the length of her body was covered in a blend of gentle switching and firmer strokes. Just when she was getting used to this and thinking it was really rather pleasant, the hot bundles of leaves were clamped without warning on her large muscles like a fluffy hot mustard poultice—shoulders, lower back, buttocks, thighs, calves and finally feet. Her skin was tingling with damp fire.

Then Dimitri yelled, "Cold shower, now, cold shower," and sent her scuttling off to shout out loud as she froze in the icy jets. By the time she emerged, she could tell from the exclamations that Rory was undergoing the same sweet torture. Lindsay went into the sauna, where the dry heat felt strange after the banya. She mused on what Rory had revealed earlier, thinking it sounded a little too pat as an explanation for her friend's violent allergy to committed relationships. Lindsay wondered if the real reason for Rory's avoidance of love was more to do with her mother's death. Losing the one person she'd loved and trusted in such a traumatic and treacherous way would leave anyone wary of a repeat experience, she thought sympathetically. She'd endured betrayal herself and understood only too well the scars it left behind. It would take Rory a long time to recover from something so profound.

Rory eventually joined her in the sauna. "They should have these in clubs instead of chilling-out spaces," she groaned comfortably. "I can't remember the last time I felt so completely laid back."

"Better than sex," Lindsay said.

"You've obviously been doing it wrong."

Lindsay giggled. "The thing with sex is you have to expend a lot of effort to feel this good. But here, somebody else does all the work." She stretched out on the top bench, enjoying the sensation of the muscles round her spine relaxing.

A few minutes later, Dimitri banged on the door. "Your time is over, ladies," he called.

As if in a trance, Lindsay and Rory made their way back to the changing room and got dressed. "Do you know, I haven't thought about Jack Gourlay since before we had our tea," Lindsay said dreamily.

Rory gave a slow smile. "Who's Jack Gourlay?"

The skies were grey over the Gulf of Finland, a Force 5 wind blowing out of the north-west. Tam Gourlay inched his way from the galley to the hatch leading to the cockpit, cradling a mug of tea in his hands. Boats like this weren't designed for men of his size, he thought as he forgot yet again to duck under the bulkhead and caught the side of his head a glancing blow. He leaned forward and held the drink aloft. Andy Gordon bent at the knees and took one hand off the wheel to take the tea, his sharp blue eyes never leaving the gunmetal swell ahead of the full belly of the genoa sail. "Cheers," he said.

Tam clambered up the short companionway and joined Andy in the shelter of the sprayhood. "How are we doing?" he asked.

"No' bad. It makes a change, having to watch the charts all the way through the archipelago. I'm used to water I know better than the back of my hand."

"Must be a bit different, sailing a wee thing like this instead of driving a big fishing boat," Tam said.

"Aye. It's like riding a bike, though. You never lose the knack." He leaned into the wheel, his shoulders bracing against the swell. It was hard to see a resemblance between Andy Gordon and his daughter. The balding man with the broad back and the short legs was a completely different physical type, and his blunt, ruddy features gave far less away than Lindsay's open countenance. Only in the eyes was there any congruence. The same spirit that lit Lindsay from within was there in Andy Gordon's blue gaze as he scanned the horizon.

Tam sat down on the damp plastic cushion that ran along the side of the cockpit, grateful for the oilskin trousers Andy had supplied him with, even if they were six inches short in the leg. He watched the fisherman standing rock-steady on the shifting deck, marvelling at such stamina from a man in his sixties. They'd hardly stopped since they'd left Glasgow. When they'd reached Helsinki, they'd had to go straight to the Russian Embassy and queue for a couple of hours to get their three-day visas. Then they'd gone to the boatyard to pick up the yacht they'd chartered from Glasgow, which Andy insisted on checking from stem to stern before he'd accept it. Andy had stayed at the wheel through most of the previous night, only dropping anchor in a sheltered cove an hour before dawn and snatching a couple of hours before they'd set off again. Tam hadn't expected to sleep, with the combination of the unfamiliar motion and his anxiety about what lay ahead, but he'd surprised himself by going spark out for over six hours. "Will you get a proper sleep tonight?" Tam asked.

Andy nodded. "We should be in clear water before too long. Then I can set the autopilot and get a few hours."

"You'll be on your knees at this rate."

"Ach, it's only a couple of nights. I can catch up when we get to port tomorrow night. And I'll have Lindsay to help me on the way back. We can split the night watch between us."

Tam shook his head in admiration. "I can hardly believe the way she's set this whole thing up. She's some lassie."

Andy's mouth twitched at the corners. "She's that, all right. Christ knows where she gets it from. Me and her mother, we've no' got an adventurous bone in our bodies. We were born in Invercross, and we'll probably die there. But ever since she was wee, Lindsay's aye been one for diving in at the deep end. And this time, I couldnae stand back and leave her to it. Not when I could do something a bit more useful than just giving her Sasha's phone number." He leaned across and checked the chart, scanning the horizon for the next landmark. "A wee touch to starboard, I think."

"I really appreciate you doing this," Tam said. "Lindsay told me you insisted, wouldnae take no for an answer. That means a lot, you know. The way you've weighed in when it's no' even your fight."

"You dinnae have to keep saying that, son. I know fine. We'll get it sorted, don't you worry. My pal Sasha, he'll see to that." He screwed his eyes up against a stray drift of spray. "Tell you the truth, I cannae quite believe I'm here myself. That lassie of mine has a way of making the world dance to her tune."

Right then, Andy Gordon's lassie was sitting in the Georgian restaurant Sasha had recommended, contemplating a dish translated on the English menu as "meat drunk on the plate." Rory, who was tucking into a grilled salmon fillet, had taken one look at the steak smothered in diced vegetables with a cream sauce and said, "I can see how it got its name. It looks like somebody threw up over a piece of beef."

"Thanks," Lindsay said, cutting into her meat. "That'll do wonders for my appetite. But you've got to live dangerously sometimes."

Rory glanced up from under her eyebrows. "Just so long as I don't have to eat things with names like that."

There was silence while they ate their food, washed down with a chewy Georgian red wine. "It's probably better if we split up tomorrow, cover our options. Sasha can take one school while we go over to the one where Jack's most likely to be enrolled. I've checked on the map and it's quite near a metro station on the same line as the one up the street. Getting there should be pretty straightforward," Lindsay said.

"Famous last words. What are we going to do if we find it?"

"Wait and see if Jack arrives. And if he does, follow the person who brings him to school back home. That should tell us where he's staying."

"And then?" Rory pressed on relentlessly.

"I don't know. We'll have to see how it goes."

"And what if he turns up at the one Sasha's watching?"

"He'll do the same thing," Lindsay said. "Then he'll come back and pick us up. And then we'll make our plans."

"Doesn't it scare you?" Rory asked, her eyes fixed on Lindsay's. "Knowing we're about to embark on a criminal act in a country that's not noted for the even-handedness of its judicial system? Not to mention the prevalence of guns?"

"Of course it scares me. That's why I'm trying very hard not to think about the possibility of getting caught. I'm visualizing the scene when Jack's reunited with his mother and I'm standing there taking the photos. It takes my mind off the alternative." It was the truth, but not the whole truth. There were other things on Lindsay's mind that had nothing to do with the fate of one small boy. But she knew she really shouldn't be thinking about them either.

"Good trick if you can manage it. But it's definitely winding me up. Shall we get another relaxing bottle of wine?"

Lindsay's expression turned quizzical. "Is the effect of the banya wearing off already?"

Rory laughed. "Listen, you don't want to go there. That banya has had some very strange side effects, let me tell you."

"Like what?" Lindsay felt the thin ice creaking beneath her words. She didn't think she was imagining the sparkle of electricity between them.

Rory held her gaze for a moment, then looked away, shaking her head. "Nothing I want to discuss in a public place." Her words were almost drowned by a noisy burst of laughter from a neighbouring table.

"Look, why don't we get the bill? We can buy a bottle of wine in the hotel bar and drink it in peace," Lindsay suggested. Rory nodded agreement.

As they strolled down the street towards the hotel, the warm evening air balmy against their faces, Lindsay was feverishly conscious of Rory's body inches from hers. It was as if she was radiating heat like the brazier in the banya. *This is crazy*, she thought. *Eight years you've been with Sophie and never once crossed the line. You're working with this woman, for God's sake. You're maybe going to be a parent. Aren't you taking enough risks already without going overboard? Put the lid on it now.* But her interior monologue had no effect on the churning in her stomach or the prickle of sweat along her spine.

They walked into the hotel and Lindsay turned towards the bar. "Another bottle of red?"

"Maybe not," Rory said. "Maybe I don't need it after all."

They didn't speak in the lift, but it was a silence that crackled with what wasn't being said. Lindsay fumbled with the key, struggling to get it into the lock. Then she managed it and they were inside the suite. "I thought I'd sleep in here on the divan, let you have the double bed," Lindsay gabbled as she flicked the switch to turn on the table lamps. She turned to watch Rory's reaction but couldn't see her eyes through the shadows.

One side of Rory's mouth rose in a knowing half-smile. "You know, I've seen you stripped to the skin tonight. But you look a hell of a lot sexier with your clothes on."

Lindsay cleared her throat. Her voice came out half an octave higher than usual. "Delirium. That would be one of the strange side effects of the banya, right?"

The moment broken, Rory walked away and feigned an interest in the St Petersburg tourist magazine on the writing table. "Right enough," she said, her tone darker and colder. "Should you maybe phone home?"

Lindsay took a couple of steps towards Rory. "I don't want to phone Sophie."

"She'll be worried about you. Running around Russia like James Bond." There was no mistaking the coolness now.

"No, she won't. I called her on my mobile when the receptionist was booking the banya. Just to let her know we'd arrived safely."

Rory turned her head, the half-smile back in place. "She really shouldn't be worried about you, should she?" This time, the tone was regretful.

"Why are we talking about Sophie?"

"Because it puts a wall between us, Lindsay. And that's the sensible option."

Lindsay ran a hand through her hair. "I'm not good at sensible."

"Neither am I. So let's work on treating this as a 'sensible' workshop for both of us." Rory swung round to face Lindsay and leaned against the writing table. The subtle light of the lamps cast the planes of her face into relief. Lindsay thought she had never wanted so badly to kiss someone.

"You think that'll work, do you? You think we can just ignore whatever it is that's happening here?" There was no aggression in Lindsay's questions, only a simple plea for answers.

Rory spread her hands. "What's the alternative? I want us to be able to work together. I like working with you. I don't want to fuck that up."

"Me neither. But we can't pretend we're indifferent to each other. It's not going to go away."

"If we don't feed the flame, it'll die," Rory said.

Lindsay shook her head in frustration. "You know that's bullshit. We'll always be wondering what it would have been like. It'll be sitting there between us in the Café Virginia every bloody day. So let's get it out of our system."

Rory laughed out loud. "You know, that's probably the least seductive thing anybody's ever said to me. 'Come on,

let's get it over with. One shag with you and I'll be cured,'"
she spluttered.

The laughter was infectious. Lindsay couldn't help herself.
All at once she was chuckling too. Somewhere in the middle
of the laughter, they fell into each other's arms. Two hungry
mouths connected.

Suddenly, sensible was history.

14

Even at midnight, it was still warm in St Petersburg. Lindsay and Rory lay tangled together, the bedclothes in a rumpled heap on the floor. Unfamiliar scents and sounds drifted in through the open window, reminding them how very far they'd come. Rory ran a fingertip along the thin white line that ran down from Lindsay's right ear to the corner of her jaw. Then, with the tip of her tongue, she traced the starburst scar above her left breast, tasting the sharp saltiness of her sweat. "Tell me about the scars," she said.

Lindsay squirmed pleasurably at the sensation as Rory's mouth moved down to her nipple. "Not very romantic for post-coital conversation," she murmured.

"You want romance? You picked the wrong lover, doll. Anyway, who said anything about post-coital?" Rory teased. "I thought this was just the first interval."

"Fine by me." Lindsay ran her fingers along Rory's side, learning this unfamiliar body. After eight years with the same woman, it felt strange to explore such alien territory. She'd thought the very exoticism of novelty would provoke guilt, but she'd been mistaken. Making love with Rory had taken her somewhere outside her past experience. Wild and dark, it had shown her a bewildering new side to her own sexuality, both scary and magical. But wrong was the one thing it hadn't felt.

"So, tell me about the scars," Rory persisted. "I'd never even noticed that one under your jawline before."

"They did a good job of stitching it up." Lindsay's hand strayed between Rory's thighs, but she clamped them shut and pulled away.

"Not until you tell me about the scars."

Lindsay groaned. "You're so bossy."

Rory chuckled. "Nothing like flipping the butch. You didn't mind me bossing you a wee while ago. Come on, tell me. It can't be that terrible."

"The one on my jaw I got when I tripped over a wall and landed face first on a broken bottle."

"Aw," Rory complained. "That's really boring."

"If it helps, I was being chased by a guy with a baseball bat at the time," Lindsay said, wincing at the memory.

"Now, that's much better. What about this one?" She kissed the circular scar lightly. "Wounded in a duel over a beautiful blonde? Stabbed by a jealous lover?"

Lindsay's face darkened. "I got shot by a murderous little shit who didn't take kindly to the idea of being found out by me."

"Bastard," Rory said lazily, apparently unsurprised by the notion that someone might have taken a pot-shot at her new lover. "It looks nasty."

"It didn't hit anything important. I just lost a lot of blood. And my left shoulder hurts when the weather's damp."

"Ouch. I tell you, by October, you'll be *really* sorry you left California. So what happened to the shooter?" Rory ran the palm of her hand over Lindsay's body, letting her fingers trail tantalizingly over her stomach.

Lindsay shuddered with a pleasure that took all the pain out of the recollection. "Life for murder, ten years for attempted murder on me. You probably remember the case—Penny Varnavides' murder?"

Rory nodded. "Only vaguely. She was killed a wee while before I won the money. I didn't know what I was going to do with it, so I rented a cottage on Skye for a month to try and figure out my future. I didn't touch a newspaper or listen to a news bulletin. I must have missed the trial. Which would be why I never realised you were involved in that."

"So now you know." Lindsay rolled over suddenly and pinned Rory to the bed, her knee between Rory's thighs. "Act two?"

"Mmm. I never had you pegged as a woman who would be turned on by talk of violence." Rory's voice was teasingly sexy.

"Trust me, it's not the past that's turning me on."

Nine o'clock in Glasgow, and Bernie Gourlay was alone with a glass of Johnnie Walker and a half-smoked cigarette. She'd been a prisoner of fear for so long now she had almost forgotten it was possible to entertain any other emotion. It had hit her all the harder because for years she thought she'd escaped the cold claw of terror. How stupid had that been, she told herself bitterly.

She should have known Patrick would never have resigned himself to letting her out of his grasp. But as time had passed and he hadn't materialized in her new life, she'd allowed herself to be lulled into a false sense of security. She had her fallback plan in place, so she thought. And for whole months at a time she'd been free of the very thought of him. But now he was back, and there was no telling how bad things would get before they righted themselves. If they ever could.

It had been bad enough when she'd only had Jack to be afraid for. At least she'd had Tam's strength to draw on. But now Tam had gone off on this crazy mission to get her son back, and all she could feel was anxiety. She knew she should be proud that he loved her enough to take such insane risks for her happiness, but instead she was overwhelmed with guilt that she'd brought this nightmare to his door in the first place.

No outcome offered her any relief. If they failed to snatch Jack successfully, Tam could end up in a Russian jail. Even if he avoided that worst-case scenario, she knew he would never forgive himself for letting her and Jack down. Remorse like that could be slow poison to a relationship, her presence in his life a constant reminder of his perceived inadequacy. And if they did bring him home, what prospects were there of happiness with Patrick Coughlan on the horizon? Patrick would do whatever it took to get his own back. Neither compunction nor compassion were concepts he'd ever embraced.

Bernie crushed out her cigarette as the phone started ringing. She turned her head and stared at it. It couldn't be Tam; as far as she knew, he was on a chartered yacht somewhere between Helsinki and St Petersburg. There was nobody else she wanted to talk to, and at least one voice she definitely didn't want to hear.

She drained her whisky in one swallow and waited for the ringing to stop.

When the alarm clock drilled through her dreams at half past six, Lindsay had been asleep for less than four hours. But when her eyes snapped open she was as alert as if she'd had a full night's sleep. Great sex would do that every time, she thought, turning her head to watch Rory struggle into wakefulness. "So, do you still respect me?" she said.

Rory yawned. "I think so. But I might have to fuck you again to make sure." She snuggled into Lindsay's side, her fingers slithering down her stomach. "Do you do mornings?"

Lindsay squirmed away. "Any other morning, but not this one. We've got work to do, remember?"

"Bo-ring." Rory planted a warm kiss on her shoulder. "Okay, Splash, you win. Race you to the shower." She rolled over and jumped out of bed.

Lindsay laughed. "We've got two showers, dozo."

"Damn," Rory said, heading for the en suite.

Half an hour later, they had said goodbye to Sasha and set off down the Seventh Line towards the Vasileostrovskaya metro

station, fuelled only by a snatched cup of execrable coffee in the
hotel breakfast room. As they passed a street kiosk selling fruit,
Rory looked longingly at the peaches and bananas. "I don't
suppose you could manage to buy us a couple of bananas?" she
asked wistfully.

"Absolutely right. I'm keeping my powder dry for the metro
station. Besides, I don't know how you can think about eating.
My stomach's churning like a cement mixer."

"I always eat when I'm nervous. And believe me, I'm nervous," Rory replied. The morning was warm and humid, the
sky a washed-out blue. The metro station was on the corner
of Sredny Prospekt, an ugly glass and concrete structure that
glared across at the McDonald's diagonally opposite. "Soviet
architecture meets Western capitalism," Lindsay commented as
they climbed the short flight of stairs that led into the station.

"Now what do we do?" Rory said, looking apprehensively
round the foyer. On one side were automatic turnstiles coping
with a constant stream of morning commuters who thrust plastic
cards into the slots.

"According to my guidebook, we buy a ten-journey ticket
for forty roubles," Lindsay said.

"Ten journeys for a quid? Hey, I could live like a king here.
On you go then, Splash. Show me how it's done."

With a feeling of trepidation, Lindsay crossed to the ticket
booth where a slab-faced middle-aged woman in a polyester flow-
ered dress sat glaring out at the world. Lindsay smiled and held
her hands up, fingers splayed to indicate ten. Then she proffered a
fifty-rouble note. The woman said something in Russian. Lindsay
told her she didn't speak Russian and stretched the smile wider.
The woman grunted, took the note and exchanged it for a card
and a ten-rouble note. "*Spasibo bolshoi*," Lindsay said, relieved.

Once they'd negotiated the turnstiles, they found themselves on the longest escalator Lindsay had ever seen. "This is
bowels of the earth stuff," Rory muttered in her ear.

"I suppose it's got to be deep, it goes under the river."

"Hey, so does the Clockwork Orange, but you don't have to penetrate the planet's crust to use the underground in Glasgow."

The escalator deposited them in a hallway. On either side, there were rows of closed doors that resembled large lifts. The only indication as to which side of the hallway their train would arrive at were two small illuminated signs hanging from the ceiling. "It's got to be the left-hand side," Lindsay said, frowning up at the station names.

"Hey, you're really good at this funny alphabet," Rory said, impressed.

"Hardly. This is the second to last stop going north, and there's only one name on the right-hand board. Whereas there's a whole list of stations on the other one. Ergo . . ."

Rory tutted. "You'd never make it in the Magic Circle, giving away your tricks like that." As she spoke, they heard a rumbling, and the doors on their side of the hallway slid open, revealing carriages that looked remarkably spacious compared to the familiar ones in Glasgow. They boarded the crowded train and grabbed a metal pole as it pulled out of the station.

"How do we know where to get off?" Rory asked when they stopped at the next station to the accompaniment of an announcement so corrupted by static that even a Russian speaker would have been hard pressed to figure out its content.

"We count. It's the third station. Ploshchad Aleksandra Nevskogo," Lindsay said, stumbling a little over the unfamiliar name. To take her mind off the nervous butterflies fluttering in her stomach, Lindsay practised her reading of Cyrillic on the handful of adverts on the carriage walls. She couldn't help smiling when, after a struggle, she finally deciphered one as being a transliteration of "Internet."

They emerged at the other end of the journey in a courtyard lined with kiosks selling soft drinks and alcohol, flowers, fruit and CDs. Lindsay took her map out of her backpack and pored over it. "I think we're on Nevsky Prospekt," she said uncertainly. "If we go up here and take a left, then left again, we should end up on the street where the school is." She looked up at the corner. "At least they seem to have street signs."

Since this was the less fashionable end of the long street that sliced through the heart of the city, the pavements were relatively quiet. Most of the people who were out and about were walking briskly with a sense of purpose, focussed only on their own business. To Lindsay's amazement, they ended up on Konstantinogradskaya Ulitsa at the first attempt. The street was lined with tall nineteenth-century apartment buildings and shaded with trees. They strolled along, trying to look casual as they scanned the buildings for any sign of an international school. Two-thirds of the way along, the apartments gave way to a walled courtyard with tall wrought-iron gates. There was nothing to indicate what went on in the rose-pink building beyond the gates and they carried on to the end of the street.

"Do you think that was it?" Rory asked.

Lindsay shrugged. "Your guess is as good as mine. I guess we'll just have to wait and see where the kids go when they start to arrive."

"We're going to look a bit obvious, standing around on a street corner," Rory objected. "Look, there's a bar on the opposite corner. With the tables outside. It looks like they're open for business. We could get a coffee and keep an eye open."

Lindsay looked doubtful. "It's too far away to be sure of identifying Jack. We've only ever seen photos of him. Kids all look the same at that age."

"Can I have a look at the map?" Rory asked. Lindsay handed it over and waited while Rory studied it. "Okay, here's the plan," she said. "We go to the café and as soon as kids start arriving, I shoot off round the block so I can come into the street at the other end. You give me a minute or two, then you amble slowly up towards the school. Then we bump into each other outside the school and act like we're old friends who've just met by accident. We can stand having a blether and keeping an eye out for Jack. What do you think?"

"It's worth a try," Lindsay said. They crossed the street to the café, but as they were about to sit down a couple of cars pulled up outside the iron gates. Three children spilled out, followed at a more leisurely pace by their drivers. They exchanged glances, each recognising the flame of adrenaline in the other's eyes. Rory took off at a fast pace down the side street that would bring her the long way round to the other end of the street, while Lindsay began to amble slowly back towards the school.

By the time she was a couple of dozen yards away, upwards of twenty children were milling around on the wide pavement of packed earth. As far as she could see, none of them was the right size, gender or colouring to be Jack Gourlay. As another couple of cars drew up, one of the gates slowly creaked open and the children flowed through, most without a backward glance at their drivers or their mothers.

Lindsay dawdled on. Then, a few feet from the gate, with no Rory in sight yet, she stooped to tie her shoe-lace. She was overtaken by three children who looked around eight years old, then by a harassed-looking teenager shouting something at them in German. Reassuringly, none gave her a second glance. Lindsay caught sight of Rory in a gap between what was now a steady stream of children, and stood up, surprised by the flash of delight that sparked inside her.

They achieved the planned rendezvous a few feet from the school gates, greeting each other with every appearance of surprise. While they pretended to make small talk, each was keeping an eye out for Jack. It was Rory who caught sight of him first. "Don't look now," she said conversationally. "But I think that's him walking towards us. Let's act like we're going to walk back to the café."

Lindsay turned and immediately saw the child Rory had identified. There was really no mistaking Jack. He looked exactly like the school photograph on top of Bernie and Tam's TV, except that then he'd been smiling and now he was scowling as he scuffed the toes of his trainers along the cracked pavement.

The woman who held his hand in an iron grip had the same dark hair and beaky nose as she'd seen in photographs of Bruno Cavadino. It had to be them.

Lindsay and Rory set off in the direction of the café, passing the woman and boy without a second glance, but Lindsay was close enough to the woman to hear her say in the irritated voice of adults being embarrassed by a small child the world over, "I don't care what your papa told you, this is not a holiday and you have to go to school." As soon as they were clear of the school, Rory glanced back. "She's virtually dragged him into the playground. Looks like he's not keen. Quick, let's duck into this courtyard," she said, yanking Lindsay by the arm and pulling her into the arched entrance to an apartment block.

"What are you playing at?" Lindsay demanded, staggering to stay upright.

"Chances are she'll come back the same way and we can tail her. Otherwise we'll have to stand around on the street corner and she might pick up on us." Rory's voice was sharp with excitement. Suddenly, she leaned forward and kissed Lindsay. "I haven't had so much fun for ages."

Lindsay grinned. "Me neither. But I don't think snogging in public is a good idea in Russia," she added hurriedly as an elderly woman turned into the courtyard laden with a basket of vegetables.

They didn't have long to wait before Maria Padovani passed the entry where they were loitering. She was walking quickly, as if she had places to go and things to do. "You go first," Rory said. "I'll follow you."

Their little procession made its way through the back streets and courtyards, finally emerging on a street about half a mile further up Nevsky Prospekt. The woman was still walking briskly in spite of the humidity. Eventually, she turned into a refurbished apartment block, complete with a doorman who resembled one of those gigantic statues of Soviet workers.

Lindsay carried on to the corner and waited for Rory to catch her up. "No way we're going to get in there," Rory said.

"Even supposing we knew which apartment was the right one."

"So what now?"

Lindsay glanced at her watch. "I'll give Sasha a call, tell him we've struck lucky. He could meet us at that nice café, then we can see how the school day pans out?"

Rory groaned. "How I love stakeouts."

"Look on the bright side. At least we've got a supply of coffee, and a toilet."

Rory grinned. "And plenty of time for you to figure out the menu."

"Why do you think I'm going to get Sasha to join us?"

15

Andy Gordon and Tam Gourlay were trying to keep hidden from each other their apprehensions about the next stage of their journey. Tam's anxieties had been tamped down on the journey by Andy's calm handling of the boat and apparent lack of concern about navigating the complex route towards Russian waters. But as the day wore on, the thin line of the horizon had gradually swelled to reveal itself as the line of the barrage that cut off Russian waters from the Gulf of Finland. Andy had explained about the massive sea defences the Russians had constructed, which left only a narrow passage for boats to enter Russian waters via the customs and immigration channel at Kronstadt. Tam had understood the principle. But seeing the reality was something else again.

He couldn't begin to imagine the feat of engineering that had gone into its construction. Andy had told him about the plans to turn the vast dam into a ring road for St Petersburg. But, as with so many grandiose Russian projects, this had ground to a halt for lack of funds. Even the barrage itself, which was supposed to prevent flooding as well as to funnel all sea traffic through one channel, had stopped a single kilometre short of the shore.

Yet more impressive than the dam was the city of Kronstadt itself, the fortifications unnervingly solid against the sky, their grey stone as forbidding as the steely waves that beat against the shore. Tam could imagine the daunting impression it must have made on the enemy. Even isolated from the city of Leningrad, its sole source of supplies, it had withstood almost three years of pounding from German guns and still remained in Russian hands, its defences largely intact. Above its grim exterior rose the vast dome of the cathedral, somehow incongruous in so obviously military a setting. "We couldn't have done this a few years ago," Andy observed. "Because it was a naval base, it was closed to civilian traffic." He looked at the chart again. "Time to get the sails down, I think."

He stayed at the wheel, shouting instructions to Tam, who crawled awkwardly around the deck desperately trying to do what he was told without causing any damage. He felt not so much like a bull in a china shop as a carthorse on a tightrope. Boats were definitely not his natural environment. But he managed to lower the sails without mishap and stumbled back into the cockpit, where Andy was studying the Admiralty chart.

"We're aiming for Fort Konstantin. See that unfinished dyke coming out from the south coast of the island? And the buoyed channel? We need to be north of there." He adjusted the course so that the bow swung round gently. Twenty minutes later, they were tied up on a pontoon, the only pleasure boat in sight.

"What now?" Tam asked, nervously fingering his passport.

"We wait for the customs to come on board." As Andy spoke, he spotted a pair of uniformed officers walk down the quay with the swagger of petty bureaucrats everywhere. He readied his own passport and the rest of the paperwork, and arranged his face into a smile of welcome as they boarded. They made an odd couple. The first was tall, blond and narrow-shouldered, his cheeks pocked with old acne scars. The other was short and swarthy, a heavy black moustache shot with silver completely obliterating his upper lip, the buttons of his tunic straining over a round little belly. The dark one said something in Russian.

Andy shrugged. "*Niet Russki*," he said in his best Argyllshire accent. He proffered both passports and the boat's papers. The blond one reached out and began to study them while the dark one continued to ask them something in Russian.

Andy spread his hands in a shrug of incomprehension. The blond man leaned over and tapped the chart. "Where from?" he said with negligent arrogance.

Andy smiled and nodded. He pointed to the chart, drawing their route with a finger. "We came from Helsinki, through the archipelago. Then we stuck to the Sea Channel and crossed the Russian border here, near Gogland Island. That's what we were told to do by the Russian Embassy in Helsinki."

The two men conferred, the dark one sounding irritated, the blond appearing completely unconcerned. Eventually, the blond one turned to Andy. "My colleague thinks you entered Russian waters irregularly."

"Now, wait a minute, pal," Tam protested. "We just did what your people told us to do."

The dark customs official glared at Tam and let fly a stream of Russian.

"Take it easy, Tam. It's okay." Andy's relationship with Sasha had given him some understanding in the ways of the Russian world as well as smoothing their path in St Petersburg. He motioned Tam to one side and opened the lifejacket locker. He took out a bottle of VSOP cognac and placed it on the chart table. "I'd like to apologize for any irregularities," he said.

"Where to?" the blond one asked, adding something in Russian to his companion.

"St Petersburg. We're going to the Navy Yacht Club, like it says in the letter of introduction."

The dark one gave a curt nod. He produced a stamp from his tunic pocket, took the paperwork from his colleague and franked their passports and visas. Then he grabbed the bottle and marched ashore. The blond one inclined his head in gracious acceptance. "Have a safe voyage," he said.

Fifteen minutes later, the Bénéteau was nosing into the harbour to refuel and fill her water tanks. While he was filling up, Andy sent Tam to the harbour office to change their dollars into roubles. He watched him go, glad he'd been able to find something useful for the big man to do. Andy wasn't given to flights of the imagination, but it didn't take much empathy to understand that Tam must feel on a knife-edge. He knew he'd have moved heaven and earth to get Lindsay back if anyone had snatched her from her home. Nothing would have stood in his way. And he understood that those emotions made Tam a loose cannon. He only hoped Lindsay and Sasha would have everything boxed off by the time they berthed in St Petersburg. Tam was so pent up, there was no telling what he might do if no easy opportunity to rescue Jack presented itself. And Russia was probably a dangerous place at the best of times, Andy thought. Not the sort of environment where you wanted to have responsibility for a guy like Tam on the rampage.

Not for the first time, Andy Gordon wondered what he'd got himself into. But he knew both his friend and his daughter too well to have stood idly by while they got themselves into trouble. Lindsay's original idea to get the boy out to Finland on a train had been doomed to failure, he'd known that instinctively as soon as he'd heard it. And his suggestion of doing it by sea could never have worked without him to skipper the boat. He'd had no real choice in the matter. He gave an involuntary shiver and went below deck to pump out the bilges. Keeping occupied, that was going to be the way to get through this. And, luckily, on a boat there was always something that needed to be done. Plenty to keep him and Tam from pondering on the illegalities they were about to commit.

Or so he hoped.

The waitress in the café bar was starting to give them strange looks. Lindsay, Rory and Sasha had been sitting at the same table for four hours without showing any signs of moving. They'd had coffee, they'd had a couple of beers, they'd had aubergines stuffed with cheese and nuts, they'd had bowls of fish *salyanka*, then they'd had coffee again. "She can't figure us out," Rory said.

"No. But she will be able to give bloody good description to the cops once they start looking for whoever kidnapped that little Italian boy from the international school," Sasha said drily.

"We'll be long gone by then," Lindsay said with a confidence she didn't really feel.

"You hope," Rory said gloomily. As she spoke, a dozen children paired up in crocodile formation emerged from the school gates, a teacher at their head.

Even from this distance, now she knew who she was looking for, Lindsay could make out Jack. She glanced at her watch. It was a couple of minutes after two. "Action," she said, turning round to catch the waitress's eye and making the universal sign of scribbling on phantom paper to indicate she wanted the bill.

The children were walking down the street towards them. But the waitress seemed to be in no hurry. She disappeared inside at a leisurely pace. "You follow them," Sasha said. "If I don't catch up, I see you back here. Okay?"

Lindsay and Rory waited till the file of uniformed youngsters had rounded the corner before they fell in several yards behind them. At the end of the street, the children crossed a narrow canal. Lindsay pulled her map out of her bag and hastily consulted it. The bridge would lead into a park alongside the Alexander Nevsky Monastery. Where else would a bunch of kids be going? "Playtime," she said to Rory as they followed.

They found themselves on the fringes of a small park. The children were running and climbing around a decrepit play area. The two women cut across one side of the park and made their way up an overgrown mound with the remains of stone terracing jutting out of the greenery. Lindsay waved an arm at the deep pink and white building nearby and read from the guidebook.

The church had supposedly been built on the very spot where Nevsky trounced the Swedes back in the thirteenth century.

"Let's take it as a good omen," Rory muttered. "We're too obvious here, let's keep walking."

They headed off into the shade of some trees, where the gloom made them harder to see. At exactly twenty-five past two, the teacher blew a whistle and the children lined up obediently. They headed off towards the bridge, obviously making their way back to school. "Do you think they do this every day?" Lindsay asked.

"I bloody hope so. Because it's the best chance we've got. A dozen kids running around like dafties, plenty of bushes for cover. It's tailor made for the job."

"We need to figure out the escape route. Let's see what Sasha has to suggest," Lindsay said, studying the map with a frown. At that moment, her mobile rang. She rummaged in her bag and unearthed it on the fourth ring. "Hello, Lindsay Gordon," she said.

"It's me." The familiar voice of her father crackled in her ear.

"Where are you?"

"About thirteen miles from St Petersburg, the wind's a nice Force 4 or 5, we should berth in less than a couple of hours."

"No problems?"

"No complaints. It's been a braw wee sail. This boat's a bonnie mover. Everything all right at your end?"

"Aye. I think we're maybe sorted. Give me a call when you're moored up and we'll come and have a debrief."

She heard a snort of laughter. "A debrief. Aye, right enough." Then the line went dead. Lindsay smiled at the phone and tossed it back in her bag. "The boys are on their way. They'll be tied up in a couple of hours. So we'd better get a move on and check out the territory."

Two hours later, Sasha was driving them down Bolshoi Prospekt towards Lenexpo, the city exhibition and conference centre, behind which sat the basin of the Navy Yacht Club. The combination of heat and humidity was draining but, in spite of that, they were in buoyant mood.

"If they do this every day, we can take the boy tomorrow," Sasha had said confidently after they'd scouted out the immediate environs of the park. "I can be waiting with the car on the far side, near Nevsky Prospekt. We will be gone before they realise anything has happened."

Lindsay couldn't help feeling a little perturbed. She never trusted easy pickings, and this all seemed to be much too straightforward.

"What's wrong?" Rory had asked her on the way back to the car.

"I keep waiting for the other shoe to drop," Lindsay said. "I can't believe how everything's falling into our laps."

Rory shrugged. "Sometimes it goes that way."

"You'd think, having gone to all that trouble to get the boy, Cavadino would have made bloody sure nobody could get to him, though."

"Maybe he figured that bringing him to St Petersburg just made it too difficult all round. And, you must admit, it's not exactly been a piece of piss to set this up. I mean, how likely is it that somebody looking for Jack would have a reliable contact in St Pete's? If your dad had been a fireman or a factory foreman instead of a fisherman, we'd have been up shit creek. Me, I'm not in the least surprised they're being a bit complacent."

It made a sort of sense. And since Rory accompanied it with a squeeze of Lindsay's hand, it performed the trick of reassurance.

They turned into the road leading to the yacht club, grateful even in the car for the shade of trees whose leaves were beginning to dry to gold and brown. A short drive brought them to a curved gateway in the pale stuccoed wall. Sasha parked and they got out. Their way was blocked by a rope slung across the entrance.

To one side, a youth in grey naval cadet's uniform slouched in a wooden chair. Lindsay looked at Rory and raised her eyebrows. Rory nodded. "Love the security," she said, as they followed Sasha, who merely stepped over the rope without a word.

"Just what we need," Lindsay said. The cadet hadn't so much as flickered an eyelid at their passage.

"They are more watchful at night," Sasha said as he strode ahead, apparently untroubled by the heat.

Whatever they'd expected of the Navy Yacht Club, it wasn't what they found. There were no retired rear-admirals in blazers with brass buttons drinking gin and tonic in the clubhouse here. Actually, there was no clubhouse. A building that looked as if it might once have housed social facilities was now a factory making sailboards. A broad tree-lined path led to the waterfront. Anyone familiar with the glossy marinas of British yacht clubs would have laughed out loud as they emerged from the trees to see half a dozen decaying wooden jetties jutting out into the basin. Tied up on the moorings was an eclectic collection of boats: a few dinghies, a couple of power boats, a handful of small sailing cruisers and one splendid racing yacht. On the furthest pontoon, Lindsay spotted a trim Bénéteau sporting a Finnish flag. On the cabin roof, Tam Gourlay sat in a folding chair, stripped down to a pair of shorts, his limbs already turning pink. Her father was nowhere to be seen.

"I see we've gone for the high end of the market here," Rory said, kicking a tuft of dandelions in the middle of the path.

"We have no commercial marinas in St Petersburg yet," Sasha said. "This place used to be pretty smart. But after *perestroika* the Navy didn't have money to maintain it."

"And anywhere on the water goes to shit really quickly if you don't do the upkeep," Lindsay sighed.

"Correct. That's why they started opening it up to private visitors."

"Still, at ten dollars a night, they're not going to make enough to turn it round," Rory pointed out. They arrived alongside the boat and Tam got to his feet, a bottle of beer in his fist.

"All right, girls," he called as they boarded. Lindsay noticed Rory looked extremely wary as she clambered carefully into the cockpit.

"Have you ever been on a yacht before?"

Rory gave her a hard stare. "Oh aye. We used to go cruising every weekend in Castlemilk. Of course I've never been on a yacht."

"You never mentioned it," Lindsay said mildly.

"You never asked. Hey, Tam, how're you doing?" she called up to where he towered above her.

"What's the news?" he asked.

Lindsay introduced Sasha and Tam then asked, "Where's my dad?" She had no intention of going through the whole thing twice.

Tam pointed to a vast wooden hangar behind the dock. "He's in there, talking to some Russian about boats."

Lindsay cast her eyes heavenwards. "So, nothing new there, then. I take it this is down to you, Sasha?"

The Russian grinned. "I told him he'd find a friend of mine in there."

"I'll go and get him, then we can discuss our options," Lindsay said.

She found her father with his head in an engine, a gnarled old man standing opposite, hands on hips, a look on his face that dared Andy to work out what the problem was. "All right, Dad?" she said.

Her father straightened up. "It's that gasket," Andy said, pointing to the offending part. "You take that out, and I'd lay money you'll find a hairline crack running through it." Andy nodded a greeting to his daughter and headed for the door of the hangar. "So. Are we going to have this 'debrief' or not?"

16

It was shortly after ten when Sasha dropped Rory and Lindsay off at their hotel. They'd had a council of war and laid their plans, then Sasha had insisted on taking them all out to dinner in a restaurant that boasted the worst cabaret Lindsay had ever seen in her life. The combination of tawdry costumes, Westernized versions of Russian music and a tenor with more eye make-up than Cher had been so bad it was almost good. But the food had more than made up for it, a constant procession of traditional Russian dishes that had left them all feeling stuffed.

The only thing that had disturbed Lindsay all evening was a look she'd caught in her father's eye. She'd been leaning over to whisper some smart remark about the dancers in Rory's ear when she'd glimpsed him sizing her up. The expression on his face reduced her to childhood. Her mother had always been a sucker for whatever line Lindsay had chosen to spin her, but Andy had always been able to see right through her. That he still had the knack to flood her with guilt infuriated her almost as much as it frightened her how easily he'd figured out that she had something to hide. Something that concerned Rory.

But he'd said nothing, and the moment had passed. The pressure of Rory's knee against hers under the table was more than enough to distract her. She'd probably only imagined it,

Lindsay told herself. She was subconsciously forcing herself to feel the guilt that hadn't come naturally.

They piled out of Sasha's Peugeot. "I pick you up at eight," he said. "So don't go drinking in the bar till late."

They waved him off. Lindsay said, "Do you fancy a drink?"

Rory shook her head. "I've had enough. All those toasts. I must have drunk a quarter-bottle of vodka. I can't figure out why I don't feel drunk."

"It's the way they pace it, with all the food in between. Or so Sasha says." They turned to go inside.

"He's a sweetie."

"You're not the first one to think so," Lindsay said. "There's a woman ten years younger than me in Invercross who has a wee boy the spitting image of Sasha. There's probably one in every fishing port between Newfoundland and Vladivostok."

Rory giggled. "Bad, wicked Sasha."

"Like bad, wicked Lindsay?" She stabbed the button to call the lift.

Rory looked aghast. "Me and my big mouth." They stepped inside the empty lift. "You're not like that, babe."

"You've only got my word for that. Anyway, is there any difference between one infidelity and a dozen?"

Rory frowned. "Of course there is. I should know. I'm the one who specializes in loving them and leaving them. If anybody's like Sasha, it's me."

They walked down the corridor to their room in silence. Lindsay unlocked the door, then went straight to the duty-free bottle of Bowmore and poured herself a stiff measure. "Sure you don't want one?"

"I've changed my mind." Rory reached for the bottle and matched her. Lindsay sat down in the armchair, Rory on the sofa. "Do you want to knock this on the head? Draw a line under last night?"

Lindsay sipped the amber malt, letting the peaty fumes clear her sinuses. She sighed. "No, I don't. It wasn't just some one-night stand, Rory. I don't do that kind of thing. It meant something to me. And I think it meant something to you too. So no, I don't want to knock it on the head. But I don't know what we call it and I don't know what we do with it."

Rory stretched out on the sofa, kicking off her shoes. "Let's get one thing straight. You love Sophie, right?"

Lindsay looked confused. "This isn't to do with Sophie."

"I know that. But you do love her, right?"

"Right."

"And you're not planning on leaving her, right?"

"I never said I was," Lindsay said, her voice defensive.

"And I'm not asking you to. That's the last thing I want. I don't do the long game, remember?"

Lindsay dipped her head in acquiescence. "That's what you said."

"But I don't want to be the Other Woman either. I don't want this to slide into some shitey-hole-in-the-corner affair where we duck in and out of bed in the afternoon and you tell lies so you can sneak off for a shag."

Lindsay winced. Rory's brutal honesty was uncomfortable, all the more so because part of her had been dreaming the impossible notion of continuing the adventure. "When you put it like that . . . So how do we go on?"

"I don't know if this makes any sense to you, but there'll be times when work takes us out of town. Either or both of us. Maybe even abroad. And then, we can be lovers."

"Out of town doesn't count?" Lindsay said incredulously. "How very male."

"I never said it didn't count. But at least it puts it in a separate box. You have Sophie, I have my little exploits and, when we can seize the moment, away from the mainstream of our lives, we do."

It did have a certain seductive logic, Lindsay had to admit to herself. "And what about if you meet somebody you want to get serious with? What happens then? 'Oh, by the way, darling, you'll have to accept my bit on the side.'"

Rory exploded in laughter. "Yeah, right, like that'll happen. Lindsay, how many times do I have to tell you? I don't do getting serious. And even supposing I did, what would change? We'd just go on being out-of-towners."

"And what if you wanted more than that?"

Rory got off the sofa and crouched down between Lindsay's knees. "I promise you I will never, ever ask for more," she said, suddenly very serious. "This is about fun. About the pleasure we take in each other. It's about a friendship that includes a sexual dimension from time to time."

Lindsay put her glass on the table and leaned forward. "Would this be one of those times?" she asked, closing in for the kiss.

"You might as well make the most of it. This time tomorrow, we could both be in a Russian jail. And I bet they don't do double cells."

Bernie put the phone down gently, staring out of the kitchen window, noticing the tendrils of honeysuckle that strayed over the edge of the frame, thick pencil lines against the glass. As they'd arranged, she'd called Tam on his mobile and been amazed by the extraordinary news that Lindsay had tracked down Jack. Not only that, but they thought it would be possible to snatch him back and make a clean escape. In a couple of days, she could be flying out to Helsinki to be reunited with her only child.

Now, her feelings were in turmoil. She was thrilled at the thought of seeing her son again. Her arms ached to hold him, and there was a permanent pit of anxiety in her stomach in his absence. She wanted him with her, no two ways about that. But, equally, she wanted him safe.

And safe was not a state he could achieve while Patrick Coughlan knew where she was. Perhaps the time had come to tell Tam the whole story. But that held its dangers too. How would he react to the knowledge that she'd been less than totally honest about her past? Could she really expect him to uproot himself from the city that had always been his home, turn his back on a successful business and go underground as she'd once had to do? And there was always the possibility that he might insist she give Patrick what he was demanding.

That was a risk she couldn't afford to take.

There was one other possibility. She had run away once before. Maybe she would have to do it again. But, if she did, she would have to take Jack with her this time. That meant she could do nothing until he was back in her arms again. And that in turn depended on whether Tam could bring him safely out of Russia.

Nothing had changed. She was still in limbo. With a sigh, Bernie lit another cigarette and picked up the phone.

⋘⋙

There was always a trade-off, Lindsay thought. Yesterday, their stakeout had been riskily conspicuous, but at least they'd had access to food and drink and a loo. Today, slouched in the passenger seat of Sasha's car, parked opposite the school, she felt a lot less noticeable, but it definitely scored short on the creature-comfort level. Already the car was uncomfortably hot. And the conversation was considerably less entertaining. She'd always liked Sasha, but they'd exhausted all common ground the day before. Somehow, she didn't think Rory would be faring a lot better with Tam at the corner café, though at least she might get some useful info on the seedier end of the second-hand car trade. Andy was back on the boat, stowing Rory and Lindsay's luggage and making sure everything was shipshape for a speedy getaway.

The pupils of the international school had started to trickle in for their morning lessons. Lindsay kept her eyes fixed on the far end of the street, straining to catch the first glimpse of Jack. She hoped Tam would stick to the agreed plan and not try anything daft. Still, if anyone could keep him under control, it was probably Rory.

They didn't have long to wait. Lindsay saw the woman, presumably Bruno's sister, round the corner first. Jack was a couple of steps behind her. But there was a change from the previous day. Where before the pair of them had been alone, now there was a third person in their little group. A burly man with the waddle of a weightlifter towered above Jack, his shaven head gleaming in the sunlight. A white T-shirt strained across pectoral muscles the size and shape of dinner plates and his forearms looked like ham hocks. "Oh fuck," Lindsay said. "Look. They've got a minder."

"He was not here yesterday?"

"No, I would have said."

Sasha shifted in his seat and frowned. "Maybe he is just an escort. Maybe the woman is going shopping and he is there to take care of her?" His optimism sounded hollow.

"You're telling me people need protection to shop in St Pete's?"

Sasha pulled a face. "Depends what you're going to buy."

They watched as the trio walked up the street and entered the school gates. A few minutes later, the woman emerged alone and headed back the way she'd come. "So much for the escort theory," Lindsay said bitterly.

"We need to revise our plans, no?" Sasha said, winding up his window. "You go off to the café, I'll park round the corner and join you there."

By the time Sasha joined them, the others were staring gloomily into their coffees. "Hey, Sasha. Any bright ideas?" Rory greeted him.

He shrugged. "The park is still the best place, I think."

"But that guy's enormous," Lindsay said. "There's no way we can take him on."

"Want a bet?" Tam growled.

"Don't be daft, Tam. For all you know, he might have a gun in an ankle holster," Lindsay protested. "Besides, even if you could take him in a fair fight, the last thing we want is a ruck in a public park. We'll have the cops all over us. There's got to be a better way of doing it. Maybe Sasha can come up with something. He knows the territory, after all."

Rory stirred her coffee thoughtfully. "I don't think familiarity is the answer."

"How do you mean?" Tam asked.

"We should be cashing in on our unfamiliarity. We're foreigners. We're tourists. And we're women. Well, at least, two of us are."

Lindsay began to have a glimmering of what Rory was getting at. "We play the stranger card."

Tam and Sasha looked bemused, but Rory beamed. "Exactly."

Five to two and everyone's nerves were shredded. Sasha sat in his car at the far end of the monastery park, his fingers beating a random tattoo on the steering wheel. Tam was loitering behind a stand of bushes on the edge of the play area, smoking frenetically, trying to look as if he was casually appreciating the beauties of nature. Rory and Lindsay were sitting in the corner café, bill paid, sipping at the dregs of the glasses of wine they'd ordered to give themselves Dutch courage.

Lindsay anxiously checked her bag, making sure they had what they needed. "God, I hope this works," she said.

"You and me both. Because we're the sitting ducks here. Once we get on that underground train after the snatch, we're rats in a trap."

"Thanks, Rory, that's what I really needed to hear." Lindsay gulped the last of her wine and grimaced at its sourness.

Rory, who had taken the seat facing up the street, straightened up. "Hey, Splash, it's showtime."

"Is the Terminator with them?" Lindsay asked.

"Walking right beside Jack." Rory leaned across the table and clasped Lindsay's hand, momentarily earnest. "Whatever happens, you know I wouldn't have missed this for the world."

Lindsay smiled. "Let's see if you're still saying that in an hour's time."

They waited till the crocodile of schoolchildren had rounded the corner before they followed. Everything was identical to the previous day, except for the presence of Jack's bodyguard. Down the street, across the bridge, into the park, then the children erupted into carefree play. Lindsay and Rory hung back, watching and waiting. The minder had taken up station on the fringe of the playing area, about twenty yards from where they knew Tam was lurking. He didn't take his eyes off Jack, who was running around in a game of tig with three other boys. Whenever Jack went more than a few dozen yards from him, the minder moved to keep him in range. The teacher had her back to them, watching half a dozen children playing a wild game of football.

"Let's go for it," Lindsay said, watching how Jack's game was taking him closer to Tam's hiding place. They walked across the grass, Rory with the guidebook, Lindsay with the map, pretending to argue about where they should be going, stopping a couple of times to look around helplessly. As they drew level with the minder, Lindsay suddenly swerved towards him, Rory trailing in her wake, doing her best to put herself between the man and the object of his attention.

"*Spasibo*," Lindsay began. "How do we get to the Tikhvin Cemetery?"

The man frowned and said something in Russian, sidestepping to bring himself closer to Jack. Rory moved nearer to him, doing the dizzy blonde. "We're lost," she said, giving him the dazzling smile that Lindsay knew only too well was a killer. "The Tikhvin Cemetery?" She pointed to the guidebook.

The bodyguard frowned and glanced down at the page.

"*Kladbische*," Lindsay said helpfully, thrusting her phrase book under his nose. *Stay, Tam, stay*, she urged him mentally. It was still too risky.

The bodyguard's face cleared and he said, "*Da, Tikhvin Kladbische*." But instead of giving them directions, he pushed between them and shouted. "Jack. Come now."

Lindsay's heart sank as Jack slowed to a halt and glared at the minder. "I'm playing," he said defiantly.

The bodyguard covered the few yards between them in seconds. He grabbed Jack's hand. "Stay with me." Then he turned back to Rory and Lindsay. He pointed to the far end of the park. "Go there, to end of street. Then right." He smiled.

Lindsay forced a smile in return and said, "Come on, Rory." She headed towards the bushes where Tam was hidden. "Abort," she said conversationally as they approached. "Stay out of sight, Tam," she added more insistently.

They rounded the bushes and found Tam crouched like a coiled spring. "Fuck it, I'm going for it," he growled.

"Don't be stupid," Lindsay said. "You'll blow the whole thing if you try it now." She took out her mobile and dialled Sasha's number. "Sasha? Abort. We'll see you back at the boat."

She turned back to find Rory and Tam engaged in furious argument. "He's my son," Tam said mutinously.

"We've all stuck our necks out to get this far, Tam," Rory said. "You've got no right to put everybody else at risk. We'll figure something else out for tomorrow. But today's a bust. Leave it."

"She's right," Lindsay said. "We need to figure out a better way of doing this. But we can't do it now. Come away, Tam," she added, taking his hand. "There's no sense in you getting arrested."

"Or worse," Rory pointed out.

The argument was settled by the blast of the teacher's whistle, summoning her charges into line for the walk back to school. Tam's head dropped and he pulled away from Lindsay, trudging despondently towards the far exit where minutes before Sasha had been waiting.

17

There was no need to take the metro now. Lindsay flagged down a passing taxi on Nevsky Prospekt and managed to communicate their destination. They arrived back at the boat to find Andy and Sasha with tumblers of whisky in their fists. The atmosphere of depression was palpable.

Lindsay poured drinks for the rest of them while they recounted the disastrous operation. Afterwards, they slouched in the cockpit in gloomy silence. It was Sasha who opened the discussion. "We have one more chance, no?" he said.

"That's right," Andy said. "We've only got three-day visas. That means we need to be back at Kronstadt by lunchtime the day after tomorrow. So, realistically, if we don't get the boy tomorrow, we'll have to leave empty-handed."

"No fucking way," Tam stated, pounding his fist against the bulkhead. "Youse can do what the hell you like, but I'm not leaving without Jack."

Lindsay felt a headache beginning at the base of her skull. "That would be one way of making sure neither of you leaves Russia for quite a while," she said tartly. "Look, can we skip the heroics and get down to brass tacks? Obviously, we need a better diversion if we're going to get Jack away from his minder. Any ideas?"

No one spoke for a moment, then Rory said, "Rather than directly approaching the minder, maybe we should try to think up something that would draw everyone's attention away from the kids?"

"Like what?" Tam demanded.

"I don't know. Maybe Sasha and Andy could pretend to have a fight?" Rory suggested.

"Who'd drive the getaway car then?" Lindsay objected.

"You could. Or I could," Rory said.

"You'd get lost," Sasha said.

"We could practise the route tonight," Lindsay countered.

"I need to be with the boat, Lindsay," her father said. "What if somebody calls the police, and we cannae get away? What happens then? You're stuck with the boy and no way of getting out."

"I can sail the boat," Lindsay said.

"I'm no' disputing that," Andy said. "But all the paperwork is in my name. They Russian bureaucrats, they're not going to wave you through if your papers aren't in order, are they, Sasha?"

The Russian shook his silver head. "He's right, Lindsay. It's too risky. We could all end up in jail that way."

"Have you got a better idea, then?" Tam challenged. Sasha shrugged.

"You know, I think we're making this too complicated. Keep it simple, that's always the best way," Andy said. They all looked at him in surprise.

"How do you mean, Dad?"

"I wasnae there this afternoon, so I'm only going by what you've all said. But from the sounds of it, this minder's a pro. Would that be right?"

Rory nodded. "He knows what he's doing."

"Right. So at the first sniff of any kind of diversion, his first instinct is going to be to protect the lad. It doesnae matter how clever we get, he's going to do his job. So there's no point in us trying to be smart. We've just got to tackle it head on." Andy's voice was quiet, but Lindsay knew from experience that his low-key approach disguised a stubbornness that nothing would shift. Whatever her father's idea, she had a sneaking suspicion that would be what they ended up doing.

"So, what are you saying, Andy?" Tam leaned forward, suddenly alert.

"Keep it simple, like I said. We've got Sasha waiting in the car, like before. But this time, we wait till the kids are running about, then Tam walks through the park, picking a line that'll bring him close to where Jack is. Then he grabs him and makes a run for it. You two," he pointed to Lindsay and Rory—"your job is to buy Tam some time. You wait by the path till Tam passes you, then you get in the minder's road. Trip him up, make him go the long way round, whatever. Just slow him down long enough, then disappear yourselves." Andy sat back and the others looked at him in stunned astonishment.

"It'll never work," Lindsay said. "They're bound to have told the bodyguard to look out for Tam. He'll recognise him."

Sasha cocked his head to one side, considering Tam. "Maybe not if we get rid of the beard and chop the hair off and put him in an FC Zenit shirt . . ."

"You really think we can hold him up for long enough to let Tam get clear?" Rory asked.

Andy shrugged. "I don't know. I've never seen the guy. But from what you said, he sounds like a weightlifter. They're no' built for speed."

Tam gave a harsh bark of laughter. "And you think I am?"

"It's amazing what the human body's capable of when it comes to your bairns," Andy said. "You'll do fine, Tam."

Tam held out his huge paw to Andy. They shook. "That's settled, then," he said.

Lindsay and Rory exchanged a bewildered look. "Out-flanked by the old man," Lindsay said, shaking her head, half-amused and half-terrified at the thought of what her father had just let her in for.

"We should go back to the park, make sure we all know the ground," Sasha said, swallowing the last of his whisky. "Andy, you must come too, give us an extra pair of eyes."

As they walked back to Sasha's car, Lindsay managed to detach her father from the group and hung back with him. "Tam's really wound up," she said. "I think you need to get him off the boat. He's going stir crazy on there. Is there any chance that you and Sasha can take him out and get him pissed tonight? Maybe the two of you could stay at Sasha's?"

"What about the boat?" Andy asked, casting an apprehensive look back at the Bénéteau.

"I'll stay on board with Rory. We've checked out of the hotel, remember? We can't go back, it'll only draw attention to us. And after we snatch Jack, the cops will be looking for two British women behaving suspiciously. We need to keep a low profile."

"And you two want the place to yourselves, eh?" Andy asked severely.

"It's a small boat, Dad. We're all going to be cooped up there for long enough as it is. But I'm not suggesting this for my sake. Tam needs to let off some steam before he blows up."

Andy stopped and stared hard at his daughter. "That better be the real reason, Lindsay. I've seen the way that lassie looks at you."

"Aye, well, Dad, if wishes were horses, beggars would ride," Lindsay said, using anger to hide her guilt. "Please yourself."

She began to walk away, but Andy put a hand on her arm. "I'll do what you suggest," he said. "Don't let yourself down, Lindsay."

Her father's words echoed in her head hours later as she made up the double berth in the forepeak cabin for her and Rory to share. Was she letting herself down, or was she finding the road back to herself, a road that had been obscured by the forces of habit and affection? It was a question that had no easy answer. She tucked the sheet in under the thin foam mattress as Rory called, "Dinner is served, madam."

Lindsay finished off and joined Rory in the cockpit, where she'd arranged a picnic with the food they'd bought from a small grocery store near Sasha's apartment. There was ham and red caviare, a sweating block of yellow cheese, various flavoured yoghurts, black bread and, improbably, a baguette. They'd supplemented this with bananas, peaches and tomatoes from a nearby kiosk, and a couple of bottles of Georgian red wine recommended by Sasha. "Looks good," Lindsay said, leaning across to kiss Rory on the mouth.

"I don't know if I can eat much," Rory said. "I never realised you could feel the boat moving even when you're tied up like this."

"You'll get used to it." Lindsay grinned. "Either that or you'll be seasick."

"Gee, thanks," Rory said, cutting off a chunk of bread and smearing it with caviare.

"Just remember it's always better up on deck," Lindsay said. "Poor Sophie gets sick as a dog when she's below. That's why she never used to come on overnight trips with me."

"Did you used to sail in California, then?"

"I learned to sail almost as soon as I could walk. When we were in America, I had a half-share in a thirty-six-foot Baltic."

Rory shook her head. "That means nothing to me."

"It's a classic yacht. A colleague of Sophie's found her languishing in a boat yard and he persuaded me to go in with him. It took us the best part of a year to get her seaworthy, but it was worth it. I had some great sails in that boat. I really miss her, especially on a night like this, sitting on the water and soaking up the peace and quiet."

"So, are you going to get a boat back in Scotland?" Rory asked, uncorking the wine.

Lindsay shook her head. "I can't afford it."

"That's a shame."

"I'll just have to try and hitch a ride crewing for some of the rich bastards who keep their boats up in Invercross. They're always desperate for an extra pair of hands."

Rory grinned. "Either that or we'll have to make lots of money selling stories."

"Maybe." Then a sudden thought stabbed her. "Except I might have another mouth to help feed." She'd managed to remain in denial about the prospects of parenthood ever since the plane had taken off from Glasgow, but now it was there between them, a monkey on her back that wouldn't stay caged.

Rory reached across and squeezed Lindsay's hand. "Hey, maybe you should try the lottery."

Lindsay burst out laughing. "I think you've used up enough luck for both of us there."

Rory winked. "You mean, you don't think you'll get lucky tonight?"

Lindsay made herself a cheese and tomato sandwich. "I intend to take full advantage of tonight. It could be our last chance for a while."

Rory frowned. "But we're going to be on the boat for another couple of nights, surely?"

"Yeah, but so will my dad," Lindsay pointed out. "Call me a coward, but that is not going to make me feel relaxed and sexy."

"Duh, silly me. You think he'd tell Sophie?"

Lindsay sighed. "No, I don't think he would. I just don't want him to know that there's anything *to* tell Sophie. It's easier all round."

Rory leaned against Lindsay. "Well, we'd better eat fast, then."

"I thought yesterday was bad, but this is hell," Lindsay muttered to Rory as Tam disappeared inside the bar in search of the toilet.

"If it gets any hotter, Tam's going to spontaneously combust," Rory agreed. They were sitting at a pavement table at a bar on a side street between the international school and the play area. From the safety of his car, Sasha had watched Jack and his minder arrive at school a couple of hours before. He'd stayed put, in case they left early, but so far, Lindsay's mobile had remained silent.

The air was heavy with humidity, the sky coppery and oppressive. It was the sort of day when a thin sheen of sweat covered every exposed piece of flesh, making bodies adhesive. The weight of the weather served only to accentuate the discomfort and drag of hanging around.

Waiting alone with Rory would at least have held an element of pleasure. But with Tam added to the mix, it was grim. He couldn't keep still. When he wasn't smoking, his fingers danced incessantly on the table top. He made Lindsay check her phone every five minutes to make sure she hadn't missed a vital call. He kept running his hands over his newly naked chin and the half-inch of hair that was all that remained of his thick auburn mop, as if he couldn't quite believe he was still in his own skin.

What was worse was that his nervousness was contagious. Lindsay had started the day feeling fairly calm, but she was growing more and more edgy with every passing minute. "He's doing my head in," she complained.

"He can't help it," Rory said. "He's scared. And if there's one thing a macho Scottish male can't acknowledge, even to himself, it's being scared. So he's hiding it behind impatience. Try and relax, Lindsay." She leaned across to massage Lindsay's neck between her fingers and thumb.

"Oh yeah, right. Relax. That'll work. How am I supposed to relax?"

Rory smirked. "Think of something pleasant. No, actually, skip that. Think of something wildly, extravagantly, sexily fabulous. You shouldn't have to search far back in your memory . . ."

In spite of herself, Lindsay smiled. Before she could reply, Tam came lumbering back to the table. With his new look and his blue Zenit shirt, nobody from Glasgow would have recognised him. Lindsay herself had had to do a double take when he'd appeared at the boat earlier with her father and Sasha. A bodyguard who'd only seen a photograph would have no chance.

"How long now?" he asked, dropping like a stone into his chair.

Lindsay checked her watch. "Fifteen minutes."

"Right. Gonnae get me a vodka?" he asked her.

"Are you sure that's a good idea?" Lindsay said.

"I need a drink, okay? It didnae do me much harm last night, did it?"

She couldn't deny that. According to Sasha, they'd been drinking vodka till well past midnight, but none of them had a hangover in spite of Tam having reportedly collapsed in a senseless heap on the floor of Sasha's living room. She signalled to the waitress and ordered a vodka, counting out the roubles to pay so they wouldn't have any delay when the time came to move.

When the drink came, Tam swallowed it in one. "Right then," he said. "I'll wait here till I see the kids passing the end of the street. You two better head off, get into position."

They stood up. Now the moment was upon them, Lindsay felt curiously solemn. It had to work this time. There would be no third chance. And if they failed, she'd have to deal with the fact that she had let the genie out of the bottle. She realised that, having come this far, Tam could never return empty-handed to Bernie. Impulsively, she gave him a quick hug and kissed his smooth cheek. "Good luck, big man," she said.

He nodded, beyond words, adrenaline and alcohol flushing his pale cheeks. Rory gripped his shoulder. "We'll get it right this time."

They walked off briskly, barely reaching the corner when Lindsay's phone rang. Sasha told her the children had left the school gates, heading in the right direction. He was going to drive straight to the far exit to wait for Tam and Jack. Dry-mouthed, Lindsay passed the message on to Rory, who nodded grimly. In silence, they entered the park and ambled across the grass to the shrubbery where Tam had hidden the previous afternoon. It ran almost to the edge of the path where Tam would attempt to escape with Jack, providing the perfect spot for them to ambush the minder.

As they took up position, a low growl of thunder grumbled in the distance and the sky seemed to darken. Lindsay looked heavenwards with a look of dawning delight. "I think we're in for a thunderstorm," she said, hardly able to believe the evidence of her senses.

"Oh, great, just what we need when we're about to go sailing," Rory said.

"Never mind that. If it hits now, we've got the perfect diversion."

Rory got the point and gave a low whoop of delight. "You're right!" Suddenly she started bouncing up and down, waving her arms and dancing in a little circle.

"What are you doing?" Lindsay said, bemused.

"Rain dance." Rory grinned. "Can't hurt, can it?"

Lindsay shook her head, amused in spite of herself. She peered through a jigsaw gap in the bushes and caught sight of the children arriving in the park. Already they were running free. Today, Jack seemed to have joined the game of football, though he was noticeably less frantic than the others in his pursuit of the ball. Another peal of thunder, this one louder than the last, caused a momentary pause in play, but they carried on instantly.

A few minutes later, she caught sight of Tam, strolling casu-ally towards the children. "Oh, smart move," she said softly as he took a line that would bring him to the edge of play. When the ball drifted towards him, he brought it under control and moved into the game, passing it to one of the children. He waved casually at the teacher, and carried on making his way through the players, gradually working nearer and nearer to

Jack. One of the boys kicked the ball to Tam and he dribbled expertly towards his stepson. For a moment, it looked as if he would feint past him. Then at the last minute, Tam stooped low, scooped Jack into his arms and took off. As if on cue, the thunder crashed again, a jagged bolt of lightning split the sky and the heavens opened.

Rain sheeted down, adding to the confusion of noise and blurring the rush of movement. Jack was screeching like a banshee, hammering his fists against Tam's shoulder as Tam pounded across the field towards the path. Hot on his heels, the bodyguard had sprung into action, roaring something incomprehensible as he went. The cries of playing children had suddenly turned into screams of panic.

Now Tam was running faster than Lindsay would have believed possible, in spite of the struggling child in his arms. Clearly, Tam's disguise had Jack fooled as much as his minder. He was giving chase, but as her father had rightly surmised, his body was built for strength, not speed and, although he was unencumbered, he wasn't gaining ground fast enough. "I think they're going to make it," she said. "You ready?"

Rory nodded, poised on the balls of her feet. Still peering through the bushes, Lindsay caught sight of the teacher. She was frantically gathering her pupils together, her face blanched as a turnip, her mouth still a round O of shock. Then suddenly Tam was thundering past them, his breathing ragged and painful. "Now!" Lindsay shouted.

Rory stepped into the path, closely followed by Lindsay. The bodyguard was bearing down on them. He tried to swerve at the last minute to avoid them, but Rory kept on walking, driving him towards the grass. He thrust an arm out, pushing her out of the way, but the edge of his foot skidded on the wet grass and sent him sprawling.

He scrambled to his feet, spitting what had to be curses at Rory, and hurtled on after Tam. But the distance was too great. There was no chance he could catch them now, Lindsay thought with satisfaction. "Act nonchalant, look a bit bemused, as if it's all nothing to do with us," she said, steadying Rory and steering her down the path in the opposite direction, taking advantage of the confusion to depart the way they'd come without a backward glance.

As soon as they had cleared the park, they picked up speed, cutting briskly down a side street to the Obvodnogo Canal. Within five minutes, the ugly concrete box of the Moskva Hotel reared up before them. There was no sign of pursuit, and they began to breathe easier as they crossed the busy intersection in front of the hotel and walked into the metro station. Jubilation welled up inside Lindsay, but she took care to show none of it.

In silence, they rode the metro to the end of the line then set off towards the Navy Yacht Club from a different direction. Now they were finally able to release some of their tension, laughing in pure delight as they relived the rescue, indifferent to the rain streaming down their faces. They had only walked a couple of hundred yards when Sasha's car drew up alongside. Holding her breath, Lindsay gave him a questioning look.

Sasha grinned and gave her the thumbs-up sign. "All aboard. They wait for you. All you have to do now is get the boy out of the country."

According to Sasha, Tam had barely made it to the car ahead of the bodyguard. "I had engine running and back door open," he said. "Tam threw the boy in and dived on top of him. Poor Jack, he was squealing like a pig, he wouldn't believe it was Tam at first. Anyway, I shot off before Tam even got the door closed. Just as well I did, because the bodyguard was close enough to hit the boot with his fist as I pulled away."

"Did he get your number?" Lindsay had asked, worried for her father's generous friend.

Sasha had tapped his nose with his index finger. "No matter if he did. I got plates from a scrap yard, six o'clock yesterday morning."

They'd never have done it without Sasha, Lindsay realised. She and Rory had been so gung-ho, so convinced they could cut a swathe through whatever Russia threw at them. But they'd been hopelessly wrong. She had to wonder if, back in Glasgow, even at some deep subliminal level, the reason she'd been so eager to get involved in Bernie and Jack's problem had been about impressing Rory. Or even about getting Rory on her own, in a foreign environment, in a strange light where recklessness might look like romance.

At the Navy Yacht Club they ran through the sheeting rain to the boat. Andy, Tam and Jack were below in the steamy cabin, mugs of hot chocolate in their hands. Jack barely looked up as they arrived. He was snuggled into Tam's side, talking nineteen to the dozen about his experiences. The tracks of his dried tears snaked down his cheeks, a vivid reminder of the terror he must have felt when Tam snatched him. "And when Papa went away, I was left with Zia Maria and she made me go to school, and it was horrible, and she wouldn't let me phone Mum, even though Papa promised I could," the boy prattled on. "I hated it. I wanted to come home, but Zia Maria said I had to stay until Papa came back. It was supposed to be a holiday," he added, self-righteous disgust in his voice.

Rory sat down on the bench seat and let out a huge sigh. "We made it."

"So far," Andy said cautiously. "Lindsay?" He gestured towards the cockpit with his head. "A word."

"You need me," Lindsay protested. "Nobody else can sail the boat with you. And in weather like this, you need another pair of hands."

Andy shook his head stubbornly. "They're going to be looking for two British women. You said that yourself. While I was sitting here waiting for you, I realised it was madness to try and take you both out on the boat."

"So I've got to stay behind? Are you sure you're not just trying to keep me and Rory apart?" Lindsay's blood was up now, the adrenaline rush of the snatch reasserting itself as anger.

"Should I be?" Andy said calmly.

"Well, Dad, you should know by now that if you want me to do something, the best way is to tell me I can't. And you should also know better than to stick your nose in my business."

"We're a family, Lindsay. Your business is my business. You should be thinking about Sophie."

Lindsay gave a harsh bark of laughter. "Yeah, right. Like Sophie thinks about me when she makes her decisions. Dad, you don't know the half of it. Everybody always assumes I'm the difficult one. Well, just for the record, it's not always me. Okay? Now, let's get this boat under way. We're wasting time we can't afford to spare."

"You're not coming, Lindsay. I've already spoken to Sasha. There's a train out this afternoon. We'll meet you in Helsinki. Just put your own feelings to one side for a wee minute and think about the boy's safety. We're going to have enough questions asked about why Tam looks different from his passport. Not to mention why we've got somebody extra on board."

"Okay. You two go back alone with Jack. Rory and I will get a flight out," Lindsay said stubbornly.

Andy shook his head. "Like I said, they're going to be looking for two British women travelling together. You need to split up."

"So let Rory fly out and I'll stay with the boat. You really could use another pair of hands. And having an extra person on board makes more sense if it's your daughter, doesn't it?"

Andy shook his head. "We thought about that. Sasha doesn't think Rory's confident enough to handle the independent travel."

"It's my story, Dad. Not Rory's."

They glared at each other, impasse reached. At that moment, Sasha's bulk appeared in the doorway leading down to the cabin.

"Your father is right, Lindsay. I know it's hard, but you're too smart not to see he's right. One of you has to stay behind." He glanced at his watch. "You could be on the quarter to five train to Helsinki."

Lindsay closed her eyes and exhaled noisily. She knew when she was beaten. The boat wasn't going anywhere while they were both on board, and they couldn't afford to let the time drift away from them if they were to make good their escape from Russian territory. She turned away and gazed across the marina to the expo centre. "Get Rory up here," she said.

Sasha called below and moved into the cockpit to let Rory up the companionway. "What's going on?" she asked, her expression puzzled.

"The boys think we need to split up. Because the Russians will be looking for two British women, after our attempt yesterday. So one of us goes with the boat and the other gets the train to Helsinki."

Rory looked stunned. "That's not what we planned."

"Plans sometimes have to change," Sasha said. "It is too dangerous to have you both on the boat."

Rory nodded, seeing his point instantly. "Okay. I'll take the train. It makes more sense for Lindsay to stay with the boat, she can help Andy."

Andy smiled in relief. "Thanks, Rory." He raised his eyebrows at Lindsay. "That all right with you?"

Lindsay shook her head ruefully, knowing when she was defeated. "Give me your keys, Sasha. I'll walk Rory to the car. We've got a bit of business to sort out."

They said goodbye in the shelter of a dripping tree that overhung the Peugeot, clinging to each other, neither willing to admit the desperation they felt at this sudden severance. "I'm sorry it's turned out like this. But we'll have a night in Helsinki," Lindsay murmured, nuzzling the soft skin beneath Rory's ear.

"Provided we all make it past the Russian customs."

"We'll make it," Lindsay said, with a confidence she was slowly beginning to feel. "And at least I'll get my copy written on the voyage without you to distract me." She kissed Rory's mouth, trying to imprint it on her memory so she could summon it at will.

They stepped apart and Rory opened the car door. "Safe journey," she said.

Lindsay nodded. "See you in Helsinki."

18

The 32-foot Bénéteau began to bounce a little on the heavy swell that was rolling in from Kronstadt towards St Petersburg. Lindsay had finished stowing her possessions and was lying back on the bunk in the forepeak cabin, trying to compose her intro and not be distracted by thoughts of Rory speeding through the streets of St Petersburg towards the Finland Station. She was interrupted by a bang on the cabin door.

"Lindsay?" It was Tam.

"You're okay, I'm decent."

The door to the tiny V-shaped cabin opened and Tam leaned in. "Andy wants you up on deck, just to run through what we've got to do at Kronstadt."

She followed him up to the cockpit, where Jack perched on a bench, dwarfed by a scarlet lifejacket that was clipped on to the boat. Andy Gordon never took chances on board. Tam sat down next to the boy, who immediately snuggled under his encircling arm. Neither seemed any the worse for their nail-biting escape, Lindsay thought.

Her analysis was interrupted by Jack. "When will I see my mum?" he asked plaintively.

"In a couple of days. We've got to sail all the way to Finland first. But we'll phone her as soon as we get you smuggled through the customs," Lindsay said.

Jack looked apprehensive. "What's 'smuggled,' Dad?"

"It's like hide and seek. You have to hide and stay really, really quiet for ages. Not a whisper. Because if you make a noise and we get caught, they might put me and Captain Andy and Lindsay in the jail. And we don't want that, do we?"

Jack's grin said he didn't quite believe what he was being told. "Then I wouldn't have anybody to take me back to my mum."

"Correct," Tam said. "So you have to listen to what Captain Andy tells you and do exactly what he says."

"Where are we going to stow him?" Lindsay asked her father quietly.

Andy tugged at the brim of his salt-stained San Francisco 49ers cap. "A wee boat like this, there's not an awful lot of choice. There's not even a sail locker. About the only option is to put him in the under-berth storage and cover him up with clothes. I hope the wee bugger doesnae suffer from claustrophobia."

"And that the Russian customs aren't having a bad day," Lindsay added darkly.

"Aye, well, there's still a couple of bottles of decent brandy to cheer them up a wee bit," Andy said. "Do you want to take the helm while Tam and I get things sorted down below?"

Lindsay couldn't help the thrum of excitement that ran through her as she took the wheel and felt the pull of the boat under her hands. There was nothing quite like sailing, she thought, scanning the set of the sails and glancing at the chart to check her course. Even in a swell like this, there was a tranquillity that was irresistible. No sounds other than the hiss of the hull through the water, the occasional slap of a wave and the crack of a sail.

These steely northern waters couldn't be more different from the blue dazzle of the Pacific. The rain had stopped and the sky was clearing now, but the weather here could turn on a sixpence, and there were treacherous currents aplenty to confuse the unwary sailor. Lindsay inspected chart and compass again, making sure she was sticking to the course her father had pencilled in. Kronstadt was fast approaching. Another fifteen minutes, she reckoned, though she'd have to change tack.

Andy's head appeared in the hatch. "How are we doing?"

"Ten, fifteen minutes. Do you want her back?"

Andy shook his head. "I think it might be better if you bring her in."

"Why?" Lindsay asked, slightly apprehensive about berthing an unfamiliar boat on a mooring pontoon.

"Well, see, Sasha explained this to me. The stamp in your passport says you came in on a plane. They might get a wee bit funny about you going out on a boat, but if you're actually sailing her, it looks more natural." Andy climbed up the companionway. "I'll do the sails when you're ready."

"Did you get Jack hidden away?" she asked.

"He's crawled right into the forepeak. He's a brave wee bugger, I'll give him that. Tam's arranging your bag and your clothes so he cannot be seen."

For the rest of the journey into Kronstadt, anxiety kept all three adults locked in their own thoughts. The silence was broken only by Lindsay's instructions to her father. Eventually, they tied up and sat waiting for the customs inspectors. This time, it was a long half-hour before they finally appeared.

As Andy had warned, they were suspicious of the fact that Lindsay had flown in and was leaving by boat three days before her visa ran out. And when they saw the contrast between Tam's passport photo and his current appearance, it was clear this wasn't going to be a straightforward passage. Neither of the officials spoke English, so there was another delay while an English speaker could be tracked down and brought to the boat.

First, he demanded an explanation for Lindsay's behaviour. "Why are you coming by plane and going by boat?"

"I wanted a little longer in St Petersburg than I would have had if I'd come both ways on the boat." She smiled, attempting innocent reassurance. "I wanted to see the Hermitage and the Russian Museum. And Pushkin's House. Too much for a couple of days."

He pored over her papers. "But you have return flight from St Petersburg," he pointed out.

"I know. It's silly really, but it worked out cheaper that way. A single fare would have ended up costing me more than the return. It was a special deal from the airline." It was bullshit, but it was the kind of bullshit that might just be true, she thought.

"Why are you with these men?" the official asked.

"The older man, he's my father. And the other one is my boyfriend." Lindsay hoped they wouldn't start asking her leading questions about Tam. It was a risky line to take, but one that made more sense than any other.

The official studied her papers again and finally nodded. "Okay. But your boyfriend, he doesn't look like his picture."

Lindsay gave an exasperated sigh. "He looks ridiculous, doesn't he? It was so hot in St Petersburg, he decided to have his hair cut and his beard trimmed. But the barber didn't understand what he wanted, and he ended up looking like this."

Tam tried to look sheepish. "I said I wanted to get rid of my hair because it was too long in the heat. Before I knew it, the guy was shaving me as well. I tell you, I'm going to suffer when I get back to Glasgow."

The official frowned. "You will suffer? How will you suffer?"

"How do you think? Everybody's going to laugh their heads off when they see me looking like this," he said. He shook his head. "I can't believe I let this happen to me."

"You can't believe it?" Lindsay said. "I can't believe I've got to walk around with somebody who looks like a moronic thug."

The customs official gave a thin smile. "Please do not tell anyone this is happening in Russia. It is not good for our reputation. Now, I must look at boat."

Eventually, an hour and a half after they had moored, they were free to go, two bottles of cognac and a carton of Marlboros lighter.

Lindsay almost wept with relief. It was only as they hoisted sail, leaving Kronstadt behind, that she realised how taut she had been holding herself. Tam hurried below decks, and she could hear him calling to Jack. The pair of them emerged on deck a few minutes later, the boy giggling in delight at being released from his damp and uncomfortable prison. They all hugged each other, grinning like fools. Andy reached into the chart locker and produced a flat half-bottle of whisky, taking a swig himself before passing it round.

"Christ, I wouldnae like to go through that again in a hurry," he said, hugging his daughter. "See you, Lindsay? You're nothing but trouble."

Tam took his mobile out of his pocket and suggested to Jack that they ring Bernie. The boy agreed eagerly.

"You'll maybe be wanting to phone Sophie before your mobile goes out of range." Andy said to Lindsay.

She shook her head. "I'll wait till we're safe on dry land."

Kevin was snoring softly in the camping chair when Michael dug him in the ribs. "Looks like we've got some action," he said, already on his feet and heading for the door. Kevin stumbled to his feet and hurried out of the flat after Michael, who was taking the stairs two at a time.

By the time they hit the street, the taxi that had pulled up outside Bernie's flat was driving off. "Shit," Michael cursed, running for the car he'd hired using the false driving licence Patrick had supplied him with. Kevin was barely aboard when they screeched out of their parking space and raced after the taxi. "She was carrying a suitcase," Michael said as he turned right in the wake of the cab, earning a blast of the horn from the car he'd cut across.

The taxi had stopped at the traffic lights, and he breathed a sigh of relief. Michael slowed down, allowing another car to slip in between them. They turned in convoy on to Great Western Road and headed out towards Dumbarton. "Where the hell is she going?" he wondered aloud.

"You think she's doing a runner?" Kevin asked apprehensively.

"Who the fuck knows? Maybe they've found the kid and she's going to fetch him? Either way, we better not lose her." He concentrated on keeping a safe distance between them and the taxi. They drove on out through Drumchapel and Clydebank, then turned off towards the Erskine Bridge.

"Isn't this the way to the airport?" Kevin asked.

Surprised that he knew that much, Michael nodded. "I think so."

Kevin's guess proved correct. The taxi dropped Bernie off at the departures entrance. "Get out and follow her," Michael said. "I'll park the car."

Five minutes later, he hurried into the terminal, apprehensively scanning the check-in queues. He spotted Kevin first, leaning against a wall, pretending to read the paper. "Where is she?" he demanded.

Kevin indicated the direction with a jerk of his head. "KLM. She's in the queue for the Amsterdam flight."

"She could be going anywhere," Michael said through clenched teeth as he clocked Bernie. There were only a couple of people in front of her now. Somehow, he had to find out her destination. It wasn't going to be easy; she was looking around constantly, her face a mirror of his own anxiety. But he didn't have a choice. Patrick wasn't a man to whom you could say, "I bottled out." He watched for a little longer, until the man ahead of Bernie handed over his passport and tickets.

"Wait here," Michael said. He noticed a stand containing film developing envelopes and grabbed one in passing. The counter next to the one where Bernie was waiting was empty and he ambled over there without a sideways glance. He leaned on the counter and began slowly filling in the required details on the envelope.

He'd timed it well. Bernie stepped up to the counter, placing her bag on the luggage belt. "Good afternoon," the man on the check-in desk said, reaching for her paperwork. He looked at the tickets, then added, "Your bags will be checked right through to Helsinki, you don't have to worry about them in Amsterdam."

It was all he needed to hear. Michael walked off towards the destination board. The KLM Amsterdam flight was due to leave in a little over an hour. He crossed to the KLM ticket counter and smiled at the woman tapping something into her computer keyboard. "Excuse me," he said. "Is there any chance of me getting to Helsinki this afternoon?"

"I'll just check for you, sir." She hit a few keys then frowned at the screen. "I'm sorry, sir. The connecting flight to Amsterdam is full." She clicked her mouse. "I can get you there first thing in the morning, but this afternoon's impossible."

"There's nothing at all? Not even business class?"

She shook her head. "I'm sorry. The flight's full and I've already got three people on standby."

He wanted to smash her stupid computer over her empty head, but instead Michael simply turned on his heel and walked away. He pulled his mobile out of his pocket and called the familiar number. "It's me," he said when Patrick answered. "We've got a problem. Our target is at Glasgow Airport. She's going to Helsinki. And I can't get on the flight."

"Why didn't we know about this already?" Patrick demanded. "She must have gone to the travel agent or something?"

"She's not been near a travel agent. I've been on the bitch's tail every time she's been out of the house. She could have booked it on the Internet or over the phone or anything," Michael protested.

"Well, this is a fine mess," Patrick said, his voice poison-ous. Michael had never heard him show his anger so obviously and it was unnerving.

"What do you want me to do?" he asked.

"There's fuck all you can do, is there?" Patrick sighed.

"We could meet every flight from Helsinki into Glasgow," Michael said. "She's got to come back sometime."

"You think so?"

"Well, either her or the husband. You don't just walk away from a house full of furniture and stuff." As he spoke, Michael knew there was a hole in his logic. If he had a vengeful Patrick Coughlan on his tail, he might be tempted to walk away from his life and everything in it.

"See what you can do, then," Patrick said grudgingly. Michael's ear tingled as the phone was slammed down at the other end. With a deep sigh, he headed back towards Kevin. He'd already had enough of Glasgow Airport. But it looked like he'd be seeing a lot more of it over the next few days.

Rory stared out of the window of the St Petersburg-Helsinki train. She'd caught the Sibelius Express with scant minutes to spare, rushing aboard with scarcely time to thank Sasha for all he'd done for them. He stood on the platform of the Finland Station, waving as the train shrugged into motion.

Rory settled into her seat and took a paperback from her bag. It sat in front of her, unopened, as she looked out across the landscape, seeing nothing. All she could think of was the confusion of feelings that had rampaged through her since she'd said her unexpected farewell to Lindsay. She felt bereft. There really was no other word for it, she realised with painful clarity. She'd never felt that about a lover before. Always, she'd been in charge of the comings and goings; always, she'd been in com-mand of her feelings.

Only once had she experienced this sense of abandonment. Gazing across the Russian landscape, Rory finally understood something about herself. She'd fought to keep the women in her bed out of her heart because she knew only too well what it felt like to be left utterly, to be stranded on the shore when the person you loved had disappeared over an unseeable horizon. She'd never recognised before that she had been building barricades to save herself from being forsaken as her mother had forsaken her.

But Lindsay had somehow crept behind the fortifications and laid claim to the part of herself she had never relinquished before. Rory even understood how it had happened. In the past, she'd always assumed control. She'd been the one who had taken care of business, looked after the details, made things happen. But the moment she had agreed to come on this crazy adventure, she had handed the reins over to someone else and, in doing so, she had ceded more than she had realised.

Fuck it, I love her. It was the one thing she had promised she would not let happen, and it had ambushed her. Instinctively she knew that, if she let it, this time it could work. But that wasn't the deal. Lindsay wasn't free. And Rory wasn't in the business of busting up other people's relationships. She wasn't about to cast herself as the Scarlet Woman of the West End.

There was only one solution. If she couldn't sleep with Lindsay without letting love come between them, she'd just have to do without her. They'd have their night in Helsinki, because it would be too complicated to explain to Lindsay what had changed. Then they'd go home and it would naturally come to an end. And in a couple of weeks, once the dust had settled, Rory would give Lindsay the brush-off. She'd find the words to let her down easy.

Anything rather than tell the truth.

Fuck it, I love them both. It was the one thing Lindsay had promised herself she wouldn't let happen, and it had ambushed her. *I
did this on purpose*, she thought, bracing herself against the deck
as the evening dwindled towards night. All those risks, all that
recklessness; it had all been about pushing herself so far away
from Sophie that there was no way back to the other side of a
chasm where love wasn't strong enough to bridge the distance.

Somewhere in her heart, Lindsay had granted victory to
the idea that there would be no future for her and Sophie once
the baby was born. On a conscious level, Lindsay didn't have the
courage—or the conviction—to make a clean break. So without
bothering to discuss it with the rest of her, her subconscious had
decided to take steps to drive her away before she had to play out the
depressing, long-drawn-out decline and fall of their relationship.

Rory had been the perfect diversion from the straight and
narrow. Rory made her laugh. She made her feel accomplished
and talented again. She even made Lindsay feel sexy, which
had been balm to a soul that felt it was taking second place to a
syringe full of sperm in the attraction stakes.

Any other time, Lindsay would have been satisfied with
those fillips to the ego. But this time she had wanted to walk
out on the high wire and to hell with a safety net.

Well, she was paying the price now. Her eyes were on the
sea, but her vision was of Rory. She sailed on automatic pilot,
her mind constantly replaying the past few days and inventing
alternate futures she knew could never happen.

For the irony was that now she understood the mechanism
behind her love for Rory, she could no longer play the game out
as Blind Man's Bluff. It was like a magic trick; once you knew
how it worked, it couldn't fool you any longer. Knowing what
Machiavellian tricks her mind had been conjuring, she couldn't
pretend fate had taken things out of her hands and left her its
helpless victim.

She had to go back to Sophie and do her best to make it
work. She'd let herself love Rory, and it was going to hurt like

hell to keep that as her dirty little secret. But keep it secret she must. Rory hadn't asked for love and didn't want it. Admitting to it would hurt everyone.

But mostly, it would hurt Sophie, who had done least to deserve it. "Time to grow up," Lindsay growled, checking the compass one more time and correcting her course accordingly.

Sophie stretched her legs out on the window seat and leaned against the wall. She wondered where Lindsay was and what she was doing now. They'd spoken briefly the previous evening, when Lindsay had told her of the failed attempt to rescue Jack. She almost wished Lindsay hadn't made the call, for anxiety had kept Sophie awake most of the night.

Partly, she was anxious for Lindsay, afraid that her lover would blunder into some disaster that would keep her from home for an unimaginable time. But, mostly, she was anxious for them both. The worst of the phone call was not what they had said, but what they had been unable to say.

Sophie was under no illusion about how hard she was driving Lindsay. If she had felt any choice in the matter, she would have backed off. But no one who had not felt the inexorable demand for a baby could begin to understand its overwhelming hunger. It informed every minute of her waking life. It was like a constant, discordant background music to every action and thought. It was implacable and inescapable. It had hit her like a tidal wave rising out of a calm ocean, and it had battered her ever since.

It had cast her uncommon decency and fairness to the winds. Sophie had lost herself to this imperative that had turned her into a baby factory. She didn't like it. In fact, mostly she hated this invasion. But it was undeniable. The only thing that would calm the turbulence was a baby. All she could do until then was cling to the wreckage and pray she would survive.

The big question in Sophie's mind was whether Lindsay would find a lifeboat and set sail without her.

19

The sun was still shining as they went about, ready for the approach into the harbour at Helsinki. The weather had meant near perfect sailing for the past three days, and the atmosphere on board had been surprisingly light and playful. Andy seemed to have relaxed once they had cleared Kronstadt and Lindsay made the most of the rare opportunity to share quality time with her father.

She sat in the bows, legs dangling over the side, enjoying the cooling spray that tickled her skin. "Lindsay, can you put a couple of reefs in the mainsail?" Andy shouted from the cockpit.

Lindsay scrambled to her feet and made for the mast, noting that Tam was putting his weight into the winch that furled the big genoa sail. It was nearly over. In a matter of minutes, they'd be tying up at the quay and the proper journalistic work would begin. Rory had called from Helsinki to say she had already negotiated a deal with the *Standard* for the full story of Jack's rescue and his reunion with his mother, while Lindsay had written the copy, leaving out her and Rory's part in the drama. All they had to do now was take some photographs with the digital camera, garner some quotes from Bernie, Jack and Tam and insert them into the story. They could transmit the whole package from Helsinki and it would be in the papers within hours of them returning to Scottish soil.

Lindsay leaned against the mast and put a hand up to shield her eyes from the late afternoon sun. They were still too far from the quay to distinguish any individual, but she felt sure Rory and Bernie would be there waiting. Tam had called Bernie at her hotel in Helsinki an hour earlier, warning her of their approach. Then he'd phoned the airport to confirm they were all on the next day's flight to Amsterdam and then onwards to Glasgow. It was going to be some celebration, Lindsay thought. And then home to Sophie. Which would be a different kind of celebration. It didn't make a lot of sense to her, but in spite of all that had happened with Rory, a large part of her was still looking forward to getting home, still eager to be reunited with Sophie.

At her father's instruction, she lowered the mainsail completely, feeling the throb of the engine through the fibreglass hull. The harbour loomed ever closer, till at last Lindsay could make out two figures standing on the quayside. "Jack," she called excitedly. "I can see your mum. Can you see her?" She pulled the small digital camera out of the pocket of her shorts and took a few shots of Tam holding Jack up so he could see Bernie. The look of sheer delight on the small boy's face was a reward in itself for the anxieties of the past week. His grin split his face from ear to ear, and he was waving both arms in a salute.

They'd barely come alongside when Tam plonked Jack ashore. Mother and son sprinted towards each other, Lindsay's camera bearing witness to every stride. Tears streamed down Bernie's face as she gathered her son into her arms and crushed him to her breast. Lindsay couldn't hear their words, but that was as it should be. Some things were just too personal.

She looked up and caught Rory's eye. The electricity between them made her feel suddenly weak at the knees. To hell with good resolutions. They could wait for tomorrow.

The "fasten seat belts" sign illuminated above their heads as the plane began its approach to Glasgow Airport. Lindsay glanced across the aisle to the line of three seats where Jack sat sandwiched between Tam and Bernie. Tam was glowing with delight and pride, but Bernie was more subdued. Lindsay couldn't quite figure her out. The woman should be overjoyed to be reunited with her son. But there was something off key in her response, just as there had been at their first encounter.

Lindsay couldn't exactly put her finger on what was bothering her, and she hadn't had the chance to discuss it with Rory, since Andy had pointedly sat between the pair of them on the flight. But it was as if behind Bernie's delight there was a lurking and continuous edge of fear. Maybe she was simply anxious that Bruno Cavadino would react badly to being thwarted. Whatever it was, it was eating her up from within. She must have lost a stone in weight since they'd first met, Lindsay thought. Her clothes were hanging loose on her, and her face had gone from pleasantly full to gaunt.

Oh well, there was nothing she could do about it, she told herself. Her involvement was over now. She and Rory were the visiting firefighters who parachuted in, did what they had to do and walked away, leaving people to get on with their lives. She didn't imagine they'd be seeing Tam and Bernie again after the follow-up stories to the rescue. The time they'd spent together had been intense and had produced a false sense of intimacy. But in her experience, once the dust had settled, the subjects of such intense scrutiny usually withdrew sharply afterwards, almost embarrassed by the extent to which they'd let strangers into their lives. It was the nature of the game, and it didn't really bother her. She understood the difference between real closeness and its simulacrum.

To Lindsay's surprise, Sophie was waiting for them at the airport. She tried to hide the awkwardness she felt introducing her to Rory, camouflaging it behind their farewells to the Gourlays, who were heading for the taxi rank. Tam engulfed her in a hug. "I'll never be able to thank you enough," he said.

"What you've done for us, it's nothing short of a miracle. Any stories I come across, they're yours."

Bernie's farewell was more formal. She hugged Jack to her and extended a hand to Lindsay, then Rory. "I appreciate what you did. It took real guts. Thank you."

Then they were gone. "I better go and get myself a taxi too," Rory said.

"Don't be silly," Sophie said. "Lindsay told me you live near us. I'll drop you off."

Lindsay realised she'd been right to think that what had seemed so simple and straightforward in St Petersburg was fraught with discomfort and danger here in Glasgow. It wasn't that she feared Rory would say or do anything that would give their secret away. It was more that having the pair of them in such close proximity made her feel confused, and confused wasn't ever the best way to steer a sensible course. "You'll stay with us tonight, Dad?" she asked as they loaded their bags into Sophie's car.

"Of course he will," Sophie said. "You're not thinking about driving home tonight, Andy. I won't hear of it. There's a leg of lamb roasting in the oven, you'll have dinner and a good night's sleep before you even think about getting behind the wheel of your Land Rover."

Andy grinned. "You'll get no argument from me on that score. Lindsay, you get in the front with Sophie, I'll be fine here in the back with Rory."

He really does know, Lindsay thought. And not because of anything he'd witnessed between them. He knew simply because he knew his daughter too well for her own good. And she minded. Not because he would ever say anything to Sophie; he was far too fond of the woman he regarded as his daughter-in-law ever to hurt her like that. But because she valued his good opinion, and knew that he couldn't understand what had impelled her into behaviour he would only ever interpret as disloyal and disreputable. Nothing, she reminded herself, ever happened in a vacuum.

They dropped Rory off at her flat and headed home. It was, Lindsay thought afterwards, one of those rare, apparently perfect evenings. The food was delicious. Sophie was relaxed and mellow, Andy was in fine form, full of tall tales and tittle-tattle about the inhabitants of Invercross. Lindsay herself was simply happy to be home, her first major story under her belt and the sense that, for the first time since she'd come back to Scotland, the prospects looked bright.

Shortly after ten, Andy yawned and stretched. "Well, I'm away to my bed. It's been a long day. Good night, girls."

He left them in the flickering light of the candles that gleamed against the rich wood of the dining table. The wavering flames cast a flattering glow on Sophie's skin, emphasizing the brightness of her eyes and the sparkle of the silver strands that shot through her curls. "You look particularly beautiful tonight," Lindsay said, surprised at the sudden flare of desire she felt for her lover.

Sophie smiled. "And it doesn't occur to you to wonder why that might be?"

"If I said the candlelight is flattering, that would spoil the moment," Lindsay teased. "I suppose it's because I haven't seen you for the best part of a week."

Sophie shook her head. "Try again."

Lindsay struggled. There was nothing obvious; no new hairstyle, no tinted eyelashes, no sunbed tan. "A clue?"

"What makes women bloom?"

Lindsay's stomach flipped and settled with the dead weight of a stone. "It worked?" she said, feeling the ground beneath her feet plummeting away from her.

"It worked. I'm pregnant."

Lindsay was waiting outside Café Virginia when it opened the next morning. After her father had left, the house had felt too claustrophobic to contain her. She'd gone for a short run, her ankle still too fragile for anything sufficiently cathartic. Then she'd showered and taken the bus into town, reluctant to meet Rory outside a work context.

She needn't have worried. By half past eleven, there was still no sign of her business partner. Lindsay felt faintly disconsolate. Her story on the rescue of Jack Gourlay had made the splash and spread of the *Standard* and she wanted to share her moment of glory. She also wanted to lay her head on the table and weep because Sophie's news had left her in the grip of a profound panic that threatened to engulf her. She couldn't deny that a small part of her rejoiced for Sophie's triumphant delight, but mostly she was scared of what this would mean.

It was so early. So much could still go wrong. Sophie could easily miscarry. There could be a problem with the foetus. Then there were all the things that could turn nasty during pregnancy. Sophie might be blooming now, but there was no guarantee that would last. And then, if she somehow made it to term, birth was still such a bloody, dangerous business. Lindsay didn't even want to look at what lay beyond birth. How could she be a parent when she couldn't even organise her own life in a sane and sensible fashion? What would she do if Sophie stopped loving her?

None of it bore thinking about.

So Sandra Singh's arrival felt like a small gift from the gods. Sandra plonked herself down opposite Lindsay and wrestled her cigarettes out of her bag. "Hiya," she said. "I see Splash Gordon's back with a vengeance," she added, prodding the pile of newspapers on the table. "Nice one."

"It's always encouraging to get a good show," Lindsay admitted. "Especially when it involved taking as many chances as this one did. Though we did have a lot of fun in between the scary bits."

Sandra raised her eyebrows. "So I hear. Rory and I went out clubbing last night. She told me all about it."

"Ah," said Lindsay.

"Don't worry, she's not a blabbermouth. But we're best pals, we tell each other everything. And it stops there. Your secret's safe with me." She shook her head as her coffee arrived. "My, but you like to live dangerously."

"Sometimes you just have to get on the roller-coaster," Lindsay said. "Life's hardly worth living if you don't take the odd risk."

Sandra spooned sugar into her coffee and stirred it. "Maybe. But I can't help thinking it might have been better all round if you hadn't got on this particular fairground ride. I don't think it's passed its health and safety inspection. And I hate to see anybody get hurt needlessly."

Uh oh, Lindsay thought. *The gypsy warning from the best friend. Break her heart, I'll break your legs.* "I hear what you're saying, and I think your concern is commendable. But there's no reason why anybody should get hurt, Sandra."

"That's easier said than done. There's more to Rory than meets the eye, you know."

Lindsay's smile was entirely spontaneous and it lit her eyes. "I think I'd worked that one out for myself. Sandra, trust me. I'm not going to break her heart."

Sandra gave her an odd look. But before she could say more, Rory herself appeared, looking hangdog and hungover. "What the fuck was I drinking last night?" she groaned as she eased herself into the booth.

"You ended up on tequila slammers with wee Ian Harvey," Sandra said. "That was after five gin and tonics, two Zombies, several bottles of that disgusting lemon alcopop and a rum and Coke."

Rory groaned. "I wish you hadn't told me that. Now I know it's going to get worse before it gets better."

Annie dumped a cappuccino in front of her and shook her head in disgust. "You need a Bloody Mary," she said.

Rory shuddered. "No, don't. Remember we've got a Human Rights Act now."

"Look, Lindsay got the splash and spread," Sandra said, waving the paper in front of her.

Rory managed a wan smile. "That should put you back on the map, babe. Me, I wouldn't have touched the story, but you were right to go with your instincts."

Sandra finished her coffee and her cigarette. "I'm out of here," she announced. "I've got to meet some guy at the modern art gallery. Apparently he makes sculptures out of sex toys. Which probably means he'll win the Turner Prize next year."

They watched her leave in silence. Then Rory looked blearily at Lindsay. "You're awful quiet for a woman who should be celebrating her return to the big league. Is that out of respect for my hangover? Or is there something I should know about?"

"There is something. But it's not what you think," Lindsay added hastily, seeing the hurt spring up in Rory's eyes. "This is not about us." She ran a hand through her hair. "Sophie's pregnant."

Rory's eyebrows arched. "Is she sure?"

"She's a fucking obstetrician, Rory. Of course she's sure," Lindsay snapped.

"Okay, okay, don't take it out on me." She reached across the table and covered Lindsay's clenched fist with her hand. "How are you feeling about it?"

Lindsay sighed. "I don't know. Scared, mostly. It's like everything in my life is going to change, and I have no idea how. I feel like I've got no choices, no control over what happens next. And I've just got to go with it."

"Sounds about right to me. Because you're not about to leave her, are you?"

"No, I'm not. I know you're the last person I should be saying this to, but I love her. I can't face the thought of losing her."

Rory shook her head. "Who else would understand that better than me? Of course you're scared. Anybody in your shoes would be. She's sprung this on you, backed you into a corner and given you no choice about something that is totally life changing.

But you've got nine months to get your head round the idea. And for what it's worth, I think you'll make a great parent."

"Thanks. Look, can we talk about this another time? I just wanted you to know, but I think I'm still in a state of shock."

"Sure." Rory rubbed her eyes then yawned. "I'm supposed to be meeting Giles for lunch. Do you think I'll live that long?"

Lindsay grinned. "Probably. I'm going to stay here and plough through the local papers. And maybe a punter will bring me a wee titbit of a story, given that we've been away for the best part of a week and there must be something somebody's dying to tell us."

Rory stretched and yawned again. "Oh God, I'd better go." She slid out of the seat and turned to go.

"You really shouldn't have got so drunk," Lindsay said, amusement in her voice.

Rory glanced over her shoulder. "You shouldn't have made me miss you." She poked her furred tongue out at Lindsay. "Only joking. But it was worth it for the look on your face."

Only joking? Lindsay thought. She fervently hoped so. Because the only way she was going to be able to keep her own divided emotions under control was by convincing herself that Rory did not, would not, could not feel the same turbulent surge of emotion and desire that had her in its grip. Believing that, Lindsay could stick to the conviction that revelation would only lead her to rejection. Keep it light, that was the way to deal with it.

How hard could that be?

Patrick Coughlan stared at the newspaper spread across his desk. He'd been relieved when Michael had called him the previous evening to report that Bernadette had turned up at Glasgow Airport with the boy and her husband and that they'd gone straight home. The couple of days she'd been out of his reach had made him edgy and tense, something which both his staff and his perpetually embittered wife Mary could attest to. Knowing she was back where he could put his hand on her whenever he wanted to was satisfying.

But he'd been horrified by Michael's call suggesting he get hold of that morning's edition of the *Scottish Daily Standard*. He'd sent one of his counter girls straight down to the big newsagent's in town to pick up a copy. And there she was, plastered all over the paper again, complete with the dramatic story of her husband's rescue of the boy from a Russian park. The man clearly had more balls than brains, Patrick thought. He supposed he should be grateful to Tam Gourlay for doing his work for him, because there was no denying that any threat to the boy was what kept Bernadette firmly in line.

But Patrick was far from happy. He had a sneaking suspicion that Bernadette was trying to outflank him. Perhaps she thought that if she kept herself in the public eye, it would make him back off.

She couldn't be more wrong, he decided grimly. If she wanted to play this game out in the full glare of the media, so be it. He'd give them something to write about. Something she couldn't argue with. Something that would surely make her hand over what was rightfully his. Something very special indeed.

Rory groaned. "It's not nice to mock the afflicted, Giles," she complained, warily sipping the glass of brandy he'd insisted she drink.

"I'm not mocking, Rory," Giles said. "I'm telling you the truth. Madonna and Guy are absolutely not buying a house in Drymen."

"Oh well, you lose some and you lose some." But even through her bleariness, Rory could tell there was more that Giles wasn't telling her. There was a twinkle in his eye that suggested there was more to come. "What?" she said. "You're not telling me the whole story here."

Giles nodded. "Well spotted. Your tip did check out, in the sense that I managed to find three top-notch estate agents who finally admitted that yes, they'd been showing properties to Madge. So I got on to her people, and they were adamant that I was mistaken. So I gave them a list of dates when my contacts said that Madonna had been in Glasgow looking at Scottish estates. And her PA came back with a list of other places where she'd definitely been on those dates."

Rory had perked up at the sniff of a mystery. "How very curious," she said.

"While you were in Russia, I made some other calls and I found an estate agent in Perth who had been approached by someone purporting to be representing Madonna. They'd made arrangements to view an estate near Gleneagles. So I turned up with a pic man and we fronted up the alleged Madonna and her PA, who had, incidentally, stayed the previous night in a suite at Gleneagles at the estate agency's expense." He paused for effect.

Rory leaned forward. "And? Come on, the suspense is killing me."

Giles grinned. "'Madonna' turned out to be an unemployed actress from Edinburgh. She and her mate had hit on this scheme for getting freebies from estate agents. They've been swagging nights in luxury hotels, free meals, limos, the lot, from these estate agents desperate to flog their prestige properties to a celeb client. A lovely little con, really."

Rory burst out laughing. "Gotta love it," she said. "So what happens now?"

"We're running the story across six and seven tomorrow."

"And what about the women? Are the agents going to have them prosecuted for fraud?"

Giles shrugged. "I suspect the estate agencies will let it lie. It makes them look too silly if they go to the cops. So, although it didn't quite stand up, we ended up with something even better."

"You know, that story is the best hangover cure I've come across in ages." She raised her glass. "You made my day, Giles."

"All part of the service. Now, tell me all about Russia."

20

Lindsay's prediction had come true. Just after the lunchtime rush, a middle-aged man with cropped hair and the smartest leather jacket she'd seen in a long time eased into the booth opposite her. "Are you Rory McLaren?" he asked.

"I'm her business partner, Lindsay Gordon. Anything you were going to tell Rory, you can tell me."

He looked slightly dubious. "I don't know. The friend who told me I could trust Rory, he didn't say anything about you."

Lindsay gave him her most reassuring smile. "That's probably because we've not been working together very long. Look, I understand your reluctance, and if you want to come back another time when Rory's here, I'm not going to be offended. But you're here now. You might as well do what you came for."

"I need to be sure you'll keep me out of this," he said. "It could cost me my job if it comes back on me."

Sensing a thaw, Lindsay nodded. "You don't have to worry about that. I've been keeping confidential sources under wraps for years." She pulled a self-mocking face. "It's got so my girlfriend complains I won't even tell her where I get my gossip from."

Forty minutes later, Lindsay was in possession of the bare bones of a story that she thought could be dynamite. Her source was a senior house officer at a city hospital, and he was concerned because surgical equipment designated for single use only was being employed several times. "It's not hygienic, and with some pieces of equipment, it's just not safe," he'd told her. "We've already had a couple of near-tragedies on the operating table, and it's only a matter of time before somebody dies." He'd given her several leads to follow up, and she was looking forward to bottoming the story.

By the time she'd finished writing up her notes of the interview, it was too late to start work on the investigation. Rory still wasn't back from lunch, and Lindsay guessed she might have taken her hangover home to bed. She might as well take an early cut herself. On the way home, she stopped to buy a huge bouquet of designer flowers for Sophie, secure in the knowledge that the *Standard*'s coverage of the kid-snatch story would mean she could pay for it out of her own pocket.

Although she was home before five, Sophie was there before her, feet up in the living room, a pile of papers on her lap. "Good to see you're taking care of yourself," Lindsay said, presenting the flowers with a flourish.

"They're beautiful," Sophie exclaimed, pulling Lindsay down so she could kiss her. "Thank you. I decided to bring some work home with me because I was feeling a bit sick. Of course, it passed as soon as I got back here, so now I feel like a fraud."

"You're pregnant, you've got to look after yourself," Lindsay said gruffly, leaving the room to put the flowers in water. When she came back, Sophie had put her work to one side.

"How was your day?" she asked.

"Did you see the *Standard*?" Lindsay asked, placing the vase on the floor in front of the fireplace.

Sophie's hand shot up to cover her mouth in an expression of horror. "Oh, Lindsay, I'm sorry. It completely slipped my mind."

Trying not to show her disappointment, Lindsay shrugged. "No big deal. It's not like you've never seen me get a splash and spread before. Besides, it wouldn't do your street cred any good in the university to be seen reading the tabloid press."

"I'm really sorry, love. I know it was important to you, I should have remembered."

Lindsay perched on the arm of the sofa. "Well, at least my business partner noticed. And was impressed."

"I'm glad. She seems like a nice kid, Rory."

"Hardly a kid, Sophie. She's been in the game a good few years; she's running a freelance business that's successful enough for her to be able to give me a job."

"I guess it's a sign of old age, when the journalists start to look like children," Sophie said, trying to make light of it.

"I told you we were too old for this parenthood business," Lindsay said, not entirely joking.

"You underestimate yourself, Lindsay. And besides, a child will keep us young."

Lindsay winced. "I'm not sure I want to be young. Rory came in this morning with the hangover from hell. You should have seen her. I swear to God her face was green, and the whites of her eyes were somewhere between pink and yellow. She'd been out clubbing with her pal Sandra till all hours. It sounds like they drank a distillery between them. I think I do old better."

"Well, that's hardly a mature attitude to business, turning up in a state like that. It's not exactly going to inspire confidence in the sources or the customers."

"Come on, you know how drinking still goes with the territory here in Scotland. Rory's perfectly capable of doing what she needs to do, regardless of how much she's had to drink or how little sleep she's had." Even as she spoke, Lindsay realised how protective she sounded. *Careful*, she warned herself.

"I didn't realise that working with Rory meant you had to become her staunch defender too," Sophie said, a spike of malice in her voice.

"Feeling a bit hormonal, are we?" Lindsay flashed back at her.

"Don't turn it back on me, Lindsay. This is your reaction we're talking about."

"Well, you don't even know her, and here you are, sitting in judgement on her. You've no idea what she's like."

Sophie cocked her head on one side. "So what is she like?"

"She's very smart, she's good company, she's very funny and she's totally professional. Believe me, we were in a couple of tight spots in Russia, and she was absolutely on the ball. I can't think of anyone I'd rather have had in my corner."

"So I gathered from your conversation over dinner last night. Rory this, Rory that, Rory the next thing. You sounded like a teenager with a crush."

Lindsay stood up abruptly and walked across the room to the window. "Now you're talking rubbish. Come on, Soph, we'd just come back from a really dangerous job, running on adrenaline. Of course I had to decompress, talk it out of my system."

Sophie raised her eyebrows a fraction. "And that's all it was?"

"I'm not even going to dignify that with a reply," Lindsay said, forcing outrage into her voice. She didn't quite know how it had happened, but she was out there on the thinnest of ice, hearing it creak under her words. She'd never believed in lying to Sophie and she didn't want to start now.

"It's not like you to be lost for words."

"Well, maybe that's a sign I'm finally acquiring the maturity I'm going to need if I'm going to be a parent."

"If?"

Lindsay sighed. "Okay, when."

"You don't sound very certain."

"I'm certain."

"You sure Rory would approve of her new employee embarking on parenthood?"

"This has got nothing to do with Rory. You know I love you. I wouldn't be here if I didn't."

"Suddenly we're on to love? Where did that come from, Lindsay? Why are you hiding behind declarations of love? More to the point, what are you hiding?"

Lindsay shook her head in frustration. "I can't talk to you when you're in this kind of mood. I'm going to cook the dinner."

"Never mind dinner." Now Sophie was on her feet, moving to cut off Lindsay's route to the door. They faced each other, a couple of feet apart. Sophie tried to keep the fear that had burned in her for days out of her voice. "We need to talk about this. I know when you're hiding stuff from me, Lindsay. Are you sleeping with her?"

Lindsay's eyes widened in shock. She'd never had any problem with avoiding the truth when bullshit was the route to nailing a story. But she had never looked Sophie in the eye and delivered absolute falsehood. "This is stupid," she said, trying to find a way round the question.

"Answer the question, Lindsay. Yes or no. Are you fucking Rory?" Sophie's face was white, her whole body tense as a gun dog on point. She'd forced this moment of truth and she couldn't back away from it now, whatever the cost.

Lindsay closed her eyes momentarily. "I slept with her."

The words hung in the air, vibrating with a terrible life of their own. Sophie gasped, then slapped Lindsay so hard her ears rang. Lindsay recoiled, her hand automatically going to her scarlet cheek. "You bastard," Sophie said in tones of utter contempt. "You absolute bastard. I'm sitting here, going off my head because I don't know if I'm pregnant or not, and you're escaping from your life, shagging some bimbo in St Petersburg."

"Look, that's not how it was," Lindsay said, groping fruitlessly for a response that wasn't a wretched cliché.

"That's exactly how it was." Tears stung Sophie's eyes and she turned away to prevent Lindsay seeing her pain.

"You make it sound like I had it all planned." Lindsay put out a hand to Sophie, who shrugged it off violently.

"Well, didn't you?"

"Of course I didn't. Jesus, Sophie, what do you take me for?"

Sophie turned back, eyes blazing. "I take you for a coward, Lindsay. Hedging your bets. 'If Sophie's pregnant, hey, that's okay, I can just run off into the sunset with Rory.'"

"You're so wrong," Lindsay said desperately. "What happened between me and Rory was not about you."

"No, it was all about your perennial bloody selfishness. You don't like your life? Trade it in for a different model. That's what you've always done."

"That's bullshit."

"Is it? Think back to when we got together. You didn't like the way Cordelia was making you feel so you cheered yourself up by diving into bed with me."

Lindsay stepped back as if she'd been slapped again. "That's not true. You think we'd still be together if you'd been nothing more than a diversion? Come on, Sophie, you know that's not how it was."

Sophie shook her head. "No, Lindsay, I don't know how it was. I thought I did, but that was when I thought I knew you. Only, the person I thought I knew wouldn't have betrayed me the way you have, so I can't trust anything I believed about our relationship now. The fact that you're shagging Rory turns everything on its head. Nothing means what it did before."

Lindsay shook her head, trying to find the words to ease Sophie's hurt. "Nothing fundamental has changed, Sophie. You're still the most important person in my life. Yes, I slept with Rory. I won't pretend it was just a bit of fun because that would insult all of us. But it was in a different dimension to what goes on between you and me. You're the one that I love. I've never doubted that, not for a minute. I'm not about to trade my life in for something else. I couldn't leave you."

Sophie flushed a deep scarlet, anger flooding her face. "How dare you? You stand there and tell me you're sleeping with somebody else and I shouldn't be worried about it because it's in a different dimension? And you're very kindly not going to leave me? Well, that's really big of you. So, what are you planning on doing? Moving Rory in here? Dividing your nights between the two of us?"

Lindsay held her hands up, palms outward in a placatory gesture. "Look, it happened. It's not going to happen again."

"You seriously expect me to believe that? When you're spending more time with her than you are with me?"

Lindsay ran her hands through her hair in a gesture of helplessness. "I made a mistake, okay? I won't be repeating it. We can get over this. It doesn't change the way I feel about you."

"It bloody changes the way I feel about you," Sophie shouted. "You expect me to forgive and forget? I don't think so."

Lindsay hung her head. "I'm sorry."

"Well, you took your time to get the apology in. Too little, too late, Lindsay. We always agreed we would be monogamous. It was basic. It was who we were. You can't break something so fundamental and expect everything to go along like it did before. This is it, Lindsay. It's over."

"You don't mean that."

"I've never meant anything more. Get out. Just get out of my sight, out of this house."

"That isn't the way to deal with this, Sophie. We've got to talk about it. I love you." Lindsay felt the ice break under her feet, felt herself falling, swallowed by the black cold of Sophie's rage.

"No, you don't. You bastard, you only love yourself. Don't you get it? There's nothing to talk about. Not any more. Just get the fuck out. Now!" She reached for a heavy pottery bowl on the nearby table and threw it at Lindsay with all her strength. "Get out!"

Lindsay dodged the missile and backed towards the wall. The dish clattered to the floor and split into smithereens on the polished wooden boards. "Listen to me," she pleaded, on the edge of tears herself now. "I love you."

In reply, Sophie picked up an African soapstone carving. As her arm came back, Lindsay dived for the door. "And don't fucking come back," Sophie screamed. The ornament hit the wall with a sickening thud.

Dazed, Lindsay stumbled for the front door, grabbing the satchel that held her laptop and her wallet. She closed the door behind her then leaned against the solid wood, hot tears spilling down her cheeks. Not for the first time in her life, she thought her heart would break. But this time she had nobody to blame but herself.

21

It was raining, of course. A bleak, dismal rain that sheeted out of a sky gone prematurely grey. After she'd stopped shaking, Lindsay had climbed into her car and stared unseeingly at the distorted world through her windscreen. How could she have blown it so badly? Why couldn't she have dredged up enough journalistic skill to lie for once? Or, at worst, having been honest, why couldn't she have found the words to explain to Sophie what she herself knew—that whatever she felt for Rory, it was irrelevant because it didn't change one iota of her feelings for Sophie?

Instead, she'd provoked the sort of explosion that would leave a permanent crater in her life. Even if she could persuade Sophie to take her back, it would always be there, a hole in the road for unwary feet to stumble into. Not that she had any confidence that she could worm her way back under Sophie's guard. Sophie might be the most generous and warm-hearted person Lindsay had ever known, but when she felt betrayed she was adamantine. She didn't so much bear a grudge as stuff it and wall-mount it in a prominent position. The despair that Lindsay felt then was no self-indulgence; it was realism.

She leaned her head on the steering wheel and moaned softly. The thing she couldn't get her head round was that, in spite of the fact that the pain inside her was as fierce as a physical injury, she didn't actually wish undone what had happened between her and Rory. Was that simply what Sophie had characterized as her perennial selfishness? That she wanted to have her cake and eat it? Lindsay thought not; she really wasn't greedy in that way. She still couldn't escape the notion that the feelings she had for Rory were too important to let them go by her. The paradox was that, equally, they weren't worth losing Sophie over.

She turned the key in the ignition. Sitting in the rain wasn't getting her anywhere. But then, where could she go? She didn't have any close friends in Glasgow any longer. She certainly wasn't going home to her parents, to face the reproach in her father's eyes. And she couldn't really afford to check into a hotel. There was only one real option, but pursuing it would be the most reckless of all her recent risk-taking. If Sophie found out she'd gone straight to Rory, she really would have burned her bridges.

Bernie sat by her son's bed, reading him a chapter of *Harry Potter and the Goblet of Fire*. Nothing measured up to the comfort of having Jack home again. Tam had called to say he was going out for a drink with a client, he'd be home soon after seven. Then they'd all be under one roof again, the way it should be. She didn't blame Bruno for what had happened, not really. He only wanted the best for Jack too. But she couldn't help being grateful for having Jack by her side. Even if that wasn't the safest option. But she'd think about that later. For now, it was enough just to luxuriate in his presence.

The ringing of the phone broke into her calm like a brick through a greenhouse. She jumped up hastily and ran through to the kitchen. "Hello?" she said cautiously.

"You've been leading me a merry dance, Bernadette."

Patrick's voice chilled like walking into a butcher's freezer. "It wasn't my fault," she blurted out.

"So you say. Look, I'm running out of patience. You had no right to behave the way you did to me. I was always generous to you and yours, Bernadette. And now I want what's mine."

"I know you do," she whispered. "I know."

"Tomorrow, then? I'll meet you when you take the boy to school."

"No," she said sharply. "No."

"You're telling me you won't hand over what belongs to me?"

"I can't." The phone slipped from her fingers and fell back into the cradle. She knew that hanging up on Patrick Coughlan might be a disastrous move. But she couldn't take his voice for a second longer.

She couldn't live like this. She had to do something. Slowly, she picked up the phone and dialled Lindsay's mobile number. But before it could connect, she replaced the receiver. She couldn't afford to ask for help this time. She had to figure out an escape route alone.

Rory opened her door, looking ten years younger than she had that morning. "Hey, Splash, come in," she said instinctively. Then she took in Lindsay's appearance. "What's the matter?" She pulled her into a hug without waiting for a reply.

At first, Lindsay said nothing. It was enough just to be held. Almost anyone would have done. But this was Rory, she reminded herself as soft lips nuzzled her neck. She took a deep, shuddering breath and said, "I'm homeless."

Rory leaned back so she could check whether Lindsay was joking. But there was no mistaking the sincerity in the red-rimmed eyes. "You'd better come and sit down and have a drink and tell me all about it." She took Lindsay's hand and led her through to the kitchen.

Lindsay slumped in a chair and said nothing while Rory poured them both a whisky. "Sophie threw me out." She swallowed half her drink in a single, eye-watering gulp.

"Do I need to ask why?"

"She asked me a straight question. I tried to dodge it, but she kept on at me." Lindsay looked up, her face asking forgiveness. "I'm sorry, but I can't do bare-faced lying to people I love."

Rory tried not to let her consternation show. "So you told her we've been sleeping together?"

Lindsay sighed. "I tried to explain how it wasn't about her, but she wasn't exactly in the mood for listening. Look, I'm sorry to land on you like this, but I don't have anywhere else to go. Can I stay here for a couple of nights till I get myself sorted out?"

"Of course you can. Stay as long as you want. No strings. But don't answer the phone, that's all."

"What? You don't want me to put your other women off?" It was a pathetic attempt at humour, but at least she was trying.

"No, moron. I don't want you to wreck your chances of getting it back together with Sophie. If she calls here, I'll just tell her I've not seen you outside work. Of course, if she turns up at the door with a breadknife, you'll have to come to my rescue."

"That would be so beneath her dignity," Lindsay said sadly.

"Well, that's a relief. Look, I'm sorry I got you into this mess. This wasn't part of the master plan."

"Don't be sorry. I'm not. I don't regret one minute of what happened between us. I only wish it hadn't blown up like this."

"Me too. I wouldn't hurt you for the world," Rory said, suddenly very serious.

Lindsay rubbed her hands over her face. "What a fucking mess. I handled it so badly."

"I don't think there's a good way to handle the moment when you tell your lover you've been shagging somebody else," Rory said drily. "Not if monogamy's the deal."

"Maybe not. Maybe your friend Sandra should have issued the gypsy warning before we went to Russia."

Rory frowned in confusion. "What do you mean?"

"Sandra gave me the hard word this morning. You know? 'Don't go breaking her heart.' That one. She should have spoken sooner. Maybe I'd have paid attention if I'd thought you and me getting it together was on the cards."

Rory felt puzzled. It wasn't like Sandra to interfere in her love life. Unless she had figured out that Rory was getting in too deep. Rory couldn't imagine how Sandra had realised something she herself had only acknowledged the night before. "Well, it's too late for that now," she said. "And speaking of late, I'm supposed to meet Sandra for a curry in twenty minutes. Come on, we'll drown our sorrows in vindaloo."

Lindsay shook her head. "I'm not in the mood. Either for curry or for company."

Rory considered for a second. "Okay. I'll give her a bell, tell her I need a rain check. I can see her any time."

"No, don't be daft. I'll be fine. You go out and enjoy yourself. I'm better on my own, honest."

"Are you sure?" Rory really didn't know what to do for the best, but she was inclined to take Lindsay at her word. She hadn't noticed her being backward in making her needs known in their short past, and she didn't see why that should have changed just because her emotions were in turmoil.

"Aye, I'm sure."

"I'll show you where things are, then." Rory gave Lindsay a whirlwind tour of the flat. "My office, use the desk if you want to plug your laptop in, there's a modem connection on the wall. Bathroom, help yourself to smellies. Spare room . . ." She looked a question at Lindsay, who shook her head ruefully. "Thought not. Okay, here's the mistress bedroom. House rule is I sleep on the left." She turned and pulled Lindsay into her arms. "I know it's a fucking mess," she said softly. "But it'll get sorted."

"You sure about that, are you?"

Rory grinned wickedly. "Trust me, I'm not a doctor. Listen, I'm off. I might be late, don't wait up, okay? I'm perfectly capable of waking you up when I need you . . ." She kissed her hard on the mouth, her tongue flickering along the inside of her bottom lip. "Take care, okay?"

Then she was gone. Left to herself, Lindsay mooched back to the kitchen and refilled her whisky glass. It felt strange being on Rory's territory without her, as if she were an intruder. At least Rory hadn't treated her bust-up with Sophie as an opportunity to move in on her. She'd obviously meant what she'd said about this being a friendship with sex as an added extra. *What a pity I can't manage to be that sanguine myself.* Faced with the events of the evening, Lindsay couldn't resist the dark truth that, somehow, she was managing to love two people simultaneously. And it was ripping her up.

She flicked through a couple of magazines but she couldn't settle. She needed to off-load the disaster on to someone else. If there was nobody available in the flesh, she'd have to make do with e-mail to bridge the distance and the time lag between herself in Glasgow and her friend Roz in California.

Lindsay unpacked her laptop and went through to set it up on Rory's desk, as instructed. She had to push a pile of papers to one side to make room, and a glossy brochure slithered to the floor, revealing what looked like a poem written in Rory's familiar hand. Curious, Lindsay glanced at it, not meaning to spy. But the title caught her eye and she couldn't resist.

Russian for Beginners

There is a word missing.
Between the wishy-washy and the helter-skelter, there exists nothing.
Avoid the dizzy plunge of the word that, once spoken,
cannot be ignored,
the four-letter word that shocks
much more than "fuck,"
and what remains?
"Fond" is for maiden aunts and pussy cats,
a faint insult lurking in its shallows.
"Care" is better, but still too burdened with the freight of obligation.
But sometimes,

*"love" is just too big,
too soon,
too terrifying to presume.
So we resort to foreign tongues,
hiding fear behind an unfamiliarity
whose very strangeness makes declaration safer.
Ya tebyeh lublu.*

Lindsay read it through twice, not quite wanting to believe the freight of meaning held captive in those twenty lines. She was surprised on so many levels; that Rory would resort to poetry; that Rory knew even one word of Russian, never mind three; but mostly that it looked as if Rory was being as cagey about her emotions as Lindsay was herself.

So where exactly did that leave them?

The rain was lashing the Clyde coast, making navigation difficult, especially when the destination was no official harbour. But the small motor boat chugged on through the waves that threatened to swamp it, eventually nosing into a small sheltered cove south of Wemyss Bay. The helmsman flashed his leading lights on and off a couple of times and a reply came immediately from the shore in the form of a powerful torch beam that cut a narrow slice in the black shoreline. The boat made for the light on the shore, the engine throttled back as far as it could go and still allow for forward passage. The hull ground on shingle and the helmsman immediately put the twin propellers into neutral.

Above the scratchy beat of waves dragging at pebbles, he shouted to the man in the bows, "That's as near as I can get her. If you jump for it, I'll pass you the stuff."

Patrick Coughlan was out of his element on the water, but he swallowed his unease and clambered over the safety rail then let himself fall into the sea. The sudden arrival of solid ground under his feet made him stagger. He'd expected the drop to be further. He looked back up and saw the helmsman looming above him, a heavy holdall dangling over the gunwale of the boat.

"Hang on a minute," he called. Turning towards the shore, Patrick bellowed, "Kevin, get your arse over here."

The torch beam split the night again, illuminating Patrick, up to his thighs in freezing water. Then he was cast into shadow once more as Kevin moved between the light and the boat. "I'm here, Patrick," he said.

"Grab this bag, will you? And don't get it wet," Patrick instructed, lurching away from the boat towards dry land. He aimed for the torch, losing his feet a couple of times in an ungainly scramble up the pebbled beach. "Jesus," he said as he drew level with Michael. "I hope you've got a towel in the car." He shook Michael's hand.

"Good to see you," Michael said.

"Everything we need is in the bag." They watched Kevin struggle out of the water towards them, the holdall clutched to his chest. "Are we all set?"

Michael nodded. "It won't take me long to put it together. Tomorrow morning, you said?"

"No time like the present. It's time Bernadette realised she can't hold on to what doesn't belong to her."

The trio headed towards the top of the beach, where the hire car was waiting. "What was it she took from ye, Patrick?" Kevin panted.

"You'll know soon enough, son." The geniality in Patrick's voice surprised Michael. Either Patrick was very confident of success, or else he was so focussed on the next step that he wasn't looking at the big picture. Either could lead to carelessness of a kind of which Michael had never suspected Patrick capable.

He hadn't been worried about the operation before. But now he was.

❧❖❧

Rory drained her bottle of beer and signalled to the waiter for another. She raised an eyebrow and Sandra shook her head. "I'm okay for now."

"By the way," Rory said, her drink replenished. "What was all that about this morning? Giving Lindsay the hard word about not breaking my heart?"

Sandra looked baffled. "What?"

"She said you were doing the protective best friend bit. You know: warning her off hurting me."

Sandra laughed so loud the couple at the next table in the Indian restaurant pursed their lips and looked away. "Talk about getting hold of the wrong end of the stick. I was warning her, right enough. But I was warning her about you. Trying to stop *her* from getting serious, getting her heart broken by the queen of the one-night stand."

"Well, thank you, Sandra," Rory said sarcastically. "Just what I needed."

Sandra gave her a long, considering stare. "My God, you've fallen in love."

Rory's glare should have been heat enough to light the cigarette Sandra pulled from her packet. "Your words, not mine."

"Maybe. But that doesn't make them any the less true, does it? Oh, Rory, poor you." Sandra leaned across and patted Rory's hand. "All those women who would have given their right arm for a relationship with you and you couldn't give a damn about any of them. And then, when you do fall, it's right into the middle of the briar patch."

Rory gave Sandra a tired smile. "Something like that. It's all too complicated, Sandra. I don't want to be the reason for her splitting up with Sophie. Because she's not ready to leave her yet, and she'd always blame me, deep down."

"That's quite an insight for somebody that makes a cult out of not doing relationships."

"The spectator always sees more of the game," Rory said.

"So you haven't told her how you feel?"

"Of course I haven't." Rory's distress was obvious to Sandra, even through the tone of irritation. She sighed. "It's chewing me up, all this pretence. I've never felt like this about anybody before, Sandra. I never let myself. But Lindsay slipped under my guard." She closed her eyes. "It's so fucking hard."

"I know," Sandra said. "So what are you going to do about it?"

Rory gave her a steady look. "Keep on lying. What else can I do?"

"You could always try telling her."

"She doesn't need that right now. And frankly, neither do I. Just let me get through this in my own sweet way. Get it out of my system and get back to normal."

"Oh, Rory," Sandra said. "I'm so sorry."

"Not half as sorry as I am." Rory made a self-mocking snort of laughter. "I should be happy, shouldn't I? The woman I love is in my bed, waiting for me to come home and make mad, passionate love to her. And instead I can't think of anything worse."

22

Bernie grabbed the two slices out of the toaster as they popped up and slathered them with butter. She put one in front of Jack and leaned against the counter, munching the other herself, waiting for the kettle to boil for a second cup of tea. Tam tucked into his scrambled egg and mushrooms, chattering away to the boy about their plans for the weekend.

"We could go to the football, if you fancy it," he said. "I can get tickets for the Jags, no bother. What do you say, wee man?"

Jack smiled through a mouthful of toast. "Brilliant," he said. "Can we go swimming on Sunday?"

"We'll see," Bernie said. "Just because you've been to Russia doesn't mean you get spoiled when you come home."

Jack laughed, knowing he would get his own way. He usually did with his mother. Suddenly, his expression changed to one of consternation and he pointed at the window. "Tam, look behind you," he said urgently.

Tam swung round, all senses alert. But there was nothing to be seen. When he turned back to the table, however, his last mushroom had mysteriously disappeared, and Jack's mouth looked suspiciously full. "Wait a minute," he complained.

Jack swallowed hard. "Too late, you missed the mushroom thief."

Tam laughed and leaned over to rumple the boy's hair. "Some places, you'd get your hands cut off for that."

"Are you taking me to school in the car today?" Jack asked, pulling away from Tam's hand.

"You know Tam only takes you when it's raining. And it's not raining this morning. I'm walking you," Bernie told him. "If you don't get some exercise, your legs will wither away and fall off."

"You're making that up," Jack said.

"No, she's quite right, son," Tam confirmed, a serious look on his face. He wiped his plate with his last piece of bread and stuffed it into his mouth. "I need to get on my way. I'll see youse tonight." He jumped up and grabbed his jacket off the back of the chair, leaning down to kiss Jack on the top of his head. He swung Bernie into his arms and planted a smacker on her lips. "Have a good day," he said over his shoulder as he hurried out.

"Are you glad to be home?" Bernie asked Jack as he drank down his milk.

He looked up at her, white moustache stretched into a smile. "You bet," he said. "You can't read what the Russian Pokémon cards say."

It took a moment for Lindsay to realise where she was when she woke. The bed felt wrong, the light was wrong, the background hum of the street outside was definitely wrong. Then memory swam into focus and the previous evening was there in the front of her mind, inescapable. She turned her head to check the other side of the bed. Rory lay sprawled on her stomach, her head turned away from Lindsay, her breathing almost inaudible. It was the only thing that didn't feel wrong, although Lindsay knew it was the one thing that should be incompatible with her desperate desire to see Sophie, to talk to her, to try to get things straight between them.

She hadn't heard Rory come home. Not surprisingly, the emotional drama of the previous evening had left her drained, and the several whiskies she'd worked her way through in the course of the evening had set the seal on a deep sleep. Secretly, she was glad Rory had let her slumber on. It would have been too easy to take the wrong sort of comfort there. It wasn't what had happened between Lindsay and Sophie that would have made it wrong; it was her new understanding of what Rory truly felt for her.

Lindsay slipped out of bed, trying not to disturb Rory. She scooped up her clothes and headed for the bathroom. Twenty minutes later, she was showered and dressed. Her first instinct was to head for home, to force Sophie to talk to her. It was still early enough to catch her before she left for the university. But that wouldn't get Lindsay anywhere. If she was going to stand any chance of persuading her lover that they still had a future, she'd have to wait for the first flare of Sophie's anger to subside. Better to find something more constructive to do with her time.

She left a note for Rory in the kitchen: Woke early. I've gone into the Standard office—I promised Bernie and Tam a set of photographs, I thought I'd go and sort it out with the picture desk. See you in Cafe Y. later. love, L. There was a lot more she wanted to say, but a scribbled note wasn't the appropriate medium. Maybe later, on the nearest they had to neutral territory, in the café.

The *Standard* office was still quiet when she walked on to the newsroom floor. Twenty to nine in the morning, and only the assistant news editor and a few reporters were at their desks. A couple were reading the opposition, and a third had a phone to his ear, doing the police station calls. Lindsay recognised him from her own days as a news hack and sketched a wave as she crossed to the picture desk. "Are you Gerry?" she asked the chubby, balding man flicking through the morning papers.

He looked up, appraised her as low value and returned to the *Herald*. "Aye, I'm Gerry," he said. "Who's asking?"

"We've spoken on the phone. I'm Lindsay Gordon," she said. "The Russian kid-snatch?"

Now she had his attention. "Oh aye. Nice pix. What can I do for you, Lindsay?"

"I wanted a set of the snaps, for the punters."

He nodded. "No problem. Can you hang on a wee bit till some of the team crawls in? Then I'll sort you out."

Lindsay nodded. "That's fine. I'll find a quiet corner." She moved over to the reporters' area and sat down at a vacant desk, grabbing a couple of papers as she went. She had just opened the *Guardian* when the phones all round started ringing. Five or six of them, all at once. Even after the duty staff picked up, there were still a couple trilling out, including the one in front of her. Lindsay picked it up. She could always take a message.

The breathless voice on the end of the phone was like a time machine. Suddenly she was back at the sharp end, a young reporter who still believed that the great stories would arrive down a crackly phone line, delivered with almost incoherent urgency. She'd learned differently since then, but this time she was listening to the exception that proved the rule. "Is that a reporter I'm speaking to?" the voice said, the words tumbling over each other in its eagerness. An elderly man, by the sounds of it.

"I'm a reporter, yes," she said calmly, automatically reaching for the pile of scrap paper on the desk and raking in her bag for a pen.

"There's been an explosion. A car bomb, by the looks of it. You should see it, it's hellish. Flames shooting up, black smoke, the whole shebang."

Startled into alertness, Lindsay said, "Where are you speaking from?"

"My house."

"Where's that?"

"Kinghorn Drive. North Kelvinside."

Cold fear gripped Lindsay. It couldn't be. It had to be a coincidence. "And you say a car blew up in the street?"

"That's right, hen. I was sitting at the window, eating my All Bran. Fellow that lives down the street on the other side, I saw him come out the door. Got intae his Jag and boom! The whole lot went up."

"I'll need to take your name and address," she said, on automatic pilot now. She scribbled down the details then got off the phone. They'd need to speak to him later for eyewitness quotes, but that would keep. She jumped to her feet and hurried towards the newsdesk, suddenly aware that everyone else was doing the same thing.

Everybody was speaking at once. "Car bomb . . . West End . . . cops aren't confirming . . . ambulance on the way . . . Where's Kinghorn Drive?"

Lindsay cut through the noise. "Kinghorn Drive is where Bernie and Tam Gourlay live—the Russian kid-snatch family."

Keith, the assistant news editor turned to her, his face blank. "You saying this is something to do with your story?"

"I don't know. It's just a funny coincidence, that's all. My caller said the car was a Jag. And Tam Gourlay drives a Jag."

Keith fiddled with his stringy ponytail. "Are you free to do a shift for us? Only, I think you should go out with the first car, take a pic man."

"I think so too," Lindsay said grimly.

Kinghorn Drive was like a war zone. A pall of greasy black smoke hung in the still, damp air, trapped by the high canyons of the sandstone tenements. Already, police crime-scene tape cordoned off the epicentre of the blast, keeping back the ghoulish spectators drawn to disaster like herring gulls to landfill. Lindsay let the photographer lead the way, pushing through the crowd until they could get no closer. She stared uncomprehendingly down the street where, about fifty yards away, a blackened chassis was all that remained of what she feared was Tam Gourlay's Jaguar. The cars that had been parked on either side were twisted

and crumpled from the impact, their window glass shattered
in sparkling shards across the road. Sniffer dogs strained at the
leash as their handlers systematically swept the area. A distorted
voice through a loud-hailer was asking people to evacuate the
buildings without panic. Anxious residents were still emerging
in ones and twos, escorted away from their homes by solicitous
police officers.

It was impossible to take in. Lindsay knew she should be
going through the motions, finding eyewitnesses and accumulat-
ing copy. But all she could do was stand and stare. As she watched,
an ambulance threaded its way down from the far end of the street
and stopped yards short of the bombed-out car. She watched as
the door of Tam and Bernie's flat opened and two policemen
emerged, almost carrying Bernie between them. A woman officer
followed, Jack a cowering bundle against her chest.

Professional responsibilities forgotten, Lindsay gave in to
purely human instincts. She ducked under the tape and sidestepped the flak-jacketed cop who tried to stop her. Picking
up speed, she made it to Bernie's side just as they reached the
ambulance. "Bernie," Lindsay gasped. There was no response.

A police officer tried to move her to one side as they loaded
Bernie in through the rear doors. "I'm a friend of the family,"
Lindsay insisted.

As if to back her up, Jack raised his head and caught sight of
her. He held his arms out towards her and screamed, "Where's
Tam? I want Tam." He wriggled free of the policewoman and
threw himself at Lindsay, who automatically folded him into
her arms and stroked his hair.

The ambulance attendant stood impatiently by the doors,
waiting to close them. "Look, either get in or move away. This
lady's in deep shock, she needs to see a doctor."

Lindsay had no intention of hanging around to argue with
the police. She struggled up the steps of the ambulance, made
awkward by her burden, and collapsed on the seat opposite
Bernie. "Bernie," she said softly. "Bernie, I'm so sorry."

This time, there was a reaction. Bernie looked up and mutely held her arms out to her son. He dived on to her lap and buried his face in her shoulder. The ambulance moved off, blue light flashing, the occasional two-tone blurt of the siren clearing their path. Bernie kissed Jack's hair, then stared bitterly at Lindsay.

"I as good as killed him," she said, her voice a strained whisper. "The day I let him into my life, I as good as killed him."

Lindsay shook her head. "You mustn't think that. Why should it be anything to do with you and Jack?"

Bernie looked at her as if she was stupid as well as culpable. "Poor, poor Tam. Never had an idea what he was getting into."

"You mustn't blame yourself. Tam loved you; he wanted to be with you and Jack. That was all he cared about." Lindsay didn't know what was going on here, only that she needed to keep Bernie talking.

Bernie shook her head in wonder. "I thought it was safe. But I was wrong, God help me, I was wrong. I told him, you stood there and listened to me telling him. But the pair of you got your teeth into it, and that was that. I should have stopped it before it started. I should have thrown you out my house."

"Are you seriously saying you think Bruno made this happen?" Lindsay didn't want to sound like a cop or a hack, but she couldn't ignore the obvious implication.

"I'm seriously saying if you and Tam had let things be, he'd be alive now." Her voice wobbled, but still the tears didn't come. Bernie rocked to and fro, clutching her whimpering son to her, her eyes like stones.

Lindsay told herself it was shock and hysteria talking. The notion that an Italian diplomat would even consider a car bomb a reasonable weapon in a childcare dispute was not only bizarre, it was ludicrous. There had to be another explanation. But what could it be?

Before she could probe further, the ambulance shuddered to a halt and the doors swung open. "Go home, Lindsay," Bernie said roughly. "Stay away from things you don't understand." She swung round and carefully clambered out of the ambulance, leaving Lindsay to stand and stare after her.

Among the cars, taxis and ambulances that drove in and out of the Western Infirmary, the Vauxhall Vectra parked in the disabled bay didn't warrant a second glance. Michael Conroy sat in the driver's seat, cleaning his nails with his penknife. Kevin leaned against the passenger door, frowning in concentration as he watched people come and go through the Accident and Emergency doors.

A taxi pulled up and Patrick Coughlan emerged, glancing quickly around before he climbed into the rear seat of the Vectra. "Neatly done, boys. At last."

"I still don't see why," Michael said.

"That's why I'm where I am and you are where you are, Michael," Patrick said, the geniality of his tone doing nothing to hide the steel beneath. "Now, boys, I want you to make sure that where the bitch and the boy go, you go too. See that you let me know what's happening."

Without further ado, Patrick got out of the car and walked off towards the street. As soon as he was a safe distance away, Michael shifted in his seat and scowled. "It's not right, this. It's too personal. And personal leaves traces."

"I don't hear you saying that to your man," Kevin said.

Michael jabbed his knife blade into the newspaper folded on the dashboard. "I want to go home in one piece."

Lindsay walked out of the A&E entrance and leaned against the wall. Since she couldn't use her mobile inside, she'd already dictated her copy from a pay phone in the waiting area, which had turned out to be a bad idea. She took out her mobile and called the newsdesk of the *Standard* to check there were no queries on what she'd already sent. "Hi, Keith. It's Lindsay."

"You still at the hospital?" he demanded.

"They threw me out. One of the cops overheard me filing copy on the phone and that was that. They had me out the door so fast I left skidmarks."

"Bastards. At least you got some good quotes off the grieving widow. Nice one, Lindsay. So what's the real story on Tam Gourlay? You've just spent three days on a boat with him, you must have got some sort of idea what the big secret was."

Lindsay frowned. "As far as I know, there is no story. He was a second-hand car dealer, that's all. A pretty straight one, by all accounts."

"No such thing," came the cynical response. "There must have been a sideline."

"Not that I know about."

"Well, what about the wife?"

"What about her?"

"She's Irish, isn't she? Car bombs, that's very IRA."

Lindsay couldn't believe she was hearing this. "So because Bernie's Irish, that makes her husband an IRA target?"

"Don't shoot the messenger. I'm just passing on the off-the-record from the cops. So far, it looks very like one of the Republican factions. Stick with the wife. See what you can find out."

"Andy, I'm not going to get near Bernie now. As soon as the doctors are finished with her, the cops are going to be all over her."

"Never mind. Just stick with it."

"Fine," Lindsay sighed. So much for the new life. She'd barely been back in the game five minutes, and already she was lumbered with exactly the kind of pointless task that had made her despair of the job all those years ago. Not only that, but she was homeless.

Where, she wondered, was the rewind button?

23

Café Virginia was half-empty, the lunchtime rush still some way down the line. Two young men gazed soulfully into each other's eyes like a pair of Labradors. A few singles read the papers and drank coffee. Annie was polishing glasses to the sound of Horse closing her eyes and counting to ten, and Rory stared gloomily at a bottle of Rolling Rock. Giles Graham slid into the booth opposite her.

"Terrible news," he said.

Rory nodded. "I keep getting flashbacks of the three of them on the plane. They were so bloody happy."

"At least he wasn't taking the lad to school."

"Fucking Pollyanna."

"Thank you, vicar. Where's Lindsay?"

"I have no idea," Rory said. "She was going into your office first thing, I'm assuming she got caught up in the story. I tried ringing her a wee while ago, but the mobile was switched off."

At that moment Lindsay walked through the door and headed straight for the back booth, pausing only to ask Annie for a large whisky. She dropped to the bench next to Giles. "Hell of a business. I just wanted to say I'm really sorry," he said before she could speak.

"It makes no sense," Lindsay said wearily. "They're saying it looks like the IRA, but that makes no sense whatsoever. Tam Gourlay was one of the least political animals I've ever met."

"The unofficial line is, 'Bernie's Irish,'" Giles said.

"Oh great. That's all right then," Rory said with savage irony. "That makes it clear, logical and justifiable. Fucking slab-faced bigots."

"You don't think it's anything to do with Jack's father? Revenge for snatching him back?" Giles asked.

"He's an Italian diplomat, not the Mafia. I know it's tempting to say the two things must be connected, but I don't see how," Lindsay said. Annie placed a glass in front of her and she sipped at it immediately. "Besides, it's not exactly going to help his bid for custody, is it?"

Rory frowned. "Maybe it is to do with Bernie. Maybe she does have a secret past life connected to the IRA. Remember how edgy she was right at the start, how reluctant she was to go for publicity? And I thought she was really off key in Helsinki. Her reaction was complicated, you know what I mean? It was more than just being thrilled to bits about getting her son back. You never know. What if she was on the run, and the story exposed her?"

Lindsay pondered for a moment. "You know, you might have something there. You're right, she hasn't been behaving naturally since that first night when Tam took us back to meet her. I wonder if she does have a past . . ."

"There's only one way to find out. Hit her while she's down," Giles said with chilling logic.

Lindsay winced. "Even if I wanted to, I don't think the cops will let me anywhere near her. I was supposed to be keeping an eye on her for the *Standard*, but I called the newsdesk back and told them I had something more important to do. Life's too short for sitting around on stories that are going nowhere."

"Giles is right, though. We're not going to find out the truth unless you get Bernie to talk. And we need to find out what's really happening here, Lindsay. Because we were there. We were in the firing line. We set up the sting that got the boy back. And if this is about revenge, we need to know if we're going to be the next targets."

Lindsay's eyes widened. "I never thought about that." A frisson of fear cramped her chest.

"Well, think about it now. I've never had any desire to be a heroic martyr for the cause of journalism. If I need to get on the next plane to the nearest faraway place, I want to know about it."

Lindsay gave a wry half-smile. "Leaving me to face the music, huh?"

"Don't be daft," Rory scoffed. "Paying single-room supplements is such a waste of money."

They exchanged a look that for once contained no hiddenness. Lindsay swallowed the dregs of her whisky and stood up. "I'm out of here. See if I can find a way under Bernie's guard. Talk to you later." She stood up and leaned across the table to kiss Rory's cheek. "Take no prisoners."

Giles watched her leave then raised his immaculate eyebrows at Rory. "Sandra says . . ."

"I don't give a bugger what Sandra says," Rory interrupted. "It's not going to happen."

Giles shook his head sadly. "You'll never forgive yourself."

"That's my problem." Rory stood up. "Now, if you'll excuse me, I've got to go and point out to David Keillor the error of his ways."

"You're turning Keillor over again?"

Rory nodded. "He's on the take from CCD. Lindsay nailed the evidence, now it's time for the showdown. I might as well try and produce something that'll cheer us both up. There's nothing else on the horizon that's likely to do that."

Lindsay didn't go straight back to Kinghorn Drive. She wanted time to think, so she caught a bus as far as Kelvingrove Park, then slowly meandered up towards the university. She got as far as the corridor where Sophie's office was, but realised she had no weapon in her armoury that would pierce Sophie's defences yet. There was no point in confrontation for its own sake, and no prospect of an encounter that could even begin to heal the damage between them. Lindsay couldn't afford to let herself believe there was no possibility of bridging the breach, but she couldn't for the life of her imagine the strategy that would achieve it. Still, the thought of failure made her want to curl up in a ball and howl like an abandoned puppy.

With a sigh, she turned away and continued on her way to Kinghorn Drive. The area cordoned off by the crime-scene tapes had shrunk to the immediate area around the explosion. Inside it, a team of white-suited Scenes of Crime officers were on hands and knees, collecting and bagging everything they could find. A clutch of journalists was still huddled in one corner, waiting for something to happen. Lindsay made her way over to them. "What's going on?" she said.

A BBC reporter shrugged. "Not a lot. We're waiting to see if the wife's going to make an appeal."

"Is she back at the house?" Lindsay was surprised.

"The cops brought her back about an hour ago. Apparently she insisted on coming home. They tried to talk her out of it, but she wouldn't have it. So we all came back here from the hospital. It's a waste of time. There's no way she's going to talk. Not today."

"Aye," Lindsay said. "Probably not." She eyed the scene. She couldn't see how she was going to get anywhere near Bernie. Her front door was flanked by two officers in full riot gear. Time for some lateral thinking.

She melted away and walked back up to the florist on Hyndland Road. "Can you make a local delivery this afternoon?" she asked.

The woman glanced at the clock. "Shouldn't be a problem. The van'll be back any minute now."

"I want a large bouquet of lilies," Lindsay said, giving the delivery details.

"Any message?"

"I'll write the card myself." The florist offered her a selection of gift cards, and she chose one with a simple spray of forget-me-nots in one corner. *I know how you're hurting. I've lost someone I loved, I understand the pain. But we need to talk about what's really going on here. Just between us. Then maybe we can stop it. Ask the cops to bring me in. Deepest sympathy, Lindsay.*

She wasn't convinced it would work. But it was worth a try. As she was about to pay, she had a sudden thought. "Have you got any yellow roses?" The florist pointed to a bucket in the corner. "A dozen, please. And can you deliver them too?" She chose another card, giving this message even more thought. *You've always known I'm an asshole. But it never stopped you loving me. I want to spend the rest of my life with you, I never meant to put that at risk. Talk to me? Please? Love, Lindsay.*

She didn't think for one moment it would change anything. But at any rate it showed she wasn't ignoring the situation. And at least Sophie was still within her reach, not like poor Tam Gourlay, lost to Bernie forever. Now she had to make sure she wasn't going to go the same way.

Jack sat on the floor, playing Nintendo with terrifying concentration. His whole world had shrunk to a tiny screen, the work of his fingers all he had space to think about. The headphones cut out any sound that might catapult him back into reality. Bernie was curled up on the sofa opposite, unable to take her eyes off him. She knew she was still in shock. She could feel nothing except a fierce desire not to let Jack out of her sight. The place in her heart occupied by Tam was frozen solid. Sooner or later it would melt and she would drown in the floodwaters of grief, but that hadn't happened yet.

It wasn't that she hadn't taken it in. She knew full well what had happened. She knew the how and she knew the why. The knowledge felt like a brooding bird of prey, perched inside her, biding its time before it ripped her heart out.

And she would deserve it. All of it and more.

The policewoman they had insisted must stay with her put her head round the door. "I'm sorry to intrude, Mrs Gourlay. But there's a gentleman on the phone for you. He says he's family, that you'll want to talk to him? He said his name was Patrick."

Bernie's heart lurched in her chest. The bastard would know they'd be monitoring her calls. He'd say nothing that would sound even slightly suspicious. But he'd want her to know that he was still there, inescapable as death. "I'll be right there," she said.

All she had left now was her son. All she could do was try to protect him.

Ten minutes later, Lindsay was sitting on a wall in Kinghorn Drive sharing a tube of Smarties with a local radio reporter who looked young enough to be her son. "See my boss? The guy that owns Radio NMC? He knew him," the lad said proudly.

"What? Tam Gourlay?"

"Aye. They were at the school together. Stayed pals, like. Used to go fishing up Loch Lomond. He cannae believe it. I had to do an interview with him, like, this morning? He was just devastated. Couldnae make sense of it at all."

"Has he got any theories?"

The lad looked self-important. "Mistaken identity. My boss reckons they got the wrong target. See, the Grand Master of the Orange Lodge, his name's Gourlay. John Gourlay. And he drives a Jag that's near enough identical to the victim's. That's the line we're going with, anyway."

"Could be," said Lindsay. *Biggest load of bollocks so far*, she thought, wishing Rory was there to share the moment. *I've got to stop thinking like that*, she admonished herself. If she was going to make it back with Sophie, she was going to have to train herself out of the habit of yearning.

Before she had to endure any more nonsense, the florist's van drew up at the edge of the cordon. An elderly man got out, carrying a lavish bouquet, and spoke to the nearest police officer. The cop took it and crossed to Bernie's door. It opened to reveal a uniformed woman officer, who accepted the flowers and closed the door firmly behind her.

Time crawled past. Lindsay chewed the skin round her nails, wondering what was going on inside Bernie's head. Eventually, the door opened again and the WPC who had taken in the bouquet spoke to one of the officers on guard. He nodded and stepped to the gate. "Is one of you Lindsay Gordon?" he shouted down to the waiting journalists.

Lindsay pushed herself off the wall and waved a hand. "That's me." Ignoring the outraged complaints from her fellow journalists, she pushed her way through and ducked under the tapes.

"I'll need ID," the officer in the gateway said. Lindsay dug her driving licence out of her wallet and waited while he scrutinised it. "Hang on a minute," he said, turning away and muttering into his personal radio. She wondered what would come up in any records search. She didn't have any criminal convictions, but she'd had some uncomfortable brushes with the law over the years. She speculated whether that information was stored on the Police National Computer, or if it was tucked away in some obscure Special Branch file.

Whatever his control told him, it clearly wasn't bad enough to prevent them letting her near Bernie. He glanced over his shoulder, nodded curtly and said, "Okay, on you go."

The WPC was right inside the door, waiting for her. She opened the living-room door and ushered Lindsay in, then left them alone. The curtains were closed and the room was dim in the light of a couple of table lamps. Jack was locked into his computer game, while Bernie seemed fixated on the cigarette she was smoking. Neither looked up when she entered. Lindsay crossed the room and kneeled down at Bernie's feet, taking her free hand. Bernie raised her head then and met Lindsay's sympathetic gaze with a bleak, empty stare.

"I do know what it's like," Lindsay said softly. "Years ago, my lover died. You feel guilty just for surviving. Never mind the hole they leave in your heart."

"Are you here as a journalist or as a friend?" Bernie asked roughly.

"I'm here because I'm part of this. Tam made me a part of this, and I need to know what's really going on."

"Oh God." Bernie shivered and pulled her hand away, covering her eyes. Lindsay got up and sat next to her, putting an arm round her shoulders. It was time to start pushing, but she didn't want to lose the fragile contact she'd established.

"Bernie, I know there's stuff you haven't told me about. I don't think you told Tam about it either. And he's paid the price, hasn't he?"

Bernie shrugged Lindsay's arm off. "Who the hell gave you the right to sit in judgement on me?" She glared at her.

"You did. When you let me put myself in the firing line right beside Tam. I don't know what's going on here, but if you want to put an end to it before anybody else dies, you better start talking to somebody. And since my neck's already on the block, it might as well be me."

Lindsay felt the long sigh shuddering through Bernie. "I don't know if I can." She looked down at Jack and her shoulders dropped in resignation. "I can't do this by myself any longer," she groaned. "He's not Bruno's son."

Lindsay frowned, trying to make sense of this bolt from the blue. "Not Bruno's? Then what . . . ?"

"You want the truth? Well, listen," Bernie said, her voice gathering strength from her determination finally to share her burden. "I grew up outside Belfast. On a farm. The man who owned the farm was called Patrick Coughlan. He was a rich man, a bookie in Belfast. But we all knew that he was a lot more than that. Strangers were always turning up at funny times of the day and night. That was one of the reasons why his marriage was so unhappy.

"Everybody knew Patrick and Mary hated each other. They say it started because she couldn't have children. And Patrick being a strict Catholic, he couldn't divorce her. Anyway, when I turned sixteen, Patrick offered me a job in Belfast, in one of his betting shops. I was glad of it, for there's not a lot of work back home. He used to drive me back to the country at weekends. And he paid me a lot of attention. And, like you do, I became his mistress. Because I was young and stupid, I fell pregnant. 'Never mind,' says Patrick. 'You'll have the baby in a nursing home in England, and me and Mary will adopt the child.'" Bernie looked beseechingly at Lindsay as she lit another cigarette.

"I couldn't let that happen. I couldn't give a child of mine to that hellish marriage. And I didn't want my child growing up thinking the IRA was a fine and noble career for a man."

"Jesus," Lindsay breathed.

"I had some money saved, and I knew where Patrick kept his emergency stash. So I took off. I got the boat to Stranraer and the train to Glasgow, and found myself a hotel job. I'd only been there for a fortnight when I met Bruno. He fell for me, and I let myself be carried along with the flow. He wanted to marry me and he was handy."

"So did he believe Jack was his son?"

"At first. It wasn't hard to persuade him." She gave a derisive snort. "You know men. They like to think they're all stud bulls. But eventually he figured out the truth. The marriage was in ruins by then anyway." She sighed again. "I should have known Patrick would find me one day. I've always lived with the fear of it."

"So what happened? How did he find you?"

"I've no idea. He started phoning me a couple of weeks ago. He said he wanted me to get used to the idea of Jack living with him. So I did the only thing I could think of to protect Jack."

Suddenly, light dawned in Lindsay's brain. "You set the kidnap up with Bruno!"

"We made the plans a long time ago. Just in case. I couldn't think of anything else, and I knew Bruno would take good care of Jack. But I underestimated what Tam would do for love of the boy."

Lindsay's mind was racing now, far ahead of Bernie's story. "So when we grabbed Jack back again, Patrick killed Tam?"

Bernie nodded. "As a warning to me not to thwart him. He phoned here this afternoon. He wants Jack. What am I to do, Lindsay?

Lindsay felt about six miles out of her depth. "You could tell the police?"

"Tell them what? I haven't a shred of evidence. I don't know where he is. The police have never been able to stop him doing exactly what he wanted to. Why should they start now? You think they can do anything? Patrick's not some toerag. He's respectable, rich, and he's never been nailed for anything more than a speeding ticket. Sure, the security forces know he's 'rA, but they've no evidence. He's got more than Tam's blood on his hands, but they've never been able to lay a finger on him."

"Then you're going to have to do a runner again."

Bernie shook her head hopelessly. "I can't. He's having me watched. He knows my every move.

When I go in, when I go out. He phones to let me know. He said he'd phone me tomorrow with instructions for the handover. If we try to get away, he says he'll have me killed and snatch Jack anyway." Suddenly, her composure cracked and fat, heavy tears spilled from her eyes. "What am I going to do?" she sobbed.

Lindsay took a deep breath. "Well, we'll just have to think of something."

24

The flat was clearly off limits now for Michael and Kevin. Everybody who lived in Kinghorn Drive would come under suspicion, everyone would be questioned, and it would only be a matter of time before the police got round to finding out about the two Irishmen in the vacant flat. Chances were that the estate agent would already have put two and two together and volunteered the details of his own venal stupidity.

This left Michael with the problem of how to carry out Patrick's orders without taking too many risks. He'd stayed out of jail throughout the Troubles simply because he was good at figuring out the odds and staying on the right side of them. He wasn't about to change his ways now. And so his first move had been to send Kevin back to the B&B to await further instructions.

It had been easy enough for a while after Bernadette had returned. There were plenty of sightseers for him to blend in with. But the gawkers had thinned out now. Probably away home for their tea, like good wee civilians, he thought with contempt. However, their desire to fill their bellies didn't help him one whit. Eventually, he'd called Patrick and made a suggestion.

So when Lindsay was picked out of the pack and shown through a front door he'd become all too familiar with, Michael was standing only yards away from her, a camera round his neck and a camera bag at his feet. He hadn't known the lad who had delivered the equipment to him on the corner of Great Western Road, but he supposed it had cost Patrick a bob or two to kit him up with something good enough to pass muster as a press photographer's gear.

It was the perfect disguise. Nobody gave him a second look. In the clannish world of news journalism, strangers stayed that way until and unless they made themselves one of the crowd. If you wanted to stay aloof, fine. All it meant was that you would be cut out of any sharing the pack decided to do with what meagre pickings they'd got.

He couldn't believe it when Lindsay materialized in front of him, carving a line through the crowd and walking straight in. He knew from what he'd read in the paper that she'd been at the heart of the operation to recover Jack Gourlay from his kidnappers. He didn't think Patrick would be pleased to find her in the thick of it again.

Michael walked a few yards away from the crowd and called Patrick. Quickly, he outlined what he'd just seen.

"Fucking bitch," Patrick grumbled. "We're nearly done here. I don't want outsiders interfering. This isn't the time for playing games."

"So what do you want me to do?"

There was a pause. "Follow her when she comes out. Persuade her to keep her nose out of our business."

"How persuasive would you like me to be?"

"She's a woman. They frighten easily. What happened this morning should be enough to keep her mouth shut, provided you give her a little encouragement."

The phone went dead. Michael allowed himself a small smile. It would be a pleasure.

Sophie locked her office door with a sense of relief. It had felt like the longest day of her life, and all she wanted to do was go home, unplug the phones and try to make up for some of the sleep she'd lost the night before, tossing and turning and crying over someone who simply wasn't worth it.

She'd almost made it to the lift when she heard her secretary call her name. Sophie thought about pretending she hadn't heard, but couldn't bring herself to be so rude. Lucy was hurrying towards her with a hand-tied bouquet of yellow roses. *My favourite, damn you, Lindsay.* "These have just come, Professor Hartley. I thought you'd want to take them home with you." She thrust the flowers eagerly at her boss.

Sophie's first reaction was to stuff the flowers in the fire bucket. But that would only provoke more departmental gossip than the bouquet itself. She forced a tired smile and accepted the offering. "Thanks, Lucy. See you in the morning." She struggled to press the call button for the lift, but Lucy reached past her and helped out.

"There you go," she said cheerfully. "You're obviously a very lucky lady," she added.

"Sorry?"

"The flowers. Somebody must think a lot of you. A dozen roses. That's special." Lucy sketched a wave and headed back down the corridor.

Not special enough, Sophie thought grimly. She'd half-expected to be showered with phone calls, even to see Lindsay waiting hangdog outside her office when she'd arrived that morning, but there had been nothing. She wasn't sure how to interpret that. On the rare occasions when they rowed, Lindsay always went over the top when it came to mending fences, as enthusiastic for reconciliation as she was for everything else she cared about. Did her silence mean she was secretly relieved to have found a fire escape from parenthood and Sophie? Or was it that she realised that this was one time where she had overstepped the mark so utterly that all normal routes to appeasement were shut off? Or was she simply too busy having fun with Rory?

Sophie ripped open the envelope stapled to the cellophane. Reading Lindsay's words, she couldn't resist either the half-smile or the prickle of tears that accompanied them. "You are an asshole," she said softly.

She wasn't ready to forgive. Not by a very long way. But for the first time since Lindsay's admission had slashed at her heart, Sophie was prepared to consider that forgiveness might be a remote possibility.

Lindsay walked along Great Western Road in the gathering shadows of early evening, oblivious to the traffic flowing past her in a stuttering stream. Her head was whirling with questions and options, trying to process the full implications of what Bernie had told her. She had the vague glimmerings of an idea that might just get them all off the hook, but it was a long way from something that could be graced with the term "plan."

Without thinking, she took the turn that would bring her back home. She was twenty yards down the street when she remembered that this wasn't home any longer. Lindsay groaned out loud and turned on her heel, marching back the way she'd come, crossing over to cut through the Botanic Gardens to Rory's flat. That was another thing she was going to have to deal with. She couldn't keep staying at Rory's. It had been almost possible before she'd found that poem. But knowing the truth about Rory's feelings had changed everything.

Head down, preoccupied with enough troublesome thoughts to occupy half a dozen heads, Lindsay turned into the entry for Rory's close. As she opened the door, she suddenly heard running feet behind her. Lindsay swivelled to see what was going on.

Two men emerged from the shadows of the trees that shrouded the street. They were going so fast when they hit her that they barged her into the mouth of the close, the door banging shut behind them. Before she could react, they had

crowded her against the inside wall. In the dim light, she could
tell them apart. One was small and ferrety, the other looked
about as friendly as a peregrine falcon who's just spotted breakfast. The ferret stepped back and brought his fist crashing into
her stomach. As she doubled over with the pain, Lindsay felt
him grab her hair and yank her head back, cracking it against
the cool tiles of the wall.

Lazily, the falcon let her see the blade of his knife before
he placed the point in the hollow of her throat. She could feel
something trickle, but had no idea if it was sweat or blood.
Lindsay knew all about fear. And this, she understood, was one
of those times when being scared shitless was the only sensible
option. When he spoke, his voice was the nasal drawl of Belfast.
"We've got a wee message for ye, bitch."

Terrified as she was, she couldn't bring herself to be craven.
"That would be from Patrick?" she managed to croak.

The falcon withdrew the knife and for a split second she
thought she'd won some ground. But he nodded to the ferret,
who smashed his fist into her stomach again. She felt as if her
lungs had shot into her throat and she fell into a spasm of retching
and coughing, limp as a sleeping child in the ferret's grasp. Her
head swam and she lost track of time for a few seconds. When
she tuned in again, the falcon's knife was at her throat once more.

"Like I said, we've got a wee message for you. Keep away
from Bernadette and the boy. Or else you'll get what Gourlay
got. Only more slowly."

Suddenly, the door behind them opened. Through the
groggy haze of pain, Lindsay recognised Rory's familiar silhouette. Before she could shout a warning, Rory dropped her
shoulder bag and screamed, "Police officer! Drop the knife!"

Taken by surprise, the falcon's knife hand shifted away
from Lindsay's neck. From a standing start, Rory took a flying
karate kick at him, screeching like a demented Amazon. She
connected mid-thigh and, caught off balance, he tumbled to
the ground, his knife clattering into the shadows.

In the confusion, the ferret released Lindsay and turned to make a move on Rory, whose momentum had taken her beyond him. As he moved towards her, she feinted to one side, then dropped into a forward roll, knocking his feet from under him. He crashed to the ground howling as Rory righted herself and landed a kick in his ribs.

Lindsay couldn't stand up any longer and she crumpled to the ground as the falcon tried to get at Rory. His feet tangled in her legs and he crashed into the wall of the close. "Jesus," he swore, spinning round and heading for the door. "Fucking come on," he yelled, yanking the door open and making for the street. The ferret hobbled after him.

"Fucking bitches, the pair of ye," he shouted as he made the safety of the street.

Panting, Rory crouched down beside Lindsay. "Are you all right?"

"No. But I'd be a lot worse if you hadn't turned up." Her final words were swallowed in a paroxysm of retching coughs. Rory cuddled her close, stroking her sweating forehead.

"That wasn't a mugging, was it?" she asked gently.

"No, it was a warning."

Rory tried to keep the jagged edge of fear out of her voice. "Just as well I did the women's self-defence course, eh?"

Lindsay nodded weakly. "Police officer? Smart move."

"I thought so."

"Do you think we could go upstairs?"

Rory thrust her shoulder under Lindsay's armpit and helped her struggle to her feet. "I suppose it would be too much to hope that those two Neanderthals were Sophie's hired muscle?"

In spite of herself, Lindsay choked out a laugh. "Oh God, if only."

☙❧

Lindsay lay on the sofa, swathed in Rory's fluffy bathrobe, her hair damp from the bath. On the table in front of her stood a bottle of whisky and a jug of water, flanked by two glasses. Lindsay wanted a drink, but she knew it would hurt too much to reach for the glass. She'd been on the receiving end of violence before, but that didn't make it any easier to deal with. Fear kept reverberating through her, as she knew it would for days, maybe weeks to come. A dark street would make her sweat until she managed to replace its connotations with something more powerful, more pleasurable. But that was in the future. For now, she had to cope with the flashbacks and the palpitations that came with them.

"And I still say you've got to walk away from it," Rory said firmly as she returned from the kitchen with a plate of sandwiches.

"And let that murdering bastard get his hands on Jack? It'd be signing Bernie's death warrant. My way is the only way to make sure Patrick doesn't come after the kid. Plus he might just get the idea that he'd be a lot safer if I was off the planet too. So I've got to do it. And I need help."

Rory shook her head. "He wouldn't come after you." There was no conviction in her voice.

"How can you say that after what happened this evening? Rory, this guy blew up Tam Gourlay in the middle of a residential street in the morning rush hour for the sole reason that he was pissed off with the man. If he thought I could finger him, he wouldn't think twice. So are you going to help me or not?"

"Lindsay, I want to help. But I'm a journalist, not an urban guerrilla."

"Have you got any better ideas?"

Rory shook her head.

"Look, forget I asked, okay? I'll work something out. And pass me that whisky, would you?"

Rory picked up Lindsay's glass and perched on the sofa arm next to her. "Okay, I'll help. I can't let you do this by yourself."

"Can't *let* me?" Lindsay was only half-joking.

"The shape you're in, I can afford to call the shots." Rory stroked the back of Lindsay's neck tenderly. "Hey, what's life without a few risks?"

"You can afford to say that, you won the lottery. This is worth doing, you know. You won't regret it. I promise."

"I have a feeling you've used that line before," Rory said. "Bet it wasn't true then, either. The one thing that still bothers me—apart from my new career as accessory to blackmail—is that it's not just you and me that's involved here."

"Bernie won't be a problem. She'll do anything to keep Jack safe." Lindsay shifted along the sofa, wincing, then patted the cover beside her. "Come and give me a cuddle. But gently," she added apprehensively as Rory slid over the edge of the arm to bounce on to the seat.

"If this is going to work, we need another body," Rory pointed out a few minutes later.

"I know. Anybody in mind?"

"I know just the man," Rory said.

"Does it have to be a man?"

"Don't tell me you're one of those lesbians that don't like men?" Rory teased.

"Oh, I like some of them fine," Lindsay said. "But I wouldn't trust them to hold the dog while I went for a pee."

"Well, I trust Giles."

"Giles Graham?" Lindsay said incredulously. "You've got to be joking. He'd get his suit creased."

Rory shook her head. "You underestimate him. He used to be in the Territorial Army, you know."

"That's meant to be a recommendation?"

Rory snuggled into Lindsay's side, taking care to avoid the area she knew was going to be a multicoloured bruise by morning. "Giles is one of the good guys. Besides, he owes me. I know where the bodies are buried."

"An unfortunate metaphor," Lindsay said. "Okay, Giles it is."

"So when are you thinking about swinging into action?"

Lindsay sipped her whisky and stared into the middle distance. "Not tomorrow. There's too much to get organised. The night after, I think. Bernie reckons she can stall Patrick until then, she'll tell him she can't get away from her police protection."

"Can you squeeze another twenty-four hours out of him?" Rory asked. "Only, I know Giles is going out of town tomorrow on a job. And we need time to make sure we know exactly how we're going to carry it off."

Lindsay considered. One more day wouldn't make any difference. Bernie could always plead fear and demand police protection for a bit longer. "I don't see why not. It'd give me more of a chance to recover. And I need to go up to Argyll before then."

Rory's curiosity was pricked. "You're not thinking about bringing your dad in on this?"

Lindsay shook her head. "No way. But there's something I need to sort out first."

"Tell," Rory demanded.

"No. A woman has to have some secrets, you know." Lindsay rumpled Rory's hair. "Thanks. For everything."

Rory snorted derisively. "What? For buggering up your life? You're going to have to talk to Sophie, you know. You've got to get things sorted out between you."

"What? Fed up of having me under your feet already?"

"Stop hiding behind facetiousness. You don't belong with me, you know that."

Lindsay took a slow, considering sip of her whisky. "It's not quite that simple, though, is it? We both know that in different circumstances . . ."

Rory pulled away and stood up, moving to the armchair opposite. "But we can only play the hand we've been dealt, Lindsay. And the bottom line is that you still love Sophie and that's too important to throw away for a maybe."

"I think it's already more than a maybe for us, don't you?"

Rory flinched, clearly uncomfortable with Lindsay's insight. "Look, I've been doing some thinking today. I don't think we should sleep together any more." Her eyes pleaded with Lindsay not to push for a reason.

But Lindsay couldn't close it there. "Why not?"

"It's not that I don't want to. I do, I really do, and that's the problem. If it were just a fling, just a shag, like it was supposed to be, that would be fine. But it's not. It has emotional content for us both. And so it's pointless, because your heart's still tied to Sophie, which is how it should be. And if I can't have everything, I don't want anything. Except your friendship. If that's still on offer." The words dragged out of Rory, words she'd never spoken before, and every one an effort.

They stared at each other for a long moment, both gripped by the inevitability of Rory's argument, both pierced by the poignancy of the decision that they knew they'd already taken. "Go and talk to her," Rory said softly. "Go and fix it."

"Maybe not tonight, eh? I'm feeling a wee bit fragile."

"Yes, tonight. You'll feel worse tomorrow, once those muscles have stiffened up. And it's not like you're going to get a good night's sleep, is it? Do it now, before you start figuring out another set of excuses. Besides, I've got some copy to write. I fronted Keillor up this afternoon. He tried to bluff his way out of it, but we've got more than enough to go with."

Lindsay managed a wan smile. "Well done. What a team, eh?"

Rory sighed. "Aye. What a team, right enough. So, come on, Splash, get some clothes on and go and see Sophie."

"There's no point, you know," Lindsay said, edging forward and working her way into a standing position.

"Of course there's a point. Apart from anything else, you need some clean knickers."

25

When the doorbell rang, Sophie was curled up in front of the fire in her dressing gown, talking to her stomach. She got up and looked out of the window. No sign of Lindsay's car. The bell trilled out insistently again. Whoever it was obviously realised she was home and wasn't giving up without a fight. It was trademark behaviour. "Lindsay," she sighed wearily.

Her first thought when she opened the door was that Lindsay was holding herself very strangely, as if she were primed to take a blow. Her face was tense, but with pain as much as anxiety. "What happened to you?" Sophie said without preamble.

"It's a long story. And it's really not important. I need to talk to you, that's what's important."

Sophie shook her head. "A dozen roses doesn't buy you access. I don't need to talk to you, Lindsay. And I don't want to." She moved to close the door.

"At least let me come in and pick up a few things. I can't keep wearing the same clothes forever." Lindsay was trying to sound appealing, but apprehension kept slipping through.

Sophie stood back, opening the door, then walked away to the living room. Lindsay followed. "Your knicker drawer is not in here," Sophie pointed out.

"Sophie, please don't shut me out."

"What, like you didn't shut me out when you were shagging Rory?" Sophie struggled to keep her face under control. She was determined not to show Lindsay how deeply hurt she was.

"I'm sorry. I've behaved badly and you don't deserve that."

"I know I don't. Which is why you'll never get the chance to repeat it. I'm not going to let you talk your way back into my life. It's over, and you better get used to the idea." Sophie turned away dismissively. She sat down and picked up a discarded medical journal from the table, flicking through the pages without seeing a word.

"Please," Lindsay said. This time, there was no disguising the pain in her voice. "Look, I did a stupid, stupid thing. I never meant to hurt you and I can't begin to tell you how sorry I am for what I've done. But you can't throw everything away just because I made one dumb mistake."

"Watch me," Sophie said. "Lindsay, sleeping with someone else doesn't come into the category of mistake. Mistake is when you put black socks in with a white boil wash. Mistake is when you put salt instead of sugar in the custard. This was not a mistake. It was a calculated bit of pleasure-taking and to hell with the consequences. Well, here are the consequences. And if you don't like them, that's tough. You should have thought about that before you seized the moment with the blonde."

Lindsay walked round the sofa to face Sophie. "I know I did wrong. But please. I want us to be together. You said you wanted us to be a family. That's what I want too."

Sophie barely glanced up. "You think I want to bring up my child with a liar and a cheat?"

"I'm not a liar," Lindsay protested. "If I was a liar, you'd be none the wiser."

"Okay, I'll grant you that. But you're a cheat. And I could never trust you again. Which is the bottom line."

Impulsively, Lindsay dropped to her knees. She almost passed out with the pain that flashed across her ribs. She folded her arms protectively over her abdomen and gasped. "Oh fuck."

Sophie couldn't help herself. In an instant, she was on the floor beside her. "Lindsay, what is it? What's wrong?"

Lindsay leaned against the sofa, her face grey and sweating. "I got beaten up, okay? It's none of your business, remember?" Somehow, she pushed herself upright and slumped into the seat. "I'll be fine in a minute. Then I'll go." She closed her eyes, waiting for the nausea to pass.

When she opened them again, Sophie was still kneeling on the floor, unable to hide her concern. "How did you get beaten up?" she demanded.

"Sticking my nose in where it wasn't wanted. I seem to be doing that a lot today." She got to her feet unsteadily. "You're all I ever wanted, Sophie. I'll never forgive myself for forgetting that, even for a moment."

Sophie watched as Lindsay staggered across the room. She listened to the sound of drawers opening and closing, then slowly got to her feet. *Only Lindsay could refuse to trade on having had the crap beaten out of her,* she thought with rueful affection. She met Lindsay in the bedroom doorway, carrying a gym bag. "I'll arrange to come for the rest of my stuff when I've sorted myself out with somewhere to live," she said, her voice dull.

"Don't do anything hasty," Sophie said. "Give me some time, Lindsay. Call me next week, okay?" The spark of hope that flared in Lindsay's eyes was hard to resist, but Sophie was determined not to cave in so easily.

Lindsay nodded and reached out a tentative hand to Sophie's belly. "You take care now. Take care of both of you."

"Don't worry about us. Just try and stay alive, Lindsay. Don't piss anybody else off between now and then."

She couldn't quite unravel the curious expression that crossed Lindsay's face. "I'll do my best," she said.

Patrick Coughlan paced the floor of his room. One Devonshire Gardens was reputedly the finest hotel in the city, but its luxury was wasted on him tonight. He'd thought that Tam Gourlay's death would settle Bernadette's hash once and for all. But she was acting as if she still had rights. Well, if she was relying on her journalist pals this time, she'd be in for a rude surprise. According to Michael, the Gordon bitch wouldn't be so keen to muscle in on his business a second time.

But that still left the problem of the boy. Bernadette had conceded that she would have to hand him over, but she claimed she couldn't make the arrangements while she was still under police protection. He could see the force of that, but it worried him all the same. She'd already tried to thwart him with that stupid kidnap ploy, and he supposed he should be grateful to the Gordon bitch and her sidekick for making sure Bernadette hadn't got away with it. She'd better not try it again.

He sincerely hoped she'd learned her lesson. Killing gave Patrick no pleasure. He had always regarded it as a necessity, no more, no less. Bernadette had once meant something to him, it was true. But, unlike many of his fellow countrymen, Patrick had no streak of sentimentality. If killing Bernadette was what it took to bring his son home, then he would have no compunction about ordering it done.

He wanted the boy with him. His absence had smouldered like heartburn since the day Bernadette had disappeared. Patrick had only begun to get used to the joyous idea of finally being a father when the bitch had snatched it away from him. She couldn't have known the pain she'd dealt him. Being a father to his own boy was the pinnacle of his ambition, and she'd wantonly deprived him of the chance to do the most decent thing he was capable of. There hadn't been a day when he hadn't wondered

where his son was, whether he took after his father, what he
liked and disliked. Without knowing the first thing about his
son, Patrick loved him with a fierce passion. Bernadette had had
no right to steal that from him.

One way or another, it would all be over soon.

Sophie rubbed her temples. She'd woken with a headache and it
seemed determined to hang around. Possibly it was a symptom
of pregnancy; more likely, it was a symptom of Lindsay. Luckily,
she had a fairly quiet day ahead, the morning devoted to writing
up some research in her office.

When the knock came at her door, she expected a colleague or a student. But in response to her weary, "Come in,"
she was astonished to see Rory McLaren walk in. "Actually,
don't bother," she said. "Just turn round and leave."

"Five minutes," Rory said. "That's all I'm asking."

"That's five more than I'm prepared to give you." Sophie
glared over her glasses. "I thought Lindsay was big enough to
fight her own battles."

"She doesn't know I'm here. She'd kill me if she knew I
was. You should know that." Rory's air of amused exasperation
struck a chord with Sophie in spite of herself.

"So why are you here?"

"Two reasons. First, to apologize. And second, to intercede."

Sophie frowned. "Five minutes. No more." Rory moved
towards the chair that faced Sophie. "No point in sitting down,
Rory. You're not going to be here that long."

Rory stopped in her tracks, looking awkward. "Okay.
Right. Look, I should never have slept with Lindsay. I don't
make a habit of trespassing in other people's lives."

"It's hard to imagine how I could care less about your
habits. And frankly it's not you who shouldn't have slept with
Lindsay. She shouldn't have slept with you."

"What happened, it was my fault. I made all the running. She was pissed and a long way from home." Rory looked at the floor. "I took advantage because I wanted her."

"She could have said no," Sophie said, not giving an inch.

"She could have. But she didn't. A moment of weakness, that's all it was. And we were both clear it wasn't going to happen again." Rory looked up and met Sophie's hard-eyed look with a half-smile. "And if she wasn't such a fool to herself, that's where it would have ended, with you none the wiser."

"You think it's foolish to be honest?"

Rory's eyebrows quirked upwards. "When all it does is bring everyone concerned a shitload of grief? Hey, Sophie, it's obvious that, whatever I say, you're going to pick a fight with me, and I can't blame you for that. Can we cut to the bottom line? Lindsay loves you. And I think you love her. If you let one colossal act of stupidity fuck that up, I think you'll both regret it for a very long time. Apart from anything else, every kid deserves two parents who love each other."

Sophie glared at Rory. "She told you I'm pregnant?"

"Of course she told me. She was thrilled. I know she wasn't very keen on the idea to begin with, but when she realised it was a reality, she was over the moon."

"Now I know you're full of shit."

"It's true," Rory protested. "That's a big part of why she's so upset now. Take her back, Sophie. She needs you." She glanced at her watch. "That's my time up. I won't keep you any longer." She turned away and made for the door.

Sophie chewed her lip. As Rory reached for the door handle, she said, "She's very lucky to have a friend like you. It's more than she deserves."

Rory flashed a smile over her shoulder. "We're both more than she deserves. And also rather less." Then she was gone.

Sophie stared at the closed door for a very long time. She recognised love when she saw it. And she was afraid that Lindsay might do exactly the same. The night before, she'd come close to offering an olive branch to Lindsay. But perhaps it was already too late for them both.

Lindsay sat on a crumbling drystone dyke that had once formed part of a sheep fold. Her ribs ached, there was a lump on the back of her head the size and texture of a fillet steak and her whole body was stiff. She'd slept badly, struggling to find a comfortable position in Rory's spare bed, and her eyes felt gritty and sore. Sitting in a car all morning hadn't helped. But she was here now, which was the main thing.

She'd parked on a forestry road about a quarter of a mile up the hill, well hidden from anyone down the glen, and now she was biding her time. Her father's boat wasn't at the quay, which meant he was out fishing and would be gone for a few hours yet. Her mother, she knew, would leave the house within the next hour or so and walk the mile into town to perform her daily circuit of the three village shops. Fresh rolls, milk, a few vegetables, maybe a bit of meat, whatever she needed for that day's meals. Getting the messages and the local gossip would take her out of the house for long enough for Lindsay to collect what she needed.

She perched on the wall, pulling the collar of her fleece closer to keep out the chill wind coming off the hill. Even on a grey day like this, it was hard not to be seduced by the harsh beauty of the landscape. The grass was fading as autumn encroached, nibbled close by Duncan Campbell's hardy mountain sheep, hefted to the hill and spared the foot-and-mouth cull that had devastated flocks further south. The village crouched below, grey harled cottages hugging the shoreline like a string of runners waiting for the starting pistol to throw themselves pell mell across the rippled grey steel of the quiet sea. Lindsay could identify every one of the buildings, though these days she couldn't say for certain who all the inhabitants were. At least three of the cottages had fallen to weekend visitors, and the old folks of her youth had been replaced by new faces she didn't always recognise.

She wouldn't swap with them for anything, in spite of her attachment to the land. She couldn't live here. She'd known that since her early teens. She needed wider horizons, different responsibilities.

She needed Sophie. *Please God, let her relent.* It was no consolation to realise that if Sophie refused to consider a reconciliation, Rory was waiting in the wings. Whatever her feelings for Rory, it wouldn't diminish the pain of losing Sophie.

Lindsay was spared any further introspection by the appearance of her mother at the end of the path leading from the family home to the main road. She watched her as far as the first house in the village, then Lindsay cut across the field and into the trees. She drove down to the house and let herself in. Fifteen minutes later, she was cruising down the main street, mission accomplished. She couldn't just turn round and drive back to Glasgow, however. Inevitably, someone would have clocked her car and a report of her presence would make its way back to at least one of her parents. The last thing she wanted was her father wondering what she might have been doing there. She spotted her mother outside the minimarket, chatting to a woman bent almost double over her walking frame. Lindsay recognised her primary school teacher as she parked and crossed the street.

Miss Macintyre caught sight of her and tapped her mother on the arm. "Here's your Lindsay," she said.

Mrs Gordon turned round, surprise on her face. "Lindsay! What a nice surprise."

"I'm on my way to Tarbet," Lindsay lied easily. She'd never had any problem keeping things hidden from her mother. It was an irony she was alive to that morning. She exchanged a few pleasantries with Miss Macintyre then led her mother back to the car.

"You look tired," Mrs Gordon said, reading the lines of strain round her daughter's eyes.

"I didn't sleep very well. I tripped on the stairs and hurt my ribs." Half a truth was better than none.

"Have you got time to stop for your dinner? I've got some lovely prawns back at the house."

Lindsay shook her head. "I just thought I'd stop and say hello. I'll drop you back home, then I'll need to be going."

"You'll have time for a cup of coffee." It was a statement, not a question.

Lindsay smiled. "That'd be nice."

"How's Sophie keeping?" her mother asked. Lindsay's heart sank. Maybe coffee wasn't such a good idea after all.

Bernie stood on a chair and took the suitcases down from the top of the wardrobe. She wanted to believe that Lindsay's plan would work. But she needed insurance. If Patrick couldn't be neutralized, then she would have to go on the run again. It would be harder with Jack in tow, but without him there would be no point.

She would pack a couple of bags, just the essentials for the two of them. She'd stow them in the boot of the car. Then if things went wrong, she could hit the road and head south. Hull would be a good place to leave from. They could cross the North Sea to Holland and make their way down to Italy. She'd learned basic Italian when she'd been married to Bruno. It wouldn't be too hard to find a decent job in some big anonymous city where Patrick and his thugs would never find her. Bruno would help, she was sure. After the initial acrimony of the divorce, he'd proved a surprisingly good friend. She supposed that was because he'd grown to care about Jack.

In her heart, she didn't want to run. She wanted to stay here in this house where she'd been happy with Tam. She wanted to mourn at his funeral. She wanted to grieve in peace, without having to look over her shoulder all the time. Bernie sat down heavily on the bed and let the tears flow. "Oh, Tam," she sobbed.

"What am I going to do without you?" Misery and remorse seized her and she rolled on to her stomach, pounding the pillows with her fist.

She was lamenting not only what she had lost but the knowledge that she could never again take the risk of allowing someone to love her. That was what had cost Tam his life. Under no circumstances could she gamble with another's. From now on, it was her and Jack against the world.

26

Giles stared at Rory. "Why me?" he asked plaintively.

"Because I trust you."

"What about Sandra?"

Rory snorted derisively. "Would you let Sandra loose on something that needed split-second timing? She'd probably chip her nail varnish or get distracted by some trainee accountant with a cute bum."

Giles smiled in spite of his discomfiture. "I see your point. But really, is this sensible?"

"Of course it's not sensible. But the thing I've realised about Lindsay is that, once she decides she's going to do something, she won't be diverted. And if she tries to do this single-handed it'll never work. I'm doing it purely for business reasons, because I don't want anything bad to happen to her." Rory avoided his eyes, not wanting him to see too much.

"And you're asking me to help because you know I don't want anything bad to happen to you," Giles said, reaching across the table and patting her hand. "Purely for business reasons, of course."

"Hey, where else would you get all the best stories? But the real reason I want you on board is that if it all goes horribly wrong, Julia can use her influence to get us off the hook," Rory said, deflecting his seriousness with flippancy. "So, are you in or are you going to make me ask Sandra?"

Giles shook his head, wondering at his own stupidity. "I'm in."

"Thanks, Giles. I appreciate it. Now, this is what you have to do." She ran through the details of the plan once more, making sure he was clear about his role. "Can you see any flaws in it?"

"Apart from the general insanity of trying to blackmail an IRA capo? No, not a thing. It all makes perfect sense," he said sarcastically.

"Lindsay will pick you up at half past seven. And we'll take it from there." Rory stood up and gathered her things. She took a theatrical look around Café Virginia. "I've loved these days," she said. "Do you think if I don't make it back they'll put a blue plaque on this booth?"

"More likely a health warning. 'Sitting in this booth may provoke the illusion that you are Don Quixote.'"

Rory grinned. "Bring on the windmills."

Lindsay checked over the electronic equipment one last time. "I've put new batteries in everything, so there shouldn't be a problem," she said. She studied Rory carefully, knowing the margin for error was small and needing to be sure of her. "You okay about this?"

Rory nodded. "Let's get on with it before my bottle goes completely."

Lindsay picked up a small radio mike with a crocodile clip and a loose wire dangling from it. "This is the radio mike. Not exactly state of the art, but it does the business. I'll have the receiver in my car, linked up to a tape recorder."

"So where do I wear it?"

Lindsay couldn't resist a wicked grin. "Experience has shown that, for women, the best place is attached to your bra."

"So much for keeping your hands off my body." Rory stood up and unbuttoned her blouse, trying to keep it as matter of fact as she could. "How much do I need from Coughlan, do you think? Is it enough if he acknowledges he's Jack's real father?"

"You have to get him to admit to being involved with Tam's murder. That's the only insurance policy that's worth anything. You get that, then you get clear."

Rory nodded. "Then you phone him and tell him that if anything happens to Jack or Bernie—if a pigeon so much as craps on their car—the tape goes to the police. And the papers." Rory opened her blouse and gave a wry smile. "All yours," she said.

Lindsay picked up the mike and stepped towards Rory. In spite of her best intentions, she couldn't avoid a nostalgic frisson of desire. Trying hard to stay businesslike, she delicately slid the mike inside the bra so it nestled neatly against Rory's left breast. Rory gave an involuntary shiver as Lindsay's hand brushed her skin. "Sorry," she muttered.

"Don't be," Lindsay said softly. She laid her hands on the soft skin stretched over Rory's collarbone. She frowned slightly, her eyes filled with sadness. "I . . ."

Rory put a finger on her lips. "Don't say it. I know. Me too, for what it's worth."

Lindsay nodded and stood back. "Make yourself decent. We've got work to do, woman."

Rory smiled and buttoned up her blouse then reached for her jacket.

"Okay, time to go. Try it out on the way down the stairs." Lindsay said, desperately wanting to give Rory a benedictory kiss but knowing it would only be another source of pain.

Rory waggled her fingers in farewell and winked. "See you in Café Virginia when it's all over."

Lindsay watched her leave, then made some adjustments to the small receiver and tape recorder. Suddenly, Rory's voice emerged clearly from the speaker. "Your mission, should you choose to accept it, is to adopt celibacy as the only safe way to live . . ."

In spite of the seriousness of the moment, Lindsay couldn't help herself. She burst out laughing. "Oh, Rory," she said out loud. "Such bad timing."

Patrick sat in the passenger seat of Michael's hired car, staring at Bernie's house through a pair of binoculars. He let them drop and pulled out his phone. The number was answered on the second ring.

"Are you free and clear now?" he said without preamble.

"They've left," Bernie said.

"Good. Where are we meeting?"

"The Charles Rennie Mackintosh multi-storey car park at the bottom of Garnethill. Top floor. Eight o'clock." Bernie's voice was flat and depressed, the voice of a woman who has given up. It gladdened Patrick's heart to hear it.

"Fine. I'll be there. And no tricks, mind, or there'll be a couple more funerals in this city before too long." He stabbed a finger at the phone, ending the call. He allowed himself a satisfied smile and said, "Charles Rennie Mackintosh car park in Garnethill. Half an hour's time. You know what to do, boys. When she comes out the house with the boy, you follow her. If she goes anywhere except this car park, you stay on her tail and call me right away. If the boy comes out with anyone else, Kevin, you follow them. And, Michael, you deal with the bitch. Is that all clear, now?"

"It's clear," Michael said.

"But she's not going to try anything on, is she?" Kevin asked. "Not after that wee warning."

"Of course she's not," Patrick said, confident and dismissive. "But I've always been a believer in contingency plans. That's probably why I'm still alive. I'll see youse later, boys." He opened the door and stepped out into the heavy drizzle, turning up his coat collar as he walked back to his car, parked further up the street. Although he had spent years battening down his emotions in favour of operational activity, Patrick couldn't suppress a surge of excitement that raised his pulse rate. Tonight, finally, he would take his son home. What better feeling could a man have?

Lindsay let herself out of Rory's flat and walked to her car. She put the receiver and tape recorder on the passenger seat, then lifted the narrow bench seat in the back of the MGB. When she'd first bought the car, she'd customized the seat with a set of hinges so the area beneath it could be used for extra storage space. She hadn't quite envisaged stowing one of her father's shotguns there, but it had turned out to be perfect for the job. She deliberately hadn't told Rory about the gun, aware that the knowledge would have made it impossible for Rory to carry out her end of the plan with anything approaching equanimity. But Lindsay didn't trust Patrick Coughlan and she had no intention of leaving Rory exposed and unprotected.

She leaned into the car and broke the gun open, slotting a pair of cartridges into the breech. It had been a long time since she'd handled a gun, years since she'd shot rabbits and pheasants with her father on the hills above Invercross, but she was pleased to find she hadn't lost the knack. Then she slammed it closed and put it on the floor behind the driver's seat, hiding it beneath a tatty tartan rug she'd borrowed from her father's workshop.

Lindsay leaned on the cloth roof of the car and tried to calm herself. It was still painful to breathe, never mind move around freely. But she had to be up to this. She had to forget her physical discomfort and focus on the plan. She reached into her pocket and took out a container of ibuprofen tablets. She swallowed 600 milligrams and hoped for the best.

Lindsay climbed into the car and pulled a ski mask out of the pocket of her waxed jacket. She'd gone back home that afternoon in Sophie's absence and chosen her clothes with care. A black cotton polo neck, the jacket, black fleece trousers, black leather gloves and rubber-soled black shoes. She rolled up the ski mask so that it resembled a watch cap and jammed it over her hair, then started the engine. She wanted some music to psych her up for what lay ahead and slotted Horse's *Both Sides* into the cassette player. "Never Not Going To" blasted out at her and she sang along with a sense of savage irony as she drove through the rainy streets in the gathering dusk to her rendezvous with Giles.

She pulled up outside the Victorian warehouse where Giles and Julia enjoyed a magnificent view of the river and the Finnieston Crane from their converted loft apartment. A tall slim figure detached itself from the shadows of the doorway and crossed to the car. Giles was almost unrecognisable in camouflage trousers, Doc Martens and a parka. "You look like Rambo on a night out," Lindsay observed as he piled into the car, shunting the electronic equipment on to his lap.

Giles raised an eyebrow. "And you don't?" he asked. "I have to wonder what I'm doing here."

"You can't resist playing cowboys and Indians."

"Hmm. Let me tell you, if Rory wasn't certifiably lucky, I wouldn't be here."

Lindsay drove off, cutting up from the quayside on the road that paralleled the motorway as far as Charing Cross, then followed the signs to the Charles Rennie Mackintosh car park.

"Why here?" Giles asked as they approached the entrance.

"Because of the system." Lindsay pointed to a sign that read PAY AT MACHINE BEFORE RETURNING TO VEHICLE. She drove up to the entry barrier, lowered her window and took a ticket. The metal arm rose and she drove through. "There you go," she said, handing the ticket to Giles. They stared at each other for a long moment then he opened the door, unfolded his long legs and climbed out, leaning back into the car to give Lindsay the thumbs-up sign.

"Good luck," he said.

"And you." Lindsay waited till she saw Giles walk over to the lifts and attach an OUT OF ORDER sticker to the doors. Then she drove on up, her damp tyres screaming on the cement as she climbed to the penultimate floor, the last covered level below the roof.

Lindsay parked near the "up" ramp and got out. She pocketed the electronic equipment, slipped the shotgun under her waxed jacket and walked cautiously up the ramp to the roof. Here, there were only a couple of other cars, and little scope for hiding. She checked out one of the parked cars, but the lines of sight were terrible. Adrenaline was making her jumpy and she began to panic at her inability to find somewhere to conceal herself. Then she spotted a large concrete bin used for storing grit near the door leading to the lifts. She hurried over there and stood by it, sighting along her arm like a child playing soldiers. This was better, she thought, dry-mouthed and sweating. She could see the ramps clearly, as well as the whole area of the roof level. Lindsay freed the shotgun and squeezed down behind the bin, gasping as her ribs protested.

Meanwhile, nine floors below her, Patrick Coughlan slowed down as he approached the barrier. He looked sharply around him, but missed Giles, who had found a patch of shadow in the lee of the entrance. Patrick leaned out of the driver's window to snatch a ticket then edged forward, aiming for the ramp that would carry him to the meeting he'd dreamed of for years.

Michael hadn't taken his eyes off Bernie's front door since Patrick's departure. He knew his life would be worth nothing if he fucked up now and he was determined not to make a single mistake. Suddenly, he straightened up in his seat. "It's them!"

"The bitch and the boy?" Kevin exclaimed.

"The same." As Bernie ushered Jack towards her scarlet hatchback, Michael fastened his safety belt and dug Kevin in the ribs. "Start her up, Kevin."

Startled by the hard edge in his partner's voice, Kevin turned the key and floored the accelerator. The engine coughed and stalled. On the third try, it finally caught. "Sorry," he mumbled.

"Just don't fucking lose them." It wasn't a command to argue with.

Bernie strapped Jack into the child seat in the back of the car, then walked round to the driver's seat. The car nosed out of its parking place and made its way down Kinghorn Drive to the junction.

"But why won't you tell me where we're going?" Jack asked plaintively.

"Because it's an adventure," Bernie said, glancing in her rear-view mirror, not in the least surprised to see a car pull out behind her.

"I don't want any more adventures. I want Tam." Jack sounded on the point of tears.

"I want Tam too," Bernie said, her voice trembling. "But we have to learn to manage on our own."

Patrick's car edged on to the rooftop level of the car park. He cruised slowly from one end to the other, pausing at each parked car to check it was empty. Lindsay crouched behind the bin, the ski mask pulled over her face so nothing was visible in the gloom except the gleam of her eyes. She could feel sweat trickling down her neck and pooling in the small of her back. "Just park, you bastard," she said under her breath.

As if he heard her, Patrick drew to a halt and reversed neatly into a slot as far away from the other cars as he could get. *Perfect*, Lindsay thought.

As the sound of his engine died in the damp night air, nine floors down Rory was driving up to the car park barrier. She took a ticket and drove in, then stopped. Giles stepped out of the shadows and gave her the thumbs-up sign. Rory flashed a grin at him and drove upwards, heart thudding in her chest. She urgently wanted to pee, but realised it was purely psychological. Almost the last thing she'd done before she left had been to use the toilet. That knowledge didn't stop her feeling desperate, however.

Giles checked his watch. It showed five minutes to eight. He took a deep breath and crossed to the machine that issued the exit permits. He inserted the ticket Lindsay had given him, fed a handful of coins into the machine and took the exit ticket. He walked briskly across towards the barrier guarding the way out and leaned against the wall, trying to look as if he was waiting for someone.

Which of course he was. Bernie turned into the street and checked the dashboard clock. Two minutes to eight. She was right on time. She drove into the entrance, checking her tail was still in place a discreet distance behind her. She took a ticket from the machine, then, as the arm rose, drove hesitantly forward. While she hovered, apparently uncertain of the direction she should take, a Vauxhall Vectra drove into the entrance lane. The driver's arm appeared, taking a ticket, and the barrier rose again. The car drove through and edged towards Bernie.

The moment the entrance barrier returned to the horizontal, Bernie's car leapt forward in sudden acceleration. She pulled hard on the wheel, swinging round and heading fast for the exit. Giles jumped out of the shadows and inserted the exit ticket as she approached. The metal arm rose and Bernie speeded through, her tyres screeching as she hit the street at thirty miles an hour. Giles took off on foot, running through an alley towards their prearranged rendezvous.

Inside the Vectra, panic was raging. "The fucking bitch," Kevin screamed over and over again.

"She's set him up," Michael raged, throwing open the passenger door. "Get after the fucking cow. Don't fucking lose her." As Kevin accelerated, he dived out of the car and rolled to the ground, twisting his ankle badly as he fell. He got to his feet, cursing and wincing as arrows of pain shot up his leg. As he stood, he realised he'd also done something to his left collarbone. He could hardly move his arm and every step he took provoked a painful grinding along his shoulder.

Kevin had the engine at screaming point, lifting his foot off the clutch and launching the car at the barrier. He hurtled forward, straight into the metal pole, expecting it to snap under the impact. Not for the first time in his life, Kevin had misjudged the situation completely. The barrier, more solid than it looked, rocked and bent slightly. The car was more vulnerable. The windscreen starred as the glass shattered and the car roof crumpled. "Jesus fuck!" Kevin wailed.

He threw the car into reverse then attacked the barrier again. This time, the pillar at the end of the windscreen bent under the impact, but the car's momentum carried it forward, only brought to a halt by the strength of the barrier. The car was comprehensively trapped. It could move neither forward nor back. Kevin struggled to open the driver's door, but it was stuck too. He couldn't squeeze over to the passenger door because the roof was crushed too low on that side. Nor could he stretch far enough to reach the mobile phone which had fallen into the footwell on the passenger side. As the magnitude of the disaster slowly began to penetrate, Kevin started to shake. "Ah, shit," he groaned.

Meanwhile, Michael had limped across to the lifts, only to discover the OUT OF ORDER sign that Giles had stuck there. He didn't even bother to try the call button, settling instead for kicking the door with his uninjured foot. Breathing heavily, one arm hanging useless at his side, he turned towards the stairwell. His good arm reached inside his jacket and reappeared clutching a Glock automatic. "Fucking bitch," he swore as he began the long ascent to the roof.

Rory had climbed the levels as fast as she safely could, swerving once to avoid a woman loading her boot with shopping. The red digital display read 7:59 as she turned on to the final ramp. It was still drizzling and visibility was poor on the roof level. But she could make out Patrick Coughlan standing in the shadows by his car. She parked about twenty feet away from him and got out, keeping her hands in sight and well away from her body. Her whole body was tense with apprehension, her blood pounding in her ears like a mad Burundi drummer. She took a few steps towards him.

Patrick remained motionless, his eyes watchful, his hands in his overcoat pockets. He said nothing until Rory was about six feet away from him. Then he spoke. "Who are you?" he said.

"I'm Lindsay Gordon's business partner."

Patrick's lip curled in a sneer. "Lindsay Gordon. The woman who can't take a telling."

Rory licked her dry lips, "Bernie asked me to come. You know she can't let you have the boy."

It felt like a long silence, but it was only a matter of seconds. "I wish you hadn't said that," Patrick said.

"Why? Because you'll have to deal with her the same way you dealt with Tam? And then me? And then Lindsay?" Rory's voice sounded far more defiant to her than she would have believed possible.

"You don't know me well enough to heed my warnings. Bernadette should know better, though."

"What Bernie knows is how her son would end up if she handed him over to you. A cold-blooded killer, fighting a pointless war, just like his daddy."

"A boy should know who his father is. I have a right to my son."

"And Tam? Didn't he have any rights?" Rory stood her ground, her eyes never leaving his face.

"He had no right to my son."

"He risked going to prison to get your son back to his mother," she pointed out.

"I've risked at least that much to put the boy where he belongs. In my house."

"Oh yeah, I forgot. Murder." It was, she knew, the key moment. She had to get the admission on tape, had to forge a weapon strong enough to keep this man at bay forever.

Patrick shook his head. "It wasn't murder. It was punishment. For taking what wasn't his."

"She won't let you have Jack. Not after what you did to Tam."

A cold smile, his teeth gleaming in the dim light. "Dead women don't have choices."

Rory started at the sound of a door smacking open against a concrete wall. She whirled round to see a figure silhouetted against the harsh fluorescence of the stairwell. An unfamiliar voice shouted, "Patrick! She's set you up! She's got away with the boy. We lost them!"

Rory's hand instinctively flew up to protect the microphone in an ambiguous gesture. Assuming she was going for a weapon, Michael's gun hand came up and he moved into the firing position. But before he could shoot, from behind the grit bin came the flash of gunfire and the backfire boom of a shotgun. Michael, blasted at point-blank range, crumpled to the ground without a sound. Shocked at what she'd done, Lindsay stood looking down uncomprehendingly at the still form at her feet.

She was brought back to reality by the sound of shots. Suddenly alert, she took in the scene. Patrick was waving a handgun around, shooting wildly in her general direction, his panic the reaction of a man who hasn't seen active service for a very long time and is unaccustomed to taking responsibility for his own protection. Lindsay didn't think he could see her and had no conviction that he would hit her even if he could.

But as she stood motionless in the shadows, she saw Rory whirl back round to face Patrick. As if in slow motion, she saw Patrick's gun hand waver towards Rory. Lindsay roared, "No," and left the shadows at a sprint, the shotgun held at waist height, her finger on the trigger.

Patrick's hand jerked and Rory staggered before crashing to the ground. Lindsay felt her chest constrict as she charged across the roof, screaming unintelligibly. Patrick turned back towards her but before he could fire again Lindsay's finger tightened implacably.

The blast caught him full in the chest and he collapsed, blood pouring from a hole the size of a football. Lindsay barely paused, knowing he was beyond help and not caring. She dropped the gun and fell to her knees beside Rory. Blood soaked her shirt and jacket, spreading from a wound high on the right side of her chest. Rory's face was parchment in the sodium lights, her eyes closed. Tears spilled from Lindsay's eyes as she checked for a pulse in Rory's neck. It was there, faint and thready, but it was there. She gently touched Rory's face with one hand, while putting pressure on the wound with the other. "Rory? Oh God, Rory, say something. Don't do this to me, don't die on me!" Her voice was agonized, mirroring the desperation she felt as Rory failed to move.

Lindsay pulled out her mobile phone and dialled the emergency services. "Which service do you require?" the anonymous voice asked kindly.

"Ambulance. My pal's been shot," Lindsay gabbled. "On the top floor of the Charles Rennie Mackintosh car park. You've got to hurry, she's bleeding badly. There's two other people hurt as well."

"That's the Mackintosh car park in Garnethill?"

"Yeah, yeah. Get somebody here, please."

"The police and ambulance will be with you shortly. Can you . . ." Lindsay cut off the call. She didn't have time for anything except Rory. She leaned over her to check she was still breathing. This time, her eyelids fluttered and opened. Rory looked dazed and bewildered.

"Rory?" Lindsay said, hardly able to believe her eyes.

"Lindsay?" It was a croak, but it was her name, unmistakably.

Lindsay suddenly remembered she was wearing the ski mask and yanked it off. "It's me, Rory. Listen, there's an ambulance coming, you're going to be okay. Just hang in there."

"Hurts . . . Did we get enough?" she groaned.

"It's sorted," Lindsay said.

"You look . . . You never said . . . a gun."

"You'd only have worried."

Rory coughed. "Cover your back . . . you need . . . cover your back."

"Never mind me." But nevertheless she took heed of Rory's concern. Lindsay slipped her hand inside Rory's bra, made even more fearful by the marble coldness of her skin. She pulled the mike clear and stuffed it into her pocket.

"Please," Rory whispered. "Gun. Get rid."

"Okay." Lindsay didn't care about the consequences for herself, but being scared for her wasn't helping Rory. She grabbed the shotgun and stood up. "Fucking carnage. How do you explain fucking carnage?" She raced down a level to her own car and wrenched the door open. She lifted the bench seat and threw in the gun, the spare cartridges and all the electronic equipment. Then she pulled off her waxed jacket and tossed it on top.

Lindsay raced back up to the roof, the sound of distant sirens cutting through the constant hum of the city at night. She threw herself down beside Rory again, leaning over to press down on the wound. Her eyes were closed again and her skin looked even paler than before. "Oh fuck," Lindsay groaned. "Don't die on me, Rory."

Rory's eyelids parted in a narrow slit. "Lindsay . . ."

"Can you hear me?"

"Yeah . . ."

"This is really important. Try to remember. We came here in your car. Together. You were meeting Patrick Coughlan. Some IRA story. You were worried and I offered to come along for the ride. Okay?"

"My car," Rory murmured.

"And then it all went off. We've got no idea what happened or who was involved. Okay?"

Rory's mouth twitched. It was almost a smile. "Not a lie . . ."

Now the sirens were close, whooping in and out in a Doppler effect as the emergency vehicles climbed through the car park. "You're going to be okay," Lindsay insisted.

"Coughlan . . . ?" Rory said so softly it was almost lost in the background noise.

"He's dead. It's all over, Rory. It's all right."

"Tell Bernie." Then her eyes flickered shut again as two police cars and a pair of ambulances screamed up the ramp. Lindsay got to her feet and waved her arms over her head. "Just don't find my fucking car, that's all," she muttered as the headlight beams pinned her like stage spotlights. There would be time enough for her to deal with what she'd done. For now, what mattered was saving Rory. And perhaps, in the process, saving herself.

EPILOGUE

It was, Lindsay thought, the most splendid bouquet of flowers she had ever spent money on. She didn't even know the names of most of the things in it. She only hoped the nurses could find a big enough vase. She walked through the hospital corridors towards the lift, still buzzy with lack of sleep and the satisfaction that comes from surviving a terrifying ordeal. She'd never been so scared in her life, nor so relieved at the outcome.

Lindsay emerged from the lift and took the short corridor that led to the private rooms. She nodded to a nurse who exclaimed at the flowers. Lindsay paused on the threshold and took a deep breath. Then she grabbed the handle and marched in.

Rory was sitting on a chair by the window, the animation on her face revealing she was in the middle of some anecdote. But Lindsay had no interest in her today. She turned to face the bed, where Sophie sat propped up, nursing Clare Julia Gordon Hartley, thirty-six hours old and the most beautiful creature Lindsay had ever clapped eyes on. A slow grin spread across her face and she leaned down to kiss Sophie and then their daughter, who remained oblivious to attention while there was milk to be downed.

Lindsay glanced up at Rory. "So, what do you think?" she said.

"She's gorgeous."

"That's the right answer," Sophie said. "You can come again."

Rory uncurled her legs from under her and stood up. "Try and keep me away. How long are you going to be in for?"

"They usually keep mothers in for five days after a section, but I'm going to try to persuade them to let me out sooner than that. Hospitals are such unhealthy places," Sophie said. "Besides, Lindsay's getting off far too lightly right now."

"Well, I'll probably wait till you're both home." Rory reached for the flowers. "I'm going off now, I'll give these to one of the nurses and get her to stick them in a vase. Lindsay, what time are we kicking off tonight?"

"Eight o'clock, Café Virginia."

"Kicking off what?" Sophie asked, curious rather than suspicious. Doubt had disappeared some months before, for which Lindsay was profoundly grateful.

"Wetting the baby's head," Lindsay said. "Work contacts, mostly. All the gang from Radio NMC, plus people like Giles and Sandra."

"I'm so glad I'm missing that one," Sophie said drily.

"See you soon," Rory said, stooping to kiss Clare's wispy black hair on her way out.

Sophie watched her leave, then reached for Lindsay's hand. "I'm glad you forced me to get to know Rory. She's great fun."

Lindsay shrugged, embarrassed. "I didn't see how I could avoid running into her, with us both so involved in the media scene. I just hoped the two of you would ignore me and get to know each other. Self-preservation, that's all it was."

"Well, it worked." Sophie shifted. "She's asleep. Do you want to hold your daughter?"

Lindsay picked up Clare as if she were a primed bomb and edged round to the chair by the window. "I can't believe how good she is. Did you get much sleep?"

Sophie grunted. "It wasn't too bad. She went three hours between feeds at one point, which was blissful. But it's not restful in here. We'll both do better once we get home."

The rest of the day passed in a drift of feeding, changing, bathing and conversation. Lindsay's parents turned up in the afternoon to drool over their grandchild, and Lindsay left her mother with Sophie for half an hour so she and her father could get some fresh air.

"It's all worked out for the best, then," Andy said as they walked along the banks of the Kelvin.

"Amazingly enough, yes," Lindsay said. "I couldn't believe it when they put Clare in my arms. It was like a hook going into my heart. Instant love."

"There's nothing like it," Andy agreed. "You forgive them anything, you know."

"Even stupidity," Lindsay said wryly.

"Even stupidity. Do you see much of Rory now you're doing the radio show?"

For the past five months, Lindsay had been the presenter of the midday news programme on Radio NMC. It was one of the few good things that had come out of her encounter with Tam and Bernie Gourlay. The station's boss had been a close friend of Tam's, and when his anchorman had left for BBC national radio, he'd called Lindsay to offer her the slot. She'd been at a loose end ever since she'd given up working with Rory as the price of reconciliation with Sophie, and it had turned out to be the perfect slot for her abrasive humour and incisive questioning. "I usually only see her when Sophie's around," she said. "It's safer that way."

Her father nodded. "Aye. Nice lassie, but trouble on legs."

Lindsay shook her head. "I'm the one that's trouble, Dad."

"Aye, well, that'll all change now. You've got responsibilities."

Lindsay grinned. "I know. Great, isn't it?"

❧❀❧

clutching a cold beer. "Mmm, that's nice," Lindsay said, rolling the bottle against her forehead.

"Bernie called today. She's finally found a house she likes and the owners have accepted her offer."

"Where is it?"

"Cornwall. Near St Ives. Jack likes the sea. She was thrilled to hear about Clare."

"I suppose that's as near as we're going to get to a happy ending," Lindsay sighed.

"All things considered, we should probably be grateful we came out of it with nothing worse than matching scars," Rory said.

Lindsay reached for her hand. "I know it's not exactly what you hoped for. I'm sorry."

Rory shook her head. "Don't be. I'd only have broken your heart. And it taught me something important too."

"What? Don't mess with married women?" Lindsay said, only half teasing.

"There's that," Rory acknowledged ruefully. "But more importantly, I learned that I'm maybe not as much of a lost cause as I thought I was. I always reckoned me and love were as incompatible as a Mac and a PC. But what I felt for you . . . well, let's just say I'm not really scared any more."

"Oh, Rory," Lindsay said, putting down her beer and pulling Rory into her arms. "You deserve better than me."

Rory grinned up at her. "You think I don't know that?" She snuggled into Lindsay for a moment, then pulled away and said briskly, "Come on. It's time to go and paint the town lavender. You've got something to celebrate, Lindsay. The new life starts here."

She left the hospital in time to get to her counselling session at half past five. She'd gone into therapy while Rory had still been in hospital recovering from the gunshot wound that was bizarrely a mirror image of Lindsay's own. When she'd woken screaming in Rory's spare room for the third night running, she'd called Sophie for help. They'd had a cautious lunch together when Lindsay had revealed the truth about the events on the roof of the car park. Sophie had been horrified at Lindsay's risk-taking and adamant that she needed professional help.

"How can I talk to a therapist?" Lindsay had demanded. "As far as the cops are concerned, I'm just a bystander who got caught up in a Republican revenge shooting by chance. Thank God the only one of them left standing kept his mouth shut or I'd be on remand at Cornton Vale right now. I can't sit down with some New Age namby-pamby and confess that I killed two men. They'd freak out."

"Leave it with me, I'll find someone," Sophie had promised. And she'd kept her word. AnneMarie Melville was a medically qualified psychiatrist turned counsellor who regarded her duty of confidentiality as highly as a priest in the confessional. Lindsay reckoned Anne-Marie had probably saved her sanity.

That evening as she left Anne-Marie's consulting rooms, she was astonished to see Rory sitting on the bonnet of her car, soaking up the sunshine. "What are you doing here?" Lindsay asked.

"Nice to see you too," Rory said, sliding off the car and giving Lindsay a hug. "I just wanted to see you on your own before we got ripped into the drink. I knew this was your night for seeing Anne-Marie and I thought I'd grab you when you were vulnerable."

Lindsay grinned and hugged her back. "Living dangerously, huh?" She moved away and unlocked the car. "Come back to the house and have a drink, we'll go into town together."

They were silent on the short drive, each keeping her own counsel till they were sitting on the living-room sofa, both